The First Verse

The First Verse

a novel

BARRY McCREA

CARROLL & GRAF PUBLISHERS

NEW YORK

THE FIRST VERSE

Carroll & Graf Publishers
An Imprint of Avalon Publishing Group Inc.
245 West 17th Street
11th Floor
New York, NY 10011

AVALON
publishing group incorporated

ISBN: 0-7394-6200-8

Book design by Jamie McNeely

Printed in the United States of America
Distributed by Publishers Group West

For Ludovico

"Did you ever happen to hear an old rhyme that begins 'Oranges and lemons, say the bells of St. Clement's?'"

Again O'Brien nodded. With a sort of grave courtesy he completed the stanza:

"Oranges and lemons, say the bells of St. Clement's,
You owe me three farthings, say the bells of St. Martin's,
When will you pay me? say the bells of Old Bailey
When I grow rich, say the bells of Shoreditch."

"You knew the last line!" said Winston.

"Yes, I knew the last line. And now, I am afraid, it is time for you to go."

—George Orwell, *1984*

"Orange and lemons," say the bells of St. Clement's.
"You owe me five farthings," say the bells of St. Martin's.
"When will you pay me?" say the bells of Old Bailey.
"When I am rich," say the bells of Shoreditch.
"When will that be?" say the bells of Stepney.
"I do not know," says the great bell of Bow.

—Traditional

Book One

Prologue

In the end, I abandoned my new life, along with the people who had helped me to put it together, and I returned to the world of strange games and secret systems they had saved me from. The summer after I left the cult, everyone was initially pleased with my progress in adjusting to everyday living: I was set up in a flat in town with my oldest friend, working part-time doing data entry in a bank and all set to go back to Trinity in October and repeat the year I had lost. But I had never really taken to the temping which had controlled the days since my rescue, and in my idle moments I let my mind turn back to the dangerous questions and mysteries, to the vanished actors and intrigues that I had promised to forget for good.

My return to the cult occurred on a warm evening, halfway through the summer of 2004, as I sat alone waiting for a text message from my new lover. I was distracted and nervous; the flat oppressed me with its spoons and cushions. I stared at the unlit phone, willing the message to arrive while there was still time. But when it did beep, buzz, and glow, instead of picking it up and reading the message, I walked, as though instructed, into

Patrick's room and stood in front of his bookshelf. In a single, illuminated instant, like the flash and tinkle of a lightbulb blowing, I knew that that fresh life, brief and safe, was over. I stood for a short time in feigned resistance, glancing now and then out the window at the cars moving regularly by on Baggot Street, following flawlessly upon one another, like the days, the minutes, the years. But I was not being persecuted or hunted down against my will; I was not suffering from love, exhaustion, or nerves. I was voluntarily lost, I was long gone.

I switched on Patrick's reading lamp, illuminating the titles on the bookshelf.

By the time I pulled the first forbidden volume down, the traffic, the hum of the fridge, the homeless couple fighting outside, the tick of Patrick's alarm clock—even, perhaps, the ring of my phone—had already woven themselves into a fine fabric of sound, the inevitable and dangerous Latin singing that had seduced me first and would now lead me away again:

ecce enim veritatem dilexisti
incerta et occulta sapientiae tuae manifestasti mihi
Asperges me hyssopo et mundabor
Lavabis me, et super nivem dealbabor.

For behold you loved the truth
And you revealed to me the hidden secrets of your wisdom.
You will purge me with hyssop and I will be cleansed:
You will wash me and I will shine whiter than snow.

One

B ut to begin with, all words. For a long time I used to lie,
and say that words had "always" been my "trade," while
in fact mine is just the rude tongue of my homeland, the
bourgeois suburbs on Dublin's southern side, a Levantine
country reaching from the tree-hushed redbrick of Ranelagh,
Rathmines, and Donnybrook, on the edge of the city centre,
stately places of canals, cornices, and quiet burghers, extending
east and southbound along a glittering Mediterranean coast.
Amphibious green trains run along its foamed edge, sliding back
and forth between the heart of the Hibernian metropolis and
the deep south, through the litorally bounded civilisations of
Glenageary, Blackrock, and Killiney, through Dalkey, Seapoint,
and Bray. The Stillorgan dual carriageway cuts across the middle
of this land, a spine laterally transversing the wild darkness of
Foxrock and Leopardstown, stretching through countless lonely
valleys and plains all the way out to the western edges, the
foothills, the ends of the earth, the literally fantastic tracts in
Three-Rock's solemn shadow. These are the boundaries of my

home, and my language consists only of its bland Neapolitan vowels, its middleclass maritime cadence and its uncertain refusal of tense.

An unremarkable swottishness and a cheap, almost corrupt knack for exams had got me easily through secondary school at the Jesuit Gonzaga College, and covered me with the scalps and headdresses of local competitions. And then in my last year of school (nine months, that is, before that evening in Patrick's flat), these mediocre gifts, in combination with a modest flair for foreign languages, had brought something more exciting my way. It took the form of a new Trinity College scholarship, only two in Ireland, the Beckett Foundation Fellowship, to study French and English literature. It entitled me to "Commons"—dinner in the huge Dining Hall every evening at six—and, more importantly, to rooms (which means a room) in Trinity, a fact which enabled me to move out and leave, after nineteen years, the draughty Victorian house of my parents and of my childhood, atop the sad swell of the sea at Dún Laoghaire.

I left home in early October, walking to the DART station through dead leaves and night rain and most likely a big orange harvest moon. The final goodbye to my parents had taken place in the worried blue light of the television, where I turned down their offer of a lift. They fussed about money and food and told me they were proud of me. I said I loved them and left.

I would have been more aware of this as a rite of passage, the extreme unction of my childhood, setting off into the city to seek my fortune, but my mind had room only for Ian O'Neill. He had returned more than a month before from interrailing around Europe, and despite near-daily calls to his mobile and messages left on the family landline, I had only seen or spoken to him once in all that time. A few days before he was to embark on his degree in Commerce at UCD, I had turned up unannounced on the doorstep of the O'Neill family's semi-detached house in Dartry, driven not even by affection or love so much as a rabid, carnal desire to feel the press of his flesh in our initial handshake. His girlfriend—Laoise, I think her name was—was there in the sitting room. He hadn't invited me in, he had kept me there on the porch for the few minutes of our conversation, but I could sense her moving round inside, like a mysterious royal prisoner in a tower. Ian's manner was friendly, what's the craic, how's the man, but his dead eyes betrayed a new knowl-edge of the true nature of my feelings for him, a full-on recog-nition, at last, of the cannibalistic fervour which had characterised my interest in him. I sensed right away in his voice that he had finally penetrated the veils of deceit I had woven around our friendship over the last two years in school, two end-less, mad years when I wandered like Lady Macbeth among the darkened rooms of our house every evening, hoping he would phone, sick with worry that he was out meeting girls or— worse—founding new confidences with other boys.

Our association was a strange one, between a quiet, mildly unpopular swot and an affable, confident, blond-haired rugby player. In the ordinary course of school events, our paths would hardly have intersected, and so our friendship was carefully and calculatingly set up by me, through a series of apparently inno-cent and random encounters at bus stops, class religion retreats, and queues in the newsagents of Ranelagh. Through these devices and designs I had become the closest friend of the object of my sexual obsession, and if he was confused by my mad jeal-ousy with regard to the social life he maintained independent of me, with his old group of friends, he had accepted it as a quirk of my personality, a sign of real friendship.

However, everything had changed in the summer after the Leaving Cert, the months between school and college, which I spent on walks on the seafront in Sandycove with my parents and sister, and he inter-railing around Europe with a mad crowd of lads from school. During these continental adventures, the distance from Dublin and the time spent with friends who didn't tearfully accuse him of insensitivity or neglect, must have caused him to rethink our strange friendship. One afternoon, drinking beer from a plastic glass on Wenceslas Square or chatting, maybe, to a group of Australian backpacking girls at the harbour in Bruges, he had been arrested by a sudden, retrospective vision of me at home on those weekend nights in Dublin when he had been out with his other friends. As he slid stoned, perhaps, down the cobbled slope of the Piazza del Duomo in Siena, or ran to validate his ticket in the Hauptbahnhof in Munich, he had been halted in his tracks by a first clear sense of how it had really been, skidding, losing his balance, and falling over a suitcase trolley as an image flared up in his mind's eye of me on a Friday night, wandering miserably from room to even-darkened room in our big old house beside the sea waiting for some sign of him, a despondent Bernadette in a rainswept Lourdes waiting uselessly for a divine apparition to burst with a ring from the silent phone.

But now, walking across the cobbles and brown leaves through Trinity to collect my keys from the porter, these recent memories fell away. I signed for my keys, and the porter pointed me in the direction of my new address, House 16, the corner entranceway in a nineteenth-century granite complex known as Botany Bay. My third-floor room was large and bright, furnished with a desk, single bed, and bookshelf, a sink in the corner and two old windows looking out onto the tennis courts and the gothic Graduate Memorial Building. I looked at the bookshelf and the bare walls, and up at the high, white ceiling, and I thought, I will furnish this room with a life.

I was disturbed from my unpacking and the pleasant thoughts that accompanied it as a bell in the room gave two long, loud rings. It was my doorbell, a shrill old-fashioned mechanism above the door. But it was impossible that I could have callers, since I myself had just found out which room I had been assigned when I collected my key. I hadn't put my name on the bell-panel at the side of the entranceway. The bell rang twice more, and I remained standing in the middle of the room, frozen in a musical-statues pose with a pile of boxer shorts in my arms. I dropped them on the floor, went over to the window, opened it and stuck my head out into the darkness. Behind me, the bell rang twice, confidently, again. Standing on the steps of the door to House 16, looking up at my window as he took his finger off the bell, was a young man. At first I took him for Ian, and then for Patrick, before realising it was neither of them, nobody, in fact, that I knew. He was a little older than me, with curly blond hair and a brown leather jacket.

"Hello?" I called down. He jumped down from the steps, walked over to stand directly beneath my window, and looked up, hands in his pockets.

"Hi," I called again.

"Niall? Niall Lenihan?" he shouted up cheerfully.

"Yes, yeah, that's me, hello," I said.

He laughed, then took a few steps back, and cupping his hands around his mouth sang up at me:

"Oranges and lemons, say the bells of Saint Clements."

"What?"

He laughed out loud and sang it again:

"Oranges and lemons, say the bells of Saint Clements."

I looked back at him, speechless, trying to imagine what it could mean.

"Who are you? What do you want?"

"Pablo Virgomare," he said, in a perfectly Irish accent, "delighted to make your acquaintance."

"Strange name," I called back, accusingly.

"Stranger than yours anyway, Niall Lenihan," he replied. "So few letters, all repeated and rearranged."

"What do you want? How do you know who I am?" I shouted. He laughed.

"All repeated and rearranged!" he said again.

The Dining Hall bell struck the half-hour. He called up:

"There's Saint Clement's calling. Take care. And look, if you need me, you know where to find me. Send me a song."

He blew me a kiss, then ran off along the edge of the tennis courts towards Front Square. I stared out the window into the wind and leaves on Botany Bay, hopelessly looking for a clue, the line of song ringing away in my head. Eventually I pulled my head back in, sat on my bed, and racked my brains, wondering if I knew him from somewhere, from school, a friend of one of my cousins, what kind of in-joke the song might refer to. Maybe just a local crazy doing knick-knocks. But he knew my name and had found out what room I was in.

I jumped with fright, heart still pounding, as the bell rang again. I sat, terrified, until it stopped, and remained there waiting stiffly for it to start again. After a long pause it did, two short rings. I gathered my courage and went cautiously to the window. I couldn't bring myself to look down, so I just called blindly and firmly up at the stars:

"Yes? Hello?"

A girl's voice replied, in the singsong accent of northern Ireland:

"Niall? Niall Lenihan?"

I looked down to the doorway. She had shoulder-length dark blond hair, and was standing with her arms folded in front of her chest.

"Who are you?" I called out.

She walked over, like the last caller, and stood beneath my window.

"I'm Fionnuala Shiel, I'm the other, you know, Beckett scholar. I got your room number off the guards in Front Arch. I just called over to say hello."

"Oh," I called down suspiciously.

"Is this a bad time?"

"What? Oh, no, not really. I mean, well, no. Hi."

"Do you want to have a cup of tea or something?" she called.

I hesitated. It still seemed quite possible that this was a trick, part of the last caller's arcane plot. Then it seemed to me that anything at all would be preferable to sitting alone in my room waiting for him to call again, so I threw down my key and invited her up.

As her slow footsteps came up the stairs I pulled my duvet from my rucksack and spread it on the bed, with the idea that a bare bed was somehow unmannerly to show a guest.

"So, you're the mysterious Niall," she said when I opened the door to her, "congratulations on your scholarship."

"Likewise." I smiled. "Why mysterious?"

"You weren't at any of the orientations. I called for you a few times over Freshers' Week."

"I skipped it," I said, ashamed of myself for lingering at home for the sake of the completely improbable possibility that Ian would phone the landline or call over to the house. "I've literally just moved in."

Fionnuala had big green engaging eyes, and she wore real person's clothes, co-ordinated and modern, selected not with the purpose of getting noticed, but rather the embarrassed teenager's goal of remaining as invisible as possible. I invited her to come in, and we sat on the chairs on either side of the gas heater, which I turned on as she looked around my room.

"Nice room," she said.

The heater finally lit, I sat down opposite her, and we inhaled a faint odour of unlit gas. I enjoyed the sound of her northern accent, the little trill at the end of each sentence, the vibrato vowels.

"You're from the north . . ."

"From Belfast, yeah. You . . . ?"

"Dublin. I'm from Sandycove, just outside Dún Laoghaire, you know, where the boat goes to Holyhead."

"Dublin's riviera."

"That's right."

She had met our French class, and said they seemed mostly nice, she had been out dancing with them in a nightclub behind Grafton Street. Break for the Border. She asked me if I'd heard of it. I had, a distant whisper on the breeze which had blown around the cold sidelines of Ian's private social world of rugby players and their girlfriends, the one from which I was miserably excluded, condemned instead to drift like the white lady of Hampton Hall through our house in Sandycove, the distant noise of the television which my parents and sister were watching not any more audible than the phantom sounds of club music and slowdances to whose rhythms Ian could have been moving with some lucky girl from Mount Anville or Muckross, sounds that would come to me across vast, unnavigable distances of the imagination, broken only by the muffled laughter of the television audience from the sitting room, or by a dull phone call about homework from one of my classroom acquaintances, boys who swapped computer games, read fantasy novels, and were afraid of their mothers.

"So anyway, some of our French class are heading to the pub tonight, do you feel like coming along? It's what, half-seven now, we can sink one before they show up."

I was feeling sensitive and unsociable, but my nerves were badly jangled by the previous caller and I didn't want to be left alone, so I said I'd be delighted.

"They're meeting in O'Neill's, do you know where it is? I don't."

"I do," I said, pleased with myself.

Although in many ways the city centre was a strange place for me, still washed in the amniotic waters of Sandycove, Dún Laoghaire and Dalkey, years of desultory Saturday afternoons wandering around town with Patrick and his friends, as well as the second-hand knowledge of pubs and clubs which was part of Ian's legacy, had left me with a decent, if largely theoretical, acquaintance with the layout of its streets and drinking places.

I relaxed with her as we walked through Trinity, across the traffic on College Green and up past proudly buxom Molly Malone to the pub, and was pleased I had gone. We added each other's numbers to our phones, a pleasant gesture of investment in the future, a fun anticipation of when our names would be flashing up on one another's screens, heralding student parties and gossip about tutorials. O'Neill's was quiet when we went in, and we took a large table near the door so the others would see us easily.

"What are yous habing?" The loungegirl was Spanish, but, rather comically, used the demotic Dublin second person plural.

"A glass of Carlsberg," Fionnuala said, "actually no, fuck it, a pint."

"A Guinness, please."

Fionnuala put her purse on the table and sat back. "In Belfast they think you're a slag if you drink pints. I've come south to liberate myself."

I paid for the drinks over Fionnuala's protests and we drank to happy undergraduate days. As we drank, things took on a happy, fuzzy blur, and, forgetting about my weird Oranges and Lemons caller, I had a surge of affection for my first new friend. We talked about our families. She was adopted, the eldest, with three younger siblings, all adopted too except the last one. She didn't know a thing about her natural parents and it didn't interest her at all ("Sure I have a Mammy and a Daddy already, Niall"). The conversation came around, of course, to sex, and I was trying to formulate a response which would be neither entirely untruthful nor a coming-out. I opened my mouth, but was saved by Fionnuala suddenly waving to a young woman walking by our table.

"Sarah!"

"Oh. Hello, Fiona."

"Fionnuala."

She was older than us, probably a little under thirty, with a ghostly pale face and two huge staring grey eyes. She had messy brown hair, swept to the side in a rather masculine-looking parting. She was holding a battered brown handbag in one hand, a cigarette in the other. She ignored me and addressed Fionnuala in an urgent tone.

"Do you know my friend John? Have you seen him?" She asked in a low, mannish voice.

"Neither, Sarah, I'm sorry . . ."

"Well, confound the things!" she exclaimed in frustration. "Damn liars!" She took her coat off and moved to throw it on the bench. I shifted over towards Fionnuala to make room and she sat down.

"Damn liars!" she exclaimed again, and then called: "Waiter! Waiter, over here!" She looked at Fionnuala and said: "That's not what you're supposed to say, is it . . . remind me how you're supposed to say it." She had a slight trace of a provincial accent, almost neutral, but not Dublin.

"Niall, Sarah, Sarah, Niall," Fionnuala introduced happily. "Niall's the other Beckett scholar."

Sarah's big eyes looked me over in a brief but dramatic grey roll. I thought I saw in them the hint of some other colour, a funny effect of the light, and I stared at her quite rudely. She turned back to Fionnuala.

"This is O'Neill's, isn't it? I was supposed to meet a friend in O'Neill's pub, he's not here."

"Why don't you text him?" Fionnuala asked, and nodded to our phones lying on the table.

Sarah ignored her and ordered a vodka and orange with a slice of lemon from the loungegirl.

"Sarah's the one I was telling you about, Niall," Fionnuala said, "the Ph.D. student who lives upstairs from me."

"What do you work on?" I asked her. "I mean, what is your doctorate in?"

"What is it in. Do I have to tell you? I suppose I do. Old

Irish." She gave the term a kind of disbelieving emphasis. "I mean, very old."

"Wow, interesting," I said.

"Do you think so? Really? Old Irish? *Wow, interesting,*" she echoed absentmindedly under her breath, then looked away and began rummaging in her bag until her drink arrived. She paid, took a gulp of her drink, and picked up her cigarette pluming away in the ashtray. "I hate a dry cigarette. *Wow, interesting,*" she repeated again, as if weighing its meaning.

"Not long now till they bring in the smoking ban," I suggested, to general silence.

After a few moments Fionnuala made another attempt:

"What's the craic anyhow, Sarah?"

Sarah was looking distractedly round the bar. Not finding what she wanted, she sighed and pulled a paperback book out of her handbag. She flicked through it, stopped about halfway through, and placed her finger at a point on the page. She read for a little bit, then closed the book and threw it back on top of her coat. She stood up, looked around again, then sat down abruptly.

"It was definitely O'Neill's, definitely. But he's not here. Not a sign. What time is it, Fiona?"

"Half ten."

"Where is he . . ."

"It was definitely O'Neill's of Suffolk Street?" I offered.

"Well, O'Neill's O'Neill's. Where else is there?"

"Is there another O'Neill's, Niall?" Fionnuala asked.

"Pearse Street," I told them, proud, for once, to be a repository of local knowledge, a wise aboriginal tracker.

Sarah thrust the book into my hands. "You," she said, "flick through this, read me out any sentence."

"Any sentence at all?" I stole a look at Fionnuala, who winked at me across the table.

"Yes, quickly," Sarah said looking round nervously.

"Um . . ." I opened the book towards the end and picked a

sentence. I started to read but stopped in shock when I saw the words under my finger. My head spun and I closed the book.

"What's wrong with you?" Sarah asked, with an odd look. "What does it say?"

"I . . ." It was too strange, I couldn't read it. I gave her the book and pointed to the passage I had chosen.

" *'Oranges and lemons say the bells of Saint Clements'* . . ." she read aloud. "What does . . . ? What's *wrong?*"

"Just a weird coincidence," I said, "really crazy."

She studied my face intensely, searching my eyes for something specific.

"What kind of coincidence?" she demanded sharply.

"Just . . . a phrase, repeated, you know, out of context. . . . The phrase came up earlier, and it's here again. . . ."

She was visibly taken aback. She left her eyes to linger on mine, hunting for an answer, and as I stared back I felt I was about to see something concrete, something like writing, emerge from the grey depths of her pupils. She snapped her eyes away from me, stuffed the book back in her bag, and stood up decisively.

"I have to go now, I'll . . . I'll try O'Neill's on Pearse . . . I have to go. Bye."

I half stood up to try and call her back, but by the time I had formulated a question, she had already stridden through the crowd and was out of earshot. I sat back, dazed.

"What the hell was all that about?" Fionnuala asked, leaning in.

I opened my mouth to begin telling her, but, for the second time that night with her, words failed me.

"Oh . . . you know, just déjà-vu kind of thing. Freaked me out."

"She's off her rocker, isn't she?"

"Loopers."

We were interrupted once again, this time by the arrival of our French class. There were five of them in all, and we stayed drinking together and introducing ourselves until closing time. I

was not used to meeting people from outside Dublin. The last
time I had mixed with the national pool had been years before, in
Irish language college with Patrick, when for three weeks we
breakfasted, dined, played sport, danced at *céilithe,* and spoke
pidgin Irish with other fourteen-year-olds from Limerick,
Thurles, Arklow and Bunclody. Just as I had clung to Patrick in
the language classes, sports, hikes, and reels at that time, now,
among this small group of departing pilgrims meeting for the
first time in O'Neill's of Suffolk Street, I gravitated towards the
only other traveller from my world, an expensively dressed and
rather self-centred girl from Foxrock called Andrea. She did most
of the talking at the table, extravagantly proportioned tales of
suburban adventure, with a cast, bewildering in its scale and intri-
cacy, of friends, cousins, ex-boyfriends, classmates, occasional bit-
players from other generations, and a category of adventurer she
referred to disparagingly as "randoms." It was impossible to tell
who was going to end up the protagonist of a story or sub-plot
("This friend of mine, right, Jen, she got *attacked* by this Spanish
guy in Paris one time, I mean like a knife and everything. So her
cousin, right, the one who used to work in The Hairy Lemon with
Feargal . . ."), nor which of the subplots would turn out to be the
centrepiece of any given cycle. I could even see Andrea, like all
true storytellers, mentally transforming the present night with us
all around the table in O'Neill's into a future story to recount to
her friends. She seemed to be one of those people who, like a
seanchaí in a village of a hundred people, have a supernatural
ability to spin the straw of uneventful passing time into narrative
gold. It gave this night around the table in O'Neill's a kind of
glamorous shimmer about it, a feeling of history being made.

Andrea was grateful to have another south county native in
this new world, and was clearly comforted when I knew of,
knew slightly, or pretended to have heard of some of the characters in her thousand and one nights. And for me too, amid the
accents and customs of people from the four dark provinces

beyond Dublin, and especially with the terrifying clanging of my visitor and his jingle constantly at the back of my mind, I felt an ex-pat's relief at Andrea's presence. Our dual carriageway-crossed land was only a few miles distant, but felt as remote from the world at the table in the pub now as any holding in the Golden Vale, any chip shop in east Galway.

Apart from her there was Harry, the only other guy. He was redhaired and nervous, I think from Monaghan or somewhere. He bit his already-chewed nails, drank Coke, and went red whenever anyone spoke to him. Andrea whispered to us all with hilarity after he had clambered awkwardly over us to go the toilet that she had "never" met anyone so strange. ("What is he *like?*" she screamed, slapping the table with hilarity. "I mean, what's the fucking *story?*") Also present, but mostly silent listeners, were Therese from Wexford, nunnish and bob-haired, wearing a white cardigan and a sad floral skirt, and Eileen, sharp and curly-haired from Carlow, who kept picking up her single glass of Ritz and observing it from different angles as if hoping to read auguries.

When closing time came round, Fionnuala, following on a text message, suggested that we go on to Hogan's on Georges Street, where a crowd were gathering to go along to Rí-Rá, a nightclub I had heard of so many times but never even seen. Harry, too traumatised by the evening to continue, mumbled mortified excuses. Therese also blankly announced she was retiring, and promptly erased herself not only from the subsequent but also the preceding section of the evening. Andrea, Fionnuala, Eileen, and I made our way down Dame Street together.

Across the road from Hogan's, lights, music, and dry ice spilled from the George, for a long time Dublin's only gay pub and still the unrivalled centre of Dublin's homosexual world, a name I had heard only in knowing jokes from the most worldly boys in my class making fun of one another, or from occasional articles in the *Irish Times* about attacks or drugs or gay rights

(". . . *in an altercation outside* The George *on South Great Georges Street, a pub popular among Dublin's gay community* . . ."). I looked over my shoulder at the steady stream of men, young and old, going past the bouncers with Mossad earpieces at the door, and wondered if I'd ever cross its threshold.

Hogan's was packed, full of people our own age, rugby-shirted guys with wise nodding smiles, jovial girls, everything a smell of designer scent, cigarette smoke, and beer. On the upper level, squashed against the rail, I saw Ian's older sister Catherine—who had always been kind to me in the days I used to go to their house, when her polite chat would save me from the surly silences meted out by her younger brother—laughing loudly in the middle of a group of friends from her law class.

Fionnuala went to buy me a pint and I stayed talking to Eileen, who was bored by me and kept drifting off mid-sentence and looking round for distraction. Fionnuala had an excited look when she came back with the drinks.

"So can you guess who just texted me to say he's here?"

"Not that crazy post-grad with the books?"

"No, no, not Sarah, the guy I snogged in Break for the Border last week! He's here somewhere. Hang on for me while I go and find him."

"Of course, good luck," I wished her, wondering what on earth I was going to talk to Eileen about. I shouldn't have worried —two minutes later, she saw her chance with a group of girls she knew from Carlow standing nearby. She politely offered for me to come and join them and could barely hide her relief when I said I thought I would go after Fionnuala instead.

So there I stood lost and drunk on my first ever time in a real nightclub, surrounded by masses of laughing coevals, making friends, flirting, and communicating, full, joyous participants in the verve of Dublin's nightlife. I felt like I was wearing my Gonzaga school uniform, standing shyly with my lunchbox and new copies while bigger boys who knew their way around pushed past me, laughing and horseplaying. In the blurry distance, in a cluster of people near the bar, I saw Fionnuala with her snog. He was tall and big, in a check shirt and jeans, could have been any one of Ian's friends, standing with feet planted widely apart, nodding and smiling silently as Fionnuala talked to him energetically, leaning in towards him, touching his sleeve for emphasis. She turned, clearly to find me and bring me over, but I felt shy and out of place, so I turned away, drained the end of my pint, and left the pub.

The cold night air in Georges Street was a shock to my system. I was unsteady on my legs, so I leaned against the wall and texted Fionnuala:

Tired gone home. Enjoy rest of night!

I looked down the road to the flashing lights of the George and the little groups of men disappearing inside. Outside Hogan's, where I was still standing, a group of guys sporting tattoos and football jerseys were drinking cans of cider, bantering back and forth in strong working-class accents (what we southsiders always called a "Dublin" accent, as though we were not Dubliners but expatriates living in an international compound, familiar with the customs, streets, and weather of our adopted city, but still smiling at the speech and habits of its natives, while clinging to the displaced, genteel dialect of our nameless old country). One of them, the one standing most directly opposite me, at the kerb, caught my attention because he looked like Ian, a bit. He had light brown hair, darker than Ian's blond, but the same soft, babyface skin with a slightly honey-coloured tint. I saw that he noticed I was staring at him and I looked away quickly, but when I looked back again he was looking at me, instead of the other three guys telling jokes. I looked away again, and again when I turned back he was looking at me. He moved away from his friends, a couple of steps nearer to me and leaned in over his cupped hands to light a cigarette. I was seized by something foolish, maybe a desire for the reality of another body, and I walked nervously over to him. The lighter glowed in the cavern of his palms. I had bought a packet of cigarettes at the DART station when I had arrived in Trinity, thinking they might come in useful as a way to bond and make friends. I pulled off the plastic and took one out.

"Sorry . . ." He didn't hear me, but when he looked up, exhaling the first brief puff of smoke, he saw me. "Sorry . . ." I said again, "do you have a light?"

"What?"

"Do you have a light?"

"Oh . . ." he pulled his lighter out and lit it for me. I leaned in with my cigarette, but the wind blew the flame out. Irritated, he lit it again, and I rested my cupped hands on his to shelter it. The end of the cigarette glowed red, smoke came, it was lit. But his hands were warm and soft like Ian's, and I let mine linger there just the shortest fraction, a gentle, bedwarm moment of past or imagined tendernesses.

He jerked it away and pushed me back:

"You're a fuckin *faggih,* aren't you? You're a fuckin *faggih!* I knew you were fuckin lookin at me!"

I stared at him in horror, the cigarette smoking away in my hand. His eyes were alight with rage, the blonde fuzz on his upper lip moved angrily as he flung his fricatives and glottal stops at me. His friends had gone quiet and had moved up to stand behind him, facing me. He turned back to them, laughing incredulously.

"I swear to yous lads, he's a fuckin arsebandit! He's a fuckin queer!"

A commotion of movement and sound, too fast for me to comprehend, was followed by a sudden, physical shock in my stomach. I had been punched, for the first time in my life. I saw my cowardly cigarette roll away on the pavement and extinguish itself with a little suicidal hiss in a puddle by the kerb. I doubled over, holding my stomach, fell down and crouched on the pavement, waiting for him to start kicking me, but there was noise

and the voices of other people around me. I could see the runners of my assailant in front of me, blue and white spotless
Adidas, get into motion and run off up Georges Street away
from me.

"Fuck off and leave him alone," I heard from behind me,
though they had already gone. Someone knelt down beside me
with an arm round my shoulders. Ian, I thought for a crazy
moment.

"Are you all right?"

I nodded. The punch had not been very hard: more of a
push, in fact, than a punch. I was a bit winded, a state of affairs
which, in combination with my panic and the alcohol swilling
round inside, made me want to vomit. I did. Without warning,
I keeled over to the side—the wrong one, my helper's shoes, not
the kerb—and emitted a satisfying wave of watery puke. The
shoes jumped back before the second gush. Big, new-looking
square-toed black shoes, flecked with little orange and yellow
lumps of my gastric remains. I retched, gurgled and rasped for
a little while, then, as I wiped my mouth with the back of my
hands, the person who had intervened put his arms behind me,
under my armpits.

"Come on, I'll get you up. One two three." He hoisted me up
and I stood leaning against the lamp-post. He was a little taller
than me, dark hair, pale skin, brown suede jacket. He brushed
his hair out of his face and looked at me, not with kindness, but
with the weary, obligatory concern of the civic-minded stranger.
A small crowd of onlookers had formed behind him at the door
of the pub, crowding forward while barmen prevented them
leaving with their pints.

"You all right, love?" a girl called to me.

"He'll be fine in a little while, don't worry, he'll be grand,"
the guy answered her, without looking over.

"Fuckin pricks annyhow," she said, and there was a general
murmur of approval.

I tried to express my gratitude to the crowd, but my throat was full of vomit and I just started coughing. The guy put a limp hand on my back and said:

"Take it easy there." Then, turning to the people standing outside Hogan's, "Go in and get him a pint of water, someone, would you?"

"Thanks a million."

"Don't mention it," he said, somewhat coldly. "Here's your water."

"Is he okay?" the bearer asked my rescuer.

"Yeah, he's grand. He wasn't really hit at all. I think he's puking from drink more than anything."

The water was lovely and cool, a slice of lemon floating absurdly in it. I swished the first gulp round my mouth and let it flood into my nose to rid myself of the stink of puke, then spat it out into the gutter. The rest I drank slowly and awkwardly before handing the glass back half full and leaning forward, hands on my knees. The guy began to pour the rest of the water on the back of my neck. I leaped with the cold.

"Stay still, it'll stop you feeling nauseous," he said.

Wincing, I let him pour it on my neck, dribbling down my back and through my hair.

"What's your name?" I asked him.

"I'm John. Where do you live?"

"Sandycove. No, Trinity. Botany Bay."

"Well, which is it?"

"Trinity, Trinity, Botany Bay, I'm just after moving—"

"Fine, I'll help you back there. Can you walk?"

I told him I could, but my legs were a bit wobbly, a combination of drink and nerves. I heard him curse under his breath.

"Right, come on, put your arm around me, yes, there, okay." He put his arm around my shoulder, mine was around his waist. "Okay, let's go."

We walked slowly and it was some time before we arrived at the gates of Trinity, where John leaned me against the railings.

"Listen, thank you for . . ."

"Okay, fine. So long," John said, "I'm away. Will you be okay?"

"Oh, yes," I said. A clever line floated into my head, like a text message, and I spoke it out loud. "Don't worry. A plurality of bottles has often induced this in me."

John snapped his head suddenly around to me again and put a hand on my shoulder.

"What? What did you just say?"

"Nothing, nothing. Drunk talk."

"No, what was it?"

"I can't remember," I said, which was the dizzy truth. He released his grip.

"Right, so."

"Thank you . . ."

"That's fine," he said. "Goodbye."

"It has been a pleasure, really," I said.

John looked at me strangely and paused as if he was about to say something, then changed his mind. I held out my hand and he shook it, brief and firm.

"Bye."

The Dining Hall was striking two.

Cle-ments

I pushed the tune from my head as I showed my key to the security guards and walked across Front Square, the white light from under the Campanile shining on the cobblestones. Front Gate creaked and clicked closed after me, but as I walked, I heard footsteps just behind me under Front Arch. I stopped and turned around, wondering who had slipped in so quickly after me, Fionnuala perhaps, returning disappointed from her tryst, or worried after hearing of my altercation. There was no-one there, but in the echo of the Dining Hall bell I thought I heard the faint strains of a song about London churches.

I shuddered and hurried across the square to Botany Bay and House Sixteen. My mind swirled with the encounters and events of this first day: my simple life was truly over. *Oranges and Lemons*, Fionnuala, her friend Sarah with the book, the man who had picked me up and brought me home. But I was drunk and sick and sad and nervous; I would go inside, climb the four flights of stairs to my room and sleep all of this off, leaving Pablo Virgomare, like John, Sarah, Fionnuala, and everyone else as just another dark shape among countless others here in the Trinity night, lying invisibly in wait for the day to come again and divide them off legibly from one another.

Two

But the madness and excitement of that first day did not continue, and I started again, as if as new, the next morning. For the next few weeks there was no sign of Pablo Virgomare and there were no mysteriously repeated phrases or songs at my window, and I even began to wonder if the whole strangeness of my first day in college had been hallucinated, the product of a nervous and lovesick mind at the outset of its big adventure.

While coincidences and serenades from strangers did not reoccur, the theme of new encounters, happily, did. Fionnuala and I became real friends. I didn't tell her about my "private life"—or rather about the kind of private life I would have had if I had acted on my secret desires. The shared context of our new life together in the closed granite city of Trinity was enough intimacy for the time being, and besides, the lack of anything like sexual tension between us indicated an acceptance, somewhere, of some sort of situation. She and I found a place to study, downstairs in the Lecky in the Anglo-Irish section, in front of a bank of windows looking on to Fellows' Square and the Old Library. When the libraries closed, at a quarter to ten, we often went for a few pints in the Buttery or in town, with people in our class, or with other members of our expanding circle. I knew potsmoking girls from Leicester, flirted slightly with six-foot Erasmus students from Bammberg, guzzled Guinness with people who studied Latin, Chemistry, and Finance. Our phones buzzed and glowed all day with incoming text messages, words flying back and forth across Trinity to make sure our paths would all intersect in some pub, at some party, outside some club at the same point in the evening, *buttery at 9, u free for coffee at 2?, crowd going to cafe en seine, party in Thall.*

Lectures started, and I became something I had never really been, an avid reader. Years of browsing the Bible and the *Encyclopaedia Britannica* while sitting on the toilet had given me a certain thin breadth of reference, but Fionnuala was sometimes shocked at my ignorance of classics or cult novels. Professor Dunne's lectures on nineteenth-century French fiction, and the English tutorials of a shatteringly sexy young lecturer fresh out of Cambridge, Jeremy Bodmoore, captured my untrained, secondary-school imagination and I let the days fall away into my lap in the Lecky Library.

Fionnuala continued to see James, the snog from Break for the Border, on and off, and it was of the results and plans of their meetings together that we mostly talked, when not about books, lectures, or—biggest topic of all—the comings and goings of our groups of friends. She introduced me to him once when his group of rowers collided, by raucous and delighted coincidence, with our French tutorial's regular Thursday night piss-up in Samsara on Dawson Street. He was all checked shirt, post-adolescent confidence, all that solidity I lacked, the same solidity that had drawn me to Ian, like, quite as the saying goes, a moth to a candleflame.

My stillborn friend from the other side, Patrick, settled into UCD pre-med. He phoned or texted me sometimes and we met once or twice for lunch, a weird adult innovation and departure from our previous round of playdates at home and in cinemas. Ordering ciabattas and coffee, paying the bill and leaving the tip, felt awkward, as if we were provincial aristocracy recently arrived in Paris, dressed up uncomfortably with our top hats and binoculars for the opera. Patrick and I had been best friends, in a titular more than actual way, for the first four years of secondary school, going to films or "into town" (dawdling in HMV, buying keyrings, eating in McDonald's, and learning the layout of the streets which was now proving to be a useful skill), staying the night in each other's houses where we played computer games, watched videos, and exchanged lightweight confidences before going to sleep. At the beginning of fifth year I had fallen insanely in love with Ian, and thus in the final year, when we were doing our Leaving Certificate, while the other swotty boys finally got it together to cobble together slightly more recognisably social lives and genuine intimacies, I had become something approaching a rugby wife, and Patrick became a dreary distraction of whom I saw as little as I could decently get away with. All my real interpersonal energies were conserved for the all-consuming project of Ian. I spent the period of Patrick's sexual awakening, if indeed he had had one, either sitting at home fretting about Ian, or, on the rare occasions when it was agreed to, sitting silently beside him in the pub at a table of his friends. All in all, Patrick and I could hardly have been called genuinely close, and our lunches consisted of an easy swapping of comparisons between UCD and Trinity, and some idle gossip about what our former classmates were up to; like all our conversations, it was akin to the knockup in tennis.

The oddball postgrad Sarah whom I had met on the first day, with her flicking through books and endless smoking, occasionally came to Commons, to which Fionnuala and I were entitled by our Beckett Scholarship and to which she, as a Foundation Scholar, was also admitted, but she didn't sit with or even greet

us. She always sat by herself with three or four books piled at her
elbow, eating very little and drinking an inappropriate amount
of Guinness, the only beverage, apart from water, served at
Commons. When dinner was over and the other Scholars lingered on the top of the steps smoking and talking, Sarah hurried
away alone. Fionnuala must have crossed her occasionally in the
stairs and corridors of Botany Bay's House 13, but Sarah's orbit
and mine never crossed.

The next time I saw, or thought I saw, Pablo Virgomare, one
smoky Friday evening around a month into term, was an
encounter that provoked another change in my life. I had a free
hour before going to join Fionnuala and the others on a night
out to the Stag's Head and Rí-Rá, and as I was sitting on the edge
of the grass on Fellows Square drinking coffee and watching the
men walking by, my attention was arrested by a blond man on
the other side of the grass, in front of the Old Library. He was
well-built and attractive, wearing big boots and a brown leather
jacket. I squinted through the night to make him out more
clearly, as he seemed to be responding to my cruisy stares. I
broke into a sweaty panic. Was I about to pick a man up? And
then what? And then it struck me that the object of my atten-
tions looked like Pablo Virgomare, a personage I had already
more or less dismissed as a mental aberration, but he left and
started walking quickly away with his back to me, so I couldn't
tell for sure. I jumped to my feet and raced across the grass after
him, but he was some way ahead and I couldn't make out his features fully. I kept him just in sight after he passed through Front
Arch and into the throngs of Friday night groups congregating
there. He crossed College Green over to the corner of Dame
Street, but I was caught by the traffic lights going green and the
evening traffic whizzing past. I threaded my way, dangerously,
through the cars and buses, to keep him in my sight as he hurried through the young drinkers along Dame Street. He turned

left up Georges Street, crossed the road, and, with a nod from the bouncers guarding the door, disappeared into the darkness and dry ice of the George. I stood across the street from the disco-thumping building and wondered what to do, if it really had been my mysterious stalker. I took a deep breath and crossed the road.

Two bouncers stopped me at the entrance.

"Been here before?" one of them, a huge, bald man, asked me.

"Yes . . . I'm meeting a friend," I stuttered.

"Yeh know what kind of club it is?" he asked.

I nodded and they moved out of my way. Sweat pricking my skin all over, I gathered my courage and went in. At first it was difficult to make anything out, because it was dark and so packed with people that the crowd overwhelmed me. As my frightened eyes adjusted, I started to make out the layout of the place and the faces of the people in it. It was a cavernous space, filled wall to wall with standing, laughing groups of men and some women, a dancefloor on a raised platform to the side, and upstairs a whole other room full of people, looming shapes barely distinguishable in the dark, dry ice and flashing coloured lights. Everything was murky and strange; the disco lights from the dancefloor blinded me. Through the beer, smoke and aftershave I smelt the smell of men, the same mysterious musk that had perfumed the sacred space of Ian's bedroom. I had never seen so many men together, not even in school. Their smell soaked into my brain, and their various pieces, their hairy fingers gripping pintglasses, the glint of the light on their gelled hair, their T-shirts, arms, shoes, cheeks, their pink tongues behind their teeth as they laughed, all of this overpowered me. Swooning lightly, I pushed my way through the warm bodies towards the bar. It was hard to move, and I was stumbling in soft, sexual shock. I knocked into a broad, muscled man in combats and a sleeveless T-shirt. He fell forward and spilt some of his pint. He turned around and looked at me, and I shrank back in fear; he was massive and rough-looking, a tattoo of a harp on his upper arm, and a chain hanging from his pocket.

"Sorry, I'm so sorry, really . . . will I get you another? It was an accident . . ." I stammered, gesturing to the bar. The man put a hand on my back and I shrank back. But he rubbed it absent-mindedly and said in soft, Dublin tones, the tones of an old woman selling cabbages and green beans on Moore Street:

"You're all right, chicken," and turned back to his friends.

I looked up at the people leaning over the upper gallery. One of them, a short-haired guy with an earring, winked at me. The whole place was immense and strange, the laughter and jab-bering of people beneath the music was a barbaric and compli-cated language, the aggressive chatter of a foreign market where the stallholders will cheat you and slim darkeyed men in the crowd will steal your wallet from your pocket.

Despite scouring the bars, dancefloor, and toilets, I failed to find Pablo or anyone resembling him in the George that night. I bought a drink; I stood at a table upstairs; through the flashing lights and music I looked through the heaving crowd for men resembling Ian. I was approached by the man with the earring. He was from Kilkenny, Paul or Martin or Vincent who worked in IT. I do not know what we talked about, but it brought me the first taste of a tongue in my mouth, and the first person to share my bed in House 16.

It was an instant conversion. From that day, for the whole of the following month, I replaced my trips to the Buttery and the Stag's in the company of Fionnuala and our new friends with solitary adventures to the George and, later, to the other bars on the gay axis of Georges, Parliament and Capel Streets. I would bring a book in the evening and sit at a table in the corner of the optimistic Front Lounge, and see who would come my way through its mock classical furniture and potted plants; I would stand among the dark wooden fixtures in

GUBU, until some drunken office-worker would talk an incomprehensible but arousing buzz in my ear.

I learned the weekly timetable of gay nights in mainstream nightclubs, an internalised sextant regulating the movement of constellations, an arcane system of seasonal rotation. During the day I would catch the eye of young men in suits who would give me a surreptitious look in the lunchtime sandwich queue, or at the bus stops along the Green after their working day was over, and imagine in advance their transfiguration according to this enigmatic calendar into sweaty dancers to Madonna on a stage, throwers of louche looks and surreptitious caresses, hungry, heaving bodies in my bed. My nights were spent in a shadowy erotic haze, a swirl of discosmoke, aftershave, and beery kissing. I, who had so recently never been kissed, became quickly used to the sight of goose-pimpled men picking their clothes off my floor and walking out of my life, and I became accustomed to their common hopes and habits, in the end hardly differentiating one from the other, so that at times I wondered if I had ever been with the same one twice without noticing, or indeed if it was just the one I was sleeping with over and over again.

I began in that month to write small fragments and then very short stories, pieces of no literary merit which I would tap out into the computer in my room, drinking coffee in the short hour or two between Commons and my excursions into the underworld. They were mostly unedited, romantic fictions about my time with Ian, which seemed now as distant and improbable as the tadpoles and guardian angels of primary school. While I always hoped for another encounter with Pablo Virgomare, I was convinced by now that the insane meetings and coincidences of my first day had been a crazed product of the tail-end of my obsession with Ian, and I thought that writing about my actual past would maintain me in normality and sanity, and perhaps help guide me through my accelerated and rather lonely sexual awakening.

Towards the end of November, I decided, on a whim of inactivity, to send a story to *A Muse*, the College literary magazine, which I had seen advertising for submissions. I sewed together a patchwork collage of my best lines from the repetitive collection of fragments I had accumulated, and I trudged through a dark four o'clock downpour to drop it in the Publications Committee mailbox. My runners were squelching and drops were running down my nose when I reached the cold shelter of Front Arch. I posted my soggy envelope in their box and stood for a while staring at the dark, drenched evening, rivers pouring from the gutters above, thinking that the George would be slow that night if it didn't ease off.

A wet slap of a human body from behind startled me and I spun around.

"Who . . . Fionnuala, Jesus Christ, you gave me a fright . . ."

The hood of her raincoat was closed tightly round her head and she looked like an alien.

"Sorry. I've run all the way from O'Connell Street. I don't think I can face any more moisture near my skin. What are you up to?"

I felt immediately guilty: for weeks I had seen her only at Commons and in class, always hurrying off before we could get into conversation. She had been texting me information about various nights out, and, when I never showed up, questions about how I had been spending my time. I had responded with a series of lies about studying and family and resting, and she must have wondered what had happened to our promising friendship. She took her hood down and shook out her bedraggled blond hair. Little drops of rain fell from her eyebrows.

"Not much," I said, "you?"

"There's a party tonight, you should come. It's in Ranelagh. Some bloke James knows."

"Will I know anyone there?"

"You'll know me, sure. And others, it's an Arts Block thing.

There'll be faces, you know the way . . . and anyway, I haven't seen you in *ages*. . . ."

Hard as it was to think of tearing myself away from the woozy pleasures of the George for even a single night, a sense of obligation, and even affection, won over, and so we arranged to meet on the steps of the Dining Hall after Commons to go to buy drink.

"See you at seven so," she called after me as she put her hood back on and prepared to run over to the 1937 Reading Room. "No excuses!"

I lay on the bed in my room for the afternoon, dozing and half-dreaming of oranges, lemons, and mysterious blond men at my window. The rain had almost completely stopped by the time I met Fionnuala on the steps, and though it was freezing cold we were still early for the party and decided to walk the half an hour through the puddles and traffic with clinking bags to the flat.

We stopped for a pint in O'Brien's in Ranelagh village, where we "caught up." I, of course, had to tell her lies to explain my abrupt disappearance from our social circle. What I told her was highly unconvincing, but she nodded and didn't object; she may even have guessed at what was going on, that I had a secret sexual life. In answer to my question, Fionnuala told me it was going fine with James. Just fine, she said, none of the crazy passion she had hoped for, but he was good enough company. I felt myself falling into the warm sense of companionship I had had with her at the beginning of the term, little more than a month ago, and regretted the manly exile I had chosen over the previous weeks, the flashing lights and smell of aftershave, ball-sweat, and Smirnoff ice. I was pleased to be here with a woman, for a change, with a friend.

We arrived at the house around half-nine. The rest of the red-brick houses were all black and quiet, slates glistening on the wet roofs, interrupted only by the occasional spectral flash of a television. Number four, where our party was on, was lit behind the closed curtains and pulsed gently with the music inside.

"Who is it lives here again?" I asked Fionnuala as she rang the bell.

"I can't remember exactly. James knows one of them from Trinity rowing or something. And his flatmate, she runs with an older crowd, apparently. So there'll be you know, real people here too."

James opened the door.

"Come in," he said to Fionnuala, "I saw you through the window." He nodded, uninterested, to me, and I raised my eyebrows to return the greeting. Inside it was like a party in a beer ad, people on the stairs, leaning the length of the wall in the hall, standing in doorways, all talking loudly above the music and drinking out of bottles and cans. Fionnuala and James conducted a playful hello beside me, punctuated with kisses, mock-reproaches, and coy smiles.

We pushed through the hall into the kitchen, where Fionnuala and I hid our cans of beer from potential thieves as best we could and opened one each. She got distracted by people she knew and left me to fend for myself. The kitchen, with all the lights on, and its white and pine furnishings, was too bright for me, and so I drifted into the sitting room.

There was something of a crowd in here, too, the sofas and chairs filled, a group half-dancing in the middle of the room to the mellow music that the two people crouching at the stereo surrounded by a pile of CDs had put on, some young star of the Celtic Tiger. I stood against a free patch of wall behind the couch, a can of Heineken in my fist, in my well-rehearsed role as the evening's audience, a newspaper critic who covered student parties, a freelancer who wrote reviews of life. I reflected that the only social skill I had properly learned since coming to college was how to cruise in a gay bar, and standing like this against the wall, hitting my hand lightly against my leg in time with the music while surreptitiously scanning the crowd, was the way to behave on a Thursday night in the Front Lounge rather than at a student house party. Out of habit I examined the room carefully for the curly head of Pablo Virgomare. Not here either, of course. I began to consider skipping surreptitiously out and heading into town to the George when my vision was arrested by the sight, not of Pablo, but of someone else I recognised and associated with him.

It was Sarah, hunched down in the other corner, beside the bookshelf, a heap of books beside her, a cigarette smoking away between her fingers. I recognised her from just the back of her head, her unkempt, boyish hair and pale white neck. She was completely out of place at the party, older than almost everyone else for a start, and totally engrossed in what she was doing at the bookshelf. If anyone could tell me anything about Pablo and his song, if anyone was involved in the setup, it had to be her, I knew. I was about to walk over and reintroduce myself, but I was suddenly greeted with a whoop of delight by another girl I recognised.

"Nialler, you big knacker!"

It was Andrea. She opened her arms, and gave me a brief, perfumed hug. Over her shoulder, I could see Sarah holding her cigarette between her lips, while she held a piece of paper covered in handwriting up to her eyes with one hand, and ran the other along the bookshelf behind her. Andrea clinked her glass against my can in a toast.

"I didn't know you were here!"

"Yeah . . . I wasn't expecting to be." I craned my neck to make out what Sarah was doing.

"What are you looking at? You look like you've seen a ghost. You *are* a ghost, actually," she elaborated, "you haven't been out with us in *yonks*."

"I know, I know, I had all this stuff on, you know, like my cousin's wedding and that kind of jazz."

Andrea, who knew all about cousins and competing social

obligations, and who was too invested in turning the current party into something to talk about the next day to be interested in irrelevant flashbacks, accepted this without question or interest and moved the conversation on to narrative material.

"Come here, *what* the fuck do you think of that guy last week?"

"Who?"

In the corner, Sarah continued to run her hand up and down the books, her face turned away from the bookshelf. She stopped near the middle and felt the spines, back and forth, of three or four, before choosing one and pulling it down from the shelf.

"You know, the American one in Dunne's class. . . ."

"Oh, Karl."

"Yeah, him. I was like yeah yeah usual Dunne shite about hills and Napoleon and all, and suddenly he's there, *whis*-pering in my *ear*! And Jayne had said to me, right—beforehand, like—you know, that American gives me the fucking *willies*, make sure you don't sit near him. And of course, like every fucking American gobshite that shows up in that kip he makes a beeline for me . . ."

Without looking at the title of the book, Sarah opened it and began flicking through the pages, her eyes turned upwards, away from it, as if she was reading the cigarette smoke spiralling up towards the ceiling.

"I mean, what the fuck was he thinking?" Andrea was saying. ". . . I mean, pa-ra-*plee*-gic . . . He was all like what did you do at the weekend and all this shite, and I'm there you're in my class not my *life*. . . ."

Sarah was flicking back and forth through the book. She stopped at a page in the middle. Still looking up at the ceiling, she ran her finger up and down the page, before fixing on a certain point and looking down to read what she had chosen.

"*Aaa*nnyway, the thing is, that happened on the *Wanz*-day, right, and me and Jayne went to this guy's party in Carrickmines on the *Fri*-day, this com-*plete* dote, Robbie, we've known him since we were in high babies, kind of thing, you know, so we're there, chillaxing like, couple of brews and you're well on the way sort of scenario, and then in walks your man, right, and me and Jayne are there, what the fuck *is* he, some kind of serial killer or whatever . . ."

Andrea's words faded from my hearing as I concentrated on observing Sarah. She was reading and rereading the line she had picked from the book. Her lips moved slightly as she went over it again and again, her eyes narrowed and staring fixedly into the middle distance, her face in an attitude of deep, almost troubled concentration. She pulled heavily on her cigarette.

". . . well it turns out he knows some cousin of Conor Connolly," Andrea was saying, starting to look a bit suspicious of what I was interested in over her shoulder.

"Oh right, yeah, Conor Connolly," I echoed.

"Yeah. So, the party goes on annyhow," Andrea continued, satisfied, "a few more Bacardis and whatever, then Jayne right *cracks* open this bottle of Tia Maria and fucking *lays* into it. And I'm there like *no*-thank-*you*. So I go to the toilet, right, and Jayne is *langers*. I mean com-*plete*-ly vagina-faced, right, and I come down and she's there . . ." she broke off, unable to contain her laughter. "She was . . ." she screamed, "*shif*-ting him! I mean like there on the couch, *snogging* the spa! I was there, oh my god, you retarded cow, and she opens her eyes and looks at me, and we both crack up laughing, and he's there like what . . ."

Sarah had added the book to the pile around her, and was writing something down on the sheet of foolscap. When she had finished, she began studying the sheet closely again, reading back over her notes from top to bottom. She stretched out her hand to choose another book.

"I need a new drink." I interrupted Andrea, hoping to use the diversion to go over to Sarah.

She sniggered.

"Alco. See you later."

I went to the kitchen and pulled out one of my cans of beer

where I had concealed them in a fridge compartment with the lettuce and carrots. Back in the sitting room, Andrea, always the social survivor, had moved on, new group, new story, her conversation with me over and forgotten.

". . . so I asked him·what the fuck do you think I am made of money and eventually he gave in, like, but *such* a fucking scab I swear to God. . . ."

I walked over and stood behind Sarah in the corner next to the bookshelf. She was running her hand along the books, and her face was turned away from it, more or less towards me, but her eyes were glazed and she showed no signs of recognition, or even of seeing me at all, until I greeted her.

"Sarah."

She jumped.

"Yes?" She dropped her hand and looked blankly at me, huge grey eyes with a strange flicker of dark green in her pupils.

"I'm Niall Lenihan. We met with Fionnuala."

She looked startled and annoyed at being interrupted, though she could hardly have expected to be left alone to consult books in private in the middle of a party.

"Fionnuala . . . Fionnuala . . . oh, right," she trailed off, uninterested, her eyes flicking greedily back to the pile of books.

I looked to the foolscap page covered in writing, on the ground beside the books. She followed my eyeline, then snatched it up and folded it away in her hand.

"What brings you here?" I asked her.

"Oh, an ill wind, an ill wind."

"And may I ask what are you doing at the bookshelf?"

"May you ask . . . What do you think? Looking for a book."

She gathered the volumes on the ground under her arm and stood up hurriedly.

"At a party?"

"Yes, at a party," she said, and started to walk away. I shifted position to block her exit. I had decided to tell her about the coincidence of my finding Pablo's song in the book she had proffered to me in O'Neill's, but, frightened by the intensity with which she looked at me with her peculiar eyes, I recalled in sudden, full detail the forgotten strangeness of that first day in Trinity, how frightening the visit from Pablo and the coincidence had been. I stared, unable to bring myself to say anything. "So . . ." I began.

"Yes?" she prompted.

"So where are you from?" was all I could finally manage.

"Where am I from. Do I come here often. Is that Chanel Number Five you're wearing. I'm from Galway."

"I'm from Dublin. Sandycove."

"Right, well, that must be lovely for you. Dublin's Riviera. Excuse me."

She pushed past me, the books piled in her arms with the folded sheet of paper between the pages of one of them. She walked out of the room and through the door into the kitchen.

I waited for a moment where I was, then went to follow her. I couldn't see her at first, she had moved fast and they had turned off the lights in the kitchen, where a guy with a guitar was sitting at the table playing a maudlin Irish song. A bit early in the night for that, I thought irritably.

On Raglan Road, on an autumn day,
I saw her first and knew

I scanned the shadowy room to see if I could spot Sarah, but she had vanished among the crowd of darkened faces. Andrea poked her head around the door to see what was going on.

I gave her gifts of the mind
I gave her the secret sign that's known

"Oh God," she groaned when she heard the singing, "I hate this diddley-eye stuff." She went back to the sitting-room, and I finally spotted Sarah sitting at a far corner of the table, one leg folded under her, talking to a man beside her. As I attempted to figure out a means of approaching her through the several groups of people standing between us without making a scene, I did a double-take. The man she was talking to, sitting back with a booted foot on the edge of the table, black hair, dark, suspicious eyes and a pale, chiselled face, around Sarah's age, was someone I recognised from the same mad, swirling day I had met Sarah and Pablo Virgomare. It was the one who had brought me home from the pub my first night in Trinity, John. I blushed with a sudden flash of desire and surprise.

> *On a quiet street where old ghosts meet*
> *I see her walking now*

Sarah was whispering frantically in his ear, and he was nodding and frowning. He looked up then, and met my eyes. I raised a hand in greeting, but he didn't notice.

> *I had wooed, not as I should*
> *A creature made of clay*

John and Sarah kept talking, every now and again pointing to something written on the foolscap. I stayed where I was near the fridge, nodding an occasional hello to a passerby of my acquaintance, watching their conversation. After some time they stood up, squeezed in behind the guitarist to get to the French windows, and disappeared into the garden.

Andrea came by.

"Well, hello, stranger! I've been having *rahlly interesting* conversations, I'd say," she said sarcastically. "Have you seen Jayne? She was supposed to be sharing a taxi with me. I bet the slut is up in a bedroom snogging some randomer," she giggled approvingly. "Come here, wait there till I find her."

Laughing to herself at these, the usual antics, *plan*-ty material for stories the next day, she went off in search of her old friend. I contemplated following John and Sarah into the garden, but wavered, fearing it would be too much stalking, and that my interest in mysterious recurrent patterns was taking over and rotting my sanity. I opened the fridge, and discovered that all the beer was gone. I wandered around searching for something to drink, rattling empty cans and holding bottles up to the lights. Eventually I found an abandoned bottle of gin on the counter beside the fridge, and camped myself beside it waiting for Sarah and John to come back in. The party was slowly ending, but there was no sign of either Fionnuala or Andrea, and so I remained there like a maître d', greeting passersby, mixing the gin with flat tonic, until it ran out and I moved to orange juice, coke, and finally tapwater. I was not used to drinking much, but I progressed steadily and unstintingly down the bottle, and an hour of lonely tippling later, when John and Sarah had still not come in from the cold, the room was an unstable fuzz before my eyes. I left the kitchen and wandered aimlessly round the house, too drunk by now to speak or really take in what was going on around me. I thought I heard Sarah and John's voices gabbling furiously behind a bedroom door but didn't have the bravery to try it. Andrea had disappeared, Fionnuala I found in a bedroom upstairs curled up asleep on a beanbag. There was another girl sleeping on the bed so I closed the door on them and left. There was no one left awake in the house but a handful of little groups talking in corners.

My head was spinning and I was unsteady on the stairs. Finally, the pink flowers on the wallpaper began to swirl around and I realised I was ill. Someone whispered with winey breath in my ear, and put a strong soft hand on my brow. I took him first for Ian and then for Pablo, but perhaps it was just one of the hosts, whom I had not met, or a kind passing reveller. He took me to the bathroom and made me induce myself to throw up.

"You'll feel much better. Honestly, trust me. Come on, count, one . . . two . . . three. . . ."

Twenty minutes later, after many loud eruptions of bitter, watery orange, my guide through this nauseous hell guided me downstairs and into the sitting room, laid me down on the couch, and pulled a blanket over me. Two guys were sitting in a corner smoking and talking in low voices and did not seem to notice or mind my arrival. My Florence Nightingale gave me a pint of water and two little white ovals of paracetmol. I swallowed them down with a gulp into my empty, quivering stomach.

"Goodnight."

I capitulated gratefully to a blurry drunken sleep.

When grey light and mumbling voices woke me some hours later, I knew exactly where I was and immediately registered hunger and thirst. I opened my eyes. At the other end of the room, three figures, all fully dressed and holding mugs, were sitting around a pile of books on the floor. The dim dawn was supplemented by a table lamp on the floor beside them. The room had been largely cleaned of empty cans and bottles and smelt of tobacco and fresh coffee. I strained to make them out. To my great surprise, I saw Fionnuala, Sarah, and John. There was a muttering which I couldn't make out, and then I heard Fionnuala saying, in a careful, important voice, the way she spoke in Trinity tutorials:

"What is my attitude to James?"

The other two repeated what she said. Then Fionnuala stood up and went to the bookshelf, closed her eyes, and picked out a book. She flicked through it, eyes closed, then read out from the page she had picked:

Iceland, too was completely unprepared for the Reformation. Its last two Catholic bishops, Ögmundur Pállson of Skálholt and Jón Arason of Hólar, were both men of note who ruled their sees

with a firm hand. Their theological training was presumably
slight, but Jón Arason was a poet of some importance.

"Wow. What do you think?"

Sarah said: "What do you think yourself, Fionnuala?"

John walked over to the window, sipping his coffee.

"Actually, it's amazing. Okay. 'Iceland was completely unprepared for the Reformation.' Well, Iceland is me, obviously, and
it's true that I'm unprepared. Does the Reformation just stand
for the relationship, do you think, or does it *actually* mean that
being with James will reform me?" No one answered her.
"Anyway, my last two boyfriends, i.e. the bishops, I suppose,
you could say were 'of note,' in that I really did fall for and
respect them. And the firm hand thing is so true, they were
really possessive and domineering. And that really is the big difference with James. Wow. This *does* work."

"Your turn, John," said Sarah.

"It's okay," he said without turning from the window. "Pass."

"I insist."

"Do I have a choice?"

"Ask that!" Sarah said. "What choice does John have?"

"What choice does John have?" echoed Fionnuala. John
glared at Sarah.

"What choice do I have?" he muttered, then walked over to
the bookshelf. He shut his eyes, twisted his head away from the
bookshelf, and ran his hand along the titles. He picked his
volume and page, and, opening his eyes, began to read.

'You are extremely kind,' said Theresa; 'but I cannot give up my
early walk. I am advised to be out of doors as much as I can, I
must walk somewhere and the post-office is an object; and upon
my word, I have scarcely ever had a bad morning before.'

He read it in a monotone, with the double vowels and airbrush consonants of the south Dublin bourgeoisie, the accent and cadences of rugby players and young bankers, Ian's talk, and it was quite amusing to hear them accommodate this prim prose. It presented quite a contrast to Fionnuala's clipped musical Belfast sentences and the studied neutrality of Sarah's speech, which, with its lost substratum of a provincial accent, had a faint whiff of heather and seasalt.

John sat down again, keeping the page.

"Give it here . . ." Sarah took the book and read through the passage carefully, then passed it to Fionnuala.

"Well," Sarah said at length, scratching her temple. "I suggest the first question is whether she is exercising a choice or refusing the possibility of choice altogether."

"But it's also not just about her," said John, "I mean, there's the question of the relationship between . . . Theresa . . . and your one who's suggesting something else. This early walk to the bank, or the post office, is at the price of the other person's wishes. . . ."

Fionnuala spoke: "But there's also the obligation of the advice, you know, the doctor or whoever tells her to stay out of doors. . . ."

"Essentially," Sarah said, "I think we must read an element of regret here. The early walk is regretfully necessary; there *is* a choice, a possibility of doing something else, anything else at all. But there must be an object. You cannot just walk, you must walk *somewhere*. A choice must be made, arbitrarily perhaps, but a choice must still be made, and it must be to the exclusion of all other choices. Once the path is chosen, here the early-morning walk to the post office, then you must act as if you had no more choice in the matter. The passage mourns the lost possibilities which choice involves; but it acknowledges its necessity."

They continued to discuss it, pulling the passage to pieces and then putting it all back together. Sarah, quick and sharp, read something almost religious in the calling to the early morning walk, and the rejection of a life of ease and leisure offered instead; the vocation might be a random one, she maintained, it might be difficult, but the advice was to choose the hard path, any hard path, and then to follow it with full devotion and commitment. John was resentful and reticent, but when he was forced to get going, colloquially insightful. He felt the walk to the post office was more considered, a choice which was constantly renegotiated, and might well change the next day. His statements were always relevant and incisive, but not as elegantly or academically put together as Sarah's.

They discussed this one for a while, and then another one about Fionnuala's attitude to money. I dozed off again; as their voices transformed themselves into dreamlike chatter, I thought it was the radio, then my parents, Patrick and his mother, a group of men around a table in the Front Lounge. I was woken by the sounds of arguing.

"Fine, then," Sarah was saying, "ask a specific question."

"About someone else?"

"Yes, ask one about the guy asleep on the couch. He's a friend of yours, isn't he? What's his name, Neil."

I closed my eyes and feigned sleep as Fionnuala looked over.

"Okay, then, I will." She paused. "Oh yeah, I know what to ask. . . . Who does Niall fancy?"

The other two repeated it after her. I heard the sound of Fionnuala flipping pages.

"Okay," she started to read.

He was prepared to give us information in exchange. And here is what it was. Berenger was consumed, as many of the monks now knew, by an insane passion for Adelmo—by the same passion whose evils divine wrath had castigated in Sodom and Gomorrah.

I gave a little jump of shame. John grunted in amusement.

"Come on, you're awake, own up," Fionnuala said.

I hesitated for a moment and then opened my eyes.

"Morning," I said.

I threw off the blankets and sat up on the edge of the sofa, in my rumpled and slightly vomit-stained clothes. I drained the pint glass of water beside me.

"Come on over," Fionnuala said. "Join the hungover madness."

"What's the book club about?" I asked them.

"I came down to get some water, and found these two playing what I can only call a literary party game."

John was standing at the window again, his hands in his pockets and his shoulders hunched.

"And then there were none," he said without turning round.

"Niall, you know Sarah," Fionnuala said. Sarah was sitting on an armchair smoking, and didn't acknowledge the reintroduction. "This is John. John, this is my friend Niall, the other—"

"Beckett scholar," Sarah finished with a roll of her eyes.

John stayed where he was looking out at the early morning street. The rain had diminished now into a steady drizzle, and the suburban birds were stirring with tentative chirps.

"Actually, we've met as well," I said. I stood up off the couch. John turned around and looked at me without recognition. He didn't say anything.

"You did me a favour once, remember?"

"A favour?" He scrutinised me for a moment, then recollected my face.

"Oh, are you the guy who fell over after the knacker looked crossways at him?" He laughed nastily and turned back to the window. "Yeah, I remember you."

"You were very kind," I answered.

"There's coffee if you want," he said then, by way, I thought, of being nice after the rather hurtful remark. I asked him for black, no sugar and he turned without a word and went into the kitchen. Fionnuala flicked through the books, while Sarah tapped her cigarette into a saucer on the arm of her chair. John came back in and handed me a mug of coffee, then, picking up his own, resumed his silent position looking out onto the street.

"Let's do some more," said Fionnuala. "I want Niall to see it."

Sarah looked over at John. He shrugged. Sarah stubbed out her cigarette and sat forward, as if she was about to deal a hand of cards.

"Okay," she said. "This is, as your friend says, just a game, but if you do it properly it is a game that can be useful and stimulating." She looked at me as if this required a response. I cleared my throat.

"I see."

"But for it to work, it requires belief. You have to forget that you don't believe, act and think from the start as if—"

"But of course it doesn't—" Fionnuala began to interject reassuringly.

"I'll do the talking, Fiona. We've been through your views already. Anyway. Just temporarily adjust the boundaries of your reality to accept that it's true."

"What is?"

"It's a form of divination known for millennia," she said, somewhat pompously. "The Babylonians, Arabs, Hebrews, Egyptians all practised it. The Romans called it *sortes,* or lots. Simply put, you ask a question and take a random quote as your answer. Everyone knows the one with St. Augustine, where a child's voice in the garden tells him to pick up a book and read. *Tolle, lege.* He reads the first lines of the Bible which his eyes fall onto, and what he reads prompts his conversion. The most famous versions which have come down to us from the Romans are the *sortes Virgilianae,* in which they chose lines from Virgil, but it's a method known in hundreds of versions: the *sortes Biblicae,* the *sortes Apostolorum,* the *sortes Sangallenses,* and so on. Synchronicity is a Jungian term for something similar, and we use the terms interchangeably, more or less. Simply put, you ask a question and believe, in advance, with complete certitude, that the right answer to it will be in a passage chosen at random from a book chosen at random. It's always the right passage."

"And how is this supposed to work, exactly?" I asked.

Fionnuala interrupted excitedly: "The way I see it, it's like the truth of a poem, you know, the conjunction of your experience with—"

"Well, that's your theory, Fiona. The individuals of antiquity who turned to Virgil and the Bible believed it was impossible for them to be in error. So the answer had to be the correct one. After all, the Gospels or the *Æneid* were hardly going to tell you lies. All that has to be done is that we believe, implicitly, that you *always pick the right passage.* You ask the question, we all concentrate on it, then you close your eyes and pull a book at random from the shelf, open it at a random page and begin reading a random sentence. And it is always the right answer, as far as we're concerned. Do you understand?"

"How long do you read for?"

"You'll feel the shape of it, you'll know when it's come to the end of the answer. Sometimes you read on a bit more if you need clarity, sometimes sentences are clearly red herrings and we can ignore them."

I nodded.

"Right, then let's begin. John, sit down." He obeyed. Sarah turned to me. "Ask something, then close your eyes, pick a book from the shelf and pick a passage."

"At random?"

"Yes."

"What should I ask?"

"Anything. Whatever comes into your head."

I thought for a while.

"Okay. What is going on here?"

I went to the bookshelf and skipped my fingers along the spines of the books. At first I thought I wouldn't be able to choose one, there was no reason to pick one more than another. Then, suddenly, like the tug of a fishing line, one of them suggested itself definitively to my hand. I pulled it down and flicked through it. My thumb stopped about two thirds of the way through the stiff yellow pages. I took a surreptitious glance at the cover. Agatha Christie, *The Pale Horse*. I cleared my throat and began reading:

> *"All this talk of remote control reminds me of something that odd Miss Grey said."*
>
> *"Ah, our dear Thyrza!" His tone was smooth, indulgent (but had there been a faint flicker of the eyelids?). "Such nonsense as those two dear ladies talk! And they believe it, you know, they really believe it. Have you been yet—(I'm sure they'll insist on your going)—to one of these ridiculous séances of theirs?"*
>
> *I had a momentary hesitation whilst I decided rapidly what my attitude here ought to be.*

"That's enough," Sarah said sharply. But I felt I hadn't got to the end of the "answer," and that, after all, was the rule. I said so and continued reading:

> *"Yes," I said, "I—I did go to a séance."*
>
> *"And you found it great nonsense? Or were you impressed?"*
>
> *I avoided his eyes and presented to my best ability a man who is ill at ease.*
>
> *"I—oh well—of course I didn't really believe in any of it. They seem very sincere, but—" I looked at my watch. "I'd no idea it was so late. I must hurry back. My cousin will wonder—"*

"Stop!" Sarah cried loudly. She walked over to me and snatched the book out of my hands.

"What's wrong?" Fionnuala asked.

"Just," Sarah said, taking the book from me and putting it back on the shelf, "ask something else."

I wanted to ask the same question, so I varied the wording a little. "What is behind all this?"

This time I picked the *Encyclopedic Dictionary of Semiotics*. What kind of people had this on their living-room bookshelf, I wondered. Sarah and John exchanged a tense glance.

(1) The INTERLOCUTOR, more or less fictive, is not indicated in the text. If he is, it is already an addition: address. *One can occasionally speak to him without naming him: it is* parabasis.

"Sorry," Sarah said. "I'll have to stop you again."

"Wait," I said, "I think it's interesting."

In conversation one begins by mentioning the name of every one: that is presentations. *If one addresses oneself to a superior, one makes him a* report *of what one has seen, or implores his* clemency . . .

John walked over to me and pulled the book firmly out of my hands. He was standing right in front of me.

"Do as she says, would you?" he said angrily. "Ask something personal. That's what you're supposed to do."

"Okay," I said. I thought for a moment. A brief, random flash of Ian came into my head, and I asked: "Will I ever find love?"

I closed my eyes and picked something else. Another Agatha Christie. I read out the passage I had chosen:

Mr. Parker Pyne drew from his wallet a cutting. He laid it on the table in front of Smethurst.

"ARE YOU UNHAPPY?" (So it ran.) "IF SO, CONSULT MR. PARKER PYNE."

Smethurst focused on it after some difficulty.

"Well, I'm damned," he ejaculated. "You meantersay—people come and tell you things?"

"They confide in me, yes."

"Pack of idiotic women, I suppose."

"A good many women," admitted Mr. Parker Pyne. "But men also. What about you, my young friend? You wanted advice just now?"

"Shut your damned head," said Captain Smethurst. "No business of anybody's—'cept mine. Where's that goddamned araq?"

Mr. Parker Pyne shook his head sadly.

He gave up Captain Smethurst as a bad job.

"Oh Christ," I said. "That's so depressing."

Fionnuala was laughing.

"If it was a palm-reader, you'd shoot her!" she said. "And what's an 'araq' when it's at home?"

"I don't think it's funny. . . ." I said, looking at the words. "Every way you look at it it's bad news. *He gave up Captain Smethurst as a bad job.* Unless there's another way of interpreting it?" I appealed to Sarah and John. They were staring tensely at the floor.

"Undoubtedly." John said, quietly, giving the briefest glance at Sarah. She looked away.

"Oh, come on!" Fionnuala said to me, "don't get upset, it's only a game. We could have picked this one for the choice or the boyfriend or any of those other questions."

"But we didn't," I said.

"Oh please!" she snorted. "You don't really believe this, do you?"

There was a silence.

"I don't know . . ." I said. "I think they know something."

"Who's 'they,' Niall? For God's sake, you can read anything into . . . oh for fuck's sake Niall, don't . . . I can't believe you're so superstitious. I bet the books'll start bending spoons and . . . and fixing broken watches. Look, scientific conditions, I'll show you." She stood up.

"What is my relationship to the man who fathered me?" she demanded of the bookshelf. She gave me a wink, her trick, I supposed, being to pick a passage which we would all see as full of father stuff and then reveal to John and Sarah that she was adopted.

She flicked through the book she chose and stopped. When she looked at the page she gave a start and said nothing.

"Read it out, Fionnu," I said. She stayed still, the book in her hand. "Come on, show me what you picked."

"Let's go home," she said, "I'm wrecked."

"No, show me. . . ." I put my hand on the book. She resisted a little, then gave it up to me. She had picked a blank page. She looked at me. "Look, it's just another coincidence. Let's go home, it's half-eight in the morning."

"I don't think it's a coincidence. And I want to know," I said, looking at Sarah and John. Neither of them looked at me. He was standing at the window again, arms folded and back to us; she was restacking books on the shelf, as if to say *the library is now closing.*

"No, I want to go back to Trinity."

"Wait, Fionnuala, one more question." I could feel my eyes shining. "Scientific conditions. Something factual. Sarah, tell me, what should I ask."

She said nothing, but I took it as tacit permission that she did not deliberately look away. I was standing at the bookshelf with the pile of consulted volumes littered at my feet. Fionnuala had gathered her coat and bag up from a chair and had her hand on the doorknob, wavering, her coat across her arm. John was at the window looking grimly over at Sarah sitting on the armchair in front of me with a worried, concentrated expression, a plume of cigarette smoke in front of her face like a snake rising from a charmer's basket.

"Just one question, Fionnuala," I said, "Okay. Where do my parents live?"

As I felt my hand falling over the bookspines I already knew that over this hung worlds. Two mutually exclusive universes were in the balance, teetering over the tiny gap in the space–time continuum which was my choice. As I went back to the beginning of the rows of books and touched each title as I ran my finger along, I knew that the passage I chose would be either ambiguous and a confirmation of what Fionnuala was saying, a triumph for Ian, for all those people, for all those adolescent dreads of emptinesses to follow; or else it would be something else, the opposite, unimaginable. I wished so deeply for it to work, a choice between a past I knew stretching drearily on out into an eternal, colourless future, and the possibility of fullness and newness and things I didn't know. I could feel the inevitability of the dull and the mundane creeping in, the ridiculousness of anything except that the world was as Fionnuala said, and these two were just arrogant and unfriendly thirty-year-olds who took their party games extremely seriously and were irritated by our undergraduate enthusiasms and fears. I tried to push that out of my mind as I stopped at a thick book, but my heart was already falling. I flicked through *Ulysses* and the probability waves all came crashing down around each other and collapsed into a singularity.

—*We can drink it black, Stephen said thirstily. There's a lemon in the locker.*

—*Oh damn you and your Paris fads, Buck Mulligan said. I want Sandycove milk.*

Three

There was a ragged and unpleasant end to the morning. Fionnuala burst into tears and screamed "I hate this!" while John and Sarah looked on, more furious at me than at Fionnuala. I was hoping to be invited to stay on with them and do more, find out if I could use the sortes to investigate Pablo—part, I was certain, of some weird interconnected chain of events. But Sarah and especially John wanted us both gone immediately, and Fionnuala was not interested in mysteries, she wanted partisanship and loyalty. She asked me defiantly through red eyes to leave with her, immediately. I looked pleadingly at John and Sarah. Sarah stacked the remaining books on the shelf and put her cigarettes into her handbag. John walked into the kitchen and started to wash the cups.

I hesitated. If I insisted on staying, Sarah and John would have to tell me more, give me some answers, but Fionnuala had scraped a tiresome pentagram on the floor and summoned up the spirits of friendship and obligations, so I left, embarrassed, with her, writing my phone-number on a piece of paper, which

I left on a table, telling Sarah to be in touch. She showed no signs of taking it, and no one offered me any numbers.

Outside, the first wintry signs of the sun were spreading from the horizon. Fionnuala and I walked against the freezing wind, hunched over, hands in pockets, by the triangle in Ranelagh, across the Canal and down Harcourt Street along the Green, aftershave-smelling men in their suits on their way in to be first into the office, girls from the country with their wet hair scraped back, hurrying along in runners, their work shoes in the little bags on their backs. We walked down Grafton Street, where the shops were pulling up their grilles and a noisy vehicle brushed the filthy gutters with swirling bristles, and into Trinity again, where a couple of zealous academics were parking, drizzle on their overcoats, in to prepare Friday morning classes. I said an ungracious goodbye to Fionnuala at the door of House 13. We had walked the whole way in silence.

"It's free association, Niall," she called to my retreating back, as she put the key in the door, "the books call up associations in your mind and stimulate it, like automatic writing or something . . ." she trailed off. We were both looking at a flock of birds fly off crying over the Old Library.

"Yeah," I said, "sleep well."

I stumbled back to my room, dazed, cold, and exhausted, and collapsed onto my bed without taking my clothes off.

Conversation with Fionnuala at Commons that evening avoided the topic by tacit agreement, though I wanted to ask her to actually consider how it would have been if the question about my parents had drawn the blank page, or the one about her father the piece from *Ulysses*. Sarah came to Commons only once that whole week and left before I had a chance to confront her. I saw her greet Fionnuala coldly on the Dining Hall steps and hurry off. That was on Tuesday. The following, freezing, night I walked over to House 13 and looked for her name on the bells.

There was a Sarah Casey and a Sarah Ní Dhuibhir, and, guessing she was the latter, I rang it. I knew I had guessed correctly, because the muffled doorbell sound came from the room directly above Fionnuala's. The curtains were pulled, but not completely, and I could see a light on. A figure peered through the curtains to see who it was, and then moved quickly away. I rang several times but received no answer. After five minutes of waiting in the cold it was clear that she wasn't going to respond, so I trudged through the icy wind to the George, in the hope that it would distract me from these mysteries, but, once there, I found my erotic thoughts so firmly fixed on the images of John and Pablo that I gave up and went back to my rooms.

I tried again to put the whole thing out of my mind, but it was impossible, and I even found myself doing the odd few *sortes* when I was hesitating about some minor decision, or just at a loose end. A letter came a few days later which distracted me a little. It contained the unexpected news that *A Muse* had accepted my story, along with an invitation to the Publications Committee Christmas do in the Atrium on the last Friday of the term, just over a week away.

I went home for the weekend. There was now a lot about Trinity I had to let settle in my head, and I wanted some distance. The weeks I had spent there already seemed divided into geological ages, the initial night of madness, started by Pablo; the first busy weeks of lectures, friendship with Fionnuala and our gang; the subsequent weeks of man-hunting in the George and elsewhere; now this. My parents were proud when I told them about the story and told me to get a few copies so I could give one to my grandparents and send one to my uncle in London. This worried me a little, given the sexual undertones of the story, but I considered it unlikely they would pick up on them. My sister Ciara had won a debating medal that week as well, so we all went out to a Chinese restaurant in Dalkey to celebrate. John and Sarah and Pablo and cryptic synchronicities faded like a dawn dream into the soft lights and humming buses of the suburbs. We sat around, swapping sweet and sour pork for chicken in black bean sauce, bickering slightly and laughing at old family stories—when Ciara did a wee in a neighbour's houseplant, when I asked my grand-aunt Elizabeth why she had so many wrinkles. Lost in here amid the rugby pitches and shopping-centre carparks, life flowed along slow and weighted, in a repetitive and scrutable cycle like the seasons. I felt protected by the chatter of the parents of boys I used to know, the wet smell of our gardens, the viscous air and bland voices of my homeland. Here I was at one with the land and people, here I was nobody, here I slept. I waited for the last DART on Sunday night to pull me north along the coast back into the confusion and lights of the city centre.

At lunchtime the following day, back in Trinity, I got a text message from Ciara saying that Ian's mother had rung the house. He had left his phone with all his old numbers in the back of a taxi and needed my mobile. About an hour later, I got a text message from him inviting me to his birthday drinks the following Thursday in Kiely's of Donnybrook, scene of several stations of the via dolorosa of my last years in Gonzaga *(Ian Leaves Without Telling Niall; Ian Buys a Drink for a Stranger and Ignores Niall; Niall Mops Up Ian's Vomit and Carries Him Home; Ian Shows a Callous Disregard for Niall in Making Transport Arrangements Home)*. I bought a new top in Dunne's on Stephens Green, and spent an hour after Commons getting myself dressed up to go, trying to strike a note of breezy independence, the outfit of a boy who has found a life, the one not to let get away. I set off to the bus stop gelled and smelled and filled with nervous hope, but ended up standing in the yellow lights of Nassau Street in the freezing cold, letting the buses go by one by one, standing still and thinking of nothing. I stayed there for three hours, until the last bus had gone by full of the inebriated of the suburbs on their way home from city revels. I walked back through the biting midnight wind to my rooms, threw my new top on the chair and went to bed.

A Muse appeared on the Wednesday, and indeed there was "'Towards the Mist' by Niall Lenihan JF." On Friday I was exhausted after four days of intense studying, preparation for the Christmas essays, so I took a long sleep in the afternoon to refresh myself for the Publications party. I sat beside Fionnuala at Commons, since I hadn't seen her much during the week, and she congratulated me on my story, which she said she was saving to read on the Belfast train on Sunday. She seemed to have forgotten, or at least forgiven, the whole incident of the books and Sarah and John. It was a Christmas Commons, which meant they lit the fire in the huge dining-hall hearth, we had Christmas food and crackers to pull, and the Chapel choir sang carols between courses, big, boisterous harmonies which filled the hall.

Field and fountain, moor and mountain, following yonder star.

Standing on the Dining Hall steps afterwards, Fionnuala, hair damp with dead snowflakes, touched me on the cheek with a cold hand and wished me a happy Christmas.

"See you in the New Year," she called as an afterthought as she turned in by the tennis courts. Disturbed by a sudden wheeling impression that I would never see her again, I went to call out to her, but Andrea, passing by on Front Square, ran up the steps to give me a Christmas hug and make me promise to go on a huge piss-up in the new year. She left to get her bus to a party in Foxrock, and left me alone to Trinity on the Feast of the Immaculate Conception, people disappearing into the frosty streets of Dublin and thence to Busáras, Parnell Square, Heuston, Connolly and the buses and trains which would carry them off far away from here to Stranorlar, Castlecomer, Carrickmines and Nenagh, places like these.

I arrived in the Atrium for the Publications party at about a quarter past eight. There were already a lot of people there drinking mulled wine out of plastic cups. The two girls at the door examined my invitation officiously and I wandered in among the crowd. It was the kind of group I expected, big girls with pierced noses wearing felt hats and colourful cloaky garments, intense, arrogant, Marlboro-smoking guys with little round glasses and shaved heads. I wove my way through the bunches of cliques to the table at the back and took a cup of mulled wine. They were only half-full, and I was feeling shy and exposed, so I took a second and poured it into the first one. A minor sentinel of the Publications Committee glared at me.

"I'd only end up coming back twice. . . ." I explained jovially, and moved away.

I introduced myself to the editor of the magazine, a loud-mouthed and effeminate northerner doing the M.Phil. in Anglo-Irish. He didn't listen to me or refer specifically to my story, but instead gave me vociferous and condescending advice along the lines of "keep on writing," put a hand on my shoulder, then drifted off outside with someone else to smoke a joint, leaving me alone again.

I bumped into a Ph.D. student who taught one of our RomVicMod tutorials, Anne, a pleasant and intelligent young postgrad whom I would have liked to have been friendlier with. She was on the committee and said she had liked my story. She thought I was talented but too sentimental, self-centred, and verbose. As she continued her advice, with specific references to the story, and in particular to my habit of describing my protagonist pacing back and forth in his room or sitting wondering what to do next, my roving gay eye spied someone over her shoulder, a good-looking black-haired man, tall and pale, in a black jacket and white shirt. I gave him the usual lustful look-over, and then as I was about to turn my head back to Anne, my heart missed a beat. It was John. He caught sight of me and moved suddenly to go.

"Anne, I'm so sorry," I said, putting a hand on her shoulder, "I have to talk to that guy over there . . . I have to catch him before he leaves, I'm sorry. . . ."

"Oh. . . ."

"I'm really sorry, look—happy Christmas," I said, as if I was giving a tip to a waitress I had spilt red wine over.

"Okay," she said and shrugged her shoulders.

I pushed my way through the crowds, knocking someone's drink out of their hands ("*Wanker!*"). I could see John pushing through at the other end, nearer the door.

"Excuse me, excuse me, sorry, I have to—, sorry, sorry, excuse me."

But I lost him, he had slipped away.

I ran out the door of the Atrium, to the stone passage between it and the chapel, beside a small plot of graves for Trinity luminaries. Beside me the Bank of Ireland Pass machine glowed, an electronic image of a bank card mechanically going in and out of the picture of the slot on the screen. *Please insert card.* I looked across Front Square, but there was no trace of him. Bitterly disappointed, I went back inside. There was a girl sitting crosslegged against the wall, reading a book. I knew what I needed to do.

"Sorry—" She didn't look up. I bent down and touched the book. "Sorry—may I?"

"May you what?"

"Look at what you're reading."

"Uh . . . okay, I suppose. . . ." She handed me *An Introduction to Modern Spain.*

"You're on page one two one," I told her, then asked loudly, to her incredulous stare, "Where is John?" I flicked through and stopped.

"*By 1937 . . .*" the paragraph under my finger began.

That was enough, I was sure I had caught him. Thrusting the book back at the girl with a thank-you, I raced out again, up the little passage and then ran sliding across the sleety cobbles of Front

Square to the 1937 Reading Room. There were two guys standing on the steps having a cigarette, but no sign of John. I walked around the back, where a girl was unlocking her bike. Determined not to give up hope, I leaned against a pillar, asked one of the guys for a cigarette and stood there smoking—a rare enough activity for me, but it reminded me of Sarah—while I waited.

Ten, fifteen, twenty cold minutes passed. The doors in front of me swung open and closed as people left. I kept a constant look around the back, but John did not appear. And then, the door opened and he came out slowly, looking furtively around. I was standing right in front of him. He looked around for a moment to see if there was a way he could escape, then threw his hands in the air.

"How the fuck . . . ?"

I didn't reply. "You fuckin stalker," John said. "What is it you want?"

"What do you think? Answers. More."

"Ah, Christ," he said to himself. He reached into his inside pocket and pulled out a book. He flicked through it and chose. He raised his eyebrows, then looked at me as he put it away. "Okay, one pint. No more, and don't expect earth-shattering revelations. Or anything else earth-shattering for that matter," he added coarsely.

"I know, I know."

The wind was icy and the cobblestones had a fresh, wet incandescence under the clear stars and campus lamps. We were the only people on Fellows Square. As we walked up the Arts Block ramp I shuddered, and wondered if it was with the cold or some other feeling brought on by the intimacy of the double track of footprints growing behind us.

In the Nassau Street tunnel I spoke.

"So how come you were at the Trinity Pubs do?"

"I was looking for someone."

"Me?"

He didn't answer.

"That was a joke," I said.

We walked on. Finally, some trace memory of politeness made him feel obliged to say something to me.

"And why were you there?" Like Ian used to do, he tried to save face by giving what was a genuine question a sarcastic, angry tone of voice.

"I had a story in *A Muse*."

" 'Towards the Mist.' "

"I didn't have you down as among their readership."

"I didn't read it."

"Let's reintroduce ourselves," I said. "Niall Lenihan, formerly of Sandycove, now of Trinity College, Dublin 2."

He paused, then grunted reluctantly: "John Bastible."

"From . . . ?"

"Donnybrook. I live in town. Well, half the time I live in Ranelagh. With my girlfriend," he added meaningfully.

"Where are we going?"

John took a book from his bag and flicked through it. He read the line his finger landed on, thought for a few moments and said:

"Kehoe's."

The mechanical puppets in the window of Brown Thomas beside us moved jerkily with fixed sociopathic smiles and obsessive-compulsive repetition to shrill American voices singing "The First Noël." Up and down went the shoemaker with his hammer, evil grin from ear to ear, just missing his shoe each time, up and down, up and down, up and down.

Born is the king of I-I-sraël.

Our reflections passed them like phantoms, a tall broad-shouldered young man, around thirty, well-dressed in a long grey coat, black hair and pale skin, and a slightly shorter companion with wild dishevelled hair, darting eyes, and crumpled chainstore clothes. I fancied there was a certain chasing symmetry which excited me a little.

We turned left onto South Anne Street and into Kehoe's, a dark, old fashioned pub with wood and cream furnishings. John pushed his way confidently through the crowd, and I squeezed after him. Immaculate Conception Christmas shoppers having their après-ski, as well as the usual Friday night groups of pinters already half geared up for the Christmas binge. We caught an enclosed snug just as it was being vacated, and John claimed it by throwing his coat across onto the bench.

He nodded at me to sit in, which I did, and he left to go to the bar without asking me what I wanted. I found a last battered cigarette in an abandoned box on the table and I smoked it while I waited for him to return. A CD of pop Christmas tunes was playing in the background.

I watched John leaning casually and laddishly against the bar, making chat with the man next to him in that code of set phrases, winks and fond insults which I have never been able to master and which is the language of real men.

He came over and laid two pints of Guinness on the table down on the table. White froth from the head ran down his fingers. He licked them clean and sat down.

"You do drink Guinness?"

"Thanks, yes."

While we waited for them to settle, I made some chat about the price of pints, the impending smoking ban, and the crowd there tonight. John ignored me. He flicked through a book, then put it back in his bag. When the Guinness was black I picked it up and took a sip.

"Sláinte," I said.

He nodded and took a long gulp.

"So," I said after a pause.

"So. Hmm. Right, well. You say you want answers. There

aren't any, let's get that straight first off. I amn't going to give you what you want." He took another draught of his pint. "There's no answers, nothing 'more,'" he made exaggerated inverted commas with his fingers. "You're obviously an excitable fella, and I know you think it's exciting and promising and all, but there isn't anything to say, I hate to tell you. The *sortes* are an ancient trick that works for us. It's our . . . our party game. Our way of making decisions, that's all. You know . . . just relax. Leave us to our games. Invent your own."

"Oh, come on," I said. "Why were you avoiding me? And why did you freak out when I picked those two passages at the party? Why does a strange man know my name, sing songs at my window, and why do the words of that song turn up everywhere I look? I mean. . . ."

"Whoa, whoa, whoa," he stopped me with his hand like a policeman directing traffic. "The idea was for me to tell you about the morning after the party in the house in Ranelagh. Whatever other paranoid delusions you are experiencing, save them for the doctor or whatever. Okay. Why was I avoiding you? I was not 'avoiding' you, I just amn't interested in you or in being your 'friend.' Do you want to know the truth? I saw you at the Pubs party and I thought oh for fuck's sake it's that little . . . that young student who will sure as anything make a beeline for me. Which you did. Why did I freak out at the party. Well, why do you think I freaked out?"

The music filled the silence while I thought of my answer.

Westward leading, still proceeding

I said, "Look, your books told you to come and drink with me. So just tell the truth. I think, I know, you're hiding something," I said bravely. "I just know. Weird things, coincidences and things, are happening, and I think you and Sarah know something about it, or could tell me something about it, and I think it's all to do with the *sortes*. I was able to find you, wasn't I? I bet if you asked your books something about me we'd get somewhere. Actually, I know what. Here, pick a synchronicity from that book in your pocket. Ask about me. Go on. Ask it about me. If it's paranoid delusions, off you go."

This caught him off guard; he was rattled. He looked at me with disgust.

"Look at the state of you, you're a bag of nerves, twitching and shaking, full of these looper ideas. You're a mess. Get yourself a . . . friends, a life, I don't know, a *boyfriend*. You are on some planet I don't even want to orbit. If you want to know the truth about those passages you picked, it was the questions you asked which irritated me, nothing else. I just couldn't face listening to you and that girl going on about them. And I can't stand being flirted with when I'm not interested, you know. The person begins to repulse and irritate me. The bottom line is, I amn't a very nice person. You and that girl . . . you're both just very . . . well, let's say you're young. Sorry," he added, looking me in the eye. "I just . . . I'm sorry. There's no mystery, except that I'm not a nice guy, you probably are, and we really shouldn't have much to do with each other."

He got up to go.

"No, wait. . . ."

"No, I won't." He was putting on his coat. "Please, end this now."

"Come on," I called desperately after him as he left the snug and began to push his way through the crowd. "I know there's something, I mean I was drunk, I know." A phrase drifted into my panicked head. "A plurality of bottles has often induced things in me, but I'm sure, I *know*. . . ." He had gone. A pattern of strange events and coincidences had woven itself around me and my paltry life, I knew this man knew something, and I had let him slip away.

And then, a hand on my shoulder.

"Niall?"

"John?"

"What did you just say?"

I thought he was threatening me.

"I said I know I'd drunk a lot the night before, but I still. . . ."

He gripped my shoulder tightly. "No, what did you say exactly? About bottles?"

"I said . . . I said I had drunk a . . . a plurality of bottles."

"Shite." He blew out a long breath and looked around the pub. Then he took his book from the inside pocket of his coat and read the customary few lines. He shook his head slowly. "Christ. . . ." He threw his coat on his chair and sat down again.

"Fuck, *fuck*, FUCK." He made his way steadily down his Guinness, looking around the pub without saying anything, glowering at me whenever I caught his eye. Bewildered, I waited for him to calm down. This went on until we had both finished our pints. He got up and came back with two more. He drummed his big white fingers on the table, ran them through his black hair. I sipped shyly, afraid of angering him again.

Eventually he sighed and said: "Okay. I'll be in trouble for this, but the signs are so bloody . . . look, so maybe there is a bit more to things than I said. I'll explain the outline of things, just so you can make something of whatever's going on with you, and then, I beg of you, fuck off and leave it alone. I really mean it this time." He leaned in and looked at me imploringly. "I just want to give you a bit of a helping hand with sorting out your . . . situation . . . you know, but then that's it, all right? All right?" he repeated.

"All right."

"OK," he said. "I can . . . shouldn't . . . but anyhow . . . I'll tell you a few things about Sarah and myself and how I got into the whole . . . yoke." He waved his hand around vaguely. "I'll begin way back, but eventually I'll explain why I lied and then changed my mind. But it's just my story, maybe it will help you out with whatever, but then that's *it*, we say goodbye for good, do you understand?"

I nodded.

"Say you understand."

"I understand."

"So don't get . . . overinvested . . . in this, will you? Christ knows, I have enough on my plate as it is without a gay fan trailing after me like a fuckin paparazzi. I'm telling you this story, just to tell you, there've been a few synchronicities about you which is why I think I can . . . but you really can't expect to *do* anything about what I tell you. I really, *really* shouldn't. And don't go acting the gobshite and spreading this around."

"Around who?" I asked, then shrugged, "Okay, grand. Whatever."

"Right, as long as that's clear. Well. How do I start? You've worked out that the whole books thing is more than . . . well, a game."

"What is it?"

"Well, yeah, the million-dollar question. I'll tell you about me, how I got involved first of all."

"Fine."

He cleared his throat and began. "So. Well, I'm not from a really literary sort of background or anything. My father's a lawyer, and my mum's like, you know, a former culchie snob, basically. I mean, we can read and write and all, but you know the way . . . we didn't laugh over Shakespearean puns at breakfast."

I knew the way. He outlined a life I knew already, tennis clubs, golf in Ballyconneely with his parents' friends and their children, and, of course, the most glamorous of the milieux of teenage middle-class Dublin, with which I had a passing acquaintance through Ian, private-school rugby and its attendant court. I made some remark about after-match sessions in Kiely's. He looked up with surprise.

"Did you play rugger?" he asked with disbelief.

"No, but I went to Gonzaga."

"Did you know a guy, big rugby fella, must be about your age, Ian O'Neill?"

I flushed with embarrassment.

"I do. Quite well, actually. How do you know him?"

"His sister used to go out with a friend of mine. . . ."

"Catherine," I said.

"Yeah . . . Katy. Katy O'Neill. I bet I knew some other guys in your year when they were kids. I used to know a good few guys in Gonzaga, Stephen O'Connor and Patrick Devlin and all them. . . ."

He looked away, almost wistfully, as if he was a lonely old veteran listing the names of his comrades fallen in the trenches sixty years ago.

"Where did you go to school?"

"Blackrock. Not quite as intellectual, I suppose. But better at rugby. We used to say Gonzaga guys were all gay—oh, sorry."

"It's fine. Most of them weren't. More's the pity. So what happened?"

"The road to Damascus. Well, so I did a pretty regular track. Commerce in UCD, two years in Oz getting locked with Blackrock guys on Bondi beach. I did a master's out with the Smurfs in Carysfort, and then you know the whole Celtic Tiger thing started to happen, and I got a job in an investment bank, and moved into an apartment down in the financial services centre."

"I get the picture."

"So then one weekend down at my girlfriend's family's holiday home in Rosslare, she was out on a walk with her folks. They were all getting on my wick, so I stayed in the house. There was no television, no radio, and nothing to read except one book, some old Agatha Christie. The same exact one, in fact, that you chose at the party. So that was . . . it was significant . . . that you picked it, I mean . . . well, I'll come to that. Anyway, I can't stand that kind of 'are there any muffins for tea' sort of stuff, and so to entertain myself I decided to see how fast I could read the thing, the *whole* fucking thing, without skipping a word. I know that for Sarah and all probably you too, speed-reading is something you do. But like I said, I was never a big reader, and I really went at it at a sprint, you know. I mean, I had read books on my holidays, and we did, what's her face, *Emma* for the Leaving and stuff, but I almost never sat down at page one and read the whole thing through. Anyhow, I didn't skip anything, just pushed my eye along through the words as fast as I could physically do it. And when I had finished I had the strangest feeling, like I was stoned. I had gone too fast to follow the plot, even, but some kind of memory of the book buzzed in my head all day and all night. I couldn't sleep, I almost had hallucinations. The next day, the feeling, the buzzing was gone, and so as soon as we got back to Dublin I sat down and did the same thing again. Only this time, I wanted to try something weirder, a dictionary or something."

"The *Dictionary of Semiotics*—"

"—*Volume II,* yes. Don't ask me where I got it. And so on. Next was *Ulysses,* as you probably guessed. If Agatha Christie was hash, that was like heroin. I lay in my room for hours and hours and speed-read all seven hundred pages. I was dizzy for days. The point being, I suppose, I got addicted to reading, if you could call it reading, to this weird, speeded-up way of experiencing books, too fast to know what was happening or what the sentences meant. The only hobby I had for weeks and weeks was this. And then, I started doing little experiments. I remembered hearing there was a book where you could pick any chapter and read the book through starting from there, and it would make sense, but you know a different book each time."

"*Catch-22,* yes," I interrupted. "Or *Hopscotch* . . ."

"Yeah, whatever, well, I didn't know, I just started trying it out with normal books. And I got really into it."

"But what about the *sortes*? How did you get into that?"

"That's all from Sarah. I'm just giving you the background.

You know, what I was looking for, or whatever. My state of mind on the eve of the crime. So then, anyhow, about, oh a year and a half ago, I'd say. Yeah, that's right, a while after I'd met Anna—that's my girlfriend. She's the one who lives in the house where the party was. I rent a room there too, kind of like a study, gives me a break from the flat in the IFSC and gives me a bit of privacy when I stay over with her. So that was me then, a poor confused rugger-bugger with no outlet. Then I met Sarah at a party in Sandymount. It was Ash Wednesday. Don't ask me how I remember that. I was langers and we were talking and then we shifted and went back to her place and . . . well, whatever."

"And your girlfriend, Anna?"

"Oh, another tale entirely. Sarah just knocked me sideways and me and Anna were on an off-patch. Anyhow, the next morning I had a cunt of a hangover, and I was picking up my clothes off the bedroom floor getting ready to go home in the rain. Fucking purgatory. I was cursing to myself and she was lying there half-asleep in the bed and asked me how my hangover was. With all my speed-reading, lines were always coming into my head, without me looking for them, or often even recognising them. And this time there was one from Flann O'Brien: *a plurality of bottles has often induced this in me.*"

He paused and looked at me. The reason for his change of heart dawned on me. I tried to think of what to say to get him to keep talking and tell me more. I wondered especially if he could tell me something about Pablo. He was animated and friendly, not from a new amicable interest in me, but from an excitement with the relief of finally telling his story. I was afraid he would remember himself and stop talking. If I pushed him I might bring him to his senses and ruin the flow. I prodded him to continue as gently as I could.

"So when I said it to you there, you felt that this meant you should tell me some more about the whole . . ."

"Well. It wasn't only that . . . but that was the final . . . all right, yeah."

"And what about the fact that I got such freakily factual answers from the *sortes,* in your house, and then again when I was looking for you tonight?"

"Well, who knows. It's not unusual. Well, not *that* unusual. . . ."

He stopped talking, as I knew he would sooner or later. Shit, I thought, I went too far. But then he took a sip of his pint and started off again as he had before.

"So anyway, I said this thing to Sarah but I couldn't remember where I'd read it, it just sort of popped into my head. So she sits up in the bed all agitated and gets me to repeat it, and I said, you know, like, oh, just something from a book I read, but she was really excited and begged me to stay."

He was talking breathlessly, with slightly glazed eyes, not addressing me, it seemed, but another, imaginary interviewer who knew him much better than I did. He reminded me, more than anyone, of Andrea. I opened my mouth to ask a question but he kept on talking at an unstoppable pace.

"First I thought, here we are, she's all in a tizzy because she thought she'd had a quick and enjoyable one-nighter with a rugby-playing body, a roll in the hay with sporty spice kind of arrangement, and didn't expect to discover a mind. But as she went on, I started to think no, maybe this is something different— I mean, she's not like other women . . ."

"Other anyone, from what I've seen."

". . . and even after one night I could see this was unusual for her. So I took the day off work, first time of many with her. She made me coffee in the kitchen and got me to tell her all about my life, and then I told her all I just told you. I must have been nearly an hour explaining it all and talking about the books I'd read and the experiments I'd done with them and everything. She was all jumpy. She kept picking up books and asking them questions. I swear, I thought she was a nut. She went into the hall to make a phone call. It was right next to the door and I could hear everything, but it was all in Spanish which I don't understand, needless to say . . . but it was clear anyhow that she was giving someone the low-down on me. And I did hear her say 'la pluralidad de bottle-itos' or whatever it is. So then when she'd finished on the phone I told her I really had to go—she was kind of freaking me out at this stage—and she asked me if I could meet her for lunch over the weekend. At first I was a bit dodge, she was really very strange, but she really insisted, and even said to me 'I hope you're not under the illusion that I intend to bed you again' or something snotty to that effect. So this made me a bit jealous, anyway . . . the truth is I would have . . . I would happily . . ."

He broke off, took a gulp of his pint and stared down at the table for a few moments before continuing:

"Well, I agreed, anyhow. I met her for lunch and she told me she was going out with this Spanish guy who was part of some group called Pour Mieux Vivre, 'To Live Better'—well, I suppose you know what it means. . . . Its whole thing is unifying art and life, expanding the mind . . . to tell you the truth, I'm not sure what its thing is exactly. Mystic intellectuals is the best I can come up with. They have theories of language, and reading, and history. They research what they think are forgotten or hidden, um, esoteric reading practices, like they go through ancient manuscripts, you know and analyse Old Irish prayers, that kind of thing. Well, I'm basically only guessing. The truth is I know nearly nothing about them, even now, only what they . . . only what we do. What they tell Sarah on e-mail. So when she told me this, of course the warning bells were making me go deaf, I've slept with a cult-woman who's trying to recruit, and for a while I was all let's not get too excited here, but again Sarah was so confident and per-suasive and everything . . . she just, you know, just laid it all out very clearly and said take it or leave it."

"Take or leave what?"

He looked around fearfully, before continuing, without answering my question. "The group has a centre in Rome, Sarah says. But we would never be allowed to go there or any- thing. I mean, we're way down the chain. You know that Mafia thing of you only know the person immediately above you and the person immediately below you. Well it's the same way. Except there's nobody below us. Well, I suppose I'm below Sarah. I've never met Luis, Sarah's supervisor. But there's no one below me."

"Yet," I said, but I said it quietly, and he really was babbling to himself by now and wouldn't have heard anyway.

"Very very few outsiders, that is, people who don't study the material themselves, are allowed join. We learn techniques and things from them, we experiment with things and e-mail them reports on how we get on. Like, I bet Luis gets stuff from who- ever's the rank above him about where to look in medieval bibles and Egyptian manuscripts, coded references to esoteric arts, but Sarah and I only get to do the basic *sortes,* or versions of it. We don't know about the other stuff. And we only know him."

His gushing narrative suddenly trailed off and the hyper, glazed look fell from his eyes. He looked at me as if waking up, realising only now that it had been me, the random stalker, that he had been talking to, who had listened to his mad tale.

He was quiet for a while, slightly ashamed and self-conscious, as if after sex with a stranger. We drank slowly and watched the pre-Christmas chaos of the pub around us. "So that's it," he said finally.

"But the special way you two use the *sortes*?" I asked. "What *is* it?"

"The *sortes* are the main method for connecting with the non-material world, the world outside your own sensory experience. The idea is you connect with this massive bank of collective humanity, a world beyond the ordinary mortal one we live in. Reawaken the whole graveyard of all human thought, ever. That's how it's supposed to work, the questions matching the answers,

it's all energy. Archetypes and energy. Like, some energy of yours
connects with some energy of this other world, the world in all
writing and art, the world of the dead. Not just dead-dead, but
also what is not directly lived, if you know what I mean. So this
means doing the synchronicities opens a channel. Oh look, forget
it. It sounds loopers, and it is. It's pure madness. That's it."

"But what do you use them *for*?"

"Nothing. Anything. Different things."

"How come you showed them to Fionnuala?"

"Big mistake. We knew it would be. It was instructions Sarah
got from Luis. It was one of the games he directed us to do . . .
involve a random stranger. That's why we went to the party, we
figured students would be the most likely to try a whim and
then forget it. But that whole session wasn't complete. In itself,
I mean. It was part of a bigger thing we were doing. We were
using the stranger like a book."

"Only the stranger turned out to be me as well. What about
those passages I picked?"

John drained down the end of his pint and stood up.

"Right, so, I'm glad we had this talk, Niall. I hope you feel
better about things, and try out the odd synchronicity for yourself. But please . . . the whole package isn't for you. Me and Sarah
aren't for you, and I promise, on my word of honour, you will
be a happier person for leaving things that way."

I pulled a pen out of my pocket and wrote my phone number
on a beer-mat. He took it, but said:

"We'll say hello if our paths cross again, though they might
not. Anyway, certainly no more than that. It's madness what
we're doing, you're well enough out of it. Good luck, you know,
ploughing your own furrow. Happy Christmas." He shook my
hand, tingle of desire on my skin, then made his way quickly
and purposefully through the laughing crowds.

Christmas taunted me. I knew very well that John would not get in touch with me, this really was supposed to be it, but still I couldn't bring myself to abandon my room and go back to Sandy-cove for the holidays. At night I watched from my desk as the number of lights on campus dwindled, as one by one the ruck-sacks were heaved onto hunched shoulders and people walked through Front Gate to find buses or trains out in that busy, bewil-dering world beyond the walls, to whisk them away to turkeys and relations off in Terenure, Dunmore East, and Carrickfergus.

My room got colder and colder. When I woke now, there was frost on the inside of the window pane. I would leap from the bed to crank up the gas bar heater in the corner and scurry back in until it had heated up the little halo around it. When I came in from the shower I would stand and try and get dressed without stepping outside the little semicircle of warmth. I some-times went to the chapel to hear the choir practising for Christmas services, but otherwise I wandered around the empty stone of campus and ceaselessly interrogated my present, past, and future with *sortes* from my bookshelf.

What was I when I was sixteen?

She was slightly afraid—deeply moved and religious. That was her best state.

And so on. I also picked passage after passage which I read as signs that I should stay in Trinity. The truth was that I wanted to go home, but the impossible lure of the world of John and Sarah, as well as a growing superstitious fear of countermanding what I understood to be the orders of the *sortes,* left me idling, waiting, freezing, and frequently offered clear suggestions of promise. ("What should I do?" *He paced up and down the room, looking at one object, picking up another. I had the impression that he had something to tell me, and couldn't find the right terms with which to do so.*)

I let the week fall imperceptibly into Monday, the twenty-second, and still I did not go home. The guilty fear that my parents felt rejected by my reluctance to go back to Sandycove led me to ring my mother in the evening. She was distracted and distant, and for the first time since I had moved out of home, three months before, I had the feeling she had forgotten me, that home was now a happily reconstructed reality in which I had no important part. She sounded busy and contented, she told me they were putting up the tree that night, that my aunt and cousins were coming for Christmas dinner, they were all going to midnight mass in the Gonzaga chapel on Christmas Eve night. She wasn't unfriendly, just not noticeably delighted or relieved to hear from me or anxious that I come home soon. She didn't even ask if I would come to the Gonzaga midnight mass. She had to go, there was a man at the door selling calendars.

"I suppose we'll see you later in the week, love. Bye."

Solitude and paralysis filled me with sexual desire, and I walked through the Christmas lights and snow-sprayed windows to the George. Instead of going into the main entrance to the club as I usually did, I sat for once in its small adjacent pub downstairs, a quiet place frequented mostly by older men, called Jurassic Park by the youth upstairs. The tinsel, plastic Santa Claus figures and coloured lights in here were like gloomy church icons. I ordered a pint and sat at the bar, watched by hungry-eyed old men hiding in the shadows underneath the tinsel. I wondered if their Christmases were as theatrically tragic as I imagined, a microwaved lasagne in a bedsit in Phibsboro with no photos on the walls. Sisters in new 3-beds in Clonee-off-the-Naas-Road, bossily inviting them over, grey-haired and awkward, afraid of their nephews, trying to make the right remarks about what was on the television, praising the food, trying not to look too greedy with the drink, desperately simulating inclusion, before running back, exhausted from the effort, to the easier, shrouded life of Jurassic Park.

As usual, I peered through the murk, looking for Pablo. But my eye was caught by someone who did not look like him at all, the only other young man in the room, a dark-haired guy across the bar, wearing office clothes. He gave me a smile which I half-returned. His sallow skin, big cheekbones and serious face were too handsome to be Irish, I thought, maybe a German or a Netherlander on business or holidays. He ordered another pint with a shake of his empty glass to the barman, and drummed his fingers happily on the bar while he waited for it, his chain bracelet chinking on the counter. He looked over and winked. I returned a raised eyebrow of greeting, then after a shy turn of my head, a smile of hello, a picking up of the leather jacket and drink, he became—*mirabile dictu!*—a breathing, fleshly presence beside me, as though I myself had conjured a spirit from the depths.

"Can I join you?"

His accent—*jine yeh?*—far from the anglo-internationalese of a Dutch or German tourist, ("What's ap?"), which I had been expecting, was working-class Dublin.

"Sure," I cleared my throat, "sure, sit down."

He sat facing me, black office shoes perched on the edge of my stool.

"Chris," he said and offered a big soft hand.

"Niall."

"Nice to meet you, Niall."

His hair, buzz-cut at the back and sides, was gelled and groomed on top, and slightly tousled from the heat of the pub. His tie was loosened, and a few black hairs protruded from the slightly paler skin of his chest where the top buttons of his shirt were undone.

"Don't tell me," I said, "you've just escaped from your office Christmas party."

He clicked his tongue and winked. "You're on de ball."

"Where you from?" I asked him.

"Out by Cabra," he said.

"Ah, Cabra," I replied, meaninglessly.

"Ah, Cabra," he repeated, imitating my south county accent. "Do yeh know the rhyme, *Abracadabra, me granny comes from Cabra?"*

I'd heard it. He was working for an IT operation out in Sandyford Industrial Estate, a "bench manager," in charge of the people on the phones or something. As I spoke, I tried to pad out my narrow, poky little vowels with a rounder, relaxed coarseness, and I thought I could sense him smiling inwardly at the attempt. He had big green-blue eyes and his aftershave swirled around us and made me slightly high. He was from Cabra originally but he lived in town, in a flat on Capel Street.

"It's a small oul pad, you know, handy enough, do yeh know the way, but it's a pain in the arse to get out to Sandyford. The 116 from O'Connell Street. But when the Luas is up an running I'll get out dere great guns, so I will."

One of his three sisters knew he was gay and was "all right" about it, but he didn't sound too convinced. For my own life, I made up dull lies, duller even than the truth would have been, I'm studying languages, very useful with the whole Europe thing and all. Chris would love to speak a language, he was hopeless at French in school.

"I had no interest in it then, do yeh know what I'm sayin, I didn't make the effort, like, but if I put de mind to it now . . . I'm a mad fan of French films and pop music from the 60s, actually, Serge Gainsbourg and all, I wish I could understand the feckin words. You'll have to translate all the songs I listen to for me some time."

"If I can," I replied. "Of course I would."

"Whereabouts are you from?"

"Near Dún Laoghaire. Glasthule," I specified (slightly less bourgeois-sounding than Sandycove), "just up from the old Forum Cinema."

"Dublin's Riviera, wha'?"

"That's right."

He looked at me uncertainly, as if confronted with an experimental painting he was about to get the point of.

"What?" I asked, slightly panicked. He narrowed his eyes and stared more closely. "What?" I repeated, "what's wrong?"

"Shut up till I kiss yeh, yeh big eejit." He pulled my face up to his. I took his hands; they were enveloping and warm. His mouth tasted of beer, his soft neck of aftershave. He stood up off his stool to kiss better, and put my hand on the crotch of his jeans to feel his erection. We kissed for a long time, twenty minutes or more, without talking. Then he withdrew and lifted my hand away. I reached out for my pint, but he pushed it away.

"Forget your oul pints," he whispered, his lips brushing my ear as he did. He invited me back to Capel Street, but I wanted my love in Botany Bay.

When the smell of strange breathing awoke me the next morning, I had no idea what it was. I touched the moving lump beside me and when I felt human flesh I recoiled in horror. The sight of the body reminded me of the lurid, yellow Christ bleeding on the cross at the back of Dalkey church. Hating my nakedness suddenly, like Adam and Eve come to their senses, I put on my underwear and a T-shirt lying on the back of my chair and opened the curtains. It was cold and bright.

"Mmm."

The man in my bed turned over in reaction to the light. I ignored him and tried to remember his name so I could ask him to go.

"What time is it?" he muttered, pretending to be sleepier than he was.

"Nine."

I heard him sit up in the bed, but I paid no attention, just stood there in my boxers and Tin-Tin T-shirt, staring at the bare trees in the sunlight.

"Jaysus, I'm wrecked," he said.

I realised with a slight horror that I was going to have to kiss him again before he left.

"Would you like some coffee?"

"That'd be lovely, thanks."

I went into the kitchen and filled up the percolator. No hangover, anyway, which made a change. As I fixed the filter paper in place and spooned in the coffee, I searched for his name. Conor? Cormac? No, not an Irish one . . . the nighttime scene replayed itself in my mind's eye. I went over some of the lines to see if I could think of one that included his name. Banter about me speaking French. And then him asking me to lick his balls. How embarrassing.

"Niall?" He was standing, naked, at the bedroom door, bedraggled and smiling, slightly dark-skinned penis flopping unashamedly against his legs.

Well, bad cess to him for remembering mine. Brian? Michael?

"Yeah?"

"Do you mind if I have a shower?"

"No, that's fine. There's a towel hanging on the door. Chris." I finished suddenly as his name bounced like a submerged cork up to the surface of my brain. I was tired and a bit chilly, but didn't want to get back into bed because the sheets smelled of Chris and were covered in his little curly black pubic hairs, so I sat at my desk and looked out onto the deserted, frosty tennis courts, thinking back on the first visitor I had had at that window and how it had led up to the apparent dead end of the strange story John had told me in Kehoe's.

Ten minutes later, Chris knocked respectfully at the door and came in dripping with my towel around his waist.

"Deadly water-pressure," he said, dropping the towel and sitting to put on his socks. He *was* good-looking, I conceded, with a sneaking pride, repelled nevertheless by the faded and hungover sight of him putting his office suit back on at half-nine in the morning of the day before Christmas Eve in a room smelling of tobacco and spilt seed. I watched him get dressed in silence, like a nun observing a child dutifully fulfilling a punishment she had assigned. He picked up his discarded tie from the floor and rolled it up.

"So," I said, as he stood up to squeeze his feet into his shoes, hoping to provoke him into some sort of a move. He held out his hands. Reluctantly I walked over to him and let him put his arms round my shoulders. I stared at the dust on the carpet while he murmured affectionately. He stroked the back of my neck. Cold fingers, smell of my soap.

"Do you feel like doing something tonigh'?" The accent . . . where was it he said he was from?

Abracadabra my granny comes from Cabra.

"Like what?"

"I don't know, a walk on Dollymount strand or something, maybe we could watch a film in the evening and go to the chipper. There's a gay night in the Ormonde Hotel. Ease ourselves into the family Christmas."

"No, no," I said, horrified, "I'm studying today. Sorry," I added in a mutter. I thought of him the night before, heaving on top of my slender body, pinning my wrists down on the bed, manoeuvring my head; now, transformed by the sunlight, his universe was delineated by these, the pleasures of an infant, beach and burgers.

"I'll be stuck up in Cabra from Christmas Eve until Stephenses night. A nightmare, the uncles all gettin soused and askin me when I'm gettin married. . . . Could do with some light relief before that, wha'?"

"I know, I know, I'd love to do something together, but I've an essay to hand in, and then Christmas and . . . look, give us your phone number and I'll text you." I really was going to have to kiss him again.

He shrugged his shoulders and searched my desk for a pen and paper.

Chris 086 611 3029

The name was underlined with a hopeful squiggle.

"Well, goodbye." I stood at the door.

He didn't move.

"So dat's it, tree days with the family and nothing to look forward to? Not even a bit of oul sodomisin?"

"I'll text. What day would suit?"

"We could go out Stephenses night. There's always an event on at the George. A drag panto, I tink." He grinned involuntarily as he said this, as though the rites and rituals of the gay scene, though fully familiar, retained a hint of shamefaced exoticism.

"Grand so," I said. "I'll text you on the twenty-sixth."

He walked over and put his arms around me.

"I won't hold my bret."

"I'll text you."

"You will in your hole."

He kissed me. Indifferently, I let his wet tongue slither around for moment before pulling back and patting him on the cheek.

"Come on. We'll be here all day, otherwise," I said.

"That's what I'd like," he breathed, stroking my neck.

"I know, I wish we could. . . . Goodbye," I whispered, guiding him towards the door. "See you."

"Happy Christmas."

"You too." I closed the door after him. I heard his footsteps on the stairs and then from the window I watched him in his crumpled bench-managing office suit, crossing Botany Bay along the side of the tennis courts, then turning onto Library Square, walking across the sun-mottled cobbles in front of the Rubrics. He disappeared round the corner, off to Capel Street to change. Maybe he would kill time by going home to Cabra a day early. *Abracadabra*. The morning sun touched the statues of angels and men on top of the Bank of Ireland. Now I too had to go back somewhere and expel him and his taste like the night, along with John and Sarah and Pablo and *sortes*, just as all the drink-fuelled words and promises of the city the night before had been expelled, foul-smelling and liquid, into the sewers and streets of Dublin.

Although the habit among Scholars and others in rooms was to return to campus after New Year, when Commons started up again, I didn't go back into college until the night before term began. Throughout Christmas, I hoped for another encounter with Pablo, but I had the vague idea that he did not roam outside the city centre, that in the suburbs he would fade away, or die, like a deep-sea creature inadvertently swept up into lighter, warmer waters. John and Sarah had occupied my thoughts like busy ghosts. I spent my free time casting *sortes* as the endless rain fell from the sky. I tried to squeeze some alchemic vision from the books on our sitting-room shelf, but the synchronicities—though with the odd resonance of wisdom they always had—were oblique and I was unable to decode the sermonising scraps they spat back at me.

The rhythms of holiday family life, Christmas visits from relations and walks on the seafront greeting neighbours, had already slipped away into work and school by the night before Hilary Term began, and I was packing to go back to my rooms. To delay my arrival in Trinity, which seemed an increasingly ominous moment, I called in to see Patrick in Rathgar, and had a catch-up chat with him in the McVeighs' traditionally chaotic kitchen, a mixture of doctors' detritus (pens and post-its from pharmaceutical companies, antiseptic swabs, *Irish Medical Journal*), and slightly exotic household clutter (bags of Thai spices, Kenyan figurines, *The Rough Guide to the United Arab Emirates*). Patrick was fine, he saw some of the guys from school, he studied very hard. I told him I'd made friends, and we discussed all getting together one of these nights. He was bringing a girl from his medicine class to the Gonzaga debs. He asked me who I was bringing—literally, our first conversation about "relationships." I told him I didn't think I would go, and he nodded.

Patrick's mother, Paula, came in from work at Tallaght hospital around ten. She was younger than my parents, still in her forties. She always had dyed blond hair and jangling bracelets, spoke at a furious pace, and had a slightly dangerous aroma about her.

"Hello, sweetheart?" she called when she came in the door.

"In here, mum."

"Niall! Lovely to see you. . . ."

She threw her bag down and collapsed into a chair. "I am *exhausted!* Fit for the grave. Patrick, *a stór,* would you ever open that bottle of wine for me? And get out three glasses."

"Oh, no, thanks, Dr. McVeigh," I said. "I have to get the bus into town."

"Paula, please, darling, Paula," she murmured over me. "No, no, you'll stay for a glass of wine. I haven't seen you in an age."

"I'm sorry, I'm afraid of missing the last bus. But thanks."

"Don't be a gom, Frank'll run you in, he'll be home any minute," she said.

There was a pop as Patrick opened the bottle. He took one glass down from the cupboard, filled it, and left it with the bottle beside the armchair his mother was sitting on. She kicked off her shoes and put her long legs in their black tights up on the coffee table in front, or rather upon the heap of papers, magazines and knick-knacks piled on the coffee table.

"Are you not having one yourself, pet?"

"No, mum, I have to study."

She took a sip. "Christ almighty, we weren't working that hard when I was in first med. Niall?"

I felt a desire to keep her company, to collaborate in her effort to liven up their red-brick routine of family dinners, overworked husbands, and studious sons.

"A quick one so."

"Frank'll run you in."

"Not at all."

"No, no, he won't mind."

Paula and I had a glass of wine while Patrick had a mug of tapwater.

"*We* never worked as hard as that in first med," she repeated.

"O tempora! O mores!" Patrick mocked.

"Oh, the benefits of a classical education. Mock your oul bogtrotter of a mother. Speaking of which, Niall, who are you going to take to the Gonzaga debs?"

The rest of the glass of wine was spent with her giving out to me for not going. Paula did not approve of anything less than full and enthusiastic participation in time-honoured festive rituals. I was promising I'd reconsider when the door opened and out of the dark and frost came Frank, who was quickly dispatched out again to run me into town in his Saab.

In the car, he turned up the radio, Vincent Browne on the Tribunals, to avoid the embarrassment of the silence and every time we stopped we stared out the window at the streetlights shining in the puddles. I felt a growing sense foreboding as we neared town, and, overcome with desperation and dread, I had a sudden urge to ask him to turn around and drive me back to Rathgar, where I would tell Patrick about Ian, Pablo, the synchronicities confess all of the many things I now feared and desired, reach out properly for once to the friend I needed to know was there, even in his absence, going about his business in the steady tick-tock of the suburbs. I said nothing to Dr. McVeigh, but I did stand at the tree outside the Nassau Street gate of Trinity and wish his little lights well for him, his son and his wife, for our whole tribe, indeed, as he moved off, relieved, into the new year, the chill night.

Book Two

Four

Afraid that I was losing my reason, I made some New
Year's resolutions before I went to sleep in my newly
unfamiliar Botany Bay room that night. Be normal:
forget the synchronicities, forget Sarah, John, and especially the
now-fading figure of Pablo. Work on my friendships: start
seeing Fionnuala again properly, invest in Patrick, come out to
them both. Find a boyfriend: no more one-night stands, find
something continuous. One night a week max in the George.
Continuity and context, that was the name of the game.

After a dream, a troubling one about something soft and dangerous, I woke up shivering with the cold. I could feel from my
body's rhythm that it was the morning, and a bleary glance at the
luminous hands of my alarm-clock confirmed that it was half-
five. I tried to go back to sleep, but instead stared wide-eyed at the
ceiling while my thoughts jumped restlessly back and forth
between icons and epochs, my grandmother, a time when I was
ten and had purposely let Ciara take the blame for something I
had done, the first time I slept in Ian's house, Pablo, Fionnuala,

Drs. Paula and Frank McVeigh, Flann O'Brien, Sarah, John, Jeremy Bodmoore, Gonzaga debating competitions. I rolled over to try and fall back into my dreams, but the freezing cold was keeping me awake.

Stressed about how tired I would be the following day if I didn't get back to sleep, I jumped out of bed into the icy room and fumbled through my rucksack for a jumper. I pulled one out from the bottom in a small shower of socks and underpants and put it on over my pyjamas. I was about to run back to the warmth of my duvet when my attention was drawn to my bookshelf. Quivering with the cold, I stopped and hesitated. I walked over and pulled something down. I chose big fat *Anna Karenina*, glancing over at my window as I did so. I read, aloud, to my gloves, pens, shoes, and the rest of the silent, unstirring objects.

> *Levin put on his high boots and, for the first time, a cloth coat instead of a fur, and went out to attend to his farm. Stepping now on a piece of ice, now into the sticky mud, he crossed the stream of dazzling water.*

I looked blankly at the tiny print for a moment, and then around the room. My attention was suddenly caught by a curious light I glimpsed through a gap in the curtain. I turned back to the passage; but once my mind began to work on its possible meanings, I looked away uneasily from it. *Stepping now on a piece of ice, now into the sticky mud, he crossed the stream of dazzling water.* Avoiding the little light I had noticed breaking the darkness, I made a few paces across the room towards my bed. I stopped again, blinking in the little spotlight of my reading lamp, listening to the regular tick tick of the alarm clock inviting me back to duvet, sheets, and pillow. But thoughts of Sarah and John and their secret mystical book club filled my head, and the synchronicity had drawn me towards the incongruous light on in a room across the way in the neighbouring block of Botany Bay.

I walked over to the window, pulled it open, and, leaning my elbows on the sill, I stuck my head out into the noiseless darkness. The stone figures of Wisdom, Justice, and Liberty stood immobile on top of the Bank of Ireland. My breath sent a plume of steam out onto the air.

All the rooms were dark with the curtains drawn, all except for one, the one whose light I had seen after reading the passage. On the top floor of House 13 there was one room lit, and the curtains were open. I counted the number of windows across and worked out the number, coming to the conclusion—inescapable, of course—that it was the room directly above Fionnuala's, the one where Sarah lived. I leaned out to see if I could spy on what she was doing inside. I could see a corner of her couch, which looked as if it was covered with books and pieces of paper, and a chair with a blue dressing gown or jacket hung over the back of it. I leaned out further on my tiptoes, edging my elbows along the granite, and saw some movement in the corner of the room. I looked on for a short while but saw nothing more, so I went over to the percolator and made myself a mug of coffee, then returned to resume my watch.

I had drunk almost half of it, wrapping my fingers tightly round the delf to keep my fingers from numbing, when Sarah finally moved into my little square. At this distance, it was difficult to make out any real detail, but she seemed to be fully dressed, and she was talking and gesticulating as she paced around. She moved out of sight then returned holding a book. She sat on the window with her back to me, her head tilted away from it, up at the ceiling. After a few moments, she paced around the room again, muttering and moving her arms around as before. She disappeared and returned with another book. She repeated the ritual three more times, while I stood with my coffee, entranced. She moved out of sight again and didn't return for some time. The light in her room went out, but I saw no sign of her emerging into the hall beside. Then I made out her dark silhouette, bending down. A dim flickering light, candles, I imagined, partially reilluminated the room, or at least gave her shadow more definition. She sat on the window again, a pile of books beside her, which she consulted one by one. Eventually, she stood up, extinguished the candles, and pulled up the window herself, leaned out as I was, and lit a cigarette. Afraid she would look over to her left, see my light on and catch me spying, I pulled myself back inside out of view.

I pulled the window down and sat on my bed, my heart beating so quickly I could see the veins in my arms pulsing. I went to the bookshelf.

"What is Sarah doing?"

—*Darren's gone to the chipper.*
—*He's back.*
—*Is he?*
—*Yeah.*
—*Why didn't yeh tell us? I'm fuckin' starvin'.*
—*Hang on. He took the book.*

I looked out the window and, indeed, saw her hurrying along Botany Bay, carrying a stack of books under her arm. She looked behind her quickly, up to her room, and walked to the corner. Here she waited, stamping her feet with the cold, looking around her anxiously. In a few minutes, striding purposefully from New Square behind her, came the tall, handsome figure of John. They didn't greet or even look at one another, she just moved into step beside him, and the two of them marched quickly away out of sight onto Parliament Square. I gazed at the space they had occupied for a long time after they had gone, until an increasing drizzle forced me back inside. They didn't want me; John had ordered me to stay away. But this brief half-glimpse into their mysterious world had lit the flames of my curiosity again, and left me wishing that I, too, was consulting oracles while the rest of Dublin slept.

Fionnuala texted me later in the morning and we arranged to meet in the Arts Block for breakfast. The rain was insistent, and the sky hardly seemed to have lightened at all since the night. College was quite full, and I had to push my way through a throng of early-morning smokers to get into the Arts Block. I met Fionnuala at the French noticeboard, and she gave me a cold rainy kiss on the cheek. She told me it was nice to see me.

"How are they all up North?" I asked.

"Oh, dodging the bombs, daubing murals, capping knees, the usual. Well, not really. How was the Christmas?"

"Great. Well, quiet, which was what I wanted. Your own?"

"Lovely. All the relations and everything, caught up with the mates. But it's nice to be back south, run with the new crowd for a while."

The day passed, as often with Fionnuala, in a pleasant flurry of administration and socialising. We got our Hilary term timetable, bought new stationery, and held court in the Coffee Dock while we caught up with the various members of our circle, Andrea, Harry, James's friends. College had a slightly hysterical atmosphere, as our classmates emerged, blinking, from the revisited childhood of the month at home, breathed again the air of freedom and re-formed themselves into their adult personae. Cara Murray from Music and her flatmates in Townsend Street were throwing a party to kick off the new term, and it was a huge and giddy crowd that arranged to meet in Mulligan's beforehand.

Sarah was not at Commons that evening. Afterwards Fionnuala and I stood on the steps with a few others in the evening rain, and arranged to see each other in Mulligan's with the rest of them at half-eight and went back to our respective rooms. I sat on my bed and looked out the window. I could see Fionnuala's silhouette behind her curtains as she moved back and forth getting herself ready. The party would be the first time she had seen James since before Christmas, and she wanted to be relaxed and nicely turned-out, as she put it herself. Sarah's window was dark and blank, the curtains open and the lights switched off. Almost automatically I walked to the bookshelf and pulled down a volume:

> . . . *j'ai quitté madame à six heures, joyeuse et contente. Ce mot produisit sur le prince un effet incroyable.* . . .

I rummaged around till I found the packet of ten Silk Cut Purple I had bought on my first night in Trinity, just before I had met Pablo and Sarah, and just before my encounter with John. I turned off the lights and lay on my bed smoking, with my CD player turned right up, filling my dark little space with the tin whistle tune, *The Lonesome Boatman,* which I used to listen to often during my religious phase in my first year in Gonzaga when I pictured myself fishing off a little boat in the Sea of Galilee. It brought me back to the fresh, leaf-smelling mornings of that time, when I would stand around with the other boys whose buses brought them in early, talking about homework and shivering in the autumn sun waiting for the school doors to open, a lost time when Ian was just another grey-uniformed classmate, throwing apple cores at the seagulls on the lawn and playing pitch and toss with coins against the granite wall of the chapel, a time still innocent of the fiery apocalypse which my love for him had been, before my betrayal of Patrick, before all of this that was happening now, whatever it was.

I left the CD player on repeat and let *The Lonesome Boatman* play over and over while I lay still on my back, an ashtray at my side, watching the pattern of waving branches in the white light on my ceiling. At nine my phone vibrated, announcing the arrival of a text message.

From: Fionnuala
  Where are you? We're about to leave

My eyes moved from the bedside table around the darkened walls of the room and rested on my bookshelf. I turned off the CD player, put out my cigarette, and stood in front of my bookshelf and spoke out loud the question I knew it was time to ask.

"Where are Sarah and John?"

In Rome, the position in the bank was not to last long.

With the book still in my hand, I grabbed my jacket, keys, and phone and ran down the stairs and outside.

The Bank, on Dame Street, a relatively new pub, had been converted from what had once been the Ulster Bank, with the cavernous ceiling and the sturdy marble and brass furnishings of the original Victorian building, in which the pub clatter echoed like a swimming pool. It was mostly an office crowd that night, the same people you got in the watering holes in and around the holy office-worker city of Dawson Street, where a beery muezzin called them in for Friday evening drinks in Davy Byrne's, Café en Seine, Samsara, Ron Black's and the Bailey. The pub was full of these men in crumpled suits, their shirt buttons undone, leaning back and talking loudly with pints in hand, mobile phones on the table, interested mostly in each other—"O'Reilly, you fuckin arsehole!," and of women in uncomfortable shoes taking the piss out of them. I looked through the crowd but didn't see Sarah or John. The thought did cross my mind, naturally enough, that this was crazy, but I resolved not to leave until I had definitively established that they were not there.

I pushed through a group of two men and a woman in their thirties to look further in the back of the pub. I thought the woman called something after me, something sexual and mocking, and I turned around, blushing, but when I looked back she was chatting easily with her colleagues and drinking her gin and tonic. I turned around again and my heart jumped. I saw Sarah climbing up the stairs at the back to the upstairs bar, overlooking the rest of the pub from behind a brass rail. I shoved my way through the throng to follow her, but lost her at the top of the stairs. I scanned the tables of drinkers, a group of four men and one glum woman, a neglected girlfriend, a raucous table, half women, half men, from a solicitors' firm. As the crowd carrying their spilling pints flowed past me, I saw Sarah again, book in hand, walking along the other side, towards the bar. Sitting at a table, in a blue shirt and red tie, was John, his grey suit jacket draped over the back of his chair. He was sitting at a sideways angle to me, leaning forward over a book.

While Sarah queued at the bar, I leaned back out of sight against the wall and watched John from behind, fascinated by the way he moved his body to accommodate the actions of the *sortes,* as he turned away to choose the passage, bent over to read it, and looked up into the distance to analyse what he found. There was a careless sensuality in the way the muscles of his upper body shifted, like a cat's, under his shirt. Such a natural lover, I thought, filled with sudden shame at my own loveless and childish fumblings with drunk strangers in the borrowed sheets of my bed in House 16. Sarah came down from the bar and sat at the table in front of John. They nodded an unsurprised greeting. He leaned down, opened a briefcase under his chair, and took out five or six more books which he stacked on the table.

If they looked up from their activities, I realised, they would certainly see me, and so I sneaked along the back of the gallery and slithered up onto an empty stool at the corner of the bar, where I was hidden from their view. I bought a pint and observed them greedily. I saw John ask a question and read out the answer. They discussed it for a long time, while Sarah took notes on a yellow foolscap pad. Nobody around seemed to think it was unusual; I suppose it looked like they were talking business. I, on the other hand, skulking, staring, and drinking alone in a very social pub, received the odd funny look. Enthralled, I watched them cast *sortes* together, so quick, serious, and assured as they pulled answers from the volumes in front of them.

For hours I stayed hidden behind the pillar at the edge of the gallery, sinking pints and watching Sarah and John, like a naturalist staking out a dangerous animal or an undercover supermarket detective monitoring potential thieves. I came close to discovery every time John came to the bar to buy a new round for him and Sarah, at least four or five times. On each occasion I sat up in the stool and steeled myself for his anger, and prepared to deliver the speech—demanding admission to their circle—I had been slowly composing in my mind throughout the night. But each time, as John stood rattling change in his pockets and waiting for his pints to be poured, he stared right through me, his brown eyes lost in the mists of words and patterns he had left at the table with Sarah.

As I watched them interact, I remembered John's story of his and Sarah's first night together, and their morning after. I tried to imagine Sarah around the time she met John, the interior of her bedroom, books on Roman divination and Irish courtly poetry in collapsing piles on the table, a dressing gown on the chair, a depression in the bed where John had been lying, he picking his clothes off the carpet and talking to himself, she curled up under the quilt, her mind wandering alone in her ghostly city of words, the literary labyrinth her Spaniard had built around her, craving the company of this young Dubliner as the colourless winter dawn filled her room.

The lights came on, and the bar staff came around asking us to finish up and go home. I got up and took my jacket off the stool, and while Sarah and John were distracted by gathering up their books and putting on their coats, I slipped down the stairs ahead of them. I mooched around on the ground floor, mentally going over the speech I was going to deliver when they saw me as I zipped up my jacket and put on my scarf. There was no sign of them coming down the stairs, so I left behind the smell of cleaning fluid and spilt beer, and the shouting bouncers ("Come on now, ladies and gentlemen, PLEASE") and emerged with a cold rush of air onto Dame Street. I stood there, huddled in my jacket, chin tucked into my scarf, waiting. Catherine O'Neill and a group of laughing law students came by. She was talking to somebody on her phone.

"We're all going to Rí-Rá! Come *on*! Ha, ha, ha. . . ."

Her voice, often the only source of kindness in the terrible prison which had been Ian's house in those days, was no use to me now, I thought.

Catherine and her friends moved along, drunk voices tinkling in the frosty night. I stood watching a steady stream of Friday-evening office drinkers come out through the door of the pub and join the intoxicated chaos of Dame Street, talking about taxis, nightclubs, or late bars as they passed me. A group of three men passed by walking towards Georges Street. Gays. And Christ, with them was the guy I had slept with before Christmas and failed to phone on St. Stephen's day, *abracadabra my granny comes from Cabra,* what's this his name was, Chris. I ducked in under the doorway, and watched them go, Chris and two slimmer smaller men with high voices and working-class accents. For a second I nearly ran after him to beg him to take me back to my bed. But I stayed where I was. In the far distance, I saw them stop and join the queue for the AIB cash machine beside Dublin Castle. Freezing, I stamped up and down, distracting myself by watching a dispute among scantily clad teenage girls in the general mayhem outside the Central Bank.

And then, eventually, they emerged together, John wearing his long grey coat and black scarf, briefcase by his side, Sarah with a navy woolly hat pulled over her head and ears. They were talking animatedly but stopped in their tracks as I stepped out of the shadows, red-nosed, teeth-chattering, and defiant in front of them.

"Hi there," I said, trying to catch a balance between the enthusiastic and the casual, and sounding like an embarrassed teacher meeting a pupil on a bus at the weekend. They looked at each other.

"What are you doing here?" Sarah asked me.

"*Ex libris.*" I used the line I had prepared during the hours watching and waiting for them inside.

There was a pause. Eventually, John spoke to her:

"Well?"

"We've no choice," Sarah said. "We bring him with us."

"Where to?" John asked. He clicked open the briefcase and pulled out a book. He cast his serious brown eyes over the passage, paused for a moment, and said: "My place. Let's get a taxi."

So that was it. No need for the rest of my speech, which had, in any case, flown the coop of my mind.

"The IFSC, isn't it?" I asked, by way of conversation. John didn't reply. He flagged taxis, in slightly aggressive competition with the crowd, while Sarah and I smoked and stamped our feet to keep warm, not looking at one another. When a car finally pulled up in front of us, John, for whom this gruff gallantry was a reflex, opened the door for me to get in first. Sarah sat in the front.

"IFSC," John told the driver, and we moved off.

On the way, Sarah chatted casually to the driver, an uncanny, completely convincing imitation of a normal passenger, interested not in ancient arts of divination, but in the Kinnegad bypass, the amount of people who took skiing holidays nowadays, the effects of the new Luas tramline on the traffic system around St. Stephen's Green. I leaned my head against the side, not daring to speak, John stared silently out his window on the other side, holding the handle on the roof, his eyes fixed on the road as it sped below. Every time we turned a sharp corner our legs touched briefly, but John did not notice, and didn't speak even as he handed the driver the money and Sarah and I got out of the car.

The glass and granite hulk of the Irish Financial Services Centre apartment complex was dotted with lights. A smell of boats and sea came from the Liffey docks, just across the road from us.

John took his cardkey out to open the gate.

"The sky has cleared," he said to Sarah, looking up.

"Come on." Sarah tugged the sleeve of John's coat, and he looked back to us. He swiped his card and the gate bleeped open. We followed John into the potted plants of the lobby, up six awkward and silent floors in the lift and then along a long white-carpeted corridor to his flat.

Sarah turned on the dimmer-switch lights and walked straight into the sitting room, which contained a sofa, armchairs, and table all covered in books and loose pages. A kitchenette in the corner looked unused, and though a musky male fragrance of aftershave or shower gel hung in the air, the bookshelves covering every wall space and the piles and piles of printed sheets and volumes gave the room the look of an archive awaiting cataloguing. Sarah got down on her knees and began rummaging in a drinks cupboard below the bookshelf. John threw his coat on the couch and pulled off his tie. Sarah stood up holding a half-full bottle of Southern Comfort. I followed them in and stood, a little formally, next to the window. John stood next to me with his hands clasped behind his back, and looked out the window at the lights on the Liffey. Sarah, at the kitchen table, poured three glasses of Southern Comfort.

She sneezed.

"The heat is timed to come on soon," John said.

"Good," she said. And then, to me: "Look—John and I need to talk alone. Wait here. We'll come out when it's time."

"Time for what?"

Without answering, she handed me my drink and walked into the bedroom carrying her own. John followed her with the bottle, and closed the door. I sipped my drink and wandered around the strange room, a fusion of a young well-off bachelor's townhouse (copies of *GQ*, a huge television, shirts and ties on chairs, weights in the corner), and the college rooms of a crazed old academic, covered by a thick layer of books and papers of all sizes, states, and ages. I heaved a pile onto the floor—I noticed some contemporary novels, an antique leather-bound dictionary, and a 1971 travel guide to San Francisco—and sat on the sofa. In the bedroom behind me, I heard soft voices and the clink of ice in their glasses.

I did all I could to eavesdrop, but they kept their voices deliberately low. I wondered for a moment if they had left me out there alone in order to make love, but the murmuring went on uninterrupted until, around half an hour later, the door opened and John came out with their empty glasses. He picked up mine and carried them over to the kitchen. Inside, there was a brief hiss of a match, and the smell of a cigarette came drifting over to me.

I walked over to the kitchen where John was rinsing the glasses, leaning awkwardly against the dishwasher, like a teenager at his first disco. I watched him scrub and swish, and, enjoying the sight of the intimate movement of his hands, I felt bound to say something to dissimulate my arousal.

"Can I help you there?"

He turned around and dried his hands on a tea towel.

"No, it's done now."

"I shouldn't be here, should I?"

"No, you shouldn't be here," he replied, putting the mugs into the cupboard. "Yet here you are. Come on."

I followed him into the bedroom. Sarah had turned off the light and was lighting a series of candles, a dozen or more, flickering creepily on the bookshelf, the bedside table, and at intervals on the floor around the edges of the room. It was neat and carefully kept, quite a contrast with the book-filled chaos of the other one. In one corner was a made bed with a navy duvet and pillow, and a desk with a single open folder and a laptop computer.

Beside me there was a small bookshelf with a half-empty bottle of Absolut Vodka on top of it, and, next to that, a battered copy of *The Golden Bough*. I picked it up and flicked through it. Every single page was crowded with notes in pencil and pens of various inks, different handwritings, languages, and alphabets, Hebrew, Italian, Irish, Spanish, French, Latin, Arabic, and Greek, and others I didn't recognise, so copious there was hardly a square centimetre of white space in any border or chapter break. On some pages, pieces of paper had even been glued on the edge to make more room for marginalia. I looked at the flyleaf. *"L. Anina Hillén, Paris 1968"* was crossed out, and underneath *"Sarah Ní Dhuibhir, Augsburg 1995"* and then *"A Sarah, mi pajarita, así volarás aún más alto—tu Luis."*

"Put it down," John said, and I obeyed.

Sarah lit the last candles, shook the match out, and stood up. In the middle of the floor, a space had been cleared for a pile of books stacked carefully on top of one another.

"How long have you lived here?" I asked John.

"A few years. That's my office, across the way." He nodded to a neighbouring building through the window. This was the first voluntary piece of conversation beyond orders and sarcastic remarks he had had with me since our pints in Kehoe's on the distant Feast of the Immaculate Conception.

Sarah turned on the computer and logged on to her e-mail while John and I stood at the door. I looked away so as not to seem nosy.

"He's replied, John," Sarah said. "He says under no circumstances." She looked wan and ethereal in the light of the tiny flames.

John nodded. "Too late."

"Yes," Sarah said, "too late."

"So, what am I doing here?" I asked.

They looked at each other.

"We'll do some *sortes* and see what happens," Sarah said. "Obviously, we have to show you something, because the books are just going to keep sending you after us. It's not what they want," she nodded towards the computer, "certainly not what we wanted, and I doubt very much this is what you want, really, Niall, but we have to pay attention to synchronicities." She sighed, as if in exasperation, and then said: "Well, I suppose we should start. Niall, sit down on the floor."

She snapped the computer shut and held out her hand.

"Phones."

We both gave her our mobiles, which she switched off and threw on the bed. She sat cross-legged, back to the window, and I sat facing her. John came over and sat beside me.

"All right," she said, "this is going to be different from what we did at the party. It's a simple variation; it's the main one we use from Pour Mieux Vivre."

"Okay."

"What we want to do is create a juncture, a fissure where one, let's call it a 'world' can flow into another. I don't mean 'worlds' in a vulgar, fantasy-novel way, I'm talking about *domains of experience*. One world we all know into another we also all know, but in a different way. All that is seen and unseen—"

"*Visibilium omnium et invisibilium,*" I interjected, excitedly.

"The benefits of a classical education," Sarah said to John, "what little learning they have, they wear on their sleeves." She continued: "We want to make a connection between the world we are living in with our five senses, and the world of art and of the dead, the world we cannot see. While you were in the other room, John and I were preparing an appropriate session for this evening. This is a difficult and, let me tell you, rather exasperating circumstance—that, I mean, of having an intruder. Anyway, as I said, we have prepared a suitable session, in accordance with our practices. In keeping with a long series of patterns we have been following for some time, we have picked these passages to start with tonight." She handed me the book, then took one each for her and John. Mine was *Peter Pan*. A page was marked with a yellow post-it. I almost smiled at the absurdity of such grave words about a children's book.

"Niall, you read out the passage I have marked for you in red pen. Then John will read his, then I will read mine. Then we will swap, passing the books to the left, so you will read the passage John just read, I will read yours, and he mine. Then we will swap again. We'll repeat it nine times in all so that each person will read each passage three times. After that, instead of taking turns, we'll start reading simultaneously, passing the books along to the left each time we finish, all reading aloud at the same time, alternating the passages. The important thing is the way you listen. You must listen to every word with the utmost care. You must concentrate on the verbal meaning of *everything* you hear, every single thing, even when you are hearing and reading several things at once. Think only of the words and think about them with all your energy. Okay? Any questions?"

"I hope I don't ruin it all," I said. "I'm not sure what you mean by the whole concentrating thing."

"Well, I hope so too," she said, and then added, a little less unkindly, "Off you go."

They looked at me expectantly. Their faces were stern and serious. I thought of the first time, aged ten, that I had read a prayer of the faithful at the children's mass in Dalkey Church. With shaking hands, I opened my book at the marked page, cleared my throat and began. My thin bourgeois voice, hollow and weak, filled the half-light of the candlelit room with the consonants of Sandycove and Gonzaga, and with them my fragile hopes, unsteady in this dark new place.

Indeed, a million arrows were pointing out the island to the children, all directed by their friend the sun, who wanted them to be sure of their way before leaving them for the night.

Wendy and John and Michael stood on tiptoe in the air to get their first sight of the island. Strange to say, they all recognised

it at once, and until fear fell upon them they hailed it, not as
something long dreamt of and seen at last, but as a familiar
friend to whom they were returning home for the holidays.
"John, there's the lagoon."

I stopped abruptly. Without a pause, John took over. The
immediate but unsudden way he did it, whatever tone or pitch or
rhythm he chose, made a seamless transition between our voices
and our persons, as if my voice had turned into his, the words of
my book into the prose John's deep vowels shaped around us.

Rastignac, now all alone, walked a few paces to the higher part
of the cemetery, and saw Paris spread out along the winding
banks of the Seine, where the lights were beginning to shine. His
eyes fastened almost hungrily on the area between the column in
the place Vendôme and the dome of the Invalides, home to that
fashionable society to which he had sought to gain admission. He
gave the murmuring hive a look which seemed already to savour
the sweetness to be sucked from it, and pronounced the epic
challenge: "It's between the two of us now!"

Then Sarah read:

"But oh!" thought Alice, suddenly jumping up, "if I don't make
haste I shall have to go back through the Looking-glass, before
I've seen what the rest of the house is like! Let's have a look at
the garden first!" She was out of the room in a moment, and ran
down stairs—or, at least, it wasn't exactly running, but a new
invention of hers for getting down stairs quickly and easily, as
Alice said to herself. She just kept the tips of her fingers on the
hand-rail, and floated gently down without even touching the
stairs with her feet.

Her voice and words merged with the echoes of John's and

mine. We passed the books around, read again, then passed and read again, then all read simultaneously. Once, twice, three times. The words began to mix.

a million arrows all alone jumping a few paces along the winding banks of the Seine back through the Looking-glass to be sure of their way before leaving the night the lights beginning to shine Wendy and John and Michael stood out in the air down quickly and easily they all recognised it the room the island between the column in the place Vendôme and the dome of the Invalides not as something long dreamt of

"Keep reading," Sarah whispered, and we went on, reading a passage and passing the books on.

"touching the stairs with her feet," I finished and passed *Alice* on to Sarah. The words continued to fuse.

John the lagoon a million paces returning back home the looking-glass island the arrows the night the lights down in the place thought Wendy and John and Michael Alice sure of their way back to the Seine in the island quickly and easily sought shine in the room the Invalides cemetery something at once the epic column John the lagoon

There was nothing in my head, in the room but words, disembodied from syntax, etymologies, or phonetic origin of any kind, words of no language, not from a book, a pen, or any other, human place. I floundered in a sea of utterances, each unrelated to the next, but each aglow with an autonomous and undivinable meaning. They enmeshed themselves around me, formed a web, a single throbbing word, a delicate cat's cradle of lexical threads.

I closed my eyes and fell forward, unsure if we were still reading or not. John touched my shoulder and pulled me back up. His eyes were shining, and so were Sarah's. I felt drunk. We kept reading.

returning home the epic room looking-glass island shine winding beginning the night John the lagoon

A soft sound startled me. There was still the mantric hum of our reading, but it seemed regulated now, governed by some internal law of metre and harmony. The three strands of our words and voices wrapped themselves together like a plait, and became a single, regularly pulsating whole. And slowly, gently, above this throbbing mesh of sounds, like static or harmonics it was generating, there came a quiet whine, an infinitesimal high-pitched wailing. I looked over at John.

"Keep reading," he whispered fiercely, and gave me a painful elbow in the ribs.

The wailing became louder and more defined. Still we kept intoning the words. It became singing, the faintest of soprano melodies on top of the heavy drumbeat of our reading. It became louder, a choir line spinning away from us, separate now from our reading, joined by a deep bass counterpoint, echoing round the bedroom, then filled out with the straining combinations of tenors and altos, an impossible choir.

"Keep reading!" John shouted. "Here, keep reading!" He thrust his book into my hand and took mine. My vision was swimming, the room was a lunatic display of watery lights and objects, and I couldn't focus on the words. I think I must have passed out, but I was revived by John, his eyes inhuman now, shining, emerald and frenzied. Sarah was much calmer, staring quietly and seriously ahead of her, like a minor mourner at a dignitary's funeral, holding her hymnbook in front of her, swaying to and fro with the music, her lips moving automatically with the page in her hands. The music was spilling now into the visual swirl of John's bedroom, John urging me between the deafening cadences of the altos to keep going, Sarah now one of the choir still steadily reading:

Rastignac, now all alone . . .

John turned back to the book he had exchanged with me.

Indeed a million arrows . . .

I needed to maintain control, to keep reading. I stared at the page, focussed, sharpened, and somehow, in the midst of all the sound and sight, managed to begin reading.

But oh . . .

I could not hear my own voice, or if I could, it seemed to be coming from one of the others. I lost all sense of time. Sometimes I was reading from one book, other times another, sometimes it seemed all our voices were one, others we fell off into separate strands with the Latin music of the choir.

incerta et occulta sapientiae tuae manifestasti

The voices seemed to slowly prepare the ground for flight, for the astonishing soar of the top soprano, keeping things going underneath, so it was safe for it to fly off to notes as high as the stars and land back again with them in security, like our reading.

"Keep reading . . ." I could hear John pleading with me, in the distance through a veil of singing, but it was too much. I let the book fall onto the floor and gave myself up to the music. It was the sound of the past, of illuminated manuscripts, draughty churches, Papal commissions, sprawling metropolises abuzz with electronic communication, blizzard-battered French mountain villages, boys playing football in dusty shanty-town sunsets,

supermarkets, the shouting sails of colonial ships, the grey ash
of Pompeii, Palmyra and Dublin, a change in the weather, a
change in the traffic lights, the sadness of waves, Ian, Ciara,
Patrick, me, everything . . . it was all too much, the room fell
silent and black.

Five

The morning sunlight made me blink as it woke me. I was in the same room, sprawled on the dark-blue duvet of John's bed, still in my clothes and boots. It took some moments for the memories of the night before to hit me. I lay still, sweating in the sun, for a time, afraid that if I moved it would all dissolve forever, as fragile dreams often do first thing in the morning. Finally, cautiously, I sat up. I found my phone on the bedside table, switched off, a fossil from the distant events of the night. I turned it on, and it told me it was half-ten and that there were two new messages in my voice mailbox. The three books were strewn on the floor, *Père Goriot*, *Through the Looking Glass*, and *Peter Pan*, and there were cold stumps of candles everywhere. Otherwise, just the twittering of birds outside, and some signs of traffic from the docks.

I stood up and looked out the window. It was bright and windy, great drying, my grandmother would have said. I turned from the window and looked around, trying to pick up some sonar echo of what had happened, but the room was now all innocence and faded reality. I moved the books around a little with my foot, as the ashes of a campfire, then I went to find John and Sarah. The apartment was completely silent. Gingerly, I checked out John's odd, book-strewn living room, but it was empty. I walked out onto his little balcony, to see if maybe they were there, but there was nothing but a single pair of FCUK boxer shorts on a clothes-horse.

My clothes smelt of smoke from The Bank and were sticking to me with sweat. I threw them off and went to the bathroom to have a shower. I used an expensive shower-gel and a damp towel hanging on the door. My clothes revolted me, so I went to John's wardrobe to find some to borrow. I took a pair of boxers and sports-socks from a drawer—I was amused to note that his underwear was all folded neatly—and found a pale green T-shirt which I liked in another. I sniffed it. It smelt of John, the same as the shower-gel and the towel. I took a pair of blue jeans—too long, too wide, of course—and a boyish-looking hoody. His weekend clothes, quite adolescent for a man his age. I felt weird, as if I was cross-dressing, and in the mirror I looked like some kind of drag parody of John.

I looked around in the cupboards in the kitchen for something to eat. I set coffee going and waited, thinking that maybe we were friends now, and they would walk in the door any minute with armfuls of croissants and the morning's *Irish Times,* like a happy rock band the morning after laying down some tracks in the studio. I poured myself some coffee and walked into the sitting-room. The church-bells outside were ringing.

Oranges and lemons, I heard, and, partially to distract myself from this I asked a question aloud:

"Where are Sarah and John?" I asked, and pulled a book from the shelf.

> *He was puzzled what to do; not the less, because I gave him my*
> *opinion that it was not safe to try to get Tom, Jack, or Richard,*

too far out of the way at present. Under existing circumstances there is no place like a great city when you are once in it. Don't break cover too soon. Lie close. Wait till things slacken, before you try the open, even for foreign air.

I replaced the book and, after folding my clothes and leaving them on the bed, I walked out of the house and into the cold sun, down onto the quays. I felt frightened and decided to leave this unfamiliar part of town, with its new business centres and dockland developments, for somewhere I knew. At first, I decided to walk to Trinity, but unable to choose between there and Sandycove, I compromised and took the bus to Ranelagh, with the half-idea that I would call in on Patrick.

I walked for a while along the main street, among the merchants and professionals of the big Edwardian houses, who mixed thoroughly in the streets, cafés and video game emporiums with the inhabitants of the working-class warrens in behind the Triangle or the council flats along the Dodder. I was still sleepy and jumpy and the crowds and cars unnerved me. I made my way through Ranelagh village, past the newsagents with red-brick upper floors, peering in at the flashing lights of Jason's video arcade and snooker hall, a place in whose clockless darkness I had often stood as a shadow at Ian's shoulder after school on Wednesdays while he played Virtua Fighter 3, for me a place of love and acute jealousy, a monument to my towering passions, a mental Taj Mahal of electronic beeps and jingles.

As I walked through Ranelagh, snatches of overheard conversations seemed to throw themselves at me like synchronicities demanding interpretation, issuing obscure commands.

"Marie, would you ever sweep up the back like a good girl."

"Right, brilliant, half-one in Fitzers, fabulous, cheers, see you then, great, great stuff, cheers."

"No, Amanda . . . the reason Amanda *rang*, is Gareth never went with her last night. He never called in to her and he . . . ."

I walked into Donnybrook along Marlboro Road. Its bare chestnut trees (I remembered Ian throwing conkers bouncing down this road one autumn) were enjoying the chilly sun, and from there, guided by inscrutable instructions from the words of passersby, down by Herbert Park and onto silent, tree-filled Raglan Road. Coming towards me from the north end of the leafy road I saw someone else, instantly familiar. My old oranges and lemons caller, Pablo Virgomare. At last. The chilly breeze danced in his curls, and he was squinting a little from the sun in his eyes. He was a little ahead of me, receding into the distance along Raglan Road, and I quickened my step in order to pursue him.

He walked quickly, too quickly for me to catch up. He didn't look when he was crossing the street, he just ploughed straight onto the road, never obstructed by any traffic. I followed him as he strode back into town, dodging cars, hailed with showers of beeping horns, along Northumberland Road and over the canal onto Lower Mount Street. I lost him for the first time on Merrion Square, where I confused him with another figure lurking in the trees of the park, but caught sight of him again and followed as he walked north, almost the way I had come, across the river and up into the north inner city, foreign place for such a deep southerner like me. Here I lost him definitively in the crowd, but continued walking nonetheless, hoping to catch a glimpse of him in one of the shops or laundrettes. I wandered, in fact, for hours, through the streets on either side of Dorset Street, around Drumcondra, Phibsboro, Seán McDermott Street and Mountjoy Square, among the babel of asylum-seekers and refugees, the shabby slip-on shoes and torn jackets of the Rumanians outside the GPO on O'Connell Street, the coloured dresses of the west African women buying fruit and vegetables from Molly Malone's descendants on Moore Street, the serious quick discussions of the Chinese on Parnell Square, past the pub that serves Nigerian Guinness. I rambled pointlessly for so long that when I crossed the river southside again, exhausted and starving, it was people leaving work who hurried by me. Men's briefcases knocked against me, women speeding along in pairs separated round me and joined again behind me without breaking their conversation.

On Grafton Street I stood at the entrance to the Stephens Green shopping centre, across the road from the Gaiety Theatre, buffeted this way and that by hurried individuals, eyes glazed or downcast, driven forth ineluctably towards their preprogrammed, singleminded destinations. I heard a clinking sound which reminded me vaguely of something, the bells, I thought first, it's Pablo and his bells.

"Niall!"

I looked up, and instead of Pablo Virgomare there was Paula McVeigh, standing in front of me with a Marks & Spencers bag.

"Oh, hi, Dr. McVeigh. . . ."

She put her bags down on the ground. "*Paula*, for the love of Jesus, I feel ould enough as it is. I'm after finishing something in the College of Surgeons, and I parked the car in Drury Street, but I simply can't face the rush hour. I simply can't face it. How are you?"

"I'm grand, you know I just live down the road now. I was going in to buy something for dinner," I invented.

"Oh, look, let's go and have a glass of wine, an aperitif, that way I can skip the rush hour, and you can relax a bit. You look a bit shook or something," she said, leaning in and looking at me more closely.

Her blond hair was slightly wild and windswept; streaks of grey were visible in patches. Her huge grey eyes, in slim dark beds of mascara, were creased, and thin, tired lines crossed her cheeks and neck, the anxious, pleasing face of a woman who was recently young.

"Oh, burning the candle at both ends, you know the way. . . ."

"I do indeed. Come on anyway, let's have a glass of wine."

I objected, feeling a generalised sense of urgency and anxiety —where was Pablo? John? Sarah? What next?—but she wouldn't hear it, and in a moment was walking with me on her arm along the Green towards Dunne & Crescenzi's on South Frederick Street. The choice of location (like her taste in clothes and shoes and her conversational references) showed a successful desire to be contemporary, not to become an irrelevant anachronism— most women of her age, the mothers of any of my other school-friends (had they had the rebelliousness or confidence to initiate an outing alone with their son's classmate in the first place) would have gone to Bewley's, time-tested default place to get together in town, a habit unchanged since they brought us, as boys in the 1980s, to see Santy in Switzer's at Christmas. Paula's eyes were alive to changes around her, new cafés, new means of communication, altered trends: she sniffed the wind with eager-ness and curiosity.

I offered to carry her shopping bags, I knew she would like that, the kind of woman who misses that sort of male attention. On the walk there she talked, about how tired she was, how the hospitals were so underfunded, how she did as much public practice as she could, private medicine ruined the lives of people in Ireland, Charlie McCreevy spent his time wheeling and dealing with thugs and culchies at the Galway Races instead of managing things in a civilised fashion.

"I mean, Niall, have you *ever been* to another European capital? I mean *have* you? I mean look at this." She swept a hand, rings glinting in the last hint of daylight along Stephens Green North, "The gridlocked traffic, the queues at the bus stops, the yobs at the taxi ranks. Where are the light-rail systems, the metros, the pavement cafes, the city-centre apartment blocks, where are the public parks, the bicycle lanes, the open-air markets, the gays out in their finery like peacocks, the Jewish bakeries, the Chinese wholesale outlets with the old fellas playing checkers outside on a little table, the lesbians running a centre with free tampons and coriander soup, where are the Arabs playing dice or whatever it is . . . where are all the beautiful people? I mean, Niall, look, look at them, where are they? *Where* are they?"

As we queued for a table in Dunne & Crescenzi's, she told me that she went there because it was the only place she could feel for a minute that Dublin was different, really had changed, or that, better still, she was outside Dublin.

"I know I sound like a bitter old hag, but you know I've lived in this country all my life, I went from Our Lady's Bower Athlone to UCD Med and an old hole in Rathmines, but I *have travelled,* and I know, I see, everything in this place is shoddy, everyone is happy with third-rate facilities, dreary streets, and third-rate lives. And fine, we had, you know, unemployment and what have you. But we had a boom! An economic miracle! And now the country awash with money and in Cork General Hospital they only give epidurals three days a week."

A handsome Italian waiter sat us at a table.

"Good evening," he said, as Paula beamed flirtatiously at him. "To drink?"

She asked me if I wanted red or white, and when I said red, she ordered a bottle.

"Let's go mad. And we'll have something to eat," she said, "just a snack."

I looked through the menu and suggested bruschetta. I pronounced it *brushetta,* as I had always heard people in restaurants do. She shook her head in pain.

"*Brusketta,* dear, *brusketta.* Ch in Italian is hard," she murmured.

Paula—which I began actually to call her, finally—was in charge of the pouring. It seemed every sentence was punctuated by a glush-glush-gloop and a full glass. She talked and talked, the different hospitals she had worked in, how she had disliked so many of the teachers and parents at Gonzaga, but she had liked me and my parents, and that woman who taught us French, Anne Evan, she had a bit of imagination, got us out of the country, at least in our heads, for a few hours a week. She had had difficulties, she didn't mind telling me, with the idea of sending Patrick to a Catholic school.

"That time it meant something, you know, that we didn't say rosaries and the like at home with Patrick. I mean it still means something," she said, leaning in on the table for emphasis, "even nowadays when no one goes to mass only the ancient or bewildered."

I tried to move her off the subject of politics and society, a little because I found the pace so breathtaking, and didn't quite know how to contribute, but mostly because I felt in a childish way that my only duty was to be as polite and grateful as possible.

"This is a lovely place," I said.

"Have you not been here before?"

"No, it's really nice."

"But you see, Niall, that's the problem, that's the whole problem with this place. It gives you just enough rope to hang yourself. There's always some thing that's great, or in the pipeline, and the Irish content themselves with that. But you can't look at these things in isolation, you have to look at the bigger picture. These exceptions . . . oh, but Dunne & Crescenzi's is lovely, the ward sister is very kind, the Blackrock Clinic has a state-of-the-art CAT scan facility, the Luas will be the best light rail system money can buy. The bigger picture, Niall, the bigger picture, and it's all decrepit and paltry and overpriced and run-down. Awash with money," she repeated, "and look at how we live. I hope, Niall, that you and Patrick will think bigger. I really do. I have never lived outside Ireland, I have travelled of course an awful lot—I'm very lucky that way—but I hope you leave, get off this windswept oul rock, move away, live in London or Paris or Berlin or somewhere. I was nine months in London when I was a student, that's it."

I told her I was thinking I'd go to Paris that summer. She was delighted. She started on again about the beautiful people, or rather the lack of them, in Ireland, and reminiscing about those nine months when she shared a flat in Hackney with another young Irish med student, Colette Ryan, still her friend, works in

Tallaght, still went on what she called "mega-lunches" a few times a year. The men, the dances, the craic. She told me she loved her husband, Frank, but god he was so *Irish*, you know. . . . All too Irish, as the man said. . . .

As we finished up the wine, Paula made a few references to the fact that I had been in such infrequent touch with Patrick, and I felt guilty. She paid, and squeezed me on the shoulder as a goodbye while she waved down a taxi on the street.

My room was old and forgotten, a hoard of relics, like my granny's house. There were clothes on the floor from days ago, and an upturned volume of Stendhal on the bed reminded me I had forgotten, or in any case been absent from, my tutorial with Professor Dunne. I switched on my neglected phone and faced the voicemails. Two where-are-you messages from Fionnuala, barely audible against the background noise of the pub and then the party, repeating directions in case I had got lost. There was also a text message from Patrick, *"I'll be in town tonight, meet up?"* I flopped down on the bed and turned over to try and sleep, but my mind was restless. I stuck a hand out to the radio and listened to farming news.

The doorbell rang, and I went to the window, hoping it was Pablo. It was Fionnuala.

"Hello stranger!" she called. "Where the fuck were you?"

"I was about to ring you," I said. "Do you want to come up?"

"Come on down for a pint."

I hesitated for a moment while my eyes lingered on the bookshelf. "Sure," I said, "one second."

I threw on my jacket and went down to her.

"So, where were you last night?" she asked.

"Would you believe I fell fast asleep?"

"The sleep of the dead, it must have been. I ran back and rang your bell before we went to the party, and again when I got back."

"I'm so sorry, Fionnu, I'll buy you a pint. Name your pub."

"We just pop over to the Buttery?" she suggested. "There'll be people from the class there."

"Grand. Was it a good night, anyway?"

"Well! You missed a heap of scandal."

"Typical."

We walked down by the tennis courts towards Front Square while Fionnuala filled me in on what had happened, shenanigans between people we knew involving locked bedrooms, much hilarity and intrigue. I began really to wish I had gone there instead of about my unwholesome business in the IFSC.

The people playing tennis hit the ball over the fence and I threw it back to them. The guy gave me a little salute of thanks. As we turned the corner of the Dining Hall I texted Patrick, out of mixed-up feelings of guilt and loyalty. He responded immediately, as he always did. He was in town, wandering around the bookshops, and would definitely join us in the Buttery.

Two eras of my life came together as I introduced Patrick and Fionnuala inside the Buttery a few minutes later, when Patrick came walking across the pub to us. At school he had been a mournful plodder, always looking at the ground, sandy-haired head bent over staring at the soggy crusts and cigarette butts in the school yard, tugging the cord of his anorak nervously. But he walked with confidence and enthusiasm over to us now, smiling and waving before he reached us, then greeted both of us energetically.

"Fionnuala, Patrick, Patrick, Fionnuala. Patrick is a friend of mine from school, Fionnuala is the other Beckett scholar."

"Oh right, great. Well done!"

"You in Trinity too?" Fionnuala asked him. Of course I had told her all about Patrick while we were waiting for him to come, but Fionnuala had rapid-fire reflexes for how to get interactions oiled and ready to run.

"UCD Med."

"Oh, right. You'll earn more money than us anyway," she joked. Patrick smiled politely and looked at his shoes.

". . . well, my parents are both doctors . . ."

The Buttery was quite full and, as always, under its low, vaulted roof, dark. We were fussing around looking for a free table to fit the three of us, when through the hubbub of clinking and laughter we saw Andrea beckoning to us on the other side. She was standing on top of her table waving at us, ignoring the security guard who was ordering her down.

"Niall! Niall! Fionnuala! Come on over! Okay, okay, *relaxez-vous*," she added crossly to the guard, as she clambered down, seeing we were coming over to join her.

It turned into an extremely entertaining evening. Andrea took a drunk liking to Patrick, who remained permanently brick-red as she let her arm fall casually on his legs when she was making a point, he staring into the bottom of his glass. Andrea's friends were fun, and between their banter and the buying of drinks I chatted a little to Fionnuala about the classes I had missed that day, and the marks for the Christmas essays (we had both got firsts; Andrea overheard this piece of conversation, and giggled through her drink "You know what Harry got? *Twenty*! That's like the lowest possible. But *literally*, like. They say the range is twenty to eighty. So I mean, if he got twenty, it means he actually got *zero*! I nearly pissed myself when Jayne told me. I didn't bother writing one," she added airily, tossing her hair to one side, and looking at Patrick out of the corner of her eye, "couldn't be arsed, like."). Patrick and I had occasional opportunities to barter information tokens about our lives, and even got into a livelyish conversation about how different the world seemed outside school. For some reason I didn't mention the bottle of wine and plate of bruschetta with his mother, something about the meeting felt illicit. But I did feel that being out and about like this in a group of wild students was one way of being faithful to Paula's desire for things to be bright, shiny, and cosmopolitan. In all, the pints, the animated talking of Andrea and her friends, the sense of a possible real closeness with Fionnuala in the future, and the presence of

Patrick, link between the past and the present, gave me a heady sense of youth and normality, and all thoughts of the *sortes* and their gloomy priests were wiped out.

As I clambered out over the others to go the toilet, it even crossed my mind that my interactions with John and Sarah, and the strange night I had spent with them in the IFSC apartment, could eventually become conversational fodder for a night like this, a crazy story to drink out on.

I leaned in over the urinal, feeling content and guilty for having been so remiss with Patrick. He was a good friend, and part of me, I thought, and he could make the transition into this life, now, come to the Buttery with college friends and have a laugh, and then we would have people in common to talk about, a whole new basis to be friends. Glasses of wine at home with Paula before the two of us headed out on the town. I began to imagine the conversation in which I would come out to Patrick.

But as I walked to the sinks, I was stopped in my tracks by a sentence written in bold blue marker on the pale yellow walls, a fresh line of graffiti, standing out in its confidence and relative elegance from the *Brits Out, Fuck B.E.S.S. Wankers, Ciarán Kelly=gay* that surrounded it. It read:

"You owe me five farthings," say the bells of Saint Martin's.

The room spun. I shut my eyes, thinking it was a drunken delusion, but when I opened them the words were still there. I looked away from the wall while I washed my hands and splashed cold water on my face. Still it remained, confidently scrawled across the wall over the faded graffiti underneath it. And then, when I had finished drying my hands and the drier subsided, I heard it coming in on the air through the back door at the edge of the bathrooms, the same voice as before, faint but definite, mischievously singing the line:

"You owe me five farthings," say the bells of Saint Martin's.

I tried to hold on, I splashed my face again with cold water, but I could hear it clearly now, singing out on the night air, across the city to me, louder than the driers, louder than the weeping urinals, the sounds of laughter, talk, and bleeping phones from the other room, louder than the voices of Patrick, Andrea, and Fionnuala, calling me back. The colours of everything, the dirty tiles of the bathroom, the buzzing fluorescent lights above, the darkness through the windows, appeared to me in a sharper, addictive focus. I peered out through the door of the bathroom. I could see our table. Andrea was gesturing madly, pressing some point home, and Fionnuala and Patrick were laughing. I left the bathroom and hesitated in the passage.

In front of me was the door which led back into the bar, through which I could see them all talking and joking at the table, my half-drunk pint waiting for my return. On my left was a fire escape, through which I had heard the voice of Pablo singing the second line of *Oranges and Lemons.*

Emergency Exit Only. Alarm will sound.

A few moments later I was running along Botany Bay with a bell screaming behind me.

In my room, face flushed with excitement, clappers clanging in my head, I almost roared at the bookshelf "Where are Sarah and John?," and knocked a pile of books onto the floor in my rush to pick one, *The Rough Guide to Spain.*

They are concentrated particularly around Plaza de Santa Ana.

I thought for a little while. Anna's place, that must mean the house in Ranelagh. I left my phone on the bed to ring away into the empty night, set off through Front Square, out into the city and across the canal to Ranelagh.

There was a waxy, flickering light coming from the window of John's bedroom, the candles they had laid for the session. I rang the doorbell, and, to my surprise, it was answered by a tall, goodlooking woman of around thirty. Her black hair was tied up, and she was wearing a *New Zealand* T-shirt, tracksuit bottoms, and suede clogs, the lounge-around-the-house outfit of someone who wears stylish and glamorous clothes in the outside world.

"Yes?" she asked suspiciously through a partially opened door.

"I'm a friend of John's."

"He's not here, sorry, bye." She began to close the door, but I stuck my foot in.

"Wait, I really . . . he's expecting me."

She hesitated. "Do I know you?"

"We might have passed each other at the party you had here in November."

She narrowed her eyes. She had light freckles around her nose.

"Really?" she said, "I don't think I recognise your face. Well . . . come in for a moment."

She closed the door behind me and brought me into the kitchen where I had seen John and Sarah together for the first time. On the table was a steaming mug with the little string and label of a herbal teabag hanging over the side, a plate with a half-eaten slice of toast and a buttery knife, and an *Irish Times* spread open at the letters page.

"Sit down," she said, but I stayed standing at the edge of the table. She sat down opposite and tried to sip the tea, but it was still too hot. She blew on it, then looked at me with her pale blue eyes.

"Are you involved in all this . . . in John's book club thing?" she asked me, quietly, like a school counsellor. I nodded. "I hope you know what you're doing. What's your name?"

"Niall."

"I'm Anna."

"Yes, I guessed that."

"Oh, so he does talk about me then."

"Look, I'm going to go up and join them."

"No, you can't. Not now, wait until they're finished. They won't even let me in."

I looked at her for a moment, the steam from the tea rising in front of her; then I turned around and ran up the stairs two at a time.

"Stop!" she called after me, but I ignored her.

I stood in front of John's door. There were people talking rapidly in loud voices. I was going to knock, but I heard Anna running up the stairs behind me, and quickly turned the handle and went in. The room was filled with candle-light, like a small chapel. John and Sarah were sitting on the floor with heaps of books and papers around them. For a single, horrified split second I saw them in full flight, glazed eyes fixed on the ceiling, both of them babbling in alien voices, a mad chatter of foreign syllables. They started and turned to me in terror when I entered.

"Get out!" John roared, and leaped over to push me roughly back out onto the landing. He banged the door shut and I heard him sitting down again. The babble did not start again. Anna was standing at the top of the stairs, leaning on the banisters.

"I told you," she said softly. She put a hand up to her forehead and shook her head. "Come on, leave," she said. "Go, now."

At that moment the door of the bedroom opened and John appeared.

"You can come in now, Niall. It's okay, Anna," he said in response to her long stare.

"Okay," she laughed bitterly. "Sure, John, it's all just fine." She turned and walked into the other bedroom. "I'm going to stay in Isabelle's."

We stood there, John at the door and I standing on the landing, listening to the sounds of her packing a bag in her bedroom, taking her washbag from the bathroom, going down the stairs, gathering her coat, keys, and phone. John didn't move or speak until the door front door slammed and we heard her footsteps clacking by on the pavement. He went into the room and I followed him.

The candles, extinguished, had been replaced by a small desk-lamp, and the books and papers had been gathered up. Sarah was standing looking out the window, smoking, holding her elbow with her free hand. She didn't react when I came in. John closed the door and stood behind me. I took off my coat and threw it on the bed.

"What was—"

"I need a drink, John," Sarah interrupted. She switched off the reading lamp.

John left and came back with a bottle of Southern Comfort and three glasses. The room was dark, a faint glow from the street outside, the angry orange tip of Sarah's cigarette, and behind John the blue-green lights of his stereo mutely alight like the console of an abandoned starship. John walked to the desk beside the window and poured us each a drink. I sat on the bed. John said:

"Never, ever do that again. Never interrupt like that."

I swished my Southern Comfort. Sarah had drained hers off in two gulps. She opened the window and tossed her cigarette out.

"Okay, back to it," she said. "John, candles."

We laid out the room as before. Sarah chose the books and passages we were to use: bizarrely, three guide books. We sat around as before, read, passed, read, passed, and so on. Again, I was to begin:

Geography and history have combined to give Paris a remarkably coherent and intelligible structure. The city lies in a basin surrounded by hills. It is very nearly circular, confined within the limits of the ring road, the boulevard périphérique, which follows the line of the city's nineteenth-century fortifications. The capital's *raison d'être* and its lifeline, the River Seine, flows east to west, carving the city in two. Anchored at the hub of the circle, in the middle of the river, is the island from which the rest of Paris grew: the Île de la Cité, home of the capital's oldest religious and secular institutions—Notre Dame cathedral and the Palais de Justice. The north or Right Bank (rive droite) of the Seine is characterised by imposing government buildings, sweeping vistas and elegant boulevards. The longest and grandest thoroughfare is the so-called Voie Triomphale, which runs from the Louvre to the Grande Arche de la Défense in the northwest . . . to the immediate north and east of the Voie Triomphale spread the commercial and financial quarters, site of the stock exchange, the refurbished nineteenth-century passages and Les Halles shopping centre.

John took over from me, as before:

Getting There & Away: Telendos is reached by a regular caïque service from Myrties (400 dr each way), running every half hour from 8 a.m. to midnight. If you are stuck after midnight, restaurant owners are usually willing to give you a lift back to Myrties.

Emborios: North of Massouri settlements rapidly thin out and a long, sealed road leads northwards to the last settlement on the island, the relaxed village of Emborios. Along the way the road curves around the fjord-like Arginonda Bay which is home to a thriving fish farming industry. The fish pens can be seen along the southern edge of the bay. The village of Arginonda itself is rather spread out but attracts a few bathers to its pebbly beach. Most visitors plough on to the end of the line past a rugged landscape that seems to support more goats than humans.

Sarah followed without pause or overlap; they were like skilful djs, I thought.

For all the gentrification of the last twenty years, Camden Town
retains a seedy air, compounded by the various railway lines that
plough through the area, the canal, and the market, now the dis-
trict's best-known attribute. Having started out as a tiny crafts
market in the cobbled courtyard by the lock, Camden Market has
since mushroomed out of all proportion. More than 100,000 shop-
pers turn up here each weekend and parts of the market now stay
open week-long, alongside a similarly-oriented crop of shops, café
and bistros. The market's overabundance of cheap leather, DM
shoes and naff jewellery is compensated for by the sheer variety
of what's on offer: from bootleg tapes to furniture, along with a
mass of street fashion that may or may not make the transition
to mainstream stores. To avoid the crowds, which can be over-
powering on a summer Sunday afternoon, you'll need to come
either early—before 10am—or late—say, after 4pm, when many
of the stalls will be packing up to go.

I started again, trying to imitate their smooth transitions:

Geography and history have combined

We went around a second time, *than humans for all the gentri-*
fication, and then a third, *packing up to go geography and history,*
and then we swapped books to the left, so that I was reading
Camden Town, John Paris, and Sarah the passage about the
Greek island. There was nothing of the intensity of the last time
we had done it; the passages were much longer than before, and
although John and Sarah's eyes flickered slightly, no effect
seemed to be taking place: the words seemed straightforward,
unshakeably themselves, and out of their context, even a little
absurd. Even when we began reading over one another, it
remained distinctly our three separate voices reading out passages, competing rather than combining, almost embarrassing. I
even started to suspect that the supernatural events of my first

sortes session had been a delusion, a madness from which I had now awoken, and Sarah and John, reading so deliberately and concentratedly, seemed like foolish teenagers at a sleepover, waiting for the glass on the homemade ouija board to spell out the name of an ancestor or a deceased rock star.

And then, after some time, I don't know how long, but after a long and nearly tedious simultaneous recital of the three extracts from the guide books, the reading and the sound took on a rhythm, a slow and regular gallop which began to imply some new meaning and context to the words and sounds.

> *history and getting away have compounded a coherent and intelligible structure. From midnight railway lines plough a basin surrounded by settlements along the lifeline the river runs by curves of bay*

I became excited and began to trip over words, but the other two, not surprised at what was happening, continued competently on, not missing a syllable and passing the books swiftly to the side and so I did my best to continue reliably, not to ruin things.

> *away Arginonda similarly oriented at the hub along site of the secular mass*

And then, with a leap and a buzz, it took on life, became a peculiarly familiar initiatory incantation of magic words:

> *Having started out, all geography and history. Every half hour from midnight, the city lies, and retains a seedy air, usually willing to combine to give a regular service, but the real home of the capital, the city's raison d'être, on the southern edge of the bay, spread out from the nineteenth-century fortifications of Telendos, Emborios and Camden Town, cobbled districts of*

canals, cafés and secular institutions, overpowering west and then northwards (400 dr each way) along a pebbly beach. Various railway lines run along the Right Bank (rive droite) of the fjord-like bay, getting there and away, making the transition between the hub of the circle and the immediate south, through the sealed settlements of Myrties, the Louvre and Notre Dame, through Arginonda, Les Halles and the lock. The River Seine carves the district in two, lifeline ploughing east to west, anchored by curve of bay and compensated for by a refurbished boulevard, flowing on to the end of the line past a rugged landscape to the last settlement on the island, running to avoid the crowds from sweeping vistas and an elegant caïque. This is a basin surrounded by hills, compounded in the middle by the river, willing to give you a lift back, packing to go.

Suddenly Sarah threw her book into the middle and said: "Stop, listen."

Obediently, but in my case rather crestfallen, John and I closed our books and put them down. In the sudden silence, the room throbbed with the echoes of the thing our reading had become.

"Are we listening for music?" I asked. No one replied. "What music are we listening for?" I pursued, "What was it last time?"

"A famous setting of Psalm 50, normally sung on Ash Wednesday. It used to be a secret piece, sung only in the Pontifical Chapel, punishments meted out for copying it, supposedly Mozart wrote it down from memory as a teenager. And if you believe that . . ." she rolled her eyes at John as she trailed off.

Even though we were sitting and talking as if everything was still normal—Sarah even lit a cigarette—a profound change in our surroundings was palpable, as though we were not in the same room as before, but in a painting or stylised photograph of it.

"That music—I hear it now." I said. Distantly, cautiously, like the sound of an ice-cream van on another child's street, I could hear the voices.

Auditui meo dabis gaudium et laetitiam

I craned my head (towards what, of course, is another question), and there it was again, slightly louder now. "Yes, I definitely—"

"Ssh!" commanded Sarah.

John got up and pushed open the window. With the sudden gust of cold air came the sound of the choir, still reticent and far, but now too solid to miss, part of the wind. Then John, with his back to me, stiffened and leaned further out the window. Sarah turned to look at him.

"John?"

I noticed him breathing deeply and sat up. He pointed to the window. I stood up and put my elbows on the windowsill beside his and looked out. Sarah walked over and squashed in on his other side.

"What? What is it, John?"

"Look." He breathed. "Look." He pointed out the window again. I looked out and saw nothing, just the implacable roofs of the houses under the dark sky. And then a movement, a slow arc of light drawn across the sky in the distance. I looked closer. It was a crane moving in the distance, somewhere on the North Strand, a crane with a light on the top moving backwards and forwards in a gentle, dignified semi-circle. And then to the left another, creaking in the opposite direction at exactly the same pace. Together they described two soft curves of light in front of us. And then behind them, another crane on a local building site. The rhythm increased in tempo, and they moved in full circles now, the trail of light they left after them lingering in the huge darkness above the city, three fading intersections above the still chimneys and apartment blocks we saw through the window of Anna's spare room. On the Docklands, a cluster of cranes slowly set themselves in motion, intersecting perfectly with the rhythm of the others. The music faded, the cranes took over, a wordless ballet, lights all over the city moving for us, until our necks were too sore to look any longer, and I fell asleep on John's bed again.

I awoke around three and hearing whispers around me, opened my eyes slightly. The room seemed to be filled with a blue light, and I thought I heard three voices altogether, first of all a strange one, an elderly female I thought, but indistinct and muttering, and kind of distorted with static. I couldn't make out what she was saying. I fell asleep again, then awoke again to the sound of the front door closing and two sets of footsteps hurrying away down the street. I got up myself and fell back through daybreak to my rooms.

I defaulted on class the next day, and wandered around town wherever synchronicities took me, a vast bank of instructions and ideas for me to connect with. I spied John and Sarah hurrying along the edge of New Square towards the Berkeley library and I ran after them but lost them. Books failed to bring me nearer to them. Instead I zigzagged back and forth across the city as literature dictated, dropping into a church for a stranger's removal at about five, where I lusted after a young mourner in a suit and tie with his arm round his girlfriend's waist.

I got back to my rooms around six. There was a note pushed under the door.

Niall, called by to see if you were OK. What happened last night? Your phone doesn't seem to be working. Talk to you soon (I hope), I'm at home all day so ring whenever you get this, Patrick. P.S. I'm worried.

I faced my phone. There was of course a rake of missed calls. *Missed 1: Patrick Missed 2: Patrick Missed 3: Fionnuala Missed 4: Fionnuala Missed 5: Patrick Missed 6: Fionnuala* . . . , text messages *Are you ok? Where are you?*, and voice-mail messages which I didn't listen to. I wrote a text message which I *Sent To Many* to Patrick and Fionnuala.

So sorry about last night. Was too drunk to go back to pub, got sick

*and went home, fell into deep sleep! Hope you weren't too worried.
Can't believe what a drunken fool I am. Talk soon. N*

I switched it off and turned over in order to sleep. The floodlights were on on the tennis courts, giving my room a ghostly
pink glow and the shadows an unlikely extension. Poc poc poc.
Pause. POC poc. I closed the curtains and turned over. I wasn't
tired. I sat up again. Patrick's note, the torn piece of foolscap,
was making me feel uncomfortable so I crumpled it up, put it in
the bin and walked out of the room into the kitchen down the
corridor. One of the girls had put up a jolly notice in marker
asking us to take our turns emptying the bins. I looked in the
fridge. Someone else on my corridor had frozen mini-pizzas,
which I would have liked. All I had was half a block of cheddar
cheese, so I stole two slices of white bread from the cupboard,
toasted the cheese on them for myself, and made a pot of tea.
Below, on Pearse Street, people hurried towards the train station. The evening air was packed with headlights and traffic
lights as the cars beeped and nudged one another along. The
granite of the outside wall was black, a skin slowly grown from
patient years of watching these tired workers making the trip
back to their children in the suburbs. What a scramble for peace
it was, an unseemly dash to quit the words and turmoil of the
city, a desperate rush to sink pints of lethe in Blackrock and
Foxrock, to chew the lotos in Rathgar, Sandymount, and Dalkey.

I took the tea back into my own room. I pulled a chair up to
the window and sat looking out. There was some shadowy
movement below in Botany Bay, as people went home and to
dinner and to call on one another. The tennis players were finishing, two middle-aged men who shook hands and walked
away together, towels and balls in hand. The statues on the top
of the Bank of Ireland, off to the northwest, were haloed with a
faint blue glow, as the sun sank off behind them, hidden by
cloud. Sarah's light was not on. Fionnuala's was: I could see her,
in fact, bent over a book at her desk in a pool of light from her

study lamp. I wondered what it was, the book that I, if things had turned out differently, would now be reading myself, from beginning to end, in logical, full order. I asked aloud:

"What should I do now?" and took a book from the shelf.

The heat was suffocating.

Totally useless. I threw the book on the floor in annoyance. I went back to the bookshelf and demanded:

"What should I do now? A real answer."

At the mere sight of Russian print an English person is apt to exclaim: "How funny the Russian letters look, rather like ours upside-down . . . "

I was going to toss this absurdity away from me in a rage, when it struck me that it was kindly advice. I had been too quick to dismiss the first one, because at first glance it appeared to have no clear meaning, gobbledy-gook in relation to what I had asked. I read on:

Nevertheless, some of them, with characteristic British determi-nation, have taken up Russian with enthusiasm as a fascinating hobby. They have done so probably because it is the language of a country which at the present time is stirring the minds of men and women in all walks of life, in England and probably the rest of the world.

At present stirring the minds of women and men . . . did this mean Sarah and John? Synchronicities they were looking up? Maybe right now? I looked back at the sentence I had chosen ini-tially. *"The heat was suffocating."* The text around it didn't feel rel-evant. Heat . . . I should go somewhere hot, eat something hot (it struck me this would have been a good idea; in more than twenty-four hours I had eaten only the cheese on toast) . . . suffocating . . . I looked again at the introduction to *Teach Yourself Russian*, thinking vaguely that I ought to give it back to Ciaran Judge who had lent it to me such a long time previously. Letters seem like ours. Something jumbled up. Suffocate. Suffolk Street? Yes, British, England—Suffolk. That was it, Suffolk Street! Walks of life, Pour Mieux Vivre, walk to Suffolk Street!

I ran down the steps two and three at a time, crossed Front Square through Front Gate. Grafton Street was wet and puddled. I turned right down Suffolk Street, where Christmas lights, dead and pocky now, were still slung over the street, dripping carcasses in an abbatoir. There was a long queue at the bus stop. I thought maybe I would see Pablo there, but they were all familiar strangers, as people at Dublin bus stops tend to be, familiar and morose. I took forty euro out of the wall beside O'Neill's, and purposely ignored the dwindled sum on the advice slip. That was a good expression for the way of things now, advice slip. I walked back down towards the Grafton Street end and looked in the door of the wood-panelled Thing Mote's. The whiff of beer and after-work laughter was warm, and I even thought about staying, but Pablo was not here either. In Pacino's across the road I frightened a couple having dinner by looking in the window. Finally I leaned against the damp stone wall of McCullough Pigott's and waited. A couple of moments later John and Sarah emerged from O'Neill's, John carrying the briefcase they used for their books. They turned around, startled, as I shouted their names and began running towards them. They hesitated and looked at one another, wondering what to do, and were saved from the choice between the indignity of flight on foot and the inconvenience of being saddled once more with the third wheel by a taxi coming down Trinity Street. John hailed it and they rushed in, Sarah pulling her coat inside before banging the door shut. It drove off. I waved down another taxi from which a foreign businessman was descending across the road from me. I jumped in, and as the driver pressed the button on the electric metre to start the fare I pointed to John and Sarah's taxi in front of us, turning left onto Dame Street.

"Follow that cab!" I said excitedly to the driver, a young man with a tattoo on his forearm. He jolted the car to a sudden stop, leaned back, and threw my door open.

"Get the fuck out, yeh muppeh," he growled, and drove away, leaving me to run after John and Sarah's disappearing taxi. I shouted and waved, but the two silhouettes in the back didn't react and had soon driven out of sight.

I walked through Temple Bar and down to the quays where I stood on Capel Street Bridge scanning the rush-hour crowds hurrying north and south on the bridge, hoping to see Pablo. A homeless boy, probably not more than ten, wrapped in blankets beside me, stared with sombre, hardened eyes. I threw him a two-euro coin.

Spatters appeared on the water. As the rain grew heavier and heavier, the people crossing began to hurry, those without hoods or umbrellas raced over the slippery black surface covering their heads with bags or newspapers. Even the homeless boy left to shelter in an awning on Ormond Quay. I stayed where I was, staring down at the ceaseless drumming on the dirty water below, watching the drops tumble in front of me, but the water began to run down my nose and neck and to leak into my shoes, and I looked around in the thundering rain, wondering where to go to shelter. I ran, splashing over the bridge. As I looked right before crossing the road, in a spinning, faint-headed sensation I saw a Paris streetname in the afternoon sun, rue de la Croix something, and two men with closely-cropped hair, white T-shirts, and jeans walked by me hand in hand, smiling at one another and looking in the window of a shop on the corner. I started to cross the street, but was greeted with a screech of brakes as a white Mercedes with a 75 registration stopped just in front of me. Fuck, I thought, the cars are driving on the right. I stood in the middle of the street looking back and forth, up and down a big Paris boulevard shimmering in the heat. The driver rolled down the window of his car and started shouting at me. On the pavement, people were stopping and looking. I saw Pablo turn into one of the shops on the street, and I ran to go after him, running into another lane of traffic and frantic beeping, only now I was crossing Ormond Quay in the heaving Dublin rain again, and I jumped back onto the curb in order not to get splashed or knocked down. My skin was cold from the wet now, but I didn't care. I crossed the bridge and the road on the other side, weaving in a wet daze through the car headlights, up Parliament Street, and found myself seeking out the warm, gay interior of the Front Lounge.

It was often full at this time of the evening, about two-thirds men, mostly gay, mostly in big, intersecting groups of regular friends. They were all drinking pints, introducing friends and throwing eyes. I sat up on a free stool at the bar at the back and ordered a Guinness, the money rattling and falling from my quivering fingers. I hoped the bitter, creamy stout would drown the growing panic within me, rising through my veins and battering the walls of my heart. My hands were shaking, and I spilt Guinness-foam on my trousers. I was afraid that my surroundings would lurch again, and I would find myself standing in the middle of a summer street in Paris.

A warm hand touched the back of my neck. Pablo? I opened my eyes. It was still the palms and white pillars of the Front Lounge. I turned slowly around in my stool.

Abracadabra

A good-looking man in a blue shirt without a tie, a nearly finished pint in his left hand, was smiling at me broadly, part mockingly.

"Well, look what the cat's after draggin in."

"Chris!"

"So you remember my name at least, you do?"

I reached out in gratitude and touched his face, just to be sure he was real, the soft skin of his cheek. He took my hand down, but held it a moment in his and squeezed.

"I'm sorry I didn't ring you," I said. "I mean, I . . ."

"Ah, save it," he said with a rueful laugh. "I'm an old hand. I know men, especially young ones like you, fateless feckers all of yous."

"No, but . . . no, I wanted to," I said, though the truth was of course that I wanted, there and then, to have done so. He gave me a friendly, knowing smile and patted me on the shoulder.

"Are you doin all right, so?"

"Not so bad, not so bad. Yourself?"

"Grand, grand," Chris said, and leaned in to give me a quick kiss on the cheek. "I just wanted to say howayeh."

"Thanks."

"Good luck to yeh, so."

He turned and left, ambling happily back to whatever group he was with, off to a full evening of banter and sex. My heart heaved like a ship in a storm.

"Hang on . . ." I began weakly, then, mustering my forces, stood up and called at his retreating figure, so neat and careful in his tieless after-work suit, so orderly and handsome, so in the world. "Chris!"

He turned around and I gestured to him to come back over. He raised an eyebrow quizzically and returned. I drank in the tiniest details of his physical presence: how his short, neat hair was slightly tousled from the heat of the pub, how his thick fingers, with their clipped, clean, well-kept nails grasped the lower section of the glass, hiding the foamy dregs.

"Allow me to buy you a drink, at least," I said, nodding towards his glass. His face broke into a tooth-crowded smile.

"All right so."

I ordered two pints. He stood next to my stool as the first pour settled. He didn't say anything, but smiled once, his eyes dancing with interior amusement as they had the night we met, and in them I saw the spark of desire. When the pints were filled and paid for, I raised mine in a silent toast. He responded, then said:

"I'm with a crowd of friends. I better go back."

"Of course," I said, as my hopes sank, "sorry, of course."

"You're welcome to join us."

I said no, but he laughed at me and said, "Come on, we're over here."

He was at a rowdy table in the back corner, by the windows looking onto South Essex Street. He introduced me round his group. By their thin and wary smiles when we shook hands, I could tell some of them knew the state of affairs, that I was a score who had promised and failed to ring. They were a mix of ages and social classes, a five-person product of the mad swirl of the Dublin gay scene. Séamus, a freelance producer, was in his late forties with a white linen jacket, grey moustache, and an RTÉ accent; beside him, fat Brendan with gold hoops in his ears and bald head shining like a silver tea service in the light, curling Celtic tattoos on each forearm, was a "community activist"; Darina, heterosexual and mid-thirties, was a co-worker of Chris's, his boss, I thought, and seemed a little antagonistic to me; Ciarán was the wit, an effeminate and working class-accented man in his mid-twenties from Clondalkin, a waiter in Café Bar Deli; at the edge, Dave, a laughing stud around my age with floppy black hair and an ambiguous sexuality looked like a junior reporter for the *Star* or assistant to an events organiser, and he spent the evening deep in conversation with Andrew and Melanie, a straight couple a bit older than me who sang in a choir and had Protestant accents. Those three, friends of Séamus, left early on. I shared a small stool with Chris, warm leg on leg. In our section, we were listening to Ciarán talking about taxi-drivers. He would tell the story in a half-banal way at first, getting slightly more ridiculous as it went on, then pausing before catapulting it with cross-references and allusions into the realm of the absurd.

"Mad hatter's tea party, wha?"

It buzzed around me and filled my head, exorcised all the ghosts and banished the other things which seemed, once again, far away and ridiculous. Chris told the others that I studied languages, and told us again how useless he was at them. Even Irish, he said, when he was a boy in school his party piece was a song everyone learnt in school, *Báidín Fheilimí,* he used sing it at family hooleys and that kind of thing, but he sang it phonetically. He knew it was about a little boat all right, but that was it, the syllables themselves meant nothing to him. He was only after discovering the other day that it was a little boat going back and forth to three different islands in Donegal. He had always thought it was a kind of nonsense song, like row row row, not about a real boat going real places. Slightly uncomfortable and not wishing to act the languages know-all, I decided against informing Chris further about the song, how the brave little boat does not go back and forth to three islands, but to two; how in the last verse it is broken against the rocks and sinks with the boatman, Felim, in it.

The night flew by, and it seemed only a short while before they flashed the lights and roared at us to leave. Our table, like many, discussed heading off for what Chris called an oul boogey in the George. Four of us walked over together, pulled yet more euros from the wall on Dame Street and then exercised wildly to Smirnoff ice- and red bull and vodka-fuelled dancing. It was all comers in the George, a ragbag collection of accent, class, and even race, united in a frenzy of rhythm, camaraderie, and sweaty sexuality. And then at four in the morning on Dame Lane, muffled memories of music still pounding in my ears, Chris asked if he could come back to mine. I thought of the room, and its books, and its lurking shadows, and asked if I could go back with him to his.

• • •

Chris's flat was in a new modern complex on Capel Street, and looked like many new apartments in Dublin, yellow walls, a pine kitchenette. It was a young gay place all right, not the way they are so often imagined or portrayed, with expensive campy knick-knacks, Japanese furniture, Mapplethorpe coffee-table books, slick antiques, interior design magazines, but the way they really are (and I'd spent the night in quite a few), rather bare, a vague atmosphere of house-sitting, as opposed to inhabiting, and instead of the queer-eye touch of perfect taste and decor, a shamefaced manliness. The glass coffee-table was covered with magazines and picture books (*Gay Community News, Hot Press, Empire, Ireland: Land of Contrasts, The French New Wave*). There was a large collection of footwear in a corner, deck-shoes, hush-puppies, square-toed leather, Caterpillars, Doc Martens, laceless boots, and white new runners. I examined his shelves while Chris boiled water in the kitchen. His DVDs included the usual working man's *Lord of the Rings* and *The Commitments*, the gay, *In Bed with Madonna*, and the girly, *Beaches*, as well as a more surprising collection of French films and music (*Jules and Jim, The Music of Georges Delerue, Best of Serge Gainsbourg, Jeanne Moreau Sings*). There was a poster of Jean Seberg in *Breathless* above the sofa.

"Tea?"

"Lovely."

He brought over two mugs and put them on the table in front of the couch, then sat beside me, his feet stretched up on a stool in front. He kicked off his shoes, picked up the remote control, and brought a CD to life. A French pop-song from the late sixties or early seventies filled the room.

"What's this?" I asked him.

"France Gall is the girl's name. Or was, maybe. I love all that old French stuff."

"So I see. How come?"

"We can read and write in Cabra, you know."

"That's not what I meant . . . I don't know anything about it . . ."

"And you studying French in Trinity College. Do you even know what she's saying? I've been dyin to know for years."

I listened.

"Um . . . *I'm everywhere at once broken into pieces of voice.* Something like that."

"*Quelque-chose comme ça,* monsieur Sandycove." He laughed, then put his arm round me and we kissed.

After making sweaty, drunken love on the navy sheets of his Old Spice–scented bed, I told him that I had rung him at Christmas but had got no answer. He replied with a gale of laughter.

"Yeh *chancer*! Are yeh mad? Do yeh tink I don't know how to use my mobile? *No missed calls.* I've been on the scene for years. As soon as I saw yeh in the George I said to myself, this one would tell yeh black was white to get a taste of your cock. Yeh got no answer. Yeh fuckin *chancer.*"

I blushed and looked away. He laughed again.

"Oh yeah, all modest like all the chancers."

"Are you working tomorrow?" I asked him.

"What do you think?"

"Oh, right, Saturday . . ."

"All the same to you, with your 'student lifestyle,' I suppose . . ."

"More or less. Have you had many boyfriends?" I asked him.

"No. None really. One treeweeker is my record. Patetic, isn't it?"

"No."

I woke with a hangover some time after eleven. We had breakfast in a café on Dame Street, and walked along the Liffey boardwalk, where Chris threw the remains of his scone to the seagulls. He talked about his family, his sisters and their husbands, his parents. I talked about mine, a little. He was clever, not too cultured, despite the very particular knowledge of 1960s

French cinema, with shamefacedly garbled pronunciation of titles and actors' names, but he had a way of quickly figuring out the circumstances behind every cryptic remark I made, interpreting what I said not from his own point of view but in terms of my quite alien background. We spent most of the rest of the day together, a pleasant, easy, sexy afternoon. When the sun started to disappear and the people started to surface from their office caves and burrows, Chris, as the one who had been rejected last time, decided to cut it short before it turned into dinner and pints and bed and a whole other evening of it.

"I think I'll head off, Niall."

I dreaded the thought of being deprived of his presence. We were standing on Capel Street Bridge, where he would go north and I south. I looked fearfully into the still-bright city behind me.

"Okay."

We hugged, and I gave him a surreptitious kiss on the neck which made him smile.

"Do you want my phone number?" I asked him.

"You have mine."

"Do you . . . do you want to meet up tomorrow? Or the day after?"

He hesitated. "All right so, the day after."

"Here," I said. "Meet here the day after tomorrow. At six."

"At six."

"Will you be back from work in time?"

"I can be. On the bridge at six. *Slán*, so."

We said goodbye and I pretended to walk away. In reality, after a few steps I stopped beside the river to watch him walk off up Capel Street, dissolving slowly into fragments among the crowd.

Six

I walked back to my rooms and did my best to begin reading a novel. I found it literally impossible: I was unable to connect any sentence or paragraph to those that surrounded it; each line or segment would congeal, contract away from the rest of the text, like a bubble of vinegar in a bottle of oil, turn itself into a discrete sphere of meaning waiting to be interpreted. The book became a series of unasked-for synchronicities, sortes I cast without wishing, and every paragraph began ex nihilo and alone. So I fell into asking questions.

"Where is Chris now?" I asked silently.

On the other side of the street, on the pavement

I was confused and asked again:

"We may never see each other again! farewell!"
  This farewell, repeated twice . . .

A chastising note, like the line from the Russian book, about paying attention first time round. I thought inevitably about Ian, the huge, buried lodestone to which my mind always returned. I consulted book after book about him, what he was doing, how he had felt about me then, did now, would in the future. Later, when I lay down on my bed and tried again to sleep, the dark room spun, helicopters such as I had never had on even my worst nights of drinking. I tossed and turned and looked over at the lights of the tennis courts coming through my window. Only it no longer seemed like the floodlights, but had a bluer glow, like a streetlamp. And the room was different, whiter, fluffier, posters on the walls, a kind of flag, a pennant hanging where the bookcase should have been. *Gonzaga High*. There was a rattle at the window. I paused, and there was another. Slowly the idea formed that I was in a 1960s American television teenager's suburban bedroom, in a white clapboard house in the suburbs, a street covered in trees, elms, I thought, growing verdant and high, casting pale shadows in the moon and streetlights, and outside, standing under them with a convertible parked behind him, was Chris, or Ian, or Pablo Virgomare, standing in a leather jacket at the white picket fence throwing stones at my window to signal to me to sneak out and go off with him to make out in his car. I felt a thrill of adolescent excitement, and even worried that mom and pop would hear the gravel hitting the window. I threw back the quilt and turned on my bedside lamp, but the room spun back into itself, House 16, Trinity College Dublin, January 2004.

A wave of melancholy swept over me, a sickening, unbearable emptiness, clawing at my lungs and stomach, crucifying void. I got out of bed and stuck my head out the window to clear my mind with the cold air, and to see the reassuring lights of other rooms, unchanging rooms, the solid shadows of other unchanging students on campus going back and forth about their ordinary business. I breathed deeply and kept my eyes open to the concrete visual reality outside, but as soon as I pulled my head back inside, the feeling began to rise up inside me again. I pulled a book off the shelf, and even at the touch of the spine could feel it retreat.

> *My God, how I these studies prize,*
> *That do thy hidden workings show!*
> *Whose sum is such*
> *No sum so much,*
> *Nay, summed as sand they sumless grow.*
> *I lie to sleep, from sleep I rise,*
> *Yet still in thought with thee I go.*

I put a little pile of books on the little table beside my bed, in case I should wake up in need of a synchronicity, rather like after nights of big drinking the way I would line up a pint of water and two paracetamol tablets. I switched off the light and tried to sleep, but my mind moved through a rapid montage of all that was happening to me now, a hyperactive MTV camera, zooming in on Chris walking away from me down Capel Street Bridge, Pablo singing through the night in at the Buttery toilets, the wan, serious faces of Sarah and John pulling endless threads of meaning from tiny fragments of prose, like silk from a silk-worm, the moving cranes, the Latin singing, and then, of course, as if he were part of it all, I thought of Ian. I would like to have slept with him, once and for all. It would have been so concrete and unverbal, so real, carnal, and, well, brutal. I thought of school, the silence of its waxed corridors when I excused myself to go to the toilet. Ian cleaning his nails with a compass. Seagulls eating discarded crusts after break as we looked out the window during Irish. *Is é an dífhostaíocht an fadhb is mó in Éirinn inniu. Is í, an fhadhb.* End of gender. In Éirinn, anyway. *Dans la France métropolitaine. L'hexagone. Savez-vous prendre le métro? Les spécialités d'Annecy. Ag Críost an Síol.* Glaciated Valleys. H_2SO_4. Boys throwing apple cores at the blackboard.

Jesus all pious and sad, hanging off the classroom cross by one arm. Pull yourself together, man. Confession. A fire drill. *Follow it up, follow it up, that's the way to win the cup.* Patrick talking to my mother, using her name, as she liked, trying to sound like an adult: "Your garden is looking great, Eileen."

I turned over. I could not sleep, and was in fear of this feeling attacking me again. An imagined sound, a far strain of Latin singing.

> *Ecce enim in inquitatibus conceptus sum*
> *et in peccatis concepit me mater mea*

I put my head under the covers. It was still there, the faintest hint of it in the air of the room, the invisible vibrato of a mosquito. I could not block it out. Chris, Chris, think of Chris, I thought, but still the sound came to me across the air, across the room, under the blankets.

> *ecce enim veritatem dilexisti*
> *incerta et occulta sapientiae tuae manifestasti mihi*

I sat up. I could not sleep. I was not tired. I switched on my reading lamp and took a book from the top of the pile.

> *Now winter nights enlarge.*

I rubbed my eyes, from habit rather than fatigue. I went into the kitchen and fiddled around with a hot milk and honey remedy for insomnia, but with such a lack of conviction that I abandoned the project halfway through. Instead, I sat up in bed asking idle questions of the books I had taken off the shelf. I asked what my name was and picked the line *"Upon the caves of Nile."* They had a sense of humour, anyway. (Who were "they"?)

"What is my best way to proceed with the *sortes*?" I asked, in what felt like a daringly intrusive question.

she was hardly ever on her own, primarily because the conventions of the dance-romance film favored teamwork over solo acts.

I moved straight to the obvious follow-up inquiry, the question which, though I did not yet know it, would become for a long time the focus of my whole existence:
"Where are Sarah and John?"

They would have reached the nursery in time had it not been that the stars were watching them. Once again the stars blew the window open.

I threw the book aside and looked out onto Botany Bay, just in time to see the door of House 13 closing. I watched and waited, and after a minute or two the light in Sarah's room snapped on, and I saw her and John come in and take off their coats. They must have finished the day's secret work, off wherever they had escaped in the taxi. Perhaps they had come back in order to make love, I thought. An image of this rose up in my head, and I suffered a sharp, unexpected flash of jealousy, the impossible excitement it would be to feel the press of John's body against your own. I shook myself out of this line of thought, an unhealthy reminder of the life—half real, half imagined—that I had led with Ian. I asked the books what I should do.

What next? I proceeded to the business centre.

So I walked through the gusted rain to House 13 and rang Sarah's bell. They were expecting me: without greeting or answer, the window opened, and they threw the key down. It was buffeted into the bushes where I had to scrabble for it in the muck.

The door upstairs was open when I got there. I knocked lightly and went in. The room was much neater than John's, three bookshelves, a carefully made single bed, and a table with papers and folders stacked in an orderly fashion. The scene that greeted me was one, almost grotesquely so, of cosy domesticity. The gas fire was on, and John was lying belly-down on the bed, leafing through the heavily annotated *Golden Bough* I had seen in his room, as if it was an Asterix or Tintin book. Sarah was pouring glasses of the usual Southern Comfort and ice.

"Sit down," she said.

I sat on the end of the bed next to John. Not daring to speak or to look at either of them, I picked up a book on Pompeii from the bookshelf next to me.

"John's fighting with his lady friend," Sarah said to the window. Of course, the sentence was aimed at John, since they would never share this kind of intimate chatter with me, but I felt constrained to say something, so I said:

"Anna?"

"Yes, Niall, Anna," John said sarcastically, without looking up.

I looked at a mosaic of two men having sex. Sarah handed the drinks round. John took his without looking up. Sarah stood at the window sipping and staring at the dark.

"I'm sure you'll work it out," she said. "After all, she is *very* charming. Very *finished*. Have you met her, Niall? She has tremendous . . . *comportment* . . ."

"That's enough, Sarah," John growled at the floor, head in hands. I put down the Pompeii book and picked up another one. This was the first time I had seen a hint of personal drama between the two. Sarah was jealous, what a strange thought. Or was it all a game . . . I wondered what activities they had been up to all day in my absence, that had made them so keen to stay away from me, and that had led to this high drama. I picked a silent synchronicity.

The kernel of all jealousy is lack of love.

Meanwhile, Sarah continued.

"Yes, I think *comportment* is the word. She could walk with a book on her head."

I held my breath, waiting for John to shout. He said nothing, but after a few moments he strode over to the bookshelf and with a violent gesture swept a whole shelf of books onto the ground, then sat back on the bed beside me. Sarah didn't react, she just stood there looking out of the window smoking impassively. When her cigarette was finished, she put it out in a cup on the table, sat across from us at the table, and began to sort through notes. This was the first and last sign of jealousy or interest in John I ever saw her manifest in all the time I was with them.

"Are we ready?" she asked. "John?"

John walked sullenly over to the pile of books he had knocked onto the floor and picked a synchronicity from it.

"You know the question," he said to Sarah.

His voice was quiet and strained, the only sign of the elevated emotion which had been running just before:

I, that did wear the ring her mother left,
I, for whose love she gloried to be blamed,
I, with whose eyes her eyes committed theft,
I, who did make her blush when I was named;
Must I lose ring, flowers, blush, theft and go naked,
Watching with sighs, till dead love be awaked?

"Right," interrupted Sarah. "The guiding question for tonight's session is 'Will dead love be awaked?' Niall, there should be candles under the bed where you are."

I reached under and found a little cardboard box filled with candles. She drained back the end of her Southern Comfort and filled us all up again.

"So . . . well, look through the bookshelf."

We chose a passage each and marked it with a red pen that

Sarah passed around. Mine was a passage from *Antony and Cleopatra*, the same play that had told me my name earlier on. Sarah lit the candles and placed them round as she had done before in John's room. John and I sat on the floor with our books ready. Sarah turned out the light and joined us.

"John, you start."

His voice, shaky this time, the uncertainty of emotion still there as he read tonelessly:

"Where will you put me?" he asked presently. "I must be put somewheres, dear boy."

"To sleep?" said I.

"Yes. And to sleep long and sound," he answered; "for I've been sea-tossed and sea-washed, months and months."

"My friend and companion," said I, rising from the sofa, "is absent; you must have his room."

"He won't come back tomorrow; will he?"

"No," said I, answering almost mechanically, in spite of my utmost efforts; "not tomorrow."

Sarah continued with the poem she had picked:

Since there's no help, come let us kiss and part.
Nay I have done; you get no more of me,
And I am glad, yea, glad with all my heart,
That thus so cleanly I myself can free;
Shake hands for ever, cancel all our vows,
And when we meet at any time again,
Be it not seen in either of our brows
That we one jot of former love retain.

Then I read my piece:

No grave upon the earth shall clip in it

A pair so famous. High events as these
Strike those that make them; and their story is
No less in pity than his glory which
Brought them to be lamented. Our army shall
In solemn show attend this funeral,
And then to Rome. Come Dolabella, see
High order in this great solemnity.

We swapped. I read the *Where will you put me*, John the first half of the sonnet and Sarah read the Shakespeare. We swapped again, and then again. After three goes each at each passage, we switched to reading simultaneously, exchanging the books in the usual pass-the-parcel manner as soon as the passages were read. The words *in spite of my utmost efforts not tomorrow* trailed on their own at the end of each round. We did this for some time, but as before, the sound of the three voices remained, self-consciously, a young woman, a young man and a very young man, reading things out in Irish accents over one another in candlelight.

"Okay, speed up," Sarah said.

We swapped. I was on *where will you put me* again, and I kept tripping over all the 's's in the middle of it. The other two raced through the Renaissance verse. We swapped again. The words were beginning to curdle.

Where will you put me in lamented Rome. Come, high order, I must be somewheres. Since there's no help attend this funeral, Dolabella. To sleep? said I and he answered glad with all my heart to sleep long and sound with this great solemnity. Shake hands for ever, cancel all with our sea-tossed vows for I've been sea-washed, months and months Be it not seen in either. My friend and companion, we, one former love, retain no absent grave upon the earth. You must have his room. Clip it, rising from the sofa kiss a pair so famous. High events strike those that make them. He won't come back tomorrow; will he? Thus said I, answering almost mechanically so glad I am you get no more of me. Their story is we meet and part again at any time, in spite of my utmost efforts; not tomorrow.

We read faster still, the words slowly began to mingle more fully, until with the now-familiar jump which made my spine quake it passed from three readings to a single living thing. I could hear and feel it suddenly burst into life, its wings beating in the air, its heart thumping in the floor and pumping in my enlivened blood. The room twirled. I pulled myself back from falling forward again, received the book thrust into my hands, and continued hypnotically to pronounce the words on the shuddering air.

Glad high order lamented Rome show my somewheres and kiss the sea-washed earth strike solemnity in one former soul their story not tomorrow

The words were lost now in the presence of the single thing they had become. The candles flickered and we kept on reading in a daze, determinedly drumming out the words and swapping the books, resisting the temptation to fall into the humming thing we were creating, to surrender to it and stop giving it its life-blood.

I had no memory of any of us stopping, but at some stage I was aware that none of us had been reading for some time. The books were on the floor and Sarah and John were staring into space. The room was silent and dark, the candles were unlit and not even smoking. Slowly we became aware of one another, like one-night stands waking up in the same bed. Sarah leaned over and switched on the desk lamp. I looked at the alarm clock beside her bed. Four-twenty. I was missing two full hours.

John sat down on the bed. As last time, the room felt different. It looked exactly the same, of course: beside the window,

Sarah's desk, covered in yellow foolscap in her slanting, anachronistic handwriting; piles of books beside the little lamp; tidy bed with a patchwork bedspread; dressing-gown hanging on the back of the door; shoes tucked in under the bed; a dressing-table with moisturiser and make-up (so incongruous for Sarah, I thought). On the walls, one framed page of Gregorian chant in black and red and a poster in German advertising a 1999 conference on Old Irish glosses. Two cardboard boxes of papers beside the wardrobe. But there was some new silence now which had grown in the room. John fiddled with the sheets on the bed. Sarah stood looking out the window.

Slowly, she lowered her glass and put it on the table.

"Look . . ."

We stayed where we were.

"Come here, look . . ." she repeated.

I walked over to the window followed by John and looked out. The sky was lightening to a navy at its far edges, but it was still night. The nets in the tennis courts swung lightly. All along the old granite of Botany Bay, curtains were pulled across windows, except in the stairwells which shone in a ghostly, antiseptic light. A security guard walked along by the bikesheds at the back of the GMB, jangling his keys.

"What?" I whispered. We were all whispering now.

"Look!" She pulled up the window and the three of us stuck our heads out. The night was black and cold. "Look." She pointed over the roof of the Dining Hall and the Chapel to the tops of the buildings on College Green. "They're moving for us."

The statues of angels and men on the roof of the Bank of Ireland, standing white and rocky against the blank dark of Dublin, had left their proud stone poses and were moving. Slowly, like figures in a Swiss clock, their heads turned mechanically from side to side, arms jerkily raising swords and shields. They moved separately, without interacting, painful machinelike gestures like the Christmas puppets in Switzer's window. Their bodies were stiff and beautiful, shapely, rigid and noble, an almost embarrassed formality in their motion. None of us said anything, we stayed as we were, three heads in the early hours of a January morning, transfixed without regard for crick or cramp, on the lifeless, soundless dancing of shy gods.

The horizon was steel-blue at the edges when it stopped. The statues were once again sitting looking unblinking over the city as before. There seemed to have been no noticeable cessation or change, they were just perched again where they belonged, distantly dreaming and patiently holding their staffs and swords. There was a soft hush of traffic now on Dame Street. In the fading night, the seagulls glowed like electric-blue arctic fragments, as they fell up and down in front of the window. We came inside and shut the window. Sarah put on her heater and we sat close to it, defrosting our hands and heads, faces washed in a pale light, staring fixedly in front of us like survivors of a ferry disaster oblivious to news crews and ambulances.

I must have drifted off to sleep, because the next thing I knew I was sitting alone on the chair and the room was filled with dawn light. Behind me, Sarah was in the kitchen making coffee. The door of the bathroom opened and John came out, towel around his waist, his thick legs glistening from the shower, water dripping down his shoulders and back, face fresh and shining from being shaved.

He ignored me as he moved around the room, transforming himself slowly from the wild adept of a mystic reading system into a smooth young Celtic Tiger banker. A shirt and suit had been carefully hung in Sarah's wardrobe, and he also had underwear, ties, socks, and shoes stored around the little flat. I followed him with silent, desirous eyes as he got dressed. He went into the kitchen, where he and Sarah began talking together in low voices. Neither of them spoke to me or offered me coffee, and so I took it they wanted me out of their hair. I muttered a goodbye and staggered down the stairs and across Botany Bay to my rooms.

I had a long shower when I got there. It had been a completely surreal scene, John and Sarah on a workday morning routine, having sat up all night watching moving statues; now John would spend the day working on the floor of a merchant bank, and Sarah would conduct research at her carrel in the Ussher Library. In this spirit, I decided to make an effort to be real myself for at least part of the day, by attending the morning's classes. From under a pile of clothes and forgotten pages I pulled a biro and a foolscap pad. I had to look up a notebook to find out where my 9 a.m. translation seminar was on. I brushed my teeth and went to the Arts Block to have coffee. I left my phone, guilt-emitting object, on the desk.

I was nervous dealing with the crowds in the Coffee Dock. I wasn't sure exactly how I would relate to anyone and I was afraid I would slip into a state of high unreality or melancholy. I sat at one of the little tables on my own, sipping the coffee and doodling on the pad. I picked up a discarded *Irish Times* and tried to read it, but my eye lighted greedily on headlines as ready-made synchronicities, sealing off crazed islands of interpretation.

Southern Cross planning a "shambles" says group; Poles in two minds about Euro-project; When love just isn't enough; Homeless in Dublin.

I turned my head to escape from it, and thought I saw something pass, like a shooting star, perhaps it was Pablo coming down the stairs from the Lecky. I had a dizzying flash-change of scenery; the shaded tables of a café on a narrow European city street, nineteenth-century buildings of yellow-grey brick, ornate iron balustrades on balconies on either side. Business pedestrians walked up and down on the pavement beside me. A waiter, a young man wearing black trousers and a white shirt, put a pink drink and a receipt on the table front of me. The sun felt uncomfortably hot in my Irish winter jumper and coat.

"Votre kir, monsieur. Ça fait quatre euros cinquante."

I opened and closed my mouth, confused, and tried to make out Pablo in the crowd across the road.

"Monsieur?" The waiter reminded me. I turned back to him to repeat how much the kir was (What else could I do? At least they used the euro) and it was the Arts Block, once again, thankfully, the Coffee Dock and, instead of the waiter, Andrea sitting down to join me.

"Well, he-*llo*, stranger!"

"How's it going?"

"Where the *fuck* have you been?" She asked with a smile. "I swear, no one knows what to do when you're not there, it's such a mare. It's like a special-needs class, I swear to God. No one knows *shite*. Well, except Fionnuala, and she's in a psycho phase. Man trouble, I'd say."

She didn't mention my recent sudden disappearance from the Buttery, even though I knew she must be curious, and I was grateful for this. I asked her if Dr. Roland had noticed my recent absences, and she didn't think so.

"So anyway, though, where have you been? Just on the piss, like?" She laughed conspiratorially.

"Oh, I needed a change of scene. You know the way."

"Too right I do . . ." she said.

I drained the end of the coffee and we walked up staircase B with the surging crowd to 4091, where we had the class with Dr. Roland. I saw Fionnuala through the glass window in the door, taking her notepad, book, and pen out of her bag and laying them on the table in front of her, familiar ritual, and I decided I couldn't face her. I turned around and pushed my way back through the crowd, Andrea half-calling me back.

I was surprised then when Fionnuala caught up with me on the ramp. She touched my shoulder, and for a single giddy instant I thought I was going to have another flash to the Paris café in the sun. It was cold and grey outside, and Fionnuala was shivering under her long raincoat.

We looked at each other in a brief stand-off of silence. It had only been a few days since we had seen each other, but in between, innumerable text messages and phone calls had arrived, unanswered, in my phone. I had hardly been to my room, and I had almost not slept. She looked me straight in the eyes, with a genuinely confused and searching expression, and it struck me all of a sudden that the self-contained, eager-to-please Fionnuala of my dismissive imagination was a lie; she really wondered what was becoming of me, she knew it was not happening to her.

"Shouldn't you be in class?" I asked her, with the absurd idea that attack was the best form of defense.

"Please, Niall, don't be thick. What's happening? Tell me, please. I just saw you turn away from Roland's class."

I didn't know what to say. She went on: "I know it's to do with Sarah and that other guy. I live underneath. I heard your voice and I saw you leave. So don't lie about that bit, okay?"

"Why should I lie?" I said, suddenly riled. "They're my friends. What do we do? We're . . . well, we do what you saw that morning with the books. The thing you didn't like," I added.

"And?"

"And nothing."

"It's drugs, isn't it? You're doing something serious."

"Oh, please, Fionnuala, for God's sake . . ." I made to move off, but she caught me by the shoulder again.

"You avoid everyone. You make up pathetic excuses. You don't reply to anyone's messages. Your face . . . has this . . . it's *unnaturally* red. You disappeared from the pub with no explanation two days ago. Niall, please. You're in some kind of drug ring or . . . or . . . or a cult. Do you understand that? That girl is *mad*, Niall. She is *famously* unhinged. In a serious way. You have to get out of this. What are you doing to yourself?"

I said nothing. She looked at me pleadingly.

"We were *friends*, Niall. We were really becoming friends."

"Not really," I said. "Why don't you just leave me alone?" A phrase I had lighted upon in the features section of the newspaper drifted into my head *("Despite everything, Angie is determined to change her life")*, and I built on it. "At last, at *least*, I'm changing my life, somehow. You're always trying to pull me down," I said absurdly, not knowing where it was coming from, some other shiny fragment my magpie mind had plucked out of something larger, but nevertheless warming to the fiction, "ever since I've known you you've preached about the way I live my life. My boundaries aren't the Beckett Scholarship. These people . . . Sarah and John . . . they're thinkers, real *livers*. Not the get my degree in modern languages, settle down with a likely lad and teach the passé composé for the rest of my life. You—oh, just leave me alone, I won't interfere with you, you don't with me, okay? We're not suited. It's not like we're even close, for God's sake. . . ."

She was staring at me in disbelief. Her eyes filled up with tears and her lips were shaking. Without saying anything, she turned and walked down the ramp towards her rooms, the wind flapping the tails of her raincoat. I watched her go, her hair tied up, French translation folder under her arm, slim bookbag slung across her front, novels to read, papers to write, and as she turned out of sight at the edge of the 1937 Reading Room I said, weakly, in a hoarse whisper: "Wait . . . I'm sorry. . . ."

I trudged up the ramp through the Nassau Street tunnel and wandered blindly up Dawson Street into the bookshops, where I spent two hours moving between Eason's, Waterstone's, Hodges Figgis, and Murder Ink trying once more to read like others, as Fionnuala was probably doing at that moment, at least a page or two, but my effort collapsed into a series of non-sequiturs and then into an intoxicated orgy of synchronicities, picking passages from shelf to shelf and floor to floor, cookery books, vampire novels, modern Irish fiction, gay anthologies, all of them collections of individual fragments, each book a chest of thousands of exquisite tiny jewels, engraved with the mysterious meanings I needed to stay afloat, to keep it all abuzz.

Drunk on *sortes,* I wandered through St. Stephens Green and along South King Street by the Gaiety theatre where I spent a long time looking at the photographs of the current production, then moved across the south city as books, signs, and random pieces of language dictated. I still had seen no sign of Pablo anywhere, except for faint hints in the pages of the bookshops. Twice when I turned a corner I found myself in Paris: walking into the blinding sun of the narrow, Roman rue St.-Jacques or the mediaeval shadows of rue du Temple; another corner again and I was back in Crown Alley or Bachelor's Walk with blue-faced begging children, Irish travellers or central European Roma, and bored Spanish shop-assistants looking out the window of Spar or Centra at the dirty streets, thoughts far off in Premià and Durango.

When I returned to House 16, pushing my way through the synchronicity-sodden world as though it were flooded with honey or glue, I expected Pablo to be in my rooms, sitting on the bed leafing idly through my letters or something, but when I went in, there was just the usual reproachful unused furniture and school equipment. I lay on my bed and closed my eyes. When I opened them again, it was dark. I switched on the bedside lamp and sat up. My phone said it was half-five. I cleaned up my room a little, a kind of concession, or, more, invitation, to normality, taking clothes from the floor and putting them in the wardrobe, sorting through my useless papers.

As my eye began greedily examining them for *sortes,* and as the giddy sensation that the room would soon spin into Paris hit me again, I thought, this has to stop. Maybe Fionnuala has a point, this is out of control. I sat on the bed and tried to take logical stock of my situation, but the room swam in a sea of fragments before my eyes. And then, a solid shape suddenly looming in the incandescent coral shades floating around me, I remembered my date at six o'clock on Capel Street Bridge. From a previous life. Should I go? I made a last, almost heroic effort to think it through in the old, bookless way, then gave up.

"Should I meet Chris?"

And if this reflection will not make you keep quiet, perhaps you will do so when you know for certain that among all those people over there, though they look like kings, princes, and emperors, there's not one single knight-errant.

Filing this away in my mind for future interpretation, I asked the rival question:

"Where are Sarah and John?"

She turned into Hyde Park, which she had known of old (beneath that cleft tree, she remembered, the Duke of Hamilton, fell run through the body by Lord Mohun).

They were in the Duke. I pressed the point.

"Should I go and meet Sarah and John?"

paresseux, euse *adj. et n. 1. Qui montre habituellement de la paresse; qui évite l'effort.*

I put on my jacket, ran down the steps of the building out into the light rain, and splashed through cobbled, semi-neon puddles onto the heavy traffic on College Green.

On my right, the spire on O'Connell Street, studded with white lights, pulled me north, and I decided to keep my date. It frightened me, the way I had spoken to Fionnuala and the way my old life was so rapidly become a distant memory. The thought of Chris, his body, warmth, and voice, pulled me down to earth. I turned right, towards the bridge and away from the

Duke where Sarah and John would now be huddled over a pile of books at a table, spinning words into gold, but I had not even got to the end of the Trinity railings when I was stopped by the buzz of my phone vibrating in my pocket. There was a new message, from one *Tadhg na Scuab,* a name I had never programmed into my phone. Tadhg na Scuab's message was empty. I looked up from the little green screen across to the curve of the Bank of Ireland, where, standing rather like a moving stature himself, I saw the damp curls of Pablo, who was leaning back beside the pass machine with one foot against the granite, smoking a cigarette and grinning. He finished his cigarette, extinguished it on the ground with his foot, reached into his pocket and threw a pile of change into the McDonald's cup of the young girl begging beside the machine. I started to turn away from him, from the statues and stone, away north, towards the river, the spire, and Chris. I took two brave steps, but Pablo cupped his hands around his mouth, and, to the slight bewilderment of the people around him, sang out across the traffic to me:

"When will you pay me?" say the bells of Old Bailey.

And so, as unstoppable as the Liffey's cold eastward flow towards England, I fell down off the kerb and into the stream of traffic dividing us, and let him lead me up, south, to the Duke. As I passed Suffolk Street, I heard, in the distance, the Dining Hall bell striking six.

The Duke was fairly empty, a scattering of small groups meeting before going on to dinner and a large table of women of mixed ages who looked like they worked together in Dunne's or Marks & Spencer's, laughing over the day's adventures in Bedroom or Men's. I spotted John and Sarah immediately, perched on stools at one of the high round tables towards the back of the pub. The scene was just as I had imagined it, five or six books, a foolscap pad, and two full pints on the table. I stood near the door and watched them for a little while, heads bent over the text in front of them, Sarah with one hand holding the book open, the other on the back of her untidy hair, a cigarette between the fingers and the smoke rising up from her head like a visitation from the Holy Spirit, John frantically jiggling a suited leg up and down as he thought through the meaning of the words in front of him, occasionally running an excited hand through his hair.

I ordered a pint at the bar, then walked over to their table. I didn't know how to greet them, and so I just stood behind them like a ghost. They continued their energetic discussion about whatever fragment was in front of them for some time, maybe a minute, before John sensed my presence and turned around.

"We were wondering when you'd show up," he said, in a neutral tone.

"So was I," I said. I thought for an instant of Chris, standing under the rain on Capel Street Bridge, realizing, as the stars came out one by one, that I would not appear, but I was already long past feeling regret. The dark, magical sight of these two, and the heap of undone *sortes* in front of them, banished Chris from my mind.

"So what's going on?" I asked, sitting on the empty stool between them.

"Don't ask us," Sarah said.

I reached for a book.

That night, I left behind the twin possibilities of my old life, one walking away from me down the Arts Block ramp, the other standing in an incipient rain on Capel Street Bridge. The session lasted well into the morning. I fell into a short slumber, and when I woke up John and Sarah had left. I spent the next day alone, wandering around the city, pulling books from shelves, trying out private new tricks, staring at hitherto invisible patterns written on the surface of the city, seeing in the to-ing and fro-ing of the citizenry a ballet choreographed in miniature detail, so clear and magnificent it was astonishing to think that I had not seen it before, and even more so that the dancers themselves seemed to be oblivious of the mandala they described. It was as if a thin veil covering everything, literally everything, had been lifted. All Dublin had a clearer, fascinating definition, every colour, every chipped detail on a granite window ledge, every ripple in the dirty river. All of the apparently empty words surrounding me in the city, advertising billboards, newspapers on stands, and the drifting snatches of strangers' speech, these were now finally legible, as if I had come into possession of an internal Rosetta stone which left all signs decrypted. Even the most banal or phatic over-heard phrase took on an urgent, fiery charge, as if it were a vital part of a single, impossibly vast poem.

We spent the first of those long white nights in Sarah's rooms, before moving to John's flat on the north quays. Anna had forbidden synchronicity meetings in the house in Ranelagh. We went through boxes of candles and libraries of books. Those nights were a blur of shooting stars, blizzards of light, and spec-tral Papal choirs whose invisible singing left cobwebs of sound in the corners of the room long after we had stopped reading. Once, a woman dressed in white entered and walked around the room blowing out the candles, and we sat until dawn watching her, sitting on John's bed, until she disappeared into the whitening morning sheets of John's bed, like an ad for washing powder.

I contacted no one, and left my phone to ring out and its bat-tery to slowly fade in the abandoned shadows of my own rooms. The aberrant flush Fionnuala had noted on my face became more pronounced. Sarah and John, as far as I could tell, never slept. I had a dull and dreamless doze most afternoons, mostly out of a nostalgic loyalty to a world I was forgetting. For the same reason, I even attended a class once in Trinity, a silent,

fidgety listener in the corner, studiously ignored by Fionnuala—
who contributed even more enthusiastically and competently
than usual in the class discussion—and watched with gruesome
fascination by Andrea. Patrick, and then, more worryingly, my
parents, in the absence of telephonic contact began to write me
concerned e-mails, so one Sunday, around ten days into this new
life, I decided I must see them if I was to avoid having the Gardaí
battering down the door of my rooms. I don't know how I managed to shake myself out of the all-consuming unreality I inhab-
ited so fully, but I did, enough to get the DART out to Sandycove
to have a Sunday dinner with them. They were pleased to see
me, and for much of the time the house with its layers of rituals
and memories kept the flapping new spirits at a distance. My
mother was even quite taken with what she called my healthy
complexion. But even out here in the old salted air of Sandycove,
the conversation around the table would disintegrate every so
often from a solid, timebound chain of sentences, of questions,
answers, and interjections, and shatter into a kaleidoscope of
intersecting meanings, a soft snow of words and phrases which
no longer belonged to my mother, father, Ciara, or me but
which seemed to come across the bay from the city, and which
mingled with the headlines on the Sunday newspapers on the
spare chair, the shopping list on a post-it stuck to the fridge, the
torn envelope revealing the words "Dear Customer." I would fall
silent, battered this way and that by the words in the air, before
fighting my way back to coherent normal consciousness to find
my family looking uncomfortably from me to each other.

My father asked me gamely how I spent my time. I told him
I read during the day and at night either studied or went to parties, which was true in a way.

"Parties!" he said triumphantly, and winked.

"That's a lie," Ciara said, looking up from her roast lamb.

I said nothing. My mother told her to stop trying to cause
trouble, and she went back to cutting her meat. Just before I left, as

I was getting my coat on in the hall, and my parents were down in the kitchen assembling a bag of food and an envelope of money to give me, Ciara came up and stood in front of me, defiant and brave in her ponytail, glittered fingernails, and sixteen-year-old puppy fat.

"What's happening?" she hissed.

"What do you mean?"

"Tell me, Niall. I know we're not . . . 'close,' " she made the quotes with her fingers. "But I know something's wrong. They just don't want to see it."

"You're mad," I said. "How's school?"

"School, Niall,"—like most siblings, it was rare and slightly disturbing to use each other's names—"is just fine. What's not fine is you."

At that point my parents creaked up the stairs into the hall, slipping the money into my pocket and giving me the plastic bag containing Superquinn sausages, mandarins, and half a fruitcake.

My mother murmured "Take care now, love," and my father jovially exclaimed "Good luck now, Niall," while Ciara stood beside them, silent and glaring.

I received a text message from her, as I walked up to the DART station to take me back into the city. *Be careful,* it said.

I texted Patrick to say I had wanted to call into him, but had spent too long in Sandycove and had to go straight back into college.

I didn't go back. The suburbs, the past, anyone outside the magic dyad of Pour Mieux Vivre, had faded irretrievably. A couple of text messages a week, when I came out of a trance enough to remember, was enough to keep my parents and Patrick from attempting any serious intervention in my life. The fits of melancholy, however, became more debilitating and frequent. I couldn't speak any more if it hit me; a sense of doom and void filled me so completely that I shook and moaned until I crawled to my shelf or, if I was out, to a bookshop or library and grabbed a random volume. I knew that a few hours away from *sortes* would invariably provoke one of these attacks. I took to buying all the pocket-size editions I could and carrying them round in my pockets. I learned to detect the warning signs, a slight feeling of distraction as if I had lost something, which grew slowly into a distinct, if unnameable agitation, after which there came a sudden lull of all feeling, followed by a sickening thump to my mind and body. But in this way, and then later by mastering the ability to divine meanings and directions from bus-tickets, advertisements, and discarded crisp-packets, I managed to eliminate them almost entirely.

Best before see reverse side. Go minic anseo, go tapaidh ansiúd. Valid till the end of the line.

Seven

I lost count of everything. I kept pulling money out of the machines in the wall, hoping that overdraft facilities and automatic Beckett stipend deposits would between them contrive to keep it flowing, but I had no idea if my account contained four hundred euro or four, or—who knew?—four thousand. The days of the week too dissolved into pale nights in John's flat or in Sarah's rooms, punctuated with private daylight meanderings around the city. A couple of times a week—no more than this, but nevertheless without fail—things would subside, and I would have two quiet hours, a weird silence at the eye of a storm, a cold spell of clarity. It was during these strange tranquil hours, empty of all feeling, that I used to phone or text my parents, to keep suspicion at bay. Revisiting the old, pre-sortes Dublin like this, I felt like an emigrant returning to his native country town on a brief visit after a long metropolitan emigration, a combination of wistful fondness with oppressive boredom and wanderlust.

The inbox in my phone was full, packed, I supposed, with messages from people who wondered why I had fallen out of touch. On my crazed daytime wanderings, I never left what I considered the city boundaries. For me the southern limit of the city was Donnybrook, where the trickling source of More-hampton Road widened into the rumbling styx of the Stillorgan dual carriageway, the location of the bus garage, of the pubs frequented by Ian and his friends, the church where I had attended my first funeral, that of Patrick's grandfather, and of the bus-stop at which I used to stand miserably waiting for the 46A on my way home from Ian's, or where I would alight, in erotic hope, on my way in to him. My fevered mind styled it the gate of the city-state, Porta Domnae Brocis, where all the roads from the rustic outlying provinces converged. I would wander down here, guided by the books, or other auguries, and stand at the edge, unable to leave, and I would always turn around and return to the ghosts, to the busy city of the dead which I inhab-ited now.

My book of days: daylight I spent on my own, wandering through a world grown strange and fascinating. The long nights I always spent in the company of Sarah and John. We would meet by unfailing synchronicities at the end of the day, in a pub, or at a monument or corner dictated to each of us, independently, by the books. I went to my rooms in Trinity now only to retrieve clothes or books. I never went to class and I never saw Fionnuala. John was fired from the bank, a development which went almost unnoticed amongst us. When I first knew them, the end of every session was marked by John washing, shaving, putting on a suit and tie and heading, sleepless and stunned, down the quays to his job at the bank. But over the weeks of my association with them, the nighttime sessions became wilder and longer, and rarely ended before the sun had started to fill the room. John increas-ingly took to leaving his suit hanging in the wardrobe, and he would remain behind with Sarah after I left. They began to spend the days together, engaged in activities I knew nothing about, and John stopped going to work altogether.

The first sign of this situation having consequences was a landlord's agent hammering on the door of John's flat one morning, we green-eyed and half-hallucinating amid a pile of books, papers, extinguished candles and empty bottles of Southern Comfort. The standing order for the rent had bounced, the landlord had found out he was unemployed, he wanted him out. Sarah and I based ourselves in Trinity rooms again, while John moved into the spare bedroom in Ranelagh. In theory, he and Anna were still "seeing each other." John had always taken the occasional evening or Sunday off the books to see her. How this worked, why either of them agreed to it, I was never sure. It struck me at the time that Anna, though she knew their relationship was over, suffered from seeing John fall deeper into his addiction and cult; she knew she was his only link to the outside world, and out of a nostalgia or fondness couldn't bring herself to abandon him entirely to his fate. And perhaps, conversely, he clung to their meetings for the same reason, because she was a last, failing connection to a life which was almost irretrievably lost for him, a last-ditch effort in a doomed, secret struggle. In any case, after he was thrown out of his flat in the IFSC, she offered him the use of the spare room he used to rent as his study in her house, the site of the party in November where I had encountered the *sortes* for the first time. The idea was that he could stay there until he "got back on his feet": she hoped, presumably, that there in the house with her, isolated from me and Sarah, he might come to his senses again.

After little more than a week of his erratic comings and goings, whole days and nights of disappearances, and, when he was there, constant consultation of *sortes*, Anna finally called it a day. She found him a flat on Northumberland Road which she said he would be able to afford for a few months anyway with the redundancy money he got from the bank, and told him to move in straight away. It transpired she had a new boyfriend already, and even in the midst of the collective delirium in which

I found myself, I did think that the kindness and patience she demonstrated towards her old lover were extraordinary. The life with Sarah and the books had long been a heavy cloud, presumably, but it was clear that the life of Pour Mieux Vivre had not dominated their lives like this before. Things seemed to have changed around the time I joined in, and I had seen Anna's life become intolerable. She rarely saw John for more than two hours a week, and when she did he was usually drunk or stunned with the literary world of synchronicities around him. She must have known he didn't sleep, she must have seen the green glow in his eyes, she must have watched in horror as his job went down the tube, and most of all, it must have hurt her as he lost all interest in her, and, like an Alzheimer's patient or a concussed child, failed to recognise or understand the world in which they had lived together before this.

Sarah and I, in one of those moments of lucidity provoked by unusual necessity, went around to Ranelagh to help John with his cases. Anna was standing red-eyed in the hall with a glass of sparkling water. She had her dark hair tied up and she was wearing a white jumper and black trousers. She looked lovely. She offered Sarah and me a drink, and left us alone in the kitchen while we had a silent glass of cold red wine. I had to go into the sitting room to get a book and Anna was sitting there, staring out the window. She watched me with curiosity as I picked up a battered old *Alice in Wonderland*. With shaking hands I groped for a synchronicity in the pages and as I greedily read through the passage I had chosen, she asked me what it said. Surprised and embarrassed, I read it out to her:

She was getting a little giddy with so much floating in the air and was rather glad to find herself walking again in the natural way.

She turned back to the window and didn't say any more, so I left.

We carried John's things out to the car she had borrowed from Alan, her new boyfriend. She drove us the five minutes to Northumberland Road and we carried the cases up the stairs to his new flat.

And that was it, no one thought of Anna again. The flat was on the top floor of a slightly crumbling Georgian house, on the front of which bullet marks and a plaque informed us it had played some important role in the 1916 Rising. The flat had two rooms, a bedroom and a living-room with a couch, table, chairs, and a corner kitchen. The apartment was sparse but had high, stuccoed ceilings, big windows, and a fire escape-balcony. It became our *sortes* base, and within days was stacked with books, first on the small shelf in the bedroom, and then in piles on the floor. Hardened drops of candlewax covered the living room table and the carpets. John had money again, his redundancy payment and some liquidated investments. Our habits and addictions were fully indulged and catered for: the table and chairs in the sitting room were laden with new books, the fridge and cupboards were filled with beer, wine, and bottles of Southern Comfort.

Sarah, and even I, began casually leaving things there, changes of clothes, toothbrushes, papers, and soon we lived there more or less all the time. It was a place not just filled with books, but one which seemed as if it were built out of them, constructed upon the earth as a tower of innumerable volumes. They covered every available surface, the floor ankle-deep in them in places. Many of them, second-hand and new, were dismembered, not worn from regular use, but deliberately cut by us into segments, sometimes several pulled apart and pasted together in a new, composite volume, a trick we had begun using frequently, pages, clumps of pages, flyleaves, half-pages stapled to other half-pages, texts of all kinds, phone-books, pamphlets, cookery-books, Russian classics, popular Irish fiction, chick lit, self-help books, dictionaries, diaries, driver's manuals, *Trees of Scotland*, *Bunreacht na hÉireann*.

I do not know what all this was like for Sarah. As John had told me, Pour Miuex Vivre worked on a Mafia-like system of cells and hierarchies. I had entered it through John and he through Sarah. Both of us, after a period of hesitation, had chosen to give ourselves over to the life of the group; we had renounced our families and our fishing and gone to follow. But the circumstances of Sarah's initiation remained for a long time unknown to me, and although I had by now built up something approaching a familiarity (insofar as such a thing was possible in the dim, partially lit world we lived in) with John, Sarah I hardly knew better than the day I had met her in O'Neill's of Suffolk Street with Fionnuala. For me, the mystery of Pour Mieux Vivre was indistinguishable from the mysterious personage of Sarah. She and John knew many things about the movement which were hidden from me, and, by the same token, I reasoned that there were also secrets Sarah and the next link in the chain held for their eyes only. The sexual dynamics of our threesome reflected this: John the object of my still-lively erotic fixation, behaved like the jealous other man in Sarah's life. The scene of jealousy she had once thrown about Anna notwithstanding, it was John who longed for closeness with Sarah, and it was she who hid her cards and withheld herself.

I set myself the task of finding out as much as I could about her. I knew that whatever there was to find out about Pour Mieux Vivre would come through her. I began trying to pry. I had very few unguarded moments in the flat, but I started taking advantage of those I did—when Sarah was in the bathroom and John busy in the kitchen, for example—to rifle through the box of folders and papers she kept in John's bedroom. She caught me in the act one day, as I was leafing through an old diary of hers, written in an idiosyncratic mixture of Irish and English in her sloped, Victorian dowager's handwriting. She had been in the shower and John had gone out to the shop to buy coffee. I became so engrossed in the material—it dated from her year in

Germany when she met Luis—that I forgot to listen out for the rush of water stopping. Wrapped in a towel, Sarah had walked into the room and found me there on my knees beside the bed, her private box in front of me, and her diary open in my hands. She said nothing at all, just looked at me and blinked as I blushed and stuttered. I replaced the diary in the box and, mumbling excuses, I got up and walked by her back into the sitting room. The incident was never referred to, but when I returned to the flat that evening, the box had gone from under the bed, and there was a locked chest in the corner of the room.

I began to pester John with questions about her, in the—again all too rare—moments the two of us were left alone together. He was, as always, a reluctant narrator, but I would quiz him tirelessly, sometimes hammering away at the same question over days until he relented. John had occasional flashes of resentment and anger at Sarah, and these sometimes transformed themselves into feelings of empathy with me: he would see himself reflected in my ignorance and curiosity, and would both punish Sarah and compensate for his own frustrations by divulging little pieces of forbidden information. About her life before or outside Pour Mieux Vivre I learned almost nothing, but through these fragments released by John, and from the odd slip Sarah herself made in passing, I gleaned a basic picture of how she had started.

In the Northumberland Road time, I was nineteen and Sarah twenty-eight or twenty-nine. She was supposedly finishing a Ph.D., but, like John's job and my degree in French and English, there was no room for this activity in our literary half-world of disembodied sentences and unreal events. She told me once that her parents had died when she was quite young, and that she had been brought up by her grandparents in Galway. Her grandmother was a teacher, John told me, and her grandfather some kind of Irish language consultant to the State who was devoting his twilight years to the compilation of an Irish-language thesaurus. I don't know if any of this was true: it all seemed a little too literary, a little too Pour Mieux Vivre, even. Moreover, Sarah was fond of lies, especially of pointless lies, such as telling me or John we needed to buy a new bulb for the kitchen lamp, when in fact it was working perfectly well, or announcing that she had read in the paper that the circumference of the globe was only three thousand miles. I don't know what satisfaction she got from telling these untruths. We always believed her, and when we arrived with the box of bulbs, or the atlas, her mind would already have moved onto something new, and she reacted not with glee or pleasure, but with indifference, resignation, boredom, attenuated only by fresh lies. I tried and failed to transform our common position as recipients of her untruths into a conspiratorial connection between John and me. Determined, in the face of her indifference, to maintain their relationship as the special bond of the house, John refused to acknowledge my secret conspiratorial looks, and, despite the ample evidence of experience, made a point of assuming, in front of me, that everything Sarah said was true.

In one of his frustrated moments of deliberate indiscretion, John had told me that she had met Luis in Germany, at a conference on Irish manuscripts. He had introduced her to the *sortes* in her dormitory room in Augsburg. In their subsequent correspondence, after he had returned to Spain, Luis began to hint at possibilities beyond plain synchronicities, and at the existence of Pour Mieux Vivre. At some point, he had started giving her instructions, the ways to read, the ways to concentrate, I presume a version of what she had outlined to me my first time in Ranelagh.

For a long time it didn't work for her: this part of the story I heard from John in a single, excitable narrative one evening when we arrived at the synchronicity-designated meeting point before Sarah. In a sudden, unsolicited moment of candour, he had told me about Sarah's first time. Something must have gone on between them during the day, since they never arrived separately, and I understood that John's telling me this was a form of private retribution. The story was that for weeks she had sat alone in her fitted room in the Augsburg *Studentenwohnheim* reading aloud and concentrating by candlelight, pulling book after book from the shelf. She would persevere until dawn when her eyes were aching and her books exhausted. Luis would reply to her despondent reports by telling her she was not concentrating properly, go over again and again the method of thinking of the words as pure meaning disembodied from context, free-floating ions, listening to each sentence as a bar or phrase in a sung Mass. Sick of her small collection of yellow German volumes she threw them all in the bin and spent the rest of her month's money on a fresh set of books. The edition of a vaguely trashy vampire novel which we frequently used in the Northumberland Road sessions had *Sarah Ní Dhuibhir, Augsburg 1999* written on the flyleaf. She put these books on her shelf, used her last few marks to buy more candles and set to once more with determination, night after night, reading small passages aloud over and over again, concentrating on the words, trying to let them take over. Then one night, at four in the morning, after five solid hours of reading and concentrating, she fell back from exhaustion, disillusion and eye-strain; her glasses fell to the floor and she shut her eyes. She heard a loud flapping of wings and felt a brush of air on her face. Opening her eyes and putting on her glasses, she saw nothing, only wan candleflame, abandoned books, and a hint of the dawn through her window from Bohemia; but she knew she was on to something, she knew that she had finally succeeded in tearing open a tiny chink in the fabric of material reality, that it was the start. She fell asleep there and then, amid the books and candles, and when she awoke, without intervening dreams, the world had changed. John had got this far when Sarah joined us, and I never managed to get him to narrate it any further.

In Northumberland Road, we lived as a nocturnal family, Sarah and John a sombre couple, and I, a presence they accepted on a fundamental, practical level, but on a moment-to-moment basis mostly ignored. There was no affection between them and me, no interactions beyond the books and visions and the rudimentary practical arrangements we needed to keep them going: laundry, maintaining adequate supplies of alcohol, cigarettes for Sarah (from whom I would take the occasional one to save to smoke whenever I had to sit waiting for them on the steps of Northumberland Road), the purchase of particular books she or her e-mail correspondent thought we needed but didn't have, or the matter of keys to the house (Sarah and John kept these and refused to make me a copy, so I always had to ring the bell for them to throw it out the window to me). Nonetheless, they were the solid centre of my world, the only humans I interacted with, excepting the text message digests of my "news" I sent to Sandycove twice a week. I felt drawn to that apartment as I had never felt drawn to home or to any other building before, even, I think, more than the violent force which had once pulled me along the 46A, and up Eglinton and Milltown Roads to Ian's house. And although Sarah and John made no bones about disliking my company, and although they could easily have found somewhere else to go, sunset saw us all faithfully drift, one by one, either back to the flat or to whatever other location in town, usually a pub, that the books nominated. If neither of them was there when I arrived, I would order a pint and sit at the bar with my little bag of books, smoking, doing *sortes,* or listening, in the new way I had learned, to the sounds of the chatter in the pub, the noise from the streets, passersby, traffic, the practical interactions of the bar-staff in front of me. *"I'll move them barrels for you so, Michelle."* From here, we moved slowly across the city, drinking as we went, towards that flat where we would spend the next twelve, fourteen hours, underneath a magic cloud, in one another's unbroken company.

Neither of them ever willingly addressed a word to me, senior executives forced to share an office with the temp. They spoke with stern enthusiasm and urgency to each other, in a quick shorthand that their long common experiences had produced and that I could easily follow but not speak. The bookless bedroom was considered their space while I stayed in the paper-strewn chaos of the sitting room. The plain white-sheeted double bed, the desk where Sarah would open her laptop to connect to Pour Mieux Vivre through the phone line, and the neat piles of clothes in the corners, Sarah's bras, John's T-shirts and old office clothes, these were for me the musky, exotic contents of a forbidden chamber, glimpsed only in illicit, stolen moments.

The most changeless part of our routine was the period between when we all were assembled back at the flat and whenever the session really got going. Sarah, of course, was in charge of the planning. Even in the midst of all the books, visions and drinking, John did a short workout in the corner every evening. Sarah, wearing her glasses, frowned into the middle distance and selected books from the collapsing heaps around the apartment, while the job of laying out and lighting the candles fell to me, always the altar boy and never the priest.

Although I accepted the situation and the role of interloper in our weird family, at a certain point Sarah and John began to surround their private doings with a much greater, almost obsessive secrecy; or, at least, their secrecy started to arouse my curiosity. In the flat, they seemed increasingly more flustered and distracted before we got down to business, and would often leave the main room for whispered conferences in the bedroom. Finally the fact that the most important things were being hidden from me became an openly acknowledged reality, and I began to think about initiating an investigation, plans which I went to great pains to conceal from them. I had always known, since the pints in Kehoe's with John on the Feast of the Immaculate Conception, that John and Sarah were party to mysteries, meanings and plans in all of this far beyond what I, observer-member only of Pour Mieux Vivre, was allowed to share, and I decided it was time to find out about them.

During the daytime, when we were separated, I began to consult the books about the activities and whereabouts of Sarah and John. Where at nighttime it took only one or two flicks through a book to find my companions, during daylight hours I was unable to track them down. The books led me on fool's errands and wild goose chases, and I even began to suspect that the other two knew ways of frustrating my efforts from afar. "Where is Sarah?" I would ask, again and again, and again and again I would be greeted with an asinine answer, *"In the water."* "Where is John?" *"Underneath."* When I kept at it, I could sometimes feel the trail warming up, I would be sent to a bookshop or monument where I chose follow-up *sortes* that emitted a distinct whiff of their recent presence, as a dog smells its acquaintances in the urine deposited at streetcorners, and I would have the definite impression that they had just left, scurried down a back-alley after a last-minute synchronous tipoff.

During the worst of those days, I feared the daylight would never end; the sun seemed to blaze with such energy even in these northern skies that I was sure it would go on forever. I circled the city's streets, waiting only for the sweet deadening of the sky downriver around St. James' Gate, the sign that the books would relent, soften in their answers and lead me to the others. In the mornings, when I finally was able to tear myself from the house and leave, as soon as I closed the door to the flat and stepped out into the corridor, I would hear the door of the bedroom open inside the flat behind me, and I would hear John and Sarah come into the main room and start talking frantically in low voices, preparing things, opening and closing drawers, and I would hear the sound of typing on the laptop Sarah kept underneath the bed.

They were so careful when I was around, and the *sortes* so obstinately refused me any useful indication as to their whereabouts before nightfall, that I changed the tack of my investigations and started making a single daily trip to the Lecky library where I would spend an hour or two asking questions about Pour Mieux Vivre. "What is Pour Mieux Vivre *really* about?," I asked once, and picked a blank page. But while the *sortes* would not lead me directly to discover Sarah and John *in flagrante delicto* as it were, and would not offer me any hint of real information about the secret society to which they belonged, the answers I got were always relevant; something was working, something was listening. Over the next days and weeks, I began slyly tailoring my questions to more specific ends, and interesting results began to be thrown up. For example:

Q: "What are John and Sarah searching for?"

A: "The End"

Q: "What did John and Sarah do today when I wasn't there?"

A: "The group remained in the drawing-room engaged in conversation for some time, before moving to the library at the gentleman's invitation."

This figure, "the gentleman," began to turn up frequently in my *sortes Leckianae,* in various guises and names, a shadowy figure in the background of the passages I picked, a man to whom thoughts and conversations turned at the most unexpected moments, who seemed to influence events at which he was not present, who haunted places, rooms, and situations long after he had left them. But I never found out more about him.

The only lucky break I had came unexpectedly, without help from the books, in Trinity, when I had left the Lecky and gone back to pick up a pair of runners from my rooms, now become a spooky mausoleum. As I left campus, with the runners in my book bag, the sun was beginning to set, and I was planning to sit with a pint in Café en Seine and open the books to join Sarah and John. At this time of day, I always went either up to the north inner city to sit among the transplanted syllables and clothes of the immigrants and refugees or, as today, to Dawson Street, to watch the Johns and Ians, their colleagues and their secretaries go about their evening round. In any case, this time, walking up the ramp to Nassau Street, I spotted Sarah inside the Arts Block. I pushed open the door and followed her, across the concourse, down through the Coffee Dock into one of the computer rooms in the basement. I waited a short time before peering carefully round the door. She was sitting at a terminal in the front row, the last one in against the wall. She logged on, inserted a floppy disk, and started working. When it seemed to me she was engaged enough in what she was typing not to notice, I slipped in and sat at a terminal in the row directly behind, where I could watch her. I craned my neck to try and see what she was typing. It was an e-mail, a long one, but she had put the text size down to the smallest setting. She tapped away at the computer with her glasses on, the e-mail screen spilling out its reflected letters in her lenses, tiny letters, like those street-vendors in hot countries use to write your name on a grain of rice. There were two others in the room, one at the front and one sitting behind me, and so I was a little wary of leaning in too far and drawing attention to my spying. But I was able to make out the name of the recipient of the last message. *"lahillen @eurosur.org."* My heart leaped when I saw the username beside it: *"L. Anina Hillén 'Luis.'"* In order to look less suspicious to the other two e-mailers in the lab, I opened a word-processing document and began typing random nonsense.

linen in a hall

A printing window appeared on Sarah's screen. She got up from her computer and walked up to the printer at the front of the room, three rows away from where I was sitting. I bowed my head as low as I could and kept typing.

níl na héin, lá

Her sheet hummed out of the machine. She picked it up, and looked at it in disapproval.

"The toner's crap in that printer," one of the other people in the room said. "Send it to the other."

"Thanks . . ." Sarah muttered. I thought I would burst with excitement as she threw the half-printed page in the bin. I kept my head down while she returned to her terminal, reprinted her document from the better printer, logged off, and left. I raced up to the bin beside the printer and took out the page she had discarded. It was faded, parts of letters and even whole words missing, but for all that largely intact. I folded it, put it into my pocket, and set off about the rest of the day's perambulations.

It was a few days before I got to look at it. During the day, I found it hard to concentrate on any piece of language longer than a synchronicity, and in Northumberland Road, I was afraid they would find it. I kept it folded up and hidden in my little wash bag, as if it were the plans for the tunnel beneath Colditz Castle. One sunset at the end of that week, I delayed going to join Sarah and John, and went instead to the Lecky, where I unfolded the greasy sheet, smelling of toothpaste and shaving foam, and went through it word by word with a dictionary and Butt and Benjamin's Spanish grammar upstairs at the back in the Spanish section. I discovered to my horror as I spread out the damp soapy sheet in front of me that the great majority of what I had obtained had been washed out by a leak—from the smell, I suspected it was the aftershave I had stolen from Ian's bathroom a long time before, so that I could conjure him up in his absence with the smell, like a genie in a bottle—leaving little more than one sentence still legible. I found translating even this slice of Spanish a painful process, involving not only lexical searches, but also laborious combing through the grammar to work out forms of verbs, tenses, and so on. I transcribed my effort to render the fragment into English, and this is the disappointing, empty prose I came up with:

From: L. Anina Hillén lahillen@eurosur.org
To: Sarah Ní Dhuibhir nidhuibhs@tcd.ie
to start with, Sarah, all those words! It is just after siesta, I have

been lying down for a long time and instead of the words of our
"trade," all that comes to me is the lazy dialect of home, the sylla-
bles of my southern country. My plan is to traverse the continent
laterally and come to visit your rainy island in two weeks' time

Faced with such fragmentary but exciting information, and
used by now to turning fragments into vast narratives, my mind
went wild. It struck me that what Sarah and John, under the
instructions of Luis, might be planning was some kind of ritual
killing, a series, even, of murders, which would fulfil some
sortes-ordained pattern, satisfying conditions of spelling or symmetry. But in the twilit cave of flickering fictions which I inhab-
ited in those days, the matter seemed of no human import or
urgency to me, rather just a flow in the direction of an interesting new genre, and our habits, nights in Northumberland
Road and epic, wandering days went on as before.

One early evening in April, I found myself, as I often did, wandering the streets around O'Connell Street, a part of town rea-
sonably comfortable for me since it attracted other, more
human sorts of drifters, asylum-seekers forbidden to work,
unemployed men from the suburbs, grey-fingered young gur-
riers, who would, in a novel of the 1930s or a bad film, be cast as
newspaper boys. Guided by my books, I idled around these
streets in a succession of slow, waking dreams, in a fuzzy interface with the reality around me. As usual, I was attracted by the
mix of old melodic Dublin fruitsellers and diffident, dislocated
Nigerians and Romanians in Moore Street, and I allowed myself
to be blown down there, where I bought an apple and a Kit Kat,
and happily ambled for some time among the stalls. Then, even
through the thick fog which surrounded me, someone caught
my eye. It was not a visual realisation, it was not related to any
one of the senses, but was rather an elemental recognition, a
sonar disturbance. At first I thought it was my old guide, Pablo,
whom I saw now only in the distance of the Paris visions which

returned from time to time, but when I turned to look at the person, stretching over with one hand to part with a jangle of euro coins, and to receive with the other, smiling, a blue plastic bag of fruit from the stallholder, I saw Paula McVeigh.

I decided, instinctively, to run away and hide from her, but I remained transfixed, two paces behind her, while she put the bag of fruit on the ground beside her other bags, Marks and Spencer's, Habitat, Hodges Figgis, picked them all up in rebalanced grip, turned to go, and saw me.

"Niall!"

It was so long since I had heard anyone say my name in this way—the text message interactions I had with my parents were as bare as telexes—that I was not only struck dumb, but deeply moved. Tears leaked into my eyeballs, and I turned my gaze to the chewing gum ossified on the ground, to hide not so much the tears, but the shameful glinting green.

"Niall!" she said again, and with a slight bend of her knees, replaced her bags on the ground. Instead of holding her arms out to invite my embrace, as my aunts did, she stepped over to me, grabbed my shoulders, and kissed me forcefully on both cheeks.

"Niall, it's lovely to see you," she said, with genuine affection, and moved my chin up with her bony ringed hand to look me in the face. "You look . . ." she stood back and assessed me visually. "You look like you're not eating," she said.

"You look well," I said weakly, the first thing I had uttered.

"No I don't," she said with a rueful laugh, "I look desperate."

She was right. Even I, long unused to really seeing people in any normal physical way, could see this, she was lined, old and exhausted, and, so uncharacteristically, had not renewed the blonde dye in her hair, to the point where it covered only the tired, split fringes.

"It's been a trial lately," she said. "A trial. An unfair trial. Patrick said you'd gone off the radar."

It was bizarre and difficult for me to have a straightforward conversation such as this. I thought that I had become invisible to the world; I assumed that, just as individuals had melted into the colourful and basically abstract tapestry around me, so would I have been transformed for them into fragments of other things, pieces of sound and sky. Our physical integrity, the stability of the two bodies now standing in front of one another on Moore Street overwhelmed me. For a moment, I missed my old life. My tears dripped onto the ground, but Paula did not notice.

"He said he was trying to get in touch with you but he thought you must have lost your phone or something."

I shook my head to keep things steady before me, gathered my forces.

"I know," I said, "I did. But I've been bad at keeping in touch anyway. I feel terrible about it. Adjusting to college has been . . . hard, you know, I just didn't feel up to. . . ."

"I know, pet, I know," she said. "Patrick is having a tough time too, you know. Maybe even tougher. Have you time for a drink with an old hag?"

I said I did. I asked her was there anywhere nearby, but she wanted to return to Dunne & Crescenzi's, back up on South Frederick Street, across from Trinity, she said we could make it "our" place, and so we walked there. At first she talked about upcoming social projects and political events, the Luas tramlines from Sandyford and Tallaght into town, Michael McDowell's racist referendum, something about smoking. It wasn't until we were seated in Dunne and Crescenzi's with an open bottle in front of us that she moved on to her own situation.

Jim had left her, she said, there was no other way to put it. No major story, nothing strange, she'd seen it in other men a thousand times, she said, they just reach an age when they don't want to be married any more. Eejits. If I would excuse her, men don't learn as life goes on. How many women do I know turn their backs on a quarter-century of struggles and companionship for a fancy little flat with dimmer switches and champagne dinners with a teenager? How many women did I know who have upped and left, leaving a man on his own? I said nothing.

"None," she surmised accurately. "Only men do the leaving. Women do the staying. And do you know why? Because women *learn*. And do you know why women learn? Because women *listen*. Men *do not listen*. Talk talk talk for fifty years, and suddenly they think they're the dog's bollocks and they go chasing young ones. Big eejits."

She could reassure herself in a way that it was nothing personal, she had seen it before, she repeated, a thousand times. Jim too had found a young one, she clarified. Making a liúdramán of himself. He had moved into an apartment in Blackrock. With her, the young one, she supposed, but she didn't know or want to know. Patrick had so far refused to see him, so he didn't know either. She hoped Patrick and me would be different.

"Jesus, I hope you're not like yere fathers. Their generation, I mean. I hope ye listen. And I do worry about Patrick," she went on, "I mean a boy and his father . . . it's so central to self-esteem and maturity, you know? I mean, it's not so much the way he's treated me, but his own son. . . ."

The marriage hadn't been great for a while, she supposed in retrospect, it was true they had stopped doing things like dinner and cinema together, but she hadn't thought anything was seriously wrong. Of course Jim was *always* at work, and she only did the three days a week. And she meant *always*, he would leave the house at six in the morning and not come back until ten at night. She should have seen it from the weekends, the way he spent the whole time playing golf, or so she thought. She was out herself having lunches with the girls, or going to the theatre, but she supposed that she just took it for granted Jim would never be available.

"But I mean, the thing is, Niall, we were always civil to one another. I mean, when we *were* together, we would have great chats, you know, about everything, have a laugh together, I mean—I mean we really *did*, you know, enjoy each other's company. . . . That's what bothers me about this. It's like we're not two individuals, we're an incidence of a widespread statistic, man hits fifty leaves wife for girl of twenty-five. It's so effing banal. . . ."

She stared miserably into the distance and I patted her hand awkwardly. She seized it and looked at me with wild, mascara-streaked eyes.

"Get in touch with Patrick, would you? Would you do that for me, please? Would you? My only son . . . a boy and his father, it's just so. . . . Would you ever do that for me? You're a good boy, Niall, a really good boy. Thanks for keeping an old crone company. You've no idea how nice it is to be able to talk to someone young about this. . . ."

I nodded, but I was finding it so hard to keep a grip on reality. At any moment, I thought, Dunne and Crescenzi's might turn into Paris, signs and symbols could start bombarding me from all sides, Paula could begin growing suddenly distant from me, as if down a telescope backwards.

"You know, he's gone, he's decided to go and that's that. I accept that. If he treats me decently in the separation, I accept it. But I need closure, Niall, you know, everyone needs *closure*. There are things I need to *know*. Questions I need answered."

Slowly, an idea inched upon me, an insight into the division between Paula's world and mine, how to bridge it. Paula was lost, and I knew what to do, what I had to offer.

"Paula," I said excitedly, "Paula, what questions do you need answered?"

She took a deep breath. "Niall, we have been married for twenty-four years. This June would have been our twenty-fifth wedding anniversary. I need to know *why* he left. *Why* our marriage made him discontent. *Why* he needed to be a teenager again."

"You, you, you can find out. . . ." I babbled. "Honestly."

"Do you think so, really?" she asked. "Everyone else tells me there are no answers to these questions. That's what all my friends tell me. It's what my sister said to me this morning. It's what Patrick, nineteen going on seventy, says."

"Yes," I said, "yes really, there's a way."

Paula was looking off out the window onto South Frederick Street where an evening drizzle was starting to graffiti the windows of Dunne and Crescenzi's. She took a sip of wine and sighed.

"I suppose if I wait, if I let things go a bit until the . . . shock . . . is over, then maybe we will be amicable enough to talk it over. Christ, I can see him now, asking me to go to a lunchtime concert in the fucking Concert Hall. . . ."

"No, no," I said, leaning in over the table and touching her arm, "you don't need him for the answers, you—"

"Arra, Patrick is the same, on at me about counsellors and psychics or whatever. I need to look to myself for answers he says. But yere young, ye don't . . . I need answers from outside too . . . it's not all feelings, you realise when you're my age, you realise it's facts too, facts exist, sooner or later you come up against the concrete wall of real life. . . ."

I reached into her Hodges Figgis bag and pulled out a book. I was flooded with enthusiasm. I had finally reached a new level with Pour Mieux Vivre, a vital rite of passage: my first convert, just as I had been initiated by John into this world from the old one, John by Sarah, she by Luis, and he in turn by someone else, and from there a link stretching back through the years, across continents, languages, and other people's troubles.

"Okay, Paula," I said, feeling again like I had the day in Ranelagh when I had first done the *sortes,* discovering the forgotten freshness and thrill of sensing the door into that other world about to open for a first time. "Paula, what would you like to know? I mean, how would you word the question?"

She stared at me, with her new paperback in my hand, in confusion.

"Niall . . . I don't think I know what. . . ."

"Trust me, really," I said, "you will be pleased with the results, honestly. Just tell me what you want to know."

"I wouldn't . . ." she began, but then said wearily, to placate me, "well, I would want to know what was it that made him leave . . . but it's not a real question, you know. . . . This is twenty-four years of marriage we are talking about . . . you are so young. . . ." She looked perplexed and frightened, but I felt a surge of energy to be with someone at the beginning again. Paula living with us in Northumberland Road? Why not?

"Why did Jim leave Paula?" I asked out loud. She was staring at me incredulously as I flicked through the book she had bought. I read aloud to her:

What a divine hour I had at Gordon Square! I enjoyed it, like Saxon's brandy—the unreality, and bloom of the sensations went to my head, but of course if I'd stayed I should have run to ground. Was it great fun all through? I hope not.

It was perfect. I could hear the music and the Latin coming in from the distance, starting to wash around us. I put the book down and beamed at Paula. She was not beaming.

"What are you on about?" she whispered hoarsely, "what in Christ's name. . . ." her voice broke. She stood up and put on her coat, gathering her bags, tears spilling full and fast onto the floor. I stood up to block her exit.

"But listen! Just listen to it and you'll see what I mean," I said, and started to read it again,

What a divine hour I had at Gordon Square. . . .

She turned and walked around the other side of the table to avoid pushing me out of the way, to avoid touching me at all, and left without looking at me. I stood at our table, helpless, with the half-drunk bottle of wine and two glasses, while she rushed out onto the street. The other customers watched me curiously. Paula stopped for a moment outside the window to wipe her streaming eyes, then ran down to Nassau Street, away from me. She had left a fifty-euro note on the table for the bill. Before I left, I put her book in my bag with the rest, the Latin music swirling around me, deafening me to everything else:

Docebo iniquos vias tuas: et impii ad te convertentur.

I will teach the wicked your ways: and the sinners will turn to you.

That evening, as the sun went down, I did not try to find Sarah and John. Instead, I moved back and forth around the city of my own volition. I began walking out to the McVeighs' house, but stopped at Donnybrook, where the rush-hour cars headed away from town were starting to switch on their headlights. I stood for a while on the edge of the dual carriageway and watched them speed, enviable southbound current. I walked back into town, slowly along the quays, and then to the Front Lounge, where I hoped to see Chris; I did, sitting in the same corner I had been with him those months before, even with some of the same people, their names and identities now long lost in the thick mist that separated me from that life. I sat drinking and doing *sortes* at the bar, watching him talking, suddenly throwing back his head in laughter or mock exasperation, flirting with the young blond man sitting across from him. Silently, I watched as he bought a round at the bar, licked excess Guinness foam off his fingers, excused himself and greeted acquaintances as he threaded his way through the gay crowd with his tray of pints. I watched, carefully hidden from his happy view, until he and his group headed out to go dancing, and I returned myself, in my own direction, into the night.

On Dame Street in front of Dublin Castle, I caught sight of someone I knew to see, a woman from the Kerry Gaeltacht who played the accordion outside Tara Street DART station, a lesbian with short blond hair and man's clothes. I used to love catching her speaking her mountainy tongue to the occasional Irish-speaking passerby, sound of turf, heather, and sea in the smoky grime underneath Butt Bridge. That night I followed her across town to O'Donaghue's on Baggot Street, where she sat in a crowd of traditional musicians having a session, watched by the early season tourists, Italian couples in their thirties, with happy wax jackets and *Invicta* bags. The bodhráns thumped in my head, I abandoned myself to the swirl of the uilleann pipes and fiddles, to the round shape of unending reels, tunes which, however far they strayed, always came home with a magical wallop to the theme. I sat anaesthetised by the music, by sounds which came from strands and valleys off in the west, and untroubled images of Irish college with Patrick floated before me. As I partially remembered the person I could have been, I felt the true size of the distance that had opened up between now and then, and the inevitability of this reprieve's quick close, a dread as silent and deathlike as that of the Romanovs in Yekaterinburg, or of a spinster Victorian governess in the last few hours of her Tuesday off.

And sure enough, my day out came to a swift close. At the height of the session, when the eyes of the accordion-player were tightly shut and her fingers were flying up and down the keys, I saw Sarah and John sitting at a table near the door, Sarah with her legs crossed, smoking and looking, bored, at the musicians, John leaning low on his elbows and staring at me grimly over the top of his pint. When the piece ended and the musicians paused to order drinks and chat, John summoned me over with a toss of his head, a gesture without a hint of request or doubt, a casual and unarguable command. Sarah went outside onto the street. I picked up my bookbag and walked over to the table, and while John stood and drained off the end of his pint, I waited, mute and docile, for them to take me back to Northumberland Road.

Eight

After that, I always returned to Sarah and John at sunset. Their private preparations were becoming more frantic, due, I supposed, to the impending visit of Luis. A new ritual was added to our daily round. When we arrived back in Northumberland Road in the evenings, Sarah and John would close themselves in the bedroom for an hour or sometimes two, typing. They muttered throughout in low voices, but the typing never stopped; they must have produced an extraordinary quantity of prose. I would sit on the sofa (the only book-free space) in the living room, or, when it was fine, outside on the little fire escape, drinking white wine and consulting a little pile of books. I asked questions of them in an offhand, practical way, almost as I used to when I first got involved with Pour Mieux Vivre.

"What must I learn?"

Interaction can give rise to an exquisite variety of form in galaxies.

And, inevitably, curious questions about what was going on behind the door:

Saint Francis, at the beginning of his religion, having gathered his companions to talk about Christ, in a moment of spiritual fervour commanded one of them, in the name of God, to open his mouth and to speak as the Holy Spirit inspired him.

Static crackle and pulsing electronic tones signalled their connecting to the Internet and the end of the private typing, and I would begin laying out the room for the night's session. Sarah would leave me with detailed instructions before they retired to their typing because the sessions themselves had become gradually more complicated and obscure, finally unrecognisably different from the original campfire circle of reading aloud. As the months had gone on, Sarah had suggested so many frills, adjustments, and accoutrements that, without my noticing it, our nocturnal activities had less to do with books than with, if not quite pentagrams and dismembered reptiles, at least odd rites and fragments of arcane tongues and superstitions. To an outsider, our flat would literally have looked more like the hidden den of a coven than the meeting place of an over-enthusiastic readers' circle. The effects became simultaneously more spectacular and strange; the daytimes commensurately more detached and dazed. Worldly reality affected us only when we found ourselves physically opposed to it, such as when Sarah was thrown out of Isolde's Tower for smoking, which the Government had, unbeknownst to us, banned from all public places.

At some point, my weekly two hours of clarity stopped coming, with the result that I stopped texting home. I realised that this had happened one grey and drizzly day when, walking across Trinity's slippery cobbles, I spied Patrick and Ciara standing together at the door to House 16. Patrick was ringing the top bell, mine, and Ciara was standing back looking up expectantly at the window. She took a phone out of her pocket, called someone, and put it to her ear, shaking her head to Patrick and putting it away. I stood in a corner of the tennis courts under the dripping cherry trees, cold droplets running down my neck, watching them ring and ring at my bell before walking off together along the side of the GMB.

I imagined them saying goodbye on Nassau Street, Patrick unlocking his bike from a lamppost, putting on his helmet, Ciara waving him off and walking back to Westland Row DART station and Sandycove. It was strangely moving to see them together, an odd couple brought together by me. In one, very limited, sense, they had known each other for many years, when Patrick and I had started visiting each other's houses for weekend visits at the age of twelve, when Ciara was a ten-year-old watching cartoons in the next room.

As I looked at the fragile pair, Ciara and Patrick, a whole human life seemed to be passing me by. Time still turned away on a reliably rotating axis, but I had jumped off, and I stood watching it revolve from a distance, distant and unreal and above all silent, just as when we were children, Ciara, Patrick and I used to see the big wheel at the centre of Funderland amusement park in Ballsbridge. Their timed world drifted across to me like faraway fairground music, indeed, heavy with nostalgia, but, compared to the life I now had, repulsive and banal.

Anyway, I knew that their interference had to stop, so I gathered what forces I still had and phoned Sandycove from the Nassau Street tunnel. My mother, who, as always, answered the phone, was worried. I told her I was fine, I had lost my phone for a while (uncertain how long I had been out of contact, I didn't specify how long), and had been staying out late at parties in people's flats. My mother was hesitant, and paused to consider whether or not to believe my account of events.

"Niall, Paula McVeigh rang here. She said she'd met you in town and she thought something was wrong."

I paused. Of course it made it more difficult now there had been an actual witness. I thought only of how to discredit the evidence, and picked on the first stratagem that offered itself:

"To be honest, I thought something was wrong with *her*," I said.

"What do you mean?"

As the cock crew three times behind me, I answered: "She was raving. Drunk as a skunk at four in the afternoon."

"Was she?"

"She always had a nose for the bottle," I said.

"I know she did," my mother said. "She was a bit slurred-sounding on the phone, all right. And I heard Jim jilted her for a young one."

"She had a big red nose on her and she was muttering to herself when I saw her on Moore Street," I went on, careful not to warm too much to my subject. "I didn't recognise her at first, I thought she was a crazy homeless woman. It's so sad."

"It's awful. . . ." my mother murmured. "Did she recognise you?"

"No, I went up to her and asked her if she was okay, but she didn't know who I was. I kept telling her over and over again, it's Niall Lenihan, Patrick's friend from Gonzaga. I got her a taxi and sent her home. She didn't even remember the address. I'm amazed she remembers she met me."

"Oh, she rang up in a state. It was all very incoherent, now I think of it. Ciara went in to your rooms to check on you."

"I'm sorry I missed her."

"Well, maybe you'll come out some Sunday for dinner, will you, love?"

"Maybe I will. I'd love to. But exams are getting closer, I'll have to get on top of work a bit first."

"I know, I know, no pressure. But it'd be lovely to see you."

I said my miserable goodbyes quickly, because the daylight was fading, the call of Sarah, John, and the books was getting stronger, an unbearable tug in my guts and organs, and the busy voices of the people walking by me between Trinity and Nassau

Street were spinning out of their separate contexts and into distant but distinct and definite fragments of the usual song, echoing in the granite tunnel:

Auditui meo dabis gaudium et laetitiam
et exsultabunt ossa humiliata.
Averte faciem tuam a peccatis meis
et omnes iniquitates meas dele.
You will make me hear joy and gladness
and the bones you have cast down will rejoice
Turn your face from my sins
and wipe out all my iniquities.

It is hard to render accurately the mix of relief and disgust I felt when I did return to them, and to the flat we would have called home if such a word had been in our vocabulary. In our world, there were no parents, siblings, or friends, no boys and girls in school uniforms, no rulers, rubbers, compasses, or deserted wives, only the three of us with books, candles, Southern Comfort, Vulgate psalms sung from the ether, and ever more improbable supernatural visions. But I did look forward to the interruption which I knew was imminent, the visit of Luis of which I had been apprised by the stolen, poorly translated and very partial fragment of Sarah's correspondence with him. I was inordinately excited by the prospect of his arrival. Sarah, John, and I lived in a profoundly isolated nucleus. Our utter disconnection from the normal outside world was not compensated for, however, at least not for me, by an involvement in the international underground of Pour Mieux Vivre. I knew that our little family was a single cell in a huge network only through the brief description John had given me of Pour Mieux Vivre before I had joined myself up, and from the electronic correspondence in which Sarah engaged through the laptop in the bedroom of Northumberland Road, but I had no direct evidence, no direct contact, and no information about the rest of the network. As time went on, our own activities began not to become repetitive, exactly, but to demand situation in a wider framework. Indeed, the thought, which sometimes struck me, that contact with the mother ship, or even with another cell like our own, might never be made, struck a cold dread in the bottom of my heart. However brilliant and beautiful the transformed world was, at a certain point the idea that we would remain its only inhabitants provoked a sense of immortal loneliness which chilled my blood.

The thought of Luis's visit, then, was a relief as much as an excitement. The matter wasn't ever spoken of directly "at home," but it was clear to me that they were making preparations. I didn't know whether or not they knew I knew what was going on, but certain arrangements, such as the booking of a hotel room, were carried out without any attempt at concealment. And then one morning, around two weeks after I had stolen the printed scrap of Sarah's e-mail, as I was preparing to leave the flat for the usual solitary synchronous encounters with the city, Sarah and John emerged from the bedroom. Sarah wanted to say something to me before I left.

"Niall, you have to go away for a few days."

I had my back to her, standing at the sink and rinsing a mug for my morning coffee. I didn't turn around, and, perfectly aware, of course, of what the matter in hand would be, I played innocent.

"Why?"

"You know well why."

A sudden spirit of rebelliousness made me resolve not to make it easier for her. "Do I?"

"Yes."

"No, I don't." I poured my coffee and turned around to face her, holding the steaming mug in front of me. She was standing in front of the door, hands on her hips and looking at me defiantly. John was beside her, barefoot, rumpled and distracted, looking absentmindedly around the room, like a sun-tired tourist examining the mosaic on a church ceiling.

"Niall!" Sarah exclaimed, in frustration. "Just do it, okay?"

"Tell me why," I said, "and I'll do it."

John, staring at the cracked ceiling, murmured something I didn't catch. Sarah exhaled angrily.

"Right, your way. As you know, of course, from your tireless spying on us, Luis, from . . . the organisation, is coming to Dublin for a few days. So that's why you have to be out of the way."

"I'd like to meet him."

"Well, you can't."

"Why not?"

"Because you can't."

"Oh, just tell him, would you. . . ." John interrupted, eyes shut, groaning voice.

"You tell him, then, John."

Sarah walked back into the bedroom, and I heard her lighting a cigarette. John looked, as he always did these days, half-asleep. He was wearing a faded blue T-shirt and jeans with an unbuckled belt. He had one foot propped against the front door behind him, one elbow against the bookshelf, the other arm lazily cushioning his head from the wall. He kept his eyes closed as he spoke. To address me at all, and especially to administer such mundane matters, weighed him down with an overwhelming lassitude. The time we spent together was a cave of shadows, in which the fire of our rites and rituals left us in a gloomy, flickering room with gigantic shadows and unnatural, shape-shifting faces. Now, in this unadorned atmosphere, John spoke as if original, communicative English, not culled from books or filtered through synchronicities, was a foreign language he partially remembered from school, a qualified barrister doing the mandatory Irish exam.

"Look, eh, Niall . . . Luis doesn't know that you, eh, follow, I mean that you . . . that you *know* anything. We asked him if we should let you in on things a bit, you know after the event, that night in Kehoe's before Christmas I mean. And he said no. He was raging with us. With Sarah, I mean. He had never been thrilled that I was in on it. So he told us to get rid of you."

"But then. . . ." I began.

"But then," he said, with a sigh, "as you know, we ended up here. And we never told him, and he can't know." He let his hands fall by his sides, and opened his eyes.

John's tone was dutiful and unengaged, but there was a sadness in him I had not seen before.

"So I have to stay out of his sight."

"Absolutely."

"And you?"

He walked back into the bedroom without answering.

The reason for this was that the answer was not what John wanted. Sarah decided I couldn't be trusted not to track them all down with *sortes,* so John was supposedly deputed to chaperone me. But it was clear that morning, as Sarah prepared a little weekend case to take with her to Luis's hotel, that an unwanted bond of mutual exclusion had been created once again between John and me, that John was also forbidden from meeting the guru. He was furious, not only at the frustration of not being able to pursue his questions and assuage his lonely, burning curiosity, the desire of an adopted child to meet his birth parent, but also at this sign, in our petty hierarchy, that in Sarah's eyes the distinction between him and me was not as great as he wished. Nevertheless, he assented, as always, and he and I headed off together with two bags of books into a sunny day in town, while Sarah put on an uncharacteristic touch of lipstick and eyeliner and went off to the airport alone.

I was thrilled to have company—company from within the family, that is—on my daytime meanderings. I always craved the society of John and Sarah, and now a suppleness in John's hands and a firmness in his walk wound me up with a fierce sexual desire. He was sullen and silent, and responded to my eager chatter with silent stares at our surroundings, as if he were a visiting businessman in a foreign city, his attention idly and half-heartedly caught by the architecture and urban layout, and I the eager young tour guide, chattering manically about everything we passed. He interacted with me only over the books. These led us to St. Stephen's Green, where we sat on the grass near the pond. It was sunny but the grass was still cold and damp, and no one joined us on the ground. John threw berries across the fence at the ducks, and I ceased my talking for a while and let the noise of the people wash around me while I looked at the clouds.

"So what is his deal?" I asked finally.

"Who?"

I didn't reply.

"Luis?"

I looked at him reproachfully.

"Well . . ." he pulled at the grass. "Well, how would I know? I'm not allowed meet him either."

Again I didn't say anything. John looked hard at the ground, and moved agitatedly. He wrenched up a big handful of grass and shook the earth from the roots as he collected himself. And then, perhaps because he had decided to accept the fraternal moment, although it had been imposed from without, he went on:

"I owe him everything. My life now is something he has taught me. As if I was born again. Literally, I mean," he added.

"Me too, I suppose."

He ignored this and went on, more to the ducks than to me: "I mean, like, the only things I know now that are important, he has told me. Through Sarah mostly, but he's the one it comes from. It all depends on him, how it happened, where it goes from here, all of it."

"What do you mean?"

Foolish question. John shook his head and sank into stony silence again.

We wandered around town for the day. We didn't talk, but efficiently and in perfectly synchronous concert sliced through books and snatches of language together, rode their waves like two surfers with sunbleached hair and tough brown skin who have spent a lifetime sharing a beach. In this sense it was a perfect, if on his side unloving, partnership, and the effects were exhilarating. In the park, crossed back and forth by so many real people on their way to coffees and meetings, I had a vision of John as he might have been had he not met Sarah, a laid-back, ambitious young man in a suit. Watching him now, I saw that potential Celtic Tiger citizen—the diligent young banker living and working in the Financial Services Centre complex, drinking pints on Dawson Street or playing rugby at the weekends, engaged to a young professional woman, a live wire from County Longford—totally transformed into an unrecognisable being with chaotic hair and wild eyes, feverishly consulting books from a bag. I think John may have had the same thought himself, because when rush hour started and the streets were filled with office people such as he might have been himself, he suggested we go for a drink. He used the phrase, "go for a drink," as a word one uses in a strictly etymological or clinical sense, invoking not its common vernacular meaning, but a medical diagnosis or an ancient Greek root. I understood from this that what he had in mind was not the beginning of the usual session, the preparation of a spectacular series of night-apparitions, such as we were accustomed to doing, but a drink in the old sense, in the manner of the old world, two people sitting down together to talk and get drunk, as I would have done with Fionnuala, or he with some Rory or Conor or Brendan or Tim. He wanted a *night off.*

It was, of course, impossible for us to be mortal men together, and his desire had nothing to do with me. Since he had sunk into the alternative universe of Pour Mieux Vivre, John had lost all possibility of connection—even more than I, or even Sarah, had—with the normal world. He experienced nothing that was not mediated or dictated by Sarah, Luis, or the books. We were certainly not friends, whatever other faster bonds tied us. But John knew no one else, and so in this sudden attempt to grasp at the fleeing shadows of his former humanity, it was me he had to invite to "go for a drink."

He more or less frogmarched me down Parliament Street, not to our favourite haunt, usual Isolde's Tower, but instead to the more mainstream Porter House. There, among the bright lights, sanded pine, and regular, run-of-the-mill weekending Dubliners, we had two pints of micro-brewed lager, while John babbled manically about colleagues in his old job, friends at school, things he had done in college. I nodded and sipped, while his talking got louder, quicker, and stranger. He looked frantically around him at the other drinkers, as if he was trying to imitate them, trying to remember how to have a human conversation.

At a certain point, the physical and mental effort of this charade was too much for him, and he fell into silence, gulping his beer aggressively. I decided to take advantage of the situation, our enforced company as well as his sudden desire to be ordinary for an evening, to try and get some information out of him.

"So what do you think Sarah and Luis are *doing*?"

He stared at me for a moment, then threw his head back and laughed a long, loud, bitter laugh.

"Is that a synchronicity, Niall? *What are Sarah and Luis doing*?" He waved his hand at a shelf of decorative books, a feature from a 1990s tax-deductible renovation.

"What are they *doing*? What are they *saying*?"

John was shouting and people were staring.

"Let's move somewhere," I said to him. I reached down to pull out a book, but John reached across and grabbed my arm in a painful grip.

"No."

I pulled my arm away and stretched up to take a book off the shelf, but the volumes were all glued together. We went across the road to the Front Lounge, where there was no space left to sit, or hardly even to stand. We stood with our pints in the middle of the crowd, bookbags on the floor.

"What will happen to us, John?" I asked, all of a sudden.

He was quiet, and for a moment I thought he might even answer me, participate in the intimacy I was proposing: I thought that maybe we would have a discussion about our future. Instead, he clapped me on the shoulder, so hard some of my pint spilled onto my hands and jacket, and I fell back slightly into the group behind me.

"What did you make of Meath in the All-Ireland last year, Niall?" he asked loudly, through a wild-eyed grin. "Crackin team, what? But you're not a gaa-man, of course, are you? You're a rugger fella. A rugger-bugger. That's what you are, isn't it, a rugger-bugger. Hand between the legs of the scrum-half, what?"

People around were noticing us, but, thinking it was friendly play between two gay friends, they smiled indulgently, and indeed enviously at me, standing in such close quarters with handsome John.

"Please. . . ." I murmured. John looked away, half-smiling to himself. I went to the bar to order fresh drinks, as instructed by John. He laughed nastily when I arrived back with them, for no clear reason. As we drank, we exchanged pieces of his pretend ordinary guys' conversation—now he had given up on actually achieving it, he continued the aggressive parody, and wouldn't allow me to drop the game, to consult the books or say anything that wasn't part of the "conversation." He got better and better and more savage at the game as the night went on, and punctuated the clichéd phrases he composed with acidic self-congratulatory laughter. It felt at times as though he had some access to my mind or memories, since he seemed to choose expressions I used to use with Patrick and especially Ian.

"Sometimes . . . sometimes . . ." he said, for example, pausing as if searching for the *phrase juste,* leaning intimately over the table towards me for mock emphasis, "sometimes I feel like I'm bottling everything up inside me, you know, like I'm corking it all inside, and I feel I'll burst if I don't let it out."

Or: "You know, Niall, I don't feel I make any decisions, it's like I'm just blown this way and that by circumstances. Will I ever find my soul-mate?" He really laughed at that one, until he was redfaced, or even more so than usual, and I thought he might even vomit.

"Niall?"

I said nothing, looking desperately around the bar hoping to catch a glimpse of Chris, but John's face inevitably drew me back from the alternative universe around me and reinstated its green-tinged brown eyes as the only reality.

"Niall, you know sometimes I feel so alone. . . ." he said, and collapsed laughing.

"Let's go," I said, and when he had finished laughing he got up to leave and I followed him.

We wandered round the city in the cold for hours. At first, we tried, for once, to move according to something other than synchronicities, but it was impossible. We were like seventeenth-century sailors, and the *sortes* were our stars, without which we were lost, purposeless, incapable of coherent movement or action. As his game of real person's conversations fell bitterly apart, John abandoned the attempt to navigate the city independently and we gave in to the books again. We walked through the cold night, never speaking, changing route and street according to the passages we picked on each exit, stopping under a buzzing streetlamp and moving the pages with numb fingers.

John sank into a resentful anger. I saw in his impotent rage that the mockery of his conversation game had stemmed from a profound fury at not being able, ever, to break out of the reality of Pour Mieux Vivre. John had realised the impossibility of this for the first time, seen the permanent nature of his prison and exile. Guided by his hated bookbag, we walked vaguely east, in fits and starts, from crowded pub to crowded pub, The Oak, The Mercantile, Brogan's, The Bank, Café en Seine, Ron Black's, and then back up west, all along Dame Street again to the Lord Ed beside the silent spires of Christ Church, down along the quays and up to the gay pubs along Capel Street. Yello, a new gay bar, was the only pub we stayed in for longer than a few minutes. John insisted we have a pint there. We stood at the bar, in a scene from my brief, old life, watched by drunk old men and skinny youngsters with bleached hair.

Men stood against the wall in a line observing the self-conscious parade of hunted-looking clients walking back and forth in front of them. John stared at me with what I fancied was a mocking smirk the whole time, examining my reactions. We were both very drunk by now, a feeling exacerbated by the pause in taking *sortes*. John mocked me by posing for the men; he was over-friendly to them when they pushed, too slowly, past. A young, good-looking guy dressed up in his best clothes, brown hair carefully gelled and styled, kept looking over at him nervously. John bought him a drink. I said I wanted to leave.

"But the boys . . ." John said slurringly. "The lovely boys. . . ."

While John was in the toilet, I left, alone, and stood on the pavement in a cloud among the throng of smokers, looking across the road at a building whose familiarity puzzled me until I realised it was Capel Court, where Chris lived. His lights were off—he was in the Front Lounge, or the George of course—or I might have rung his bell. In any case, it was not long before John came running out after me, shouting sarcastic farewells to the young man inside he had deliberately confused. We walked, sick and unsteady, up the quays and boardwalk back to Dame Street. The queue at the taxi rank was long, so we stumbled all the way to Northumberland Road on foot, the sky like us, black and numb and starry, John muttering the whole way about Sarah and Luis and their hotel.

When he pushed open the door and we entered the familiar, bookfilled lair, he shouted: "Back to prison!" We were too drunk to light candles in the flat. I turned on the light, but the bulb flashed and tinkled into darkness, leaving us to stumble over the books and glasses. It was too cluttered to negotiate without light, so we went into the bedroom, usually forbidden territory for me, and I sat on the corner of the bed, never slept in, with only the slight yellow glow of the streetlights against the darkness. John lay down and sang aggressive snatches of songs about prisons, his mind, despite himself, still working on the principle of synchronicities:

A hungry feeling came over me stealing
And the mice were squealing in my prison cell
And the old triangle went jingle jangle
All along the banks of the Royal Canal.

I moved off the bed and sat on the deskchair at the table where Sarah typed her e-mails to Luis. Behind me John sang into his pillow:

As we gather in the chapel here in old Kilmainham Gaol
I think about the past few weeks, oh will they say we've failed?
From our schooldays they have told us we must yearn for liberty
Yet all I want in this dark place is to have you here with me.

I picked up a book from the floor and went over to hold it to the streetlit window. It was a second-hand souvenir edition of *David Copperfield*. I picked a line at random and read it with difficulty in the yellow light.

A dissolution of partnership.

I sat back on the chair.

"Let's rest," John mumbled from the bed. "I'm tired."

I knew he wasn't; we never were any more. I didn't reply. He said: "Let's sleep."

"Fine," I said, "sleep away."

There was a silence while John, I think, really did try to fall asleep as he would have done in his old life. I sat in the dark corner watching him lying stretched out, fully clothed apart from his shoes kicked off onto the floor beside him, his eyes closed, trying to deepen and regulate his breathing into that of a sleeper. His tossing and turning, his desperate wish to simulate the most ordinary activity of the human world, reminded me of Peter Pan, and I felt a wave of miserable pity for both of us.

After a while he opened his eyes, looked over at me and said: "Niall, you lie down too."

My heart started to beat faster. I looked at the outlines of his shape stretched out before me in the close night air of the flat, solid, gently heaving contours, apart from the tousled fuzz of his hair above the pillow. I remained as I was. He sat up a little. He patted the sheets beside him.

"Come on, Niall," his voice was slurry and strange, "lie with me."

Silently, uneasily, I crawled along the bed and squeezed myself between him and the wall. I looked at the blank white in front of me, I felt the warmth of his face breathing near my neck.

"Turn around," he whispered. I manoeuvred myself around to face him. His eyes glinted in the darkness, staring at mine. He put a hand to my cheek and stroked it slowly. He took it away, and then gently held the back of my neck. I did not react. Then, suddenly, with a jerk, he pulled my head towards his, turned down on top of me and kissed me. He kissed me for a long time, holding my head pressed against the pillow. My heart excitedly pumped blood through my veins, I forgot everything but the faint smell of whiskey from his breath, the warm pressure of his hands, and his tongue plunging my mouth. He stopped and lifted his head to look at me, his hands still on my cheeks, with a faintly quizzical air. And then I saw clearly what ought to have been obvious, the slightly triumphant look in his eyes, and I realised that this was only a selfish revenge. He moved his face down to kiss me again, but I overcame the thundering desire in every inch of my body to give myself to him, to fall fully into the pleasures I had imagined so many times, and I turned away towards the wall. He tried to turn me back around again to face him, but I pushed his head away—feeling the soft, sexual stubble on his face—and told him no. He stared, blinked, and tried again; I pushed him more forcefully this time and shook my head. He sat back and looked at me. I got out of the bed, clambering awkwardly over his body.

"Not this," I said; "instead, tell me what's going on."

He said nothing. I went on:

"I need to know more. Tell me the meaning of it all. Tell me what it's all about. Where did it start. Where does it go. What does it mean."

He remained silent, and continued watching me as I got my jacket and took a pack of Sarah's cigarettes from the bedside table. He hugged the pillow, his back to me, his face to the wall. I closed the door on him and left. I walked through night rain and lonely labyrinths back to Trinity, where I had not spent a night in months.

I locked the door and pushed my desk against it. Dressed and in the dark, I lay on the bed, over the covers, watching the window through the open curtains.

As the slow dawn rose from across the sea, I nearly wished, for the first time, that I was able to sleep again.

The following evening, as night fell, I made my way back, like a homing pigeon, to Northumberland Road. I had tried *sortes* locating either Sarah and John, but the answers I got *("The President*

*was waiting for us at the entrance to the magnificent reception rooms, sur-
rounded by all the Port-au-Princiens and –Princiennes")* let me know I
would find them already at "home."

A whole night spent away from them had left me jittery and
twitching, and it was with a species of relief that I greeted John
when he came down and opened the door. He didn't respond to
my greeting, nor did he say anything about what had happened
the night before.

"Come on," he said gruffly, and gestured to me to walk up the
stairs in front of him while he marched behind me, as if
escorting me, a prisoner of medium rank, to my cell. There was
a new quiet in the house. I asked him if Sarah was there. He
nodded his head in the direction of the bedroom, from which I
heard typing. John did not go into the bedroom to join Sarah this
time, and while we sat opposite one another in the living room
waiting for her to emerge, though we didn't speak, I felt that he
was almost relieved to see me, and that my presence had taken
the edge off some new anxiety. When Sarah did come out, I
arranged the books and candles as usual. She and John did not
speak over the course of the preparations, or even look at one
another. We proceeded in efficient silence until Sarah, in the disconnected voice of one making a tannoy public service
announcement, outlined new regulations and strategies we
were to use. I cannot remember much of the session that followed except that it was more affecting and extravagant than any
that had come before. I recall that the three of us were struck
dumb and immobile, and remained frozen, three emerald-eyed
sculptures, for hours. When I melted into consciousness from
this petrified state the next morning, as the sun came through
the window, Sarah and John had already left the house.

The air of unreality that hung over my daytime walk that
day was thicker and heavier than ever before. It was with a
stony-limbed eagerness that I sat down with my books at a
table in a café across the road from the Passport Office on

Molesworth Street to seek out Sarah and John that evening. The first passage I chose, however, offered nothing to my imagination:

> Now they could hear the carriage rumbling behind them, bearing along poor frail Cam and the argus-eyed Levasseur, frustrated that he was separated from his hero even for an hour. Fanny knew that she and the General had only another moment together unobserved and unlistened to.

The passage seemed clearly to refer not only to Sarah and John, but to my search for them; something was working, but it was useless insofar as finding them went. I walked up, unconvinced, to the Carriage Office in Dublin Castle, but indeed there was no sign of them, and the *sortes* I chose there, sitting on a bench outside the Chester Beatty Library, were even more impenetrable:

> But even in this intensely focused present they had still managed to quarrel. His children wanted their father's name unclouded by scandal, he himself wanted to honor his pact with his long-dead wife—and America wanted its French great-uncle neutered.

I read and reread it, added in the sentences just before and after it, but it failed to yield any information I could use as to their whereabouts, in this, a system which had up to now been as infallible and easy as e-mail. With fear growing inside me, I picked another passage:

> Indeed, one of the ways that The Lady Eve *defines its characters, especially its men, is to ask what each is hungry for. The answer to that question is often unsettling: they might be starving, Sturges insinuates, for something that does not exist. Loving what does not, nor never can, exist can have dreadful consequences, but then again it can also be the source of much fun.*

Once more the passage, while apparently referring to the dynamics of our group, yielded nothing but a vague sense of dread. I tried a fourth, a fifth, and a sixth synchronicity, but all the passages I chose failed to offer the usual easy interpretations leading indisputably to pubs, street intersections, buildings, and monuments. This had occasionally happened from time to time on a first or second reading, but never before like this. Always before, in the evenings at least, I would have to read a passage at most four times before the meaning came to the surface and became as clear as an address or a signpost to the location of Sarah and John. But this time, the books offered me no directions at all, only unspecific and sinister omens.

After more than an hour of panicked consultations and wild-goose chases, I walked out on my own initiative to Northumberland Road and rang the bell. No one answered the bell. Our downstairs neighbour arrived laden with bags of shopping, and by helping her carry them up the front steps, got myself in the front door with her. She watched me with unnerved fascination (*"one of the cult that lives in the top flat,"* I could imagine her saying in conversation to another neighbour). I climbed the stairs to our flat, where I found the door unlocked but no one in, the white curtains blowing in the wind. I opened the door of the bedroom: empty too, and the computer and the locked chest of papers had both disappeared. Another synchronicity pulled in panic from a book on the living-room floor sent me to Davy Byrne's pub on Duke Street where I had two pints while looking anxiously through the crowd of young financial services executives to find them. I used one of the decorative volumes there to find a new direction, and I waited for a hopeless hour at the base of the Daniel O'Connell statue, swung by the Spike and the Jervis Street Centre, but the locations I was directed to were all as bare of Sarah and John as the flat. In despair, I ran to Trinity, where I rang and rang on Sarah's bell, but it echoed with a wilful futility into the unlit square of her window.

My temples were throbbing in panic. I raced through the twilight to the Berkeley, the nearest library. I ran up the steps and rushed inside the library, waving my ID at the security guard at the entrance. I stumbled up the stairs and pulled a book from a shelf with trembling hands; I picked a blank page. Shoving the book back on the shelf, I grabbed something else.

Mr. Clarke's improvement consists in attaching a ring of zinc by zinc rivets to the top part of the outside of the hollow cylinder of zinc used in the arrangement of Mr. Mullins, and drawing a bladder over this cylinder, to which it is secured by a cord

I looked at the page in horror. The words were not making sense. The native ability I had long since acquired to spin the coarse thread of random passages into the golden filaments of meaning was lost. I read on, cold sweat now dripping onto the page in front of me, sensing with a rising terror the fast gallop of despondence. It was useless, some demon of dyslexia had cursed these books, the words in front of me failed to cohere, they remained disconnected from me, rooted in a specific, separate context of their own. I closed my eyes and breathed deeply; I thought, I am creating a juncture in my life, I am opening a gap in the world and I will allow these words to enter it. I will concentrate on the meaning of the words, the meaning in isolation from everything but this moment. I ran to another shelf and took a new book:

It would be easy to subscribe to the theory that the game David proposes is only an expedient way of getting rid of the woman he regards as a petty thief and now a major nuisance. Yet given that we have just made the acquaintance of a shrink, we shouldn't summarily dismiss the possibility that David may have unconscious motives for suggesting this particular game. We might infer, for instance, that David is summoning an

ancestral memory of a game the baby learns, indeed often exis-
tentially needs to play.

Useless, completely useless. It remained irretrievably itself, rooted to its pages, impossible to interpret as a synchronicity. I dropped the book to the floor and grabbed another, but it was the same:

The names and order of all the BOOKS OF THE OLD TESTAMENT
Genesis p. 1
Exodus p. 41

Melancholy was now pulsing round my body like a disease of the blood, the quick action of a snakebite, monstrous spiked cells pumping gleefully through my veins, cramping my speedily beating heart. Book after book I took passages from, but it was only ever a fragment of some narrative, a list of something else, a line of someone else's poem. I stumbled and leaned against the shelf. I felt physically weak. Law students around me were looking strangely.

"You okay?" a guy with an earring and a northern accent asked me. I nodded, and, gathering all my remaining forces, hoping that my own books would not be deactivated in the same way, I somehow managed to pull myself outside, across New Square and Botany Bay and up the stairs of House 16 to my rooms. I fell in, useless and incapacitated. I lurched over to my bookshelf, but, knowing it was useless, fell back in dismay against the wall. I sank to my knees, dizzy and fainting. Would this mean death? I thought, then hit on a final, desperate, stratagem. Turning around and supporting myself with one arm on the windowsill, I used the other to push up the window. I heaved myself forward and stuck my head out. With the very last reserves of energy I had, I managed to sing out these lines on the indifferent air:

"When I am rich," say the bells of Shoreditch.

I fell down on the floor among the upended drawers, socks, and folders of my long-abandoned room, and waited for the world finally to end.

And then I heard footsteps. Someone entered the room and closed the door. From where I lay, I saw two brown boots appear at the doorway and walk slowly across the carpet to where I was.

"Pablo . . . ?"

It was him. He walked over and crouched down beside me. He put a hand on my forehead.

"Niall. . . ." he murmured. He looked at the pile of clothes and bed-linen and picked up a few T-shirts, which he threw on the bed.

He crouched down beside me again. He had a book in his hand.

"Here, I have one for you."

I tried to sit up on my elbows, but I was weak. I took the book and looked at the passage he indicated, but I was unable to focus on the words. I fell back down and gave the book back to him.

"Okay," he said, and read the passage out to me in a soft voice. He knelt close to me, so close his lips brushed against my ear like a kiss, and my eardrum vibrated gently with the warmth of his voice. They were the words of an Irish song, one I remembered distantly from school or Irish college. He spoke only the first verse, in a slow whisper, but the words transformed themselves smoothly into a clear meaning I could feel. They entered my ear on the quiet breath of Pablo and filled my body, the room, with a gentle light. The gloom faded, dissolved at the sound of this first verse which once again contained, as words had for so long now, firm, geographical guides.

When I sat up, Pablo was gone, the door was swinging in the breeze, and my keys were on my desk. My clothes and other things had been tidied away and the mattress replaced. I sat on the bed. The fabric of my universe had been rent asunder and sewn back together. I knew it was temporary stitching and that it wouldn't hold for very long, but for the moment I was safe, functioning freely once again.

The world had fallen still. The trees no longer moved in the night breezes, there was no more sound of traffic from Dame Street. I looked out the window at the night silence of Trinity and felt a singular peace throughout my body, a wavy fondness for the world, a slender sense of words. In this floating way I left my room, hardly touching, it seemed, the banisters or the steps, gliding the four flights into the cold outside. I continued to drift, smiling slyly, through the streets, threaded to the moon, apart from the people. I glided with the soft winds along by the buses on Nassau Street, and quietly, quickly, the air tossed me up Kildare Street, past the Alliance Française, Dáil Éireann, and blew me, insubstantial light thing, back along Merrion Square. In among the dark trees and lonely bushes of the park I saw Pablo, in a green jacket and pink cravat, skin white as marble, lounging on top of a rock. He winked and waved me on, and the wind caught me again, blew me through the streets like an unfastened star, guided me on up past Mount Street, where the breeze fell and left me still smiling on the nightbanks of the Canal.

There was no sound but a dubious rustle of water and some movement of ducks in grass. The water rippled slowly, carelessly reflecting moon and neon, a single shimmering substance. I sat on a bench and watched. To my right I heard my name, but distant, as if through a wall, and I turned. John, in jeans and a long raincoat, was walking noiselessly towards me. His face was washed out in the moonlight and he had an uncertain smile on his face. I moved up the bench and he sat down beside me.

"Someone took. . . ." I whispered. He smiled strangely.

The water was still. The ducks, startled, took off in a scramble from the rushes and flapped up over the houses and the stars. There was no traffic, or none that we heard, on Haddington Road in front of us. We sat and waited in the moony calm. Then, in the distance, a soft splashing. John looked, and I followed his eyes. Far off, plish, plish, regular watery intervals. We looked and saw nothing. It became louder, still slow like a heartbeat, plish, plish, plish. We walked down the slope a few steps towards the edge of the canal and looked through the overhanging branches, waited while the sound came nearer. It was Sarah, walking purposefully towards us on the surface of the canal, each step bobbing unsteadily on the water, each one a slight splash. She stopped in front of where we were, standing still, moving slightly up and down on the curving swell of the canalflow. The dark water braided round her feet, flowing on around her. She raised a hand in greeting, then beckoned to us to join her. We didn't move. She walked a few steps towards the shore, smiled, and beckoned again. Hesitantly, John began to make his way through the grass and reeds to the water's edge. He stood there and looked back at me. Seagulls were flying over the houses towards Donnybrook. He looked back at Sarah; she waved at him energetically to come. She swayed with the rippling of the water moving slowly under her Converse runners. John looked back at me again, then placed one shaking foot over the edge into the water.

"Oh!" He gave a little cry as it plunged gracelessly under the surface, and he moved back, his shoe dripping. He looked up at Sarah. She smiled and beckoned to him again. He dipped the toe of his runner in but stood back on the bank and shook his head. Sarah walked slowly across to him, with a gentle shushing of disturbed water. Standing in front of him, she held out her hand. Slowly he stretched out to grasp it. He placed his foot gingerly on the water, and again with a gloop it went under, but Sarah pulled him in, taking his other foot after him, and hauled him up, where he too stood cautiously on the flow beneath, still holding on to her. With his other arm, he gestured to me. I climbed down too, leaned out and held John's warm hand, white with moon, staring at their rubber soles gently hugging the surface of the murky canal. I looked doubtfully up at him. He nodded, encouragingly. I put one foot out and tried to lean its weight on the water, but it went under and I withdrew it. The cold water began to seep through my socks.

Sarah grabbed my hand. I took a deep breath and put my boot out again. She pulled me forcefully and I tumbled into the cold water, sinking up to my knees, before she grabbed me up and I stood there beside the two of them. It was a giddying, wobbly, light-headed feeling, the sensation of thin flow underneath. We walked together to the centre of the canal and began making our way towards the lock, our six feet making a slight splashing noise against the yielding current, much faster and more forceful than it had looked, foaming, even, around our shoes. A rat scurried away in the undergrowth of the bank. Then we stopped and stood in a ring, all holding hands and looking at the sky and the water.

We remained there, standing in silence on the water of the Grand Canal. I wondered, idly, what it was we were waiting for, where it would go. The synchronicity of the night before drifted into my mind, *a dissolution of partnership.* I realised then, floating on the surface of the dirty canal water, that I was waiting for a vision, a crack of thunder in the sky which would make me change my name, re-convert me back out of this. For a long time it didn't come; I stood in the unbroken, dreamlike trance with the others, bobbing slowly up and down on the water. I feared then that it would not come at all; that I had gone too far in and would now never leave. The moonlight seemed perma-nent and timeless. I heard bells ringing in the distance. I cocked my head to listen, but the other two didn't react. I expected to hear the usual sounds drifting across the roofs to me, a verse of *Oranges and Lemons* or *Miserere Mei.* But the bells played neither of these things. I listened more carefully; it was a more chaotic, disordered metallic sound, the sound, I suddenly thought, of jewellery, of bracelets jangling. Then it seemed to me that across the rooftops from Rathgar there came the sound of Paula McVeigh getting ready for an evening out, an evening in the past, the ice cracking in a gin and tonic beside her on the dressing table, her husband conferring with Patrick's babysitter down-stairs. Slowly, the sound of Paula's rattling jewellery began to transform itself into singing, not the Latin harmonies I expected and feared, *cor mundum crea in me, Deus: et spiritum rectum innova in visceribus meis,* but the thin, shouting voice of a young working-class Dublin boy, scratchy and flat on the high notes, singing phonetically, without understanding them, the words of an Irish song he had learned in school:

Báidín Fhéilimí, d'imigh go Gabhla
Báidín Fhéilimí 's Féilimí ann.
Felim's little boat went to Gola
Felim's little boat with Felim in it

With a violent shock, the song roused me from my long slumber among the literati. As soon as I awoke, the bells were no longer ringing and the imagined singing was gone. Now there were only the real sounds of the city night, cars going by over the bridge, wind in the trees, an ambulance in the distance.

I sank with a greedy rush of freezing, dirty water, and gracelessly half-swam, half-waded to the bank where I dragged myself up, spluttering and dripping, my clothes sticking to my shivering body, covered in slime and leaves. Like frightened statues, Sarah and John remained, unable or unwilling to move, looking at me with wide, blank eyes, hands held limply between them. The ripples I had left spent themselves beneath their buoyant feet. Eventually, I pulled myself up and took one last look behind at where my companions stood, mesmerised, on the water. I trudged, drenched and freezing, back towards Trinity, leaving a single sodden trail of footprints behind me. The guards at Front Gate stared at me when I knocked, but let me through. Shaking, wet and cold, I made my way to Botany Bay and to the door of House 16. But when I looked up to my own room, I saw the light on. Through the window I could see three tall suited men walking back and forth in my room, moving things, searching. One of them came to the window and saw me; he beckoned to the others. I started to back away, squelching, and saw them move across the lighted space of the windows towards the door. I heard their footsteps battering down the stairs, so I turned and ran.

Still soaking, I ran across Front Square and out of Trinity, through the streets, guided by some new internal compass, gasping past puking revellers on Dame Street, Temple Bar, clusters of laughing gays on the pavement outside the George, up past drug pushers and chip eaters on Aungier Street, and over to Richmond Street, not looking down the canal for the silhouettes of Sarah and John. New tramlines had been laid down for the Luas light rail system, and I followed them as though they had replaced synchronicities and Pour Mieux Vivre as tracks to guide me through the world, until, almost dead with fear and fatigue, I arrived at my destination, the only place I could think of. I heard the quiet redbrick household awake a few moments after I pressed their bell, sensing the commotion before one, two, three, lights blinked on, with increasing intensity, bedside, landing, hall. Someone cautiously opened the door with the chain on, standing in her dressing-gown and nightdress.

"Yes?"

"It's Niall," I said.

"Niall! . . . what . . . ?" Paula took off the chain and let me in. "Are you okay?"

I didn't say anything.

"Come in, come in. Patrick! Patrick! Patrick, could you come down, please?" she called upstairs.

"You're soaking wet," she said. "Will I ring your parents?"

Patrick appeared at the door in his childish orange and yellow pyjamas.

"No, Mum, leave it. Niall . . . what happened?"

"I'm just . . . I can't sleep," I said.

"Patrick, bring him to the shower and get him something dry to put on."

I followed him upstairs to the McVeighs' bathroom, chaos of

brushes, magazines, bubble-baths, and half-empty bottles of hotel shampoo. Shivering, I peeled off my wet clothes, covered in slime and pieces of vegetation from the canal. My hair had pieces of branches in it, and my body stank of the dirty water. A dead worm was washed down the plughole. I gasped with relief as the steam hugged my body and the warm rivers cleaned my hair and revived the shrivelled skin of my body. Patrick gave me clean, hot press-smelling pyjamas to put on and brought me back down to the kitchen. Paula sat me down on a chair and felt my forehead.

"You might need to go the hospital. Can you tell me what happened? Did you take anything?"

I shook my head. "I was out of my mind . . . I fell into the canal. I just . . . I can't sleep . . . that's all . . . I can't sleep."

She took my temperature, then rummaged under a pile of magazines until she found a blood-pressure gauge. As it grasped me and hissed, she said it was fine. She checked my reflexes then, hitting my knees with the little hammer, knock-lift, knock-lift, like the clappers of a bell. She listened to my lungs and heart with a stethoscope, made me swear I hadn't taken anything.

"I swear."

"I'll ring your parents in the morning," she said. "You need to rest, I think that's all. And maybe to talk. Not now, of course."

She made up the bed in the spare room and brought me a glass of water.

"Call if you need anything," she said as she went to bed.

Patrick said good night to me and turned off the light.

I fell asleep.

Book Three

Nine

I thought that the story would end here, with the hallucinated fragment of an Irish children's song leading me
"home." This is not how it turned out: my association with
Pour Mieux Vivre was far from over, its many songs were still
unfinished. But for the time being, as I woke from my first real
night's sleep in nearly half a year, I was also waking from the
long, weird doze that had been my whole reality for so long, a
tired, dazed Rip Van Winkle. When I opened my eyes that
morning, far from being disoriented, it had seemed natural and
expected that I was in Patrick's, the usual pattern of the sunlight
dappled on the carpet by the trees in the McVeighs' big garden.
The room had the air of all guest bedrooms, silent and strange,
a chapel-like alienation from the rest of the house. In the corner
was a pile of old shoes, Paula's knee-high boots from the seventies, Patrick's old school runners. The desk beside the bed was
covered with a stack of folders and papers, a pile of Patrick's
school copies and textbooks.

Patrick McVeigh

Senior 2A

Latin

All this seemed right and familiar, and Pour Mieux Vivre entirely forgotten for the first minutes as I lay awake in bed. My initial instinct, the habit I had picked up during my long, lonely passion for Ian, was to feel for the latest scars and burdens of unrequited love, as a soldier in a field hospital checks, as his concussion fades, for where he has been hit by shrapnel. My first realisation was that I was no longer in love with Ian, a piece of knowledge which engulfed me in a huge white wave of relief. Feeling furiously light and unencumbered, I reconstructed my reality. Slowly, I grew to the knowledge that I was no longer seventeen, and began to move slowly ahead in time. I remembered leaving school, being rejected by Ian on his doorstep, moving into Botany Bay, meeting Fionnuala, being almost beaten up outside Hogan's, saved and taken home by a passing stranger. I remembered the short time of a busy social and academic life in Trinity, the parties in flats, the nights of drinking in the pubs of Dame and Dawson streets. I remembered the George, and I remembered Chris. I tried to remember what had happened with that story, if we were still seeing each other, and in an instant the whole of Pour Mieux Vivre, Sarah, John, all those months spent in waking trances, walloped me. A dream, I wondered for a moment, and when I realised it was no dream, the knowledge was too big; I could not look at it.

I heard Patrick downstairs. I took the towel and the clothes he had left for me on the chair, had a long shower, and went downstairs. I ate cereal at the table with Patrick while Paula moved around the kitchen behind us, avoiding me the way I was avoiding memories of the recent past. She left us alone. Patrick asked me if I had slept well, if I wanted anything more to eat. I asked him how he was, and he talked about Medicine in UCD, his classmates, his exams. I didn't even know what month it was. Ashamed to ask, I surreptitiously looked at the mast of the *Irish Times* lying on the table. It was May. Finally Patrick overcame the awkwardness and asked me if I was feeling "better." I said I was. There was a silence between us. He thought, I realised, that my jump into the canal had been a suicide attempt.

"I suppose you were depressed?" he tried. "And overworked. Mum said she ran into you in town and she thought you were overworked."

"Yes," I said, "I think I was."

"We were . . . I was worried when we didn't hear from you."

"Sorry. Yes, I think I was depressed. And drinking too much."

These things I said were as true as anything else, but in fact I found myself unable to think back at all except in little pieces; the last months were a dark shadow in the corner of a room which I could not look at—a little like the absence of Patrick's father, who was now a looming, ignored spectre in the house. I did finally say to Patrick that his mother had told me that he had gone. He nodded slowly, then paused, as if he was about to say something, thought the better of it and nodded slowly again. We moved back to talking about me.

I had attended more or less no classes since Christmas. This meant, Patrick pointed out, that even if I had been able to cover the material in the few weeks that remained, I was in any case barred by attendance regulations from sitting my final exams.

"I bumped in Fionnuala a few times," Patrick said. It was kind, somehow, the way he said her name so familiarly, as if to reassure me that our mutual world had moved on, had new characters we could refer to casually, as when we spoke of the boys from Gonzaga. It was as if to tell me I had survived. And this is how I felt, when he said it, looking at me with his brooding eyes, I felt I had only just about survived, washed up by luck on a hospitable island, concussed and confused, unsure of what ship I had been on or where it had been going when the typhoon struck. "She said the French and English departments were going mad looking for you."

"God, I suppose they were."

"Fionnuala thought I would know where you were; I thought your parents would know. They thought you were in college. I didn't let on there was trouble."

"Thanks."

An image flashed, sickeningly fast and bright, into my head, of an emaciated young man with boiling red cheeks, matted hair, and reptilian eyes pouring perfect lies into a public phone at the bottom of Grafton Street, a bag of books spilling onto the street at his feet. My stomach moved.

"Excuse me . . ." I began to Patrick, and, helping myself to my feet with the table, pulled open the french windows, and leaned over the edge of the McVeighs' patio to puke up my breakfast, soggy and white, onto Paula's flowerbeds. I leaned against the wall of the house with one arm, spitting the remainder into the drain. When I stood up, Patrick was standing at the open door with a glass of water and some tissues.

"Are you okay?"

"Yeah . . . it just kind of hit me . . . you know, that I behaved so badly."

"People were worried."

We went back inside and talked about my "situation." I could not sit the exams, and would have to repeat the year. If I repeated, however, I told Patrick, I lost my Beckett fellowship.

"Really?"

"Yes. I suppose I've lost it."

He looked at me with a hazel-coloured gaze of incomprehension. The Beckett was the me he knew, academic prizes, medals, head always down in the books. The thin, mad person who had managed to lose it was someone he didn't know.

Paula had come back into the room and was making tea. She dried her hands on the tea towel and sat down on the chair beside Patrick, opposite me. She sat on the edge, sort of sidesaddle, a noncommittal way of sitting down. It was a hot morning, a heat that seemed so unnatural for Ireland, that I had thought up to today that it was a result of the Pour Mieux Vivre hallucinations, rather than fossil fuels. Paula was wearing a thin black dress with no sleeves, under which I saw she had recently shaved her armpits. Sweat glistened on her temples under the sticky grey strands of her hair. She looked down at the table while we talked, Patrick asking me what exactly the regulations were, et cetera. When we reached, once more, the conclusion that my Beckett was gone, she said, rather wearily:

"Coffee?"

We sat drinking it, waiting for Paula to speak; she was the adult, after all, even if she had somehow been rendered less so since her abandonment. She clanked her rings against the mug, slowly and regularly. Clink. Clink. Clink. Clink. She was still wearing her wedding ring. She took a tired breath.

"Well, Niall, you *were* sick, weren't you?"

"I don't know . . . I suppose so. I don't know what it was." Again the dark shapes of the recent past shifted position a little in my mind, like sleeping dragons in their cave, and I waited a little before speaking to allow them to settle down, for fear they should make themselves visible. I cleared my throat. "I really don't know. I just lost the plot."

"I think you had some kind of nervous breakdown," Paula said. "In which case, it might be possible for me, acting as your doctor, to talk to Trinity and arrange something."

She looked into my eyes with her solid grey stare. Her eyes were deceived, tired, knowing, had seen it all. My memory of our last encounter was sketchy and unexamined, but her eyes held no affection for me, something even like distaste. She removed a stray lash from the corner of one of her eyes, making a long face and showing the yellowish edges of her eyeball as she did so.

"But I have a few conditions." She spelt them out on three ringed fingers. "One, I must talk to your parents about you.

Two, you must see a counsellor. I'll put you in touch with a girl I know out in Stillorgan who's very good. Three, if you feel something like this coming on again, you must talk to someone right away. And you go to your bloody classes next year. Is that agreed?"

"Thanks. Yes. Thank you so much."

"Don't thank me yet."

She called me a taxi to bring me home, and gave me thirty euro to pay for it. I offered to take the Luas into town and get the DART home, but she dismissed the suggestion with an impatient wave. As I said a clumsy goodbye in the hall, I saw the winter coat of a middle-aged man hanging on the stand, and a man's pair of galoshes in the corner. He would come back for them in the winter, I supposed, or buy new ones and let them gather dust here like a shrine. Now they were a phantom trace of an entirely different life, at once recent and prehistoric. Paula caught me looking at them and made a face, a thin grin referring to some irony which had more to do with the situation between her and myself than with Jim. Her final goodbye was quick and hard.

But she did save the day. She went in to talk to them in Trinity, outlining my medical condition, as she saw it, and made the case for my repeating the year and keeping the fellowship, and they agreed. I had two awkward meetings, one with Professor Dunne from French in her office smelling of photocopier and rosewater, who looked out the window at the five o'clock sun and shook her head sadly, as if what we were talking about had nothing to do with either her or me, but was a distant tragedy, beyond the influence of individuals, the cost of space exploration or the fate of Africa. She adorned her otherwise academic conversation with polished relics of slang, always somewhat dated and slightly inappropriate, like pieces of pop art among the watercolors of an underfunded local art museum.

"Attendance at classes and seminars is the name of the game. The *name of the game*." Or: "When I examined your file, Niall, it made me feel *blue*. It made me feel *very* blue."

The other interview, down the corridor in the School of English, was actually with sexy Jeremy Bodmoore, who was standing in for the Beckett Fellowship rep, Richard Ivory. Dr. Bodmoore tried to talk man-to-man, youth-to-youth with me, and did his utmost, with a distinct streak of almost pornographic voyeurism, to make me tell him exactly what had happened. Thrown into violent mental disarray at the thought of actually narrating what had gone on, I responded by flirting extraordinarily inappropriately with him, leaning over to touch pencils on his side of the desk as I emphasised a point, once tapping him on his inky hand to express my gratitude for his support, and a few times jestingly making fun of his upper-class British speech ("Well, it would be jolly rotten of them, I should think!"). When he asked direct or personal questions ("But if you don't mind me awsking, aw you *clase* to anyone in paticula?"), instead of answering, I giggled and blushed like a shy schoolgirl, all with the result that when I left his office, he was certainly left with the impression that the jury was out on my academic promise, but that what my doctor had been trying to hint to him was that in other respects I was not the full shilling.

My parents, naturally enough, convened a solemn meeting in the kitchen, while Ciara was sent over to her friend Anne-Marie's for the evening. They asked me what had been wrong, what I had been doing, who I had been seeing, how I had been feeling. They were of course deeply troubled by events, but this was, I suspected, tinged with a certain amount of jealousy for my having gone to Paula McVeigh and not to them in my time of distress. I underlined, or rather exaggerated, the random nature of my crossing paths with Paula, the odd pattern of coincidence which caused me to run into her. And I also told them how the text messages to them (the deception involved in these being one of their most wounded concerns) had been my major solace, my only point of contact with reality. In a weird way—not the way I implied, obviously—this was true, but I had not the strength or stomach to pull up the actual technicolor memories before me, and so this account came as easily to me as any other.

I moved home, back to my own bedroom with its view of the garden and childish posters on the walls. I came just with what I had, my canal-fouled garments in a Marks & Spencer's bag, and an outfit borrowed from Patrick. For around a week I survived on my father's socks and adolescent clothes I hadn't bothered to bring in to Trinity, but finally mustered the courage before the weekend and asked Patrick to come in and help me move out of Trinity.

The resentful look and smell of the room unnerved me. As we gathered up my boxes and papers, I did my utmost to stow the memories and doubts deep down in my mind, just as we packed my clothes, bedding, and toiletries into a series of bags and boxes to carry back to Sandycove on the DART.

The following weeks of living back there were restful and in ways idyllic. I had a routine—what depressed people needed, Paula had told me—in synch with my parents and sister, coffee and radio in the morning, a walk to Caviston's delicatessen to buy lunch, where I stood in line with old people and housewives to buy sausage rolls and sun-dried tomato salad, walks on the seafront in the afternoon, my mother's dinner in the evenings, tea in front of the television with my parents and Ciara at night. I kept myself on a secret diet of strictly no reading, despite the kind-hearted gifts of books from relations who had heard I had had what my mother called "a turn." Patrick was studying for and then doing his exams, but we met up once or twice a week for a cinema excursion. He always came out to me, on the Luas and DART, and we watched something in the omniplex in Dún Laoghaire. The sound of that time is the ring of Patrick at the door as I sit at the kitchen table with my parents and Ciara, drinking tea, surrounded by the remains of dinner, a few stray green beans on the plate, small pools of melted ice cream with crumbs of apple tart at the bottom of our bowls. Our expeditions were always arranged in advance, so Patrick's ring was always known and expected, a predicted jangling which signalled the regularity of the world of the southern suburbs, schoolfriends growing older, like their fathers, solid red-brick terraces, immutable, immanent repetitions, the sound of the ancient Gregorian chant we repeated in the Gonzaga choir. *Resurrexit! sicut dixit.* We stayed away from Patrick's not only because of a tacit understanding that now Paula and I did not get on, but also because I was keeping so resolutely away from town that Rathgar seemed dangerously close to its gates, and thus to those of my own memories. In Dalkey, Blackrock, and Carrickmines there were no memories, only the slow ticking of the days, unpunctuated by pealing bells.

My only moment of energy or creativity was on Tuesdays and Fridays when I got the 46A into Stillorgan to see Deirdre, my counsellor. She received me in her yellow-walled office, full of what I had expected from such a place, boxes of tissues, comfortable, non-confrontational seating arrangements, cheery posters with morale-boosting slogans—a cat suspended from a washing line saying "Hang in There"—and books with titles like *Boys' Talk, Old Age and How to Survive It* or *You and Your Teenager.* Deirdre was around forty, slim and slightly nunnish. She had a stale, sweetly perfumed sense of humour, and her little jokes—I could tell that in her mind she called them her "little jokes"— had the feel of the air in a soap shop, or an incense-heavy occult bookstore. ("Well, you're the first nineteen-year-old I ever heard of to have a conflict with his parents, so you are!" "So what attracted you to this Ian? Did he look like *Tom Cruise?*")

Her strategy was to make me talk, and in this I offered no resistance. I poured lies into her ears, painted them energetically over the bright walls of that office, into its potted plants and radiators, things I knew she wanted to hear, extravagantly expanded and elaborately refined. She wanted to know what had happened. I had no intention of splashing around in even the shallowest waters of that murky sea, and so Deirdre sat through hour after hour of my own inventions. I would plan them on the 46A on the way in to her, recalling what I had told her the week before and how she had reacted. I wanted her to feel she was helping me make progress (I liked her enough to want to boost her professional self-esteem), that what I said was profoundly painful to go over, and especially that it was unexpected, a surprise even to me.

I became more ambitious and set myself the goal in each session of moving myself to tears with my own lies. Most days I managed a trickle; some days, when the muse got me and the stories really flowed, I would sob until I lapsed into an asthmatic wheezing and leaked snot onto her carpet. On days when I was tired or off form, or when the truth of Pour Mieux Vivre and the rest of it threatened to bubble up in my brain and its suppression demanded all my forces, and my eyes remained obstinately dry, I would try and look pale and shocked, speak in a deep, gravelly voice: this is too serious for tears, I would imply. Deirdre loved my custom. The talk she elicited from me was flowing, improving, and above all full of precisely those themes she had been trained to look out for, which her usual run of fat or bullied twelve-year-olds and needy spouses did not always provide. I thought through plausible but interesting explanations for what had gone on in my second and third terms at Trinity. I told her I had had a breakdown because I couldn't cope with being gay; for no good reason I decided to give Ian a starring role in my mental life, and told her after a few weeks that, with her help, I was realising that I had a lot of "baggage" (I thought that word would be a hit with Deirdre and I was not wrong: "So Niall, getting back to this *baggage* . . .") left over from my friendship with him. I said I was paranoid, and at her suggestion affirmed ("You know, Deirdre, I think you might be right there,

God I never looked at it that way before . . .") that I had difficulty distinguishing fact from fiction, suffered from insomnia and hallucinations, that I told lies.

Deirdre was the focal point of whatever creative energies I had left, but she also provided the possibility of construing for myself a narrative of the recent past that avoided the truth. This way, the actual facts pursued me less when I was at home or out with Patrick, and my days were largely peaceful ones. I enjoyed the familiarity of all the people I met, my parents' friends who came to the house, or whom I encountered in the tennis club when I went down with my mother in the evenings sometimes to watch my father play, and Ciara's friends from Muckross, some of them sisters of my old Gonzaga classmates. I liked asking about them, what they were doing now, if they liked college, who they still saw from school, tell them I said hello. I felt angry at myself for losing a year like this, and hated the feeling of being out of synch.

I e-mailed Fionnuala and asked her if she would come out to Sandycove and meet me for lunch beside the sea. It was a few days before she answered. She agreed, tersely, to meet, but said she was busy studying for the exams and couldn't come out all the way to me, and suggested we meet in the Buttery. I didn't want to go into town, and so suggested a compromise in a cafe in Donnybrook, at the perilous edge, which she agreed to. She arrived a little late, looking slightly nervously from side to side, a face that made me feel she had only finally decided to come at the last minute. I was sitting at the window beside the zooming cars, but she couldn't see me when she came in and stood at the counter scanning the room.

"Fionnuala . . ." I half-stood and called to her. She came over and took her coat off. Her hair was tied up.

"Hi," I said. She gave a tight smile and sat down.

"Thanks for coming."

"Sure. I can't stay long . . ."

"I know, exams. I'm not . . . you might have heard."

"I presumed."

The Italian waitress came over and we ordered. I asked her how the exams were going, and—decent, intelligent Fionnuala! —she used the opportunity to shift the focus from the apology she knew would be the centrepiece of our meeting. She filled me in on what had happened during the semester, what courses had gone well, who had been a bastard in the correction of Hilary term essays, what lectures had been inspiring, brilliant, or boring. She told me what papers she would have to sit and when, how she was prepared. She'd applied for a scholarship to go to Paris during the summer. Finally, however skilfully crafted her conversation was in weaving something in common between us, the weight of what had happened was too much. The knowledge between us of our prematurely terminated friendship, my unkind behaviour and slide into madness, was too heavy, and the talking ground to a halt. I blurted out to her that I was sorry and she nodded.

She was a pleaser, but also a person with real, if few, limits, and she was not going to shoot off into a cheery flow of Belfast diphthongs and ironic asides. Her eyes grew wider and looked me up and down, as if I were a strange animal uncovered in a garden shed. I repeated it. She paused, reflected, then said:

"Okay."

"I'm ashamed. I was sick."

"I know. Patrick told me. Are you . . . better?"

"I think I was depressed. I just couldn't handle things. I lashed out," I went on, thinking how quickly I had absorbed Deirdre's vocabulary, "I lashed out at those closest to me. Which includes you, of course. I'm seeing a counsellor. But I needed just to snap out of a spiral, you know."

"To mix metaphors," she said, and gave a sad smile. This joke, once the stuff of our interactions, here, in the postlapsarian world of coffee in Donnybrook, made our friendship seem so irretrievably lost.

"I am sorry for how I treated you," I said. "It wasn't me. Can I ask you to think of it that way? It was someone else."

She didn't say anything to this, just steered the conversation back to the common ground, how James was (dumped, by her), gems of Andrea's, inane, funny, cutting, or spot-on in a way no one else would have noticed, romances of classmates, big nights out. All I had missed but all, she was trying to make it clear, still there for me to come back to. We parted without making any new arrangement to meet. I wished her luck in the exams, and told her to let me know how she got on.

"Good luck," was what she called to me as we parted. I hurried to the 46A bus stop as quickly as I could. It was midday, and the Angelus was being rung from steeples in town. I wanted to go before I could hear names of London churches being sounded in the peals, baroque harmonies beginning to be added to the plainchant.

I stayed away from town, and between the calm passage of the Sandycove days and the frenetic, colourful outlet of my mendacious two hours a week in Stillorgan with Deirdre, threatening thoughts of Sarah, John, and Pour Mieux Vivre began to recede into the distance. I even started to read a little, tentative excursions with newspapers and novels, but I was always careful to keep a flow and uninterrupted rhythm, not to focus on any word or sentence out of the absolute context of what came before and after it.

By the time the Trinity exams were over, in June, and Fionnuala texted me asking me to come into town to celebrate with her and the others, I felt I could safely venture in, and that the city as I had lived it through Pour Mieux Vivre would remain securely obscured beneath the palimpsest of this new life. I asked Patrick to come along, partly as a precaution, and partly as an alibi of sorts, since my relationship with Fionnuala was of course strained, and my acquaintance with the rest of the

Trinity crowd now long out of date. Patrick had finished his exams a few days previously and was enthusiastic about the plan, most likely relieved that we were doing something to break the tedium of my halfway-house accompanied trips to the cinema.

We met in O'Neill's on Suffolk Street, in a way the primal scene of all the trouble, where I had witnessed my first *sortes*, so I started the evening nervous and afraid. I dreaded flashbacks to the forbidden memories of my time with John and Sarah. But our group was sitting in a snug at the window, and the flashbacks remained at bay. As I hoped, the old voices of the place were drowned out by the louder shouts of this rediscovered vernacular reality, its signs overwritten by new symbols, larger and inkier; it was as if the smoking ban had chased those old ghosts away along with the ashtrays and clouds of tobacco. Andrea was delighted to see Patrick; his shyness, awkwardness, and unexpected sullen silences had given him something like a cult status with her. She made him sit with her and her friends, and he turned scarlet while they complimented his clothes and tan and haircut and shoes, even his "muscles." Fionnuala and I relaxed with one another a little by virtue of the mediation of the alcohol, atmosphere, and most of all our classmates. She even sang her party-piece, *Carrickfergus*, with another girl from the north, in defiance of the hushing of the bar-staff. Most of us joined in, along with a few smiling strays from neighbouring tables.

> I wish I was in Carrickfergus
> Only four nights in Ballygrand
> I would swim over the deepest ocean
> The deepest ocean my love to find

It was pleasant, nearly moving, to hear the two girls sing in their shared accent, the vowels of their own place, their own childhoods and pasts, far from here.

But the sea is wide and I cannot swim over
And neither have I the wings to fly
If I could find me a handsome boatman
To ferry me over to my love and die.

Even Andrea, who hated pub and party singing above almost anything else, knew the chorus and enjoyed the rebellion of the event, banging her glass in time. I felt warm and involved and full of quiet hope for what might come of this, Fionnuala and I friends again, Patrick here, out with my college friends, years of this camaraderie.

We left the pub early to join the Students' Union end-of-the-year party, the usual lowest common denominator of '80s and '90s music, in Club Nassau across the road from Trinity. On the way there, Andrea, slightly hyper from the singing in O'Neill's, insisted we sing an Irish song, and chose the most well-known, Chris's childhood party piece. The northerners did not know it. Andrea and the others only knew a sketchy outline of the lyrics; Patrick and I, ever the swots, had to lead the way as our group banged out the first verse raucously along Nassau Street.

Báidín Fheilimí d'imigh go Gabhla
Báidín Fheilimí is Feilimí ann

Felim's little boat went to Gola
Felim's little boat with Felim in it

The nightclub was full of acquaintances from our year, for me a strange reunion from the distant early weeks of Michaelmas term, before the George and before my life in the cult, as I now called it to myself. I had a long shouted conversation with Jayne at the bar, about guys and college and life and parents, and I thought that maybe next year I might even come out to her and Andrea and Fionnuala, maybe even to Patrick and

Ciara. We joined the others on the dance floor. Fionnuala and her northern friend Caroline were organising some kind of line of dancing moves with clapping and turning and hand gestures, and Andrea was getting stiff-limbed Patrick to dance *Pulp Fiction*-style with her.

The music changed to something slower and contemporary, and we all stayed, swept up and engulfed by the beat, moving and interacting in a tight, happy circle. I was interrupted as Eileen from Carlow tapped me on the shoulder and said something in my ear. I couldn't hear her above the music.

Pass me your hand, show me your face
Now that the day's run out of pace
"What?" I leaned my ear down to her.
Love is what I ask, no less
"There's someone . . ." Her words degenerated into an itchy buzz in my ear. She tried twice more, and when I still couldn't follow what she was saying, she pulled my sleeve and pointed to a man standing on the edge of the dance floor, a man standing rigidly still, not moving in any way to the music or in reaction to the people pushing to and fro past him. Eileen left me to join the others. I squinted at the man through the lights and dry ice, standing like the silhouette of a statue, his gaze fixed straight ahead, as if he were the only person in the room, and I made my way cautiously through the dancers towards him. I dropped my vodka and tonic on the floor when the figure focused into a recognisable shape. It was John.

I stopped dead in my tracks, the unnoticed broken glass on the floor in front of me. Hard to make out in the midst of this massive laughing, dancing crowd, he sporadically disappeared into blackness and was lit up suddenly by the white flash of the strobe light, so that with the ultraviolet blue of his light-coloured T-shirt and his dark hair, he looked headless, a terrifying visitation from my past, illuminated by lightning in instantaneous but full bursts of vision.

You know what I want to know

I stood still, transfixed with horror as John flashed on and off in front of me, unsure if it was one of the violent mental reappearances of the past which I feared, the underground spring of memories finally bursting through, or if it was really him, returned from the underworld to call me back. I looked behind me, saw Patrick, Fionnuala, and Andrea in jerky, electric tableaux of laughter and dance, then walked forward to John.

He looked at the ground, then asked me with a movement of his head to follow him away from the dance floor. We left the main room, closed the door on the noise of the music, and stood in the lobby, watched by the bouncers at the door to the street and the girl at the cloakroom desk. John looked like a shipwreck. His hair was in wild disarray, his eyes were dark-ringed and bloodshot, he had lost weight and his clothes were crumpled and frayed. His bottom lip was cut. I wondered how they had let him in.

"I don't want to see you," I said to him. "I can't see you. . . ."

He stared at the ground.

"I mean it, really, John. This will kill me. I've nothing to say to you. It nearly ruined my life and I'm out of it. I don't even remember what went on between the three of us, and I'm trying to make sure I forget it forever. It's over, over, *over*, I'm rebuilding the bridges I—"

"Okay, okay, I get the message. I didn't come here for one of your speeches." John continued to stare at the floor. Then, suddenly he lifted his head and looked directly at me, dark eyes surrounded by millions of tiny swollen veins of red.

"Niall—"

"What?"

He looked at the floor again. "I have to ask you for help," he muttered.

"Money?"

He shook his head.

"So what is it?"

He said nothing.

"John, I'm in a new life now, goodbye, don't come near me again," I said with conviction, and opened the door to go back into the club. The sound of the disco came rushing out into the lobby. John put his arm across the door in front of me, barring me from opening it any further. The bouncers looked at one another.

"Steady there, lads . . ." one of them said threateningly. John dropped his arm.

"Please, Niall, wait."

Inside, I caught a glimpse of my friends—as I now, rather prematurely, thought of them, on the dance floor. Andrea was leaning on Jayne's shoulder to shout something in her ear. Harry and Eileen were queuing at the bar. Fionnuala, Caroline, and a self-conscious but increasingly daring Patrick were doing Cossack dancing together in a circle. John pushed the door shut. I hesitated for a moment, then thought of them all swept up in the eddies and whirls of their interactions inside, thought of John and Sarah staring like zombies at me from the surface of the Grand Canal, and I pulled the door open again.

"Come on now, lads, make up your minds," one of the bouncers said. "In or out."

I stared defiantly at John.

"I've made up mine," I said.

"Niall . . ." he croaked, "listen, please."

Again I hesitated. "Quickly, then, tell me what you want."

He looked to the bouncers and then the cloakroom girl and then at me, pleadingly, indicating the door to the street with a nod.

"Come back to the flat," he said.

"No, tell me here or don't tell me at all."

He mumbled something hoarsely. I closed the door behind me and asked him to repeat it.

"Sarah's gone," he said.

"What do you mean, gone?"

He looked pleadingly again from the bouncers to me and indicated the door outside again.

"Okay, but make it quick," I conceded.

John and I walked up the steps and through the usual cluster of smokers standing on the path outside the club, talking and laughing loudly. The weather was so unusually warm that we were not cold, even in our T-shirts.

"Can we move a little away from the crowd?"

"If you want," I said indifferently.

We walked a little up Kildare Street, away from the smoking clubbers, and stood outside the Earl of Kildare hotel. The sleepy young man attending the phone and bell behind the desk looked at us for a moment without interest. John stood with his arms crossed and his hands under his armpits.

"Well?" I demanded.

"I told you . . ." he started impatiently, raising his voice, then stopped and calmed himself. He said slowly, with a painful patience: "Sarah is missing."

"What are you talking about? What do you mean, missing? Since when?"

"For about two weeks."

"Go on."

"I . . . she . . . we . . . I mean, she hasn't shown up for two weeks."

"You mean the synchronicities are broken? You could always meet like everyone else, John. Text each other."

He ignored this, and went on:

"She left the flat one morning and she never came back."

"Just like that."

"She had started going off on her own. And sometimes I wouldn't be able to find her with the books. She got all secretive. She had stopped letting me read the e-mails to Luis. One day, she slipped out the door with a suitcase while I was distracted. We were in the flat together and she packed in front of me. I didn't know what she was doing until I realised she was gone. She got me to do some bullshit job out on the balcony, pulling the ivy off the windows, and when I came back inside she was gone."

"Her rooms in Trinity?"

"Empty. All her stuff is gone. She surrendered her keys. They've already rented it out to tourists."

"Galway?"

He shook his head, then exhaled and looked up at the sky.

"Luis?" I asked. The names of this lost world, *sortes, synchronicities, Luis,* were sunk deep down, to find them I had to drag the lightless depths, net them and haul them up with a creaking winch. But then when they fell off my tongue, they were light and quick, with a silvery sheen, like stars, a seductive twinkle. "Email him."

laninahillen@eurosur.org, I remembered to myself.

"No answer."

"Well, ring him, or whatever."

"I have no way of getting in touch with him. I've never met him either," he added defensively.

"Neither do I," I said. "So maybe this is your cue to leave, like I did. No more books. Get a job. Get some friends."

He shook his head.

"No. It's too late for me. I have to know more. I have to go on. They can't just leave me like this. *This is death.*" His eyes were wild with panic.

"What do you want me to do, John?"

He stared at me pathetically, imploringly.

"Help me find her, Niall. Come back. Please. You're the only one who can help me find her. I need her. Without it, without her, there is nothing."

"Where do you think she is?"

"I don't know."

"Have you been to the Gardaí?"

He shook his head.

"Why not? It's the Guards you need, John, not me."

He turned away, looked over at the buildings on the other

side of the street, the quiet red brick of the Alliance Française. He cleared his throat and, still looking away, said:

"You know very well. Look, Niall . . . we were . . . we . . . it looked like Luis was going to start telling us stuff. You know, the important things. Bring us to the next level. I think she's gone after him to find out herself. The Guards would only fuck things up . . . Niall, help me. I need to know. You can help me find her. The books lead me nowhere."

He gulped down a loud sob and turned away again to stare at the dark windows of the Alliance, ashamed. I reflected. My mind was strangely empty, apart from the sight of the street, which seemed like two streets, layered one on top of the other, the solid surface street I had so recently regained, and a sleek, shining darker one beneath, from which John had come. Seconds, minutes passed, John breathed loudly, and still I didn't answer him. Finally, I turned to him and opened my mouth, unsure what would come out.

"No, John, I won't help you," was what I said, in a voice which was definitive, deliberate, unadorned and univocal, where around the figure of John the world was becoming vacillating, swirling, complex and polyphonic. "No," I continued in this plain and direct tone I recognised from certain conversations I had had with Deirdre. "My only solid recollection of what it was like when I was playing book-club with you is that it was, as you say, death. I'm not going back to it, not for anything. I am finished with your underworld. I choose life. It has been a pleasure, really. Now good luck."

I turned away from him and stood still before walking away, slowly and purposefully, towards the club, waiting for him to call me back. If he does, I thought, just one more time, I know I will give in. I stopped at the edge of the group of smokers, breathing in the tobacco on the summer air, lost in their chatter. Before I went down the steps inside, I cast a last backward glance up Kildare Street. John was sitting on the path slumped against the railings, his head in his hands, motionless. I paused, looking at him, at the two streets swimming before my eyes, old Kildare and new Kildare. I turned around, showed my stamped hand to the bouncers and walked back into the club. Through the crowds of rising senior freshmen I saw Patrick, Fionnuala, Andrea, my future, dancing and drinking. The music swelled in my ears. I let the door swing closed behind me and walked in, with the surreal impression that the bouncers were bystanders who knew more than they let on, surly guardian angels sighing with relief for my decision.

Then, perhaps it was some faded memory of the day he had plucked me, a stranger, from the concrete of Georges Street and carried me home, or perhaps a re-remembered sexual desire, or just the obvious and dangerous pull of the *sortes,* but, in any case, gripped with a sudden change, or doubt, of heart, I stopped in my tracks, turned around, and ran back up the steps, outside. The bouncers looked at one another and raised eyebrows. I emerged onto the street and looked up to where he had been, but he had gone. I stood where I had left him in a heap against the railings and scanned the empty granite pavement. I walked a little way up the street, calling his name, stony echo, softly and then louder. I walked as far as the corner of Molesworth Street, watched with mild interest by the Garda on duty outside Leinster House, then turned to go back to the disco lights and my friends, for he had gone, off towards the canal, into the darkness, alone.

Ten

This incident, too, my first temptation, was surprisingly easy to suppress from my conscious mind. After I returned to the club I danced the night away with the others without a further thought for John; in fact, by the end of the night I was not at all convinced that he had really shown up. Once or twice I thought I saw Pablo Virgomare through the dry ice, dancing on his own, or grinning down at me, smoking in the middle of the group outside, but they were apparitions, fleeting and false. Fionnuala was going to Belfast the next day and flying straight from Aldergrove to Paris for the summer the following week, so we said goodbye on the pavement outside, a quick and uncompromising hug with ringing ears and vodka-tonic breath. Patrick said his own goodbyes, with much kissing and laughing, and headed up Kildare Street towards the Canal and Rathgar. I got a taxi, the way I supposed John would have gone, if he indeed had been there at all, along Merrion Square and Lower Mount Street, shared as far as Foxrock with Andrea. Bravely, I looked out at the old flat on Northumberland Road as we drove by, but the lights were all out; it did not look like anyone was at home.

By now the problem of the Beckett, thanks to Paula, had been resolved: it would start again in October and I wouldn't lose the year. It did leave, however, the problem of the summer. I had no savings, and for the past month had been surviving on handouts from my parents. Concerned as they were for my well-being after what my aunt described as my "few nerves," they would have made no complaint had I continued my convalescence in this way until term, rooms, and Beckett started again in October. It was a comforting thought and a surprising relief to me, that the leaves would fall, that a new season would, as sure as death, come around again. But I decided that I was now well enough to embark on a more normal and full life than the gentle round of charity at home could provide. Ciara, who was working full-time in Dunne's Stores in Dún Laoghaire, was irritated by my constant idle presence, and I could see my parents worried that I would slide into a stupor from which I might never recover. So I started looking around for a job near me, left in an application at Spar in Sandycove, at Bulloch Harbour old folk's home in Dalkey, braving the eagle-eyed, corporate nuns who ran it, and at print shops, pubs, and supermarkets in Dún Laoghaire. My parents were keen for me to work in a bookshop, since it seemed more fitting for a scholar than selling *Lotto* tickets or mopping up octogenarian urine, but however much I felt I had found the straight road again, this seemed a risk hardly worth taking, a dried-out alcoholic accepting work behind a bar.

Patrick phoned me at the beginning of July, as I dithered about these local activities, to tell me his father had decided to rent him a flat in town. The reasons for this were not immediately clear. His father, from the bachelor comforts of his new apartment in Mount Merrion and the arms of his nubile companion, felt guilty about leaving him behind to be the man of the house, I supposed. More interestingly, it turned out to be

Paula's idea. Patrick told me she had decided that "to get on with her life," she needed her son out of the way so she could face up to the reality of the empty nest. Otherwise (I quote from my imagination), she would become "an oul one muttering about things that happened twenty and thirty years ago." She needed the clean break to accept the change, she told Patrick, and I was sure it was true: Paula was, above all things, determined to be absolutely up to date, not to be left in the slipstream. But I also knew, as Patrick did, without saying so, that she did it mostly for him, so that he wouldn't waste his time and energy with guilt and self-recrimination, forced to be the man of the house just when he should be off sowing his wild oats. Anyway, the point was that in the end, someone, Paula, Patrick, or Jim, had found this two-bedroom basement flat below an office on Baggot Street, at an extraordinarily low rent for the location, and Jim was to pay Patrick's half of the rent for at least the summer. The idea was that I would move into the other room, and Patrick and I would live like two unmarried gents from Dickens or Wilde, rooming together in the city. When Patrick suggested it to me, during a walk up to the Martello tower on the Sandycove seafront, I saw us dressing for dinner, dining in the Savoy, and drinking champagne backstage with disreputable actresses. So vivid were these improbable imaginings, in fact, that I almost hesitated to accept for fear that it was a return to the intrusions of unreality from which I had suffered before. But it did not seem premature to leave Sandycove and go back to town. So I said yes.

I found a well-paid part-time job as a data-enterer and occasional teller in the Educational Building Society on Westmoreland Street, within almost literal view of the back wall of my building in Botany Bay. It was an undemanding enough job, we had two days' training in, and then I entered names and addresses in the back room, or occasionally helped facilitate deposits in the front. I worked only three days a week, Tuesdays,

Wednesdays, and Thursdays, but the money was good. The work unfailingly kept up my interest, and in fact the whole mechanism of the place was a human, sane, daylight version of the *sortes,* whereby the undifferentiated crowd which surged up and down Westmoreland Street to and from O'Connell Bridge would manifest itself before my glass pane in the form of an individual, whose provenance, class, accent, age, and bank balance were entirely unpredictable. Broken off from the pack, they became numbers, values, genealogies of deposits and withdrawals, with strange meanings and histories of their own.

Our flat was small and bright, for a basement, with a sitting room facing out onto the street railings, in which Patrick and I would drink tea or beer at nights, a kitchen where we tried to cook dinners in a rota, and in the back, looking out onto an abandoned yard, our bedrooms, Patrick's neat, well-decorated and nicely furnished, and mine, a vigilantly bookless space with a bed, chair, table, and the adolescent touch of a pile of clothes on the floor.

I met Paula once. I phoned her at home in Rathgar, but she was reluctant to meet; she pretended to be pleased that I had phoned. She said she'd ring me the next time she was in town, I could meet her after work for a drink. Of course I never heard from her, so the following Monday, a day I didn't work, I stole into Patrick's room and went through his address book to find her mobile number. I called her the next day at half-five when I left the EBS. Her "Hello?," that of someone who doesn't recognise the number flashing on their mobile screen, was apprehensive, but, I thought guiltily, a little hopeful. Perhaps she thought it was Jim on a new phone, with a new heart, or some independent interest of her own, a divorced man she knew from the hospital. Or just the slim but appealing possibilities of any mystery in a daily round where all names are preprogrammed. The hope failed when she heard the voice of her son's unstable schoolfriend.

"Oh, hello, Niall."

I told her I had just finished work and, if she was in town, maybe we could have that drink. She hesitated, deeply unwilling, but the noise of people and traffic in the background made it obvious she was in town. She thought for a moment about inventing an excuse, but instead resigned herself to an hour in my company, I thought because the pretexts which suggested themselves to her were either so dull or so fantastically divorced from mundane reality that she could see no bearable alternative. She said since I worked straight across from it we could go to Bewley's on Westmoreland Street; I suggested Dunne & Crescenzi, and we met there twenty minutes later. I said I would murder a glass of wine after work, would she share a bottle.

Paula had a cappuccino and nothing to eat while I had a desultory single class of Chianti and *brusketta*. She looked tired, not the dramatic exhaustion of the time our paths had crossed on Moore Street just after Jim had left, but a bored weariness, the look of someone who has calculated, as in the religion-class conundrum, what eternity is. I chattered away about my job, gas tales of mad clients, was vulgarly effusive in my thanks agains to her for saving my skin, was shrill and brittle in my gossiping about the few mutual acquaintances we had, boys and their boring parents from a dead world, who meant little to me and nothing to her. She gave me only the responses and thin smiles needed for a minimum level of politeness, and seemed embarrassed by me in front of the other tables. She visibly wished me to keep my voice down and to cut out the slightly camp affection and intimacy I was trying to show between us. I asked how she was coping without Jim. She said it was difficult to explain the ins and outs of a quarter century-long marriage to someone as young as me, and that she had to go, she had a friend coming over to dinner. I walked her to the carpark on Drury Street. On the way, now the embarrassment of the other diners' listening was gone, she made some conversational effort with me, but whereas in our early meetings she had reached across the barriers between us, now she talked to me in the withered talk of mothers to their children's schoolfriends, how was I enjoying my independence, when did college start, what did I want to do afterwards, if Ciara was doing the Leaving this year, tell my mother she was asking for her. When we said goodbye at the entrance to the parking lot, she patted me on the shoulder in a distant way. I realised that she was not withholding, that she held no grudge against me, things were not in any crisis that would be resolved: she was just someone starting to live out a long epilogue to her story.

I walked home to Baggot Street, thinking of her and her place in my cosmology, with the idea that she, or at least someone else on her behalf, had made false promises. Paula was a disappointment, I said, almost out loud, to myself. Or rather not Paula, but this whole other story of which she was supposed to be a cardinal point of reference, the patron saint. The lights were not on in the flat; Patrick was out. It was around eight, still bright, but the shadows were long and streets peaceful, starting the patient wait to nightfall. Instead of going in, I kept on walking, allowing my feet to take me wherever they wanted, something I had not been able to do when my thoughts and movements had been ruled by the *sortes*. I crossed the canal and soon found myself walking steadily down Northumberland Road. I stopped at the old house, and looked up at the side window of our flat. The thin white curtains were drawn; there was no light on inside. I walked up to the front door and looked at the names on the bell. Our one, which used to have a crumpled scrap with *"PMV"* written in biro, was now empty. I rang the bell and heard it sound in the distance. No one came down. I rang and rang, but I had the definite impression that it was ringing into a void, a long-forgotten mess, a plurality of bottles and books left to their own silent and inhuman devices. I stayed ringing for some time, taking my finger off only when the shrill sound was likely to start offending the neighbours. As I walked back to Baggot Street, it continued to ring in my head, slowly morphing itself into the beginnings of the psalm for Ash Wednesday.

incerta et occulta sapientiae tuae manifestasti mihi

I was relieved to find the light on and Patrick in, waiting for me. As with the earlier chance meetings, I instinctively and inexplicably kept him in the dark about seeing his mother. He had plans for the evening, which he wanted me to participate in, a crowd of UCD people going to a gig in Whelan's, a girl he was interested in would be there. He said it to me, I thought, in a way that did not assume a mutual interest, a hint, I thought, that he knew I was gay and could come out to him whenever I wanted. No rush, he seemed to say, there's time enough between us, time enough. In our to-ing and fro-ing between bathroom and bedrooms, casual shirts and aftershave, and the sound of Patrick inexpertly mixing himself a gin and tonic, trying to follow unclear memories of how his mother did it, and of his phone bleeping with messages from the others who were to join us there, my melancholy, Paula, her oldness, and especially John and the flat in Northumberland Road, sank out of my consciousness again. I really am cured, I thought, I amn't going back, it really is over. Paula had disappointed me, but this kind of night, the whirlpool of my coevals in Dublin pubs on a midsummer's night, contained an essential core of attraction, the sense that I might find something I was looking for there. At least here, the sense of a story continuing.

And as it happened, I did find something I was looking for, another loose end to be tied up, or rather a knot which needed to be undone. At the gig, I saw Chris in a group. I was afraid to approach him, since, after all, our last interaction had been my leaving him standing waiting for me on Capel Street Bridge. Instead, I watched him from afar, in the usual pose, carrying pints through the crowd from the bar. Finally, I took my phone out and called his number and waited to see what he would do.

He felt it vibrating in his pocket as he distributed the last of the drinks to his friends. I watched as he took it out and saw the surprise on his face when he saw my name flashing on the screen. He hesitated and was, I thought, about to put the phone back in his pocket to let me ring out, but with a change of heart he pressed the answer button and held it to his ear. I hung up and pushed through the crowd of Patrick's friends to go over and greet him.

He laughed when he saw me, and patted me on the shoulder in greeting.

"I don't fuckin believe it. Yeh brassnecked oul hussey!"

The band was playing, so he had to cup his hands around my ear and shout. The soft touch of skin on skin and his warm breath caused me to remember our two nights together and to wish for a third. I asked him if he wanted to stand in a quiet corner and catch up. I knew I owed him an apology, I said. He told me he was "with people" that night, but that we should get together. We made an arrangement to meet for a pint after the weekend, after work some evening, I promised to text him with particulars. He laughed and said he knew my promises, but good luck to me anyway.

Of course, Chris didn't realise that I was a changed man, that I was now, in fact, a man. I texted him the following Sunday night and we arranged to meet in the bar of the Irish Film Institute for a pint on the Thursday. Patrick knew something was up, probably even guessed that I had a date. Things had gone well between him and Melanie, the med student he had been interested in. The three of us, in fact, shared a taxi back to Baggot Street, and had a nightcap in the living room together. I pleaded tiredness halfway down the rather tepid gin and tonic, and left them to it. I crossed her, a smiling and confident person who made me feel steady on my feet, in the kitchen early the next morning, as, with hangovers, we drank the coffee I made before running out to our respective summer jobs. Sex was extraordinarily taboo between

Patrick and me, and it was with some embarrassment that I broached the subject and told him I "liked Melanie." It was almost in response to this, as I was saying, that he seemed to notice a jittery edge on my optimism that week, as I waited for the day of my assignation with Chris to arrive, but he smiled and left me in peace.

The point of narrating these encounters, of which this is the last, is to show that though the dark hound of the *sortes* was in actual fact still snapping at my heels, I did manage to keep myself facing ahead, in the other direction. To really move on and leave the ghosts behind me, I was sure that what I needed to do, more than anything, was to fill out the rather lifeless portraits I had of the characters who came in and out of my reality, make them flesh and blood, and from them, build up a complete picture of the world which I felt I was missing.

I arrived a little before Chris, and sat with a pint at one of the tables in the lobby opposite the ticket booth, where I could watch people coming in down the long passage from the street. I suspected that Chris would not show up, and of course who could blame him. But fifteen minutes after the appointed time, he came walking unhurriedly over to my table, wearing a striped short-sleeve shirt, brown slacks, and immaculate black shoes. He laughed out loud when he saw me, surprised that I had bothered showing up, but I was starting to see that this laugh, which had for me been part of the wild, divil-may-care raggle-taggle-gypsy image I had had of the goodlooking working-class gay man playing the Dublin scene, was in fact a nervous one, a laugh that disguised hurt and fear.

First off, he asked me, with a hint of real concern, how I was. We were having a catch-up conversation, and the thought of this gave me pleasure. The scene seemed to come straight from a repertoire of actual, real-time human life, a snapshot of my future. Of course, I couldn't tell Chris the truth of what had gone on, any more than I could anyone else, and I enjoyed spinning a fiction for him almost as much as I had the production of lies for Deirdre. What I liked was not the fact of lying, but the potential, human truth of the things I told him (had a lot of baggage about the whole gay thing, was depressed, found the move into town difficult, got in with a bad crowd). Because, it seemed to me, even if they were technically lies with regard to the recent past, in the larger context of my new life, they were instances of truth, false in their specific details, in their accidentals and grace-notes, but together manifesting a more general truth, parts of the new real melody.

Quite apart from the matter of what I was saying, talking to Chris in this way engaged me absolutely. He looked great. He had let his hair grow a little, and gelled it into an impeccable tousle. His skin was soapy and scrubbed, and with his ironic half-smile, long eyelashes, and collarbone just visible under his shirt, he looked glowing with sex.

I invited him to tell me his news. His news was, he had got a promotion. The pay was only a bit more, and he sometimes had to work late, but it was a "good sign annyhow."

"And have you been . . . are you seeing anyone?" I asked.

He smiled and winked.

"Well, have you?" I pushed.

"Ah, I've kept meself busy, you know the way. I've only had the one fling since I saw yeh last, a fella I've seen a few times since, but he lives up in Drogheda and he commutes into town. It would be hard to work out long term, you know what I mean, but sure you never know."

I felt a sharp jab of jealousy at this news. Chris seemed to be fully absorbed in our interaction, his green-blue eyes were locked, almost unblinking, onto mine, and he leaned in over the table close to my face so that occasional flecks of Guinness passed between us like, I thought, kisses. There was no doubt from the slightly guarded tone he used with me, and a tinge of sadness in his eyes, that my behaviour had wounded his pride. But, I thought, if I had stood him up twice I had also sought him out deliberately three times. He seemed interested in, or at least curious about me, but then Chris was so used to the maypole dance of men on the Dublin gay scene that he probably thought of the protagonists of past nights as acquaintances rather than exes. He was sharing the news of this new relationship with me as with a friend, or a cousin one doesn't see often, and I tried to be pleased for him. The fling from Louth was called Paul, they had met in the George six weeks before, and it was "very nice" when they were together.

"Real easy, you know."

His Cabra accent got its tongue so easily around the consonants of love, in a way my genteel, fault-finding Sandycove speech never could, I thought.

"He's a lovely fella."

I imagined his flat with another layer of man, the pile of shoes twice the size, two toothbrushes in the bathroom surrounded by twice the amount of scents and gels. In my mind's eye I saw them on a Sunday afternoon with hangovers flicking through the straight men's magazines on Chris's white sofa, going to the IFI, where Chris and I were now having pints, to watch a French picture in the evening.

Nevertheless, Chris touched me more than was strictly necessary for politeness when I walked him through the end of Temple Bar and down to Merchant's Quay, across the Liffey from where he lived. We stood at the edge of the water for a few minutes, exchanging gay banter with no content, talk which was a kind of required metaphoric expression of our standing together. He pretend-slapped me round the head when I lit a cigarette (the only Pour Mieux Vivre habit I hadn't entirely abandoned) and I tossed it into the water unsmoked. Finally he did the old trick of asking the time and lifting my hand up to look at my watch. Late, he said, he had to go. But before he left, he told me he was having a party for his birthday the following Saturday, in the flat, from about nine. I said I'd come.

"Yeah, well you'll excuse me if I don't hold me bret," he said, before kissing me on the lips and turning around to walk across Capel Street Bridge.

When I got home the lights were on, and Melanie was leaving.

"Hi, Niall," she said with a smile when we passed on the steps.

Inside, Patrick, having seen her to the door, was lying on the couch, opening up the *Irish Times*. He refolded it and threw it down on the coffee table when I came in.

"How was your night?" he asked.

I told him it had been great to catch up with this friend, another one I hadn't seen since before my troubles. I'd had a chance to rebuild bridges and explain myself a bit and so on. He made tea and we sat chatting in the small living room until two in the morning, when I absolutely had to go to bed in order to be decent at work the following morning. He told me things were going great with Melanie, and that they were going to go on a trip to Paris the following weekend, for his birthday, a bit soon to go on holidays together, a week was long enough to spend just the two of you, but she had found amazingly cheap hotel rooms on the Internet and they might not be there again. So it was a make-or-break holiday, really. We talked about Melanie in the only way we knew, that of polite south Dublin boys: what she did, where she was from, who she knew, where she drank. Patrick imposed no reciprocity in the story, didn't offer to introduce me to her single friends—I was certain, again, that in his quiet way he was giving me space to tell him my secrets. I went to bed happy, planning all the new steps to come.

For Patrick's birthday, I bought him the *Rough Guide to Paris*. I had taken many *sortes* from this book in the Northumberland Road days, and I was obscurely glad to see that the one I bought him was a new, updated edition, from which many of my old oracle's answers were hopefully excised.

"Thanks, man," Patrick said to me when I gave it to him, the American phrase a sign of a newly acquired confidence and worldliness, of a freshly invented masculinity, but also of a quickly maturing rapport, the seeds of an adult understanding, between the two of us. This was on the Thursday night, the day before his birthday. He left at cock-crow in order to meet Melanie at the airport for the 7 a.m. flight to Beauvais. I missed him in the morning when I got up for work and saw the signs of his hurried departure, the smell of coffee and the banana skin in the bin. I mooched around the apartment a bit before leaving for Westmoreland Street, walked into Patrick's room, which I usually never did, and looked at the forbidden fruit of books on his shelf, speckled with thin morning light. Books discovered in UCD: *Stupid White Men*, *Darwin's Worms*, *The Dice Man*, *A Brief History of Time*, some volumes which belonged to our common past, *The Secret History*, *Interview With the Vampire*, *The Hitchhiker's Guide to the Galaxy*, *The Colour of Magic*, *Great Expectations*, and some touching relics from prehistoric childhood, taken from Rathgar to Baggot Street for what could only have been purely sentimental reasons, *The Magic Tinderbox*, *The Indian in the Cupboard*, *The Phoenix and the Carpet*, *The Island of the Great Yellow Ox*. I touched the spine of one of them with my fingers, and briefly let them slide along the volumes next to it before pulling my hand away. Slowly, forbidden temptations began to seep through the floorboards and drip from the ceiling, like a leak. I remained before the bookshelf, hand half-raised, but was distracted suddenly by buzzing of my phone announcing a text message from Chris, which brought me to my senses, and I hurried out to work, late.

I went for drinks that night in the Palace Bar with people from work. A little like the George, they were a mixture, student summer-jobbers like me, and the younger echelons of the permanent staff. None of us summer people knew anyone, apart from what we gleaned in brief snatches of interbooth banter when the bank was quiet, and so the night in the Palace was a mélange of customer anecdotes and get-to-know-your-neighbour conversations.

I arrived home drunk but bored, and stood again in front of Patrick's bookshelf for a few minutes while I drank down a pint of tapwater. When the glass was empty, I placed it on the shelf and continued staring at the books until the lights of a passing car on the ceiling pulled me out of the trance and into my room and bed.

I managed to devote most of Saturday to preparing for Chris's party. I bought him the DVD of *Day For Night,* which I had seen with Fionnuala in the French department cinéclub at the beginning of the year. I found it in the IFI shop, right beside where we had had our drinks the previous week, and the place filled me with a regretful jealousy about his new flame. I tried to imagine Paul, blond and skinny, I thought, Louth accent carefully papered over with a generic oriental Hibernian, a bit self-centred in conversation at first, a few too many stories of himself and his mad aunts in Termonfeckin, but with a curiosity that opened up with time. Lack of evidence put paid to these conjectures, but images of Chris with another, any other, filled my mind. I could see now exactly what someone would love about Chris, that is, if one were passionately in love with him (as I had been with Ian, say, or perhaps Paula with silent Jim), the things which would be transubstantiated from normal individuating characteristics, regular human habits and traits, into throbbing nuclei of longing: his fine body, for a start, his easy, confident air, his dark skin, his big hands, his fussy, slightly feminine attention to clothes and appearance, his curiosity about the thoughts and lives of others, and with this, his natural acceptance of human difference and diversity, his working-class childhood on a rough enough street in the north inner city, his passion for French films. He would be the best kind of company, I thought, in body and in spirit, always interested, always on the move.

After buying the DVD in the IFI I went shopping for clothes.

During the Northumberland Road days, I had changed my clothes irregularly, and my few favourite outfits had either been there when I left, and thus irretrievable, were now too ragged and frayed, or else reminded me too much of that time. And even at my best, I looked like a scarecrow next to Chris. I bought an electric-blue shirt, campers and a pair of slacks, and when I modelled them in front of Patrick's full-length mirror that evening, my back to the bookshelf, I was almost pleased with the result. I looked like someone else, someone older, someone new. It was the first time I had examined myself closely in a mirror in a long time. The red flush had gone from my face, leaving me if anything a little too pale. There was no hint of the green light which had once emanated visibly from behind my eyes. When I pulled down on my upper cheek with my finger to expose the lower eyeball, I thought I could just about make out the traces of a last, vanishing hint of jade, but it had grown so faint it was on the point of disappearing for good.

I walked slowly to the party, with a six-pack of Beck's, a humorous card, and the DVD wrapped in teddy bear–adorned paper. It was close to ten by the time I arrived. I pressed the bell and was buzzed in without an answer. Upstairs, Chris's apartment door was ajar, and the sound of roaring laughter and chatter spilled out onto the hallway. The flat was packed with people, including several faces I recognised from the George. They lined the walls of the small apartment drinking from and ashing into blue plastic cups.

I wandered around a little, looking for Chris, then went into the kitchen and put my beer in the fridge. On the table, amid the fallen towers of plastic cups and sliced limes, oranges, and lemons, there were water filter jugs full of pink liquid. A short guy with a receding hairline and bright white shoes was standing, talking to a tall woman wearing a peaked cap.

"Wanna sea-breeze, dahlin?" he called to me in a cockney accent, which I wasn't sure was his own, and when I nodded, he poured me one from one of the jugs, talking all the while to the woman with the cap. The accent was his own.

"I just fought 'e 'ad it comin, didn' 'e? She was like, I'm dahn five grand, when the *fuck* are you going to pay me. Next stop Old Bailey."

I took the cup and wandered around the flat looking for Chris. I found him talking to some people in the queue for the toilet.

"Chris!"

"Just one second," he said to the man he was talking to. The man was definitely gay, thirtyish and blond. He looked at me with pale blue eyes, almost familiar, while Chris came over and put his arm around my shoulders.

"Niall, tanks for coming."

"Happy birthday," I said, and held out the parcel. I'd expected him to kiss me, but he didn't even let his arm stay around my shoulders for long.

"I'll open it later," he said. "Thanks a million. Did you get a drink?"

"Yes." I held up the cup of sea-breeze. "A Londoner poured it for me."

"Right, right. Help yourself."

He drifted back to his conversation with the blond guy. I loitered beside them for a while, hoping to be introduced—Paul?—but their conversation was quiet and serious, not designed for nomadic revellers.

In the living room I found Ciarán and Darina, the camp comedian and the straight woman who played his straight man, whom I had met in the Front Lounge the second time with Chris. They were rather cold to me, presumably because they knew I had stood Chris up two days after our night dancing in the George together, but they were the only people I knew, so I clung to them like a limpet. Ciarán was telling stories about his visit to the Gay Man's Health Centre because of his small bladder.

"The norse says to me she says how often do you go so I says to her around twenty, says she, an hour? *An hour,* she asked me. Jaysus, can you imagine? *Twenty times an hour.* Once every tree minutes. . . ."

Eventually they joined others in a group moving to another room and I was left alone. I got a cup of tapwater in the kitchen and sat on the white sofa—where Chris and I had kissed to the singing of France Gall and Jane Birkin. My hope was that Chris was hoping for more private circumstances to talk to me. The likely thought of Chris, though, I thought, was that when the guests had pulled out like the tide, he and Paul, would be the lone pieces of flotsam left on the shore. This was not the kind of party to thin out quickly, however, and at midnight, after I had been drinking only water and reading magazines for over an hour, people were still arriving. I decided I was being ridiculous and self-centred, acting as if the party was all about me, and should go home. I walked around looking to say goodbye to Chris, but when I noticed my present tossed on the table in the corner, still wrapped in the teddy-bear paper, and the card envelope with his name on the front still unopened, I decided just to slip out. As I unlatched the door, however, a warm hand landed on my shoulder and a voice denounced me as a traitor:

"Niall! Yeh tray-er!"

I turned around and looked into the smiling face of Chris. He was drunk. His eyes had a happy glassy look and his cheeks were red. He moved his hand up and touched my face briefly, drunkenly, before letting it drop to his side.

"Yeh big *tray-er,*" he repeated. "Were you going without saying goodbye? On me *bairt-day!*"

I couldn't help smiling, looking at him standing in front of me in his expensive shoes, his shimmery silk shirt half-undone, his hair in a sweaty mess, face like a bold boy. I thought of his childhood party piece, the one verse about the little boat and its owner that he never knew he was sinking and drowning each time he sang it.

"Sorry. . . ." I said. "I just didn't know anyone. . . . Come on, it's after midnight!" I laughed in response to the face he made.

"Ah go on, stay a little while. Sure the dancing is only starting now, Cinders." The volume of the music in the other room had been put up, and its rapid, regular heartbeat was filling the flat.

"Go *on!*" he said, taking me by the hand.

"Be careful," I said. "Paul might get the wrong idea."

He let my hand fall and grinned at me.

"Paul?"

"Yeah."

He took a step closer to me, so our noses were nearly touching.

"Paul's not here," he said.

I could smell a sweet and sour mixture of sea-breeze and hash off his breath.

"No?"

"Mm-mm." He shook his head and moved his lower body against mine. I could feel the beginnings of an erection through his trousers.

"So where is he?"

"Away . . ." he waved his hand in the air. "Away. . . ." He moved his face towards me and kissed me on the lips. Reluctantly, I pushed him away.

"No, really, Chris, where is he?"

He laughed and stood back.

"He's nowhere, Niall."

"What do you mean, nowhere?"

"I mean Niall, he's no one. He's not real. I made him up. Puff the Magic Dragon."

His accent, out of the parts of Dublin I never went, where the buses are all prime numbers, softened me. *Poof de maggic draggen.*

"You mean it was a lie?"

"Yeah, a white one."

He leaned his unsteady body against mine. His erection was

big and hard, and pressing against me caused my penis to start growing. He kissed my neck.

"Why did you lie?"

"Why do you think?"

"Because I stood you up?"

"Twice."

"To make me jealous?"

"It worked, wha?"

He pushed his face into mine and we kissed, for a long time, a taste of grapefruit, aftershave, marijuana, vodka, and tobacco, but most of all, the warm misty smell of Chris.

There were still guests in the other room, and Chris, a good host, was not willing to give in to temptation by retiring to the locked bedroom with me, and led me by the hand back to the living room where a group was dancing. I was the only sober one there, but, inebriated with the joy of being with Chris, danced along with them, the small adolescent repertoire of moves I had. Chris was too drunk to take charge of the music, a young skinny guy with a shaved head sat DJ-ing in a heap of CDs, like a tropical islander opening oysters to find pearls. After some time we moved to Chris's French pop collection, and we danced close together, catching each other's eyes, smiling when we touched, an illegitimate conspiracy. Chris kept coming in and out of the kitchen to fill everyone's drinks, and I made a show of accepting, in order to be spirited company, but I left cups untouched on tables and shelves: I had no desire, for once, to get drunk. As the hours passed, the dancing turned into Brendan strumming the guitar and people singing.

"If you have to sing a song, sing an Irish song," Brendan said.

A slurring Chris tried a blast at the syllables of his party piece but was hushed by the others. They sang the usual *Fields of Athenry*, then passed on to lyrically impaired Leonard Cohen, passing round the last bottle of wine. When the darkness started to bleach out of the sky, the remaining people started to leave in earnest. Chris had fallen asleep on my shoulder, so they let themselves out, while I made the decision to stay and be the last guest remaining. Brendan and Darina exchanged what I thought was a knowing and disapproving look as they saw me settled on the couch with Chris asleep on my shoulder. *Chris the big eejit is falling for that gobshite again.* I didn't care. They walked around the flat with bin-bags clearing up the bottles, cups, and ashtrays, while I let Chris sleep on me.

As they left, they asked me, in a tone of warning and admonition, if I would make sure he was okay. I said I would. When they had gone, I hoisted Chris up and walked him slowly towards the bedroom.

"How are you?" I asked.

"Drunk," he said. "I amn't usually . . . I'm locked . . . God I'm so locked. . . ."

I laid him down on his bed and took off his shoes, socks, and belt, pulled down his trousers, extricated the duvet from underneath him, and covered him in it. I filled a pint glass of water from the kitchen and put it on the bedside table, between the digital alarm clock and the book he was reading, *Last Chance Saloon* by Marian Keyes, a book for girls. I kissed him on his sweaty forehead and said goodbye.

"Stay," he grunted. "Please stay."

I undressed to my boxers and got into the bed beside him, lay close to him so I could feel his warm breathing body the length of mine. An erection grew almost immediately, but Chris had fallen asleep and was snoring.

I woke up with an early morning sun in my face; for a single hellish second I thought we had just come through an all-night session in Northumberland Road and that it would be soon be time for me to betake myself away, alone, into the city with my books. It was an almost instantaneous realisation, when I opened my eyes, that it was over, I was in Chris's flat, in Chris's bed. I was pleased, and even more surprised, to have drunk almost nothing and not have a hangover. The bed beside me was empty. I sat up. The clock said 06:58; I had only been asleep for a few hours. Did Chris have to go to work? No, it was Sunday. A grotesque sound came from the direction of the bathroom, a canine roar. I got up and walked over to the bathroom. I pushed open the door and looked in to see Chris on his knees in front of the toilet, wearing his boxers and bottle-blue silk shirt, heaving waves of pink-coloured vomit into the bowl. I put my hand on his neck. He looked up at me, pale and shivering, then roared and gushed again. I stayed with him there, got him water and tissues, put him back to bed when he was emptied, then mopped up the mess he had left in the bathroom with kitchen paper, before climbing in beside him and going back to sleep.

I was woken again during the late morning, this time by the movement of Chris's body against mine, kissing the back of my neck and caressing me all over my body, my sleeping penis cradled in his palm, he panting furiously, inhumanly. He pulled me towards him when he sensed me wake.

"How are you feeling?" I whispered.

"I was going to do you while you were asleep," he breathed onto my face. "Wait dere." He threw back the duvet and left the room. I made a movement of surprise, but he had only gone into the bathroom to brush his teeth and he was back in a few minutes, on top of me, as if to stop me from escaping again.

We got up at two, covered in sweat and dried semen. We showered together, and Chris turned me around to face the tiled wall while he soaped my hair, back, and legs. He made coffee in a stovetop espresso pot, like in French films, something you didn't see too often in Dublin, and I felt the grand rush of emigration in his flat.

Damn you and your Paris fads

It was a hot day, so we went downstairs with the mugs and two bananas to sit out on the doorstep on Capel Street, grubby and cheerful in the sun. We sipped in silence, looking at what came by, two Chinese guys on bicycles, a woman pushing a pram and talking on her mobile, a black BMW driven by a grey-haired man in his fifties. Another Jim McVeigh on his way to a romantic assignation.

"Thanks for lookin after me this morning," Chris said at length, slapping me on the knee, the chain around his wrist clicking on my trousers. "I don't let myself get that way very often."

"Don't worry. . . ." I said. "A. . . ."

plurality of bottles has often induced this in me

"I've often been on the other side," I finished.

"I can tell," Chris laughed.

"What does that mean?"

"Only slaggin, only slaggin."

We finished the bananas and sat in sunsplashed, happy silence, our shoulders and knees touching.

We cleaned the flat properly, windows opened to let the stale cigarette and hash-smoke out, and the sun and summer air in. For a while our complicity vanished, or really, I vanished for Chris, as he focused all his energies on the cleaning of the flat. He scrubbed skirting and draining-boards, filled sack after sack with rubbish long after I thought it had all been cleared away, and hoovered with such a ferocity that the carpet fibres seemed to jump to attention. Chris was a man transformed, in a trance, scurrying with the furrowed brow of a real char, from room to room with rubber gloves and sponges until the whole place was transfigured into fullness and whiteness, into his flat. I had been struck when first in the flat by the way in which Chris was foreign to it. Now as I watched him perform this determined, energetic transformative magic on it, I thought of my places, the long-abandoned walls of the room in Trinity, floor covered with unworn clothes and pointless papers, of my bedroom in Baggot Street, a single bed with the sheets half on the floor, clothes still tossed in a suitcase in the corner, and I saw and loved in another a kind of passion I had never myself felt.

We went to Bewley's on Westmoreland Street for breakfast, brass rails, dark wood, coffee-heavy air, sugared cherry buns. Here we uncovered the shared memory of being brought here with our mothers and siblings at Christmas time when we were in town to see Santy in Switzer's. I wondered aloud if we had ever been there at the same time, seen each other. I imagined it silently, Ciara and our mother and I sitting in a red-cushioned booth, my mother with her mug of coffee and a currant bun, Ciara and I with Fanta and a custard slice, fascinated and a little afraid of the noisy working-class family beside us, a girl and a younger boy, bossed around by his big sister. The boy standing on the seat, looking over the ledge at the three of us, Ciara and I wide-eyed and slightly thrilled by their dangerous-sounding accents. The mother: "Christopher! *Chri*-stopher! Would yeh get *dow*-en! Get down off dat seat before I brain yeh." Sharp slap and bawling. "I *told* yeh to get *dow*-en, Christopher." Our mother: "Niall, would you stop gawking at people. Eat your custard slice."

By the time we had finished eating and talking in Bewley's it was dusk, and I wanted only this. The sky could be light or dark, the sun east or west, the streets crowded or empty; the buskers could play anything. I wanted to feel the shape of his difference nearby, dig around in the soft topsoil of the inexhaustible mine of Chris's self and history, his childhood, opinions, turns of phrase, parents, schooldays, coming-out, eating habits, traumas, forgotten friends. We stood on the street outside Bewley's, unsure what to do: every direction was equal.

"Let's go for a walk," Chris said at length.

"Where?" I asked.

I must walk somewhere and the post-office is an object

"Home."

I stayed that night too, and got up at seven and left with Chris, who had to go to work. We had coffee together in a café in Temple Bar before separating, the freshly showered, pink-faced

masses of the morning work rush swarming around us. Chris
was in his suit and tie, hair wet and face smoothly shaved, young
working man, my young working man, and I was wearing
clothes of his he had lent me. We couldn't see each other that
night: he was going over to his sister's after work, she wanted to
see him for the birthday, and he hadn't seen his niece and nephew
in a while anyway. He was going to go out at lunch and buy them
some little thing, he had got into the habit of bringing sweets or
toys when he went to see them and now they would "ate" him if
he showed up empty-handed. Lucy and Daragh. On Tuesday I
had work, and Ciara was leaving for France the next day, to stay
with a family for three weeks, and they wanted me out in Sandycove for a goodbye dinner in the evening. So Wednesday, we said,
we would see each other on Wednesday straight after work.
There's time enough, Chris said, time enough.

The goodbye in the café was awful. We couldn't kiss or hold
hands in the crowd, a quick embrace or handshake too casual for
the momentous two nights we had spent together, and so we
hugged tightly, which made it feel like an anguished parting, an
emigrant turning from a face he knows he will not see again
before he dies.

I saw him on Wednesday, for dinner in his flat. I stayed there that
night, going to work the next morning wearing boxers and socks
belonging to him underneath my EBS uniform, and met him for
lunch on the Liffey Boardwalk. That evening, too, we met on Capel
Street Bridge as St. Michan's, Christchurch, and St. Patrick's were
striking six, and parted again at a quarter to nine in the same place
the following morning. Patrick came back from Paris all loved up
on Friday. Chris went out to meet his friends in the Front Lounge
and I stayed in at home with Patrick to drink tea and debrief. Paris
had been brilliant; he had written down a list of places they had
found to give to anyone they knew who went there. And it had
gone great with Melanie. Bravely, I told him I was seeing someone.

"Who is it?" he asked, carefully avoiding the personal pronoun.

"I'll introduce you after it's gone on longer," I answered. "There's time enough."

For these two weeks, Chris and I led a regular life, a Dublin life. During the week we met at six o'clock nearly every evening on the bridge, ate dinner in his flat, and watched a video or just had sex. Most nights I stayed with him, as Patrick did with Melanie, so our flat was empty and abandoned for much of the time. On Mondays and Fridays when I didn't work, I would see Patrick, or my parents, when we would phone Ciara in Lyons together. Patrick and I both knew I was about to come out to him, but neither of us felt there was any rush. All my higher mental energy was focused on the miracle of Chris, his body, his voice, his accent, his secrets, and I had no room yet, I thought, to get into it with Patrick. I wrote Paula a letter, thanking her formally, once again, for the way she had helped me, and saying I hoped she was not finding it too difficult to adjust to her new situation, although Patrick had in fact told me she was finding it harder, not easier, as time went on. No one invited her anywhere now she wasn't half of a couple, he said. At the weekends, Chris and I went out with his friends. He encouraged me to introduce him to mine, especially to Patrick, whom he found an intriguing figure, but I resisted, saying I need to find the right moment to come out to them, which was true. On Fridays we went to the Front Lounge and got drunk with variations on the crowd I had met him with. They were polite and sometimes almost cordial, but never really opened up to me, not believing I was not about to leave Chris standing again, and I was always the shy outsider, encouraged and protected by Chris but not really capable of surviving on my own two conversational feet. On Sundays we went to see a film in the IFI in the late afternoon, went home for dinner with our respective families, meeting up again later in the George, though we drank little and didn't stay late, as Chris could no longer handle work with a hangover. Age, he told me, I would see when I was his age.

Time ticked by at a regular rate; it did not shrink and expand or disappear as it had for so much of my previous year. I was in love with the routine, as well as with Chris, the regular way in which the day's light and the week's shape were punctuated and predictable, and also in love with the city which I had discovered and re-entered.

Nevertheless, on those days, Mondays and Fridays, when I didn't go to work, and was left to my own devices during office hours, I was increasingly assailed by weird, uncanny sensations, feelings which I knew came from Pour Mieux Vivre, either from my repressed memories or sent as sinister messages to me from John or Sarah, wherever they had ended up. Seeing Chris dispelled this buzzing background interference. In fact, in the very instant I set eyes on him, or heard his voice on the intercom outside his flat, I would forget it had ever been there. As the weeks progressed, the buzzing became louder and began to set in always sooner after we parted. Patrick, too, kept it at bay, and when he was around the flat, talking and laughing, and planning cinema trips from *The Ticket* it was absent. But Patrick worked part of the week in a sinecure his guilty father had obtained for him in the College of Surgeons, and much of the rest of the time he was doing things with Melanie, with their mutual friends, or else was out in Rathgar keeping his bereft mother company. So I was often alone, and in this circumstance the feeling became domineering and frightening; the invisible presence in the flat, caused my attention to drift slowly back to the old life and to its unanswered questions. I began to fall into automatic tendencies of response, old and dangerous habitual reactions. I would try and distract myself first by wandering around the flat or venturing out onto Baggot Street. I would phone Chris, and if he answered, the presence would vanish immediately, but he left his mobile off for most of the working day, and anyway as time went on, his anaesthetising effect was an ever shorter-term solution.

I took to turning on the radio and filling the flat with the endlessly talkative RTÉ Radio One. During the first moments, this stratagem always worked, and following the dialogues of the programmes, Morning Ireland, Marion Finucane (most effectively), Pat Kenny, and the lunchtime news shows, occupied my attention and filled the space around me. After only a matter of minutes, however, an idle and tormented part of my mind zoned out of the substance of the conversations, lost the running thread, and started jumping instead from fragment to fragment like a mad mountain goat from crag to crag. Without noticing it, I zoomed in on individual phrases or sentences, and began the work of transforming them into something new. Obviously, I was not insensible to the implications of this. I would switch off the radio and go outside, but here, too, my mind began to assemble provocative montages of quotations from advertising billboards, sounds in the distance, the conversations of passersby.

I told Chris nothing about this, partially because I had told him nothing of my time with Sarah and John at all, except for the likely lies I had manufactured in Deirdre's surgery in Stillorgan, but also because his presence was so effective at banishing the phenomenon that I would quite literally forget about or disbelieve its existence when we were together. Soon I began to resist the old tendencies less. The feeling became too substantial to ignore or drown out, and I began looking at it, as it were, understanding its form and meaning. *This is not enough,* it said. *Unfinished business.* Patrick noticed a change in me. He said I was pale.

"It must be love," I had replied, switching the focus to my other secret in order to deflect his attention from this one.

"I'm looking forward to hearing about it."

I had dedicated myself fully to the patterns, people, and cosmologies of the waking, sunlit Dublin of Patrick, Chris, my family, and Paula—no one could have made a more valiant effort than I to keep it watertight and real!—but as the summer latened, it became clear to me that the other one, the murky, multicoloured world of Pablo Virgomare and the rest of its vanished citzenry, was bleeding slowly into it.

The day I had been fearing came in the middle of July, a hot, greenhouse day. I had spent the night in Capel Street in the arms of Chris, and we had parted in a café just up from the quays at a quarter to nine, as he left, suited, for work. It was a Friday, and Chris was going out to his sister's. He didn't know when the brother-in-law would give him a lift back into town, but it could be late. He would text me as soon as he got back in, maybe nine or ten, and we would meet in the Front Lounge. I wasn't working that Friday, so I went back to Baggot Street.

"Hello. . . ." I called as I went in.

Patrick's bedroom door was open and the bed was cold, empty and uncrumpled: he must have spent the night in Rathgar to keep Paula company, as he often did on Thursdays. The disappointment provoked by his absence slowly grew into a kind of panic at being alone in the flat so early in the morning, with nothing to fill the day. I even thought briefly of showing up at work to see if maybe someone had called in sick, or if they could do with help, but I knew it was a foolish idea. I made coffee in the percolator and wished I was doing so in an espresso pot like Chris's. Maybe he and I would see Paris for the first time together I thought, and imagined it, to distract myself.

I sat at the kitchen table, blinking in the morning sun, and listened to the morning radio, a ritual I had seen my grandmother perform all her life, back in the days of that lost civilisation when the Irish summers were not so hot, sitting down after her breakfast and Mass to hear the country talk to itself. *Abracadabra me granny comes from Cabra.* Anne in Sligo town. "I believe you fell afoul of the smoking ban, Anne?" Pádraig in Drumcondra, Breda in Tralee, Agnes in Dunmore East, Margaret in Mount Merrion, Chris in Montparnasse.

Faced with the long day before the sun would set and I could meet Chris, I phoned home, thinking I would propose a visit out to Sandycove. The phone rang out to my sister's voice:

Hi, this is the Lenihans. I'm sorry we aren't able come to the phone at the moment but please leave a message and we'll get back to you. Thanks a million.

I called my mother's mobile. She was on the DART and we had to shout over the noise of the train. I asked her if she was free for lunch.

"Oh, I'm sorry, love, I've arranged to meet Nuala. She wants to get the book club going again. What about tomorrow?"

"I'm working. Don't worry about it, I was just at a loose end."

"What?"

"I'm at a loose end."

"Send you what?"

"A loose end." Pause.

"I can't hear you. Have you any recommendations for the book club, something light but not pure rubbish?"

The Golden Bough

"Nothing comes to mind. But how are you all anyway?"

"What?"

"How is everyone?"

"What? What? Hello? Niall? I can't hear you. Hello? Niall?" She buzzed and crackled into the ether as the connection failed.

The flat bore down upon me in its emptiness, each little thing, the plate of seashells on the mantelpiece, the watercolour painting of the sea at Sandycove on my wall, all seemed shoddy and paltry things, fakes, forgeries, flim-flam. I sat on the sofa and thought of Chris, imagined him at work, talking to his colleagues, playing with his niece. I imagined him sitting at his desk, the creases of his palm as he held the phone to his ear, or at lunch, sitting on a bench on the Liffey Boardwalk to take advantage of the sun, mouth open wide and unworried to take a bite of his sandwich, dreams of Paris in the '60s drifting through his head, "New York Herald Tribune, New York Herald Tribune . . ."

But I found it hard to picture his face; the flat oppressed me with its spoons and cushions.

I rang straight to his message-minder to hear his voice.

Hello, dis is Christopher Mooney, please leave a message, tanks beep.

The sound of his voice earthed me, cemented the fragmenting room around me into a concrete whole. I rang it again, and then a third time, and then again and again and again. click *Hello, dis is Christopher Mooney, please leave a message, tanks* beep . . . click *Hello, dis is Christopher Mooney, please leave a message, tanks* beep . . . click *Hello, dis is Christopher Mooney, please leave a message, tanks* beep . . . click *Hello, dis is Christopher Mooney, please leave a message, tanks.*

The transformation performed by the words faded instantly each time, futile flame.

Exasperated, I sat on the couch listening to Raidió na Gaeltachta until after lunch. I left the flat and spent the afternoon on a long, aimless walk, but my feet took me to dangerous locations: the Canal, Trinity, Northumberland Road. Even at five, when I thought I could distract myself from the dangerous static around me by going for a lone pint among the after-work people, the idea being that their suits and banter would remind me of Chris, I found myself standing at the black and white entrance to O'Donoghue's, the place from which I had once been frogmarched back to the *sortes*. I hung around at the door for a while, but finally decided not to go in.

Stepping now on a piece of ice, now into the sticky mud, he crossed the stream of dazzling water.

The sun was hot and high, emphasising the long stretch of time remaining until my meeting with Chris; it lit up the world with such ferocity I thought it might never go down. I went back home and ate pasta and Dolmio sauce off my lap on the couch, reading the accommodation ads in the *Evening Herald*, but the words, captions, and sentences started to separate, break away from one another and regroup in illegal constellations before my eyes, so I folded it up and stared at the wilting light out Baggot Street. I chewed slowly, trying to keep the holographic image of Chris flickering before me, willing the sun to drop faster, to allow in the shades of Chris and life. Choirs were beginning to gather in the gold-lit corners of the ceiling, starting to mutter their Latin harmonies. The evening sun was beginning to weave itself into the commanding face of John. *Die, fade, darken,* I willed it. If I could just get through these last few hours, until Chris was back in town, then I would survive for good, never go back.

De l'autre côté de la rue

At eight, the sky still pale, I texted Chris, Patrick, and even Fionnuala who was in France, a desperate search for a saviour who was free.

Ring me when you get this. N

I stared at the phone, wishing it would light up and bleep; but whereas it remained silent, the flat was starting to fill up with chatter and religious singing.

Instead of going back to the couch where it was flashing up the caller's name on its little green screen, I walked, almost idly, into Patrick's room and stood in front of the bookshelf. In a single, illuminated instant, like the flash and tinkle of a lightbulb blowing, I knew that that fresh life, brief and safe, was over. I stood for a time in feigned resistance, pretending to be opposing the shining, timeless world I had so recently escaped from, by my glances out the window to the cars moving regularly by on Baggot Street, out in the world of the living, following flawlessly upon one another, like the days, the minutes, the years.

Abracadabra

I switched on Patrick's reading lamp, illuminating the titles on the bookshelf. When I looked back over my shoulder, a familiar, outlawed male figure, not Chris, was framed at the window, his face almost pressed to the glass, looking in at the living room and at me, kneeling in a small semicircle of lamplight at the edge of my bed. I raised a solemn hand and greeted the long-lost face of Pablo Virgomare, who smiled and walked away. My brain and my body were gone, softly bathed in the sweet, perilous knowledge that it was all to start again, that I was going back.

By the time I pulled the first forbidden volume down, the traffic, the hum of the fridge, the homeless couple fighting outside, the tick of Patrick's alarm clock—even, perhaps, the ring of my phone—had already woven themselves together into a fine fabric of sound, the inevitable and dangerous song which would lead me away again:

ecce enim veritatem dilexisti
incerta et occulta sapientiae tuae manifestasti mihi
Asperges me hyssopo et mundabor
Lavabis me, et super nivem dealbabor.

Eleven

That old world bled slowly into this one. Gradually, unstoppably, it poured up through the plughole of the sink in the kitchen, spilling down onto the linoleum kitchen floor; outside from under the granite flags, it rose, silent floodwater, leaking up through gutter grills, manholes, and drains, a glistening film, submerging the paths, roads, and pubs. With the flood, the names, Chris, Patrick, Fionnuala, became mere syllables, bobbing with a collection of other objects on the surface, before softly sinking to the silent and forgotten depths.

I was standing in a chamber of soft golden light: I was long gone. I cleared my throat like a tenor back on stage for the first time after a long career break, and asked loudly to the unechoing room:

"Where are John and Sarah?"

At the sound of the question, I had a rush like that of being in a plane taking off, the world suddenly shrinking and the body soaring. I twisted my body away from the bookshelf and put out my hand to feel, blissfully, the cold hard spines flipping under my fingertips once more, feeling the old instincts again as I waited for the jerk that announced the answer, as the line of a fisherman wakes him from despondent dozing.

They stared into the blinding event.

Of course, they were no longer together. I would have to look for them one at a time. I let the book drop to the floor and asked the supplementary immediately.

"Where is John?"

The pink cubicle had winked out of existence, the monkeys had sunk away to a better dimension. Ford and Arthur found themselves in the embarkation area of the ship.

These were just the kind of answers I had been expecting, and I realised that somewhere below my conscious mind all the last, rehabilitated while, I had been making dark plans for departure. I moved fast and methodically through Patrick's bookshelf, steadily, competently, towards the truth. The pleasure of the interrogation was intense, and I kept it under skilful control, never jumping ahead too quickly, always keeping carefully in mind what the books said, using their answers as a springboard to the next question.

By the time it had grown fully dark, I had left a pile of consulted books on the floor of Patrick's room. I was nearly there, and so I moved to my own room, feeling it would be a betrayal of some kind to use Patrick's small collection of books to track down Pour Mieux Vivre, and I upended on my bed the small box of books I had taken from home but hadn't touched. Having no bookcase of my own, I piled them into three roughly equal piles on the bed.

"What should I do to find them?"

My hand flicked down the sides of the piles of books, up and down, then from pile to pile, eventually abandoning two of the stacks, going up and down the same pile over and over again, then up and down the top few books. My fingers finally rested on the top two, and after a moment's hesitation I picked the second volume from the top. Proinsias Diarmaid Mac Suibhne, *Is Maith an Scéalaí an Aimsir—The Weather is a Good Storyteller: Irish Proverbs and Sayings*. I flicked through the pages and chose:

Is fearr rith maith ná drochsheasamh
A good run is better than a bad stand

"Where?" I asked straight away, and picked the anthology of selected prose we had used in Professor Dunne's class.

Beauvais

I hesitated for a moment. John was in a small town in Picardy. . . . But no, I had asked where I should go to. Beauvais was where economy flights to Paris landed: this is what it meant—I would find what I was looking for in Paris, I had known that all along.

I took three sheets of paper and a biro from the drawer of Patrick's desk and sat down to write three letters. Before I began each, I choose a guiding synchronicity for each. I wrote first to my parents, after reading a short paragraph from Balzac. *Dear Mum and Dad, Please don't be alarmed when I tell you I have gone to Paris.* I said that a close friend from college who was living in a luxury apartment in Paris belonging to his uncle had phoned and asked me to come and mind it with him. The other house-sitter, another friend of ours, had dropped out at the last minute. The offer was too good to turn down, I wrote, but the snag was I had to go immediately, as the first friend was going away for a few days and the place couldn't be left on its own. I was going on the first Ryanair flight the next morning, and I would be in touch as soon as I got there.

For Patrick's letter, I chose a line from *Pride and Prejudice*.

Style and deceit flowed so easily from my pen that I knew I really was over the other side again. I wrote to him that I was sorry to tell him what he knew already in this way, after so many years of friendship, but anyway, I was gay, had fallen in love with a French man whom I had been seeing for about as long as he had been seeing Melanie, and that I, too, was to go to Paris with my loved one. If it went well, I wrote, I might stay a month or two. Obviously I would appreciate if he kept this fact to himself, and I told him what I had said in the letter to my parents so that if they met or talked he would be able to confirm the story. I had left the standing order from the Bank of Ireland for my portion of the rent in place and there was enough accumulated in my account (I had been prudent with my wages from the EBS, and there was still a remnant of my Beckett) to pay it for three months. *It has been a pleasure,* I wrote, *now good luck! N*

Dear Chris, I wrote before choosing his synchronicity. My hand felt up and down the piles of books several times, but I found myself unable to choose. I concentrated and tried again, but it was impossible. All the quick energy I had had for the previous two letters had drained from my mind and body. Even now, in the swirling and transfigured room, even now, back in the old magic world, words, in all forms, failed me. In the end, I put pen to paper without a synchronicity, and as my heart heaved, I left Chris the only thing that would come to mind, a transcription and translation of the last verse of a children's song in a dying language:

Báidín Fhéilimí, briseadh i dToraigh
Báidín Fhéilimí 's Féilimí ann
Báidín Fhéilimí, briseadh i dToraigh
Báidín Fhéilimí 's Féilimí ann
Báidín bídeach, báidín beosach,
Báidín bóidheach, báidín Fhéilimí
Báidín díreach, báidín deontach,
Báidín Fhéilimí 's Féilimí ann.

Felim's little boat was broken off Tory
Felim's little boat with Felim in it
Felim's little boat was broken off Tory
Felim's little boat with Felim in it
Tiny little boat, lively little boat,
Lovely little boat, Felim's little boat
Unswerving little boat, determined little boat,
Felim's little boat with Felim in it.

I did not sign it. I took an envelope from Patrick's room and sealed it inside.

Christopher Mooney
Apt. 6 Capel Court
Capel Street
Dublin 1

I put a P.S. to Patrick's letter asking him to post the other two for me. Then I threw bed linen, a towel, and whatever clothes I found into my rucksack, took a sports bag for books, and fled the flat.

I walked first to the canal, grey under the moon as it had been the night I had left Sarah and John standing there. I stood on the bridge, put my bags on the ground, and threw my phone over into the canal, watched it splash and sink. I walked down to the coast and waited on Ringsend Road for a taxi to take me to the airport.

So that was my last image of Chris, straight from the early eighties, the time of my birth, a fresh-faced eight-year-old who was afraid of football and big boys and liked to play skipping with his sisters' pals, bawling out unfamiliar syllables in his little blue jumper and tie, among finger paintings, crucifixes, and pine cones of the classroom in Christ the King Boys' National School,

Cabra. In my opinion, here is the real end of the story, a sad end, a pointless end, a weak, unlearning, young man throwing his phone into the Grand Canal over Baggot Street bridge.

"Are you off on your holliers?" the taxi driver asked as we rolled north along the coast.

"I am," I answered, in the breezy, unbothered voice of an ordinary person, "I'm going to France to see my girlfriend. She's teaching over there."

"French, is she?"

"Spanish, actually."

He laughed congratulatorily, man to man.

"Pity for you!" he joked, "pity for you! I've taken a fair few of them myself in the car, over the years, the Spanish girls . . . great people, very like the Irish. The eye-talians too, very like the Irish. They have the bit of craic, you know what I'm saying. Wherever you go on this earth, the Irish are welcomed. . . . Take the Germans now . . . a very cold race. The Germans and the Slavs, cold peoples. But they do say Russians are great drinkers."

"Vodka."

"That's right. I had a coloured chap in the car once, full of talk he was. He told me that where he came from, a man can have as many wives as he wants. But he had only the one. *Too expensive,* he says! *Me I have only one,* he says, *more eet ees too expensive.*" He looked at me in the mirror to see if I would laugh or join in, but I was bored of my pretence and itching for a book. "Now the yellow man on the other hand I know very little about. . . ."

He spoke no more but contemplated inwardly the mysteries of the inscrutable oriental as we sped up along the coast, through Ringsend and across the East Link bridge, the last light just falling at the edge of the still sea. We passed the Dockers, an early house, which in the morning would be serving pints to the men who in a few hours would be there in the grey dawn unloading freight off the river, and to the hard core of the night's drinkers. We drove by the pubs of Drumcondra and the north-side onto the M50 and then the airport, a live galaxy of lights at this time of year.

I went straight to the Ryanair ticket counter, queuing behind the miserable line of customers waiting patiently to pay their excessive excess baggage charges. It was half-ten and I was not sure I would make it onto the Beauvais flight. It was high season, and a Friday. I didn't mind the thought of waiting in the airport until the first plane of the morning, at six or seven, except for the worry that someone, tipped off by Patrick, and fearing for my psychiatric well-being, would come out to the airport to try and dissuade me from leaving.

Marie, the Ryanair attendant at the desk, tapped on the key-board for a time with her long red nails, then put me on standby. I went straight to Hughes & Hughes, where I bought six books, a streetmap and guide to Paris, then waited until my name was called out in the chaos, which it was. I did everything with a patient placidity, no emotion, impatience, or stress, and my mind was untroubled with thoughts of the living.

The unassigned herd pushed and elbowed in the Ryanair scrum for seats, and I allowed myself to end up somewhere at random, at a window near the back. I watched the lights of Dublin shrink, shimmer, and vanish below me. Beside me sat an obviously American freckled girl around my age, reading *Ulysses*. She made it clear with her bright smiles that she was hoping for a bit of chat. Instead, I glared out the window at the winglights on the nightbanks of cloud, ignoring the highly priced offers of food, beverages, and trinkets passing up and down the aisle. I thought of taking out my books and beginning work, the primary stages of the search for my fugitive compan-ions and their lost world, but found it better for the time being to sit and stare and allow the memories of things recently come to pass to filter through and out of my mind. Images of Dublin appeared before me, in slow succession and in no particular order, Patrick, Paula, Chris, my parents, Ciara, Andrea, Fion-nuala, Ian, but the situations in which I saw them were car-toonish and unreal, they had already taken on the over-coloured resolution of caricatures, distant, dreary fictions.

After we landed and I boarded the Ryanair coach from Beau-vais to Paris, I took out three books and placed them on my lap in front of me; but by now everything seemed like it was offering *sortes,* the black fields on either side, the stretch of the lights on the autoroute and the low murmur of the other Irish passengers around me uprooted from their native island.

"Where am I going?" I asked a crumpled sheet printed from the Web, left muddied and footprinted on the floor of the bus.

a few streets bear the names of the people's leaders

The coach disgorged us outside a conference centre on the Boulevard Gouvion-Saint-Cyr, on the edge of the city centre, cars with yellow lights and 75 registrations thundering away up towards what I thought might be the Arc de Triomphe. The warm blast of air when I stepped off the bus smelt of garlic and petrol, and made me dizzy with distance from Dublin, as if it were heavy with laudanum, or opium, or some amnesiac potion. It was one in the morning. I walked with my bags down along the boulevard, and stopped at the James Joyce pub, pre-senting itself to me as a synchronicity in the night. It was cool and dark, and decorated quite like a pub at home. A girl of about my age with a short blond ponytail and tough green eyes, was standing behind the bar talking in a Dublin accent to a large blushing youth with wide, shy country vowels.

"No, I knew Lisa in Artane," she was saying, "she was a fuckin mad thing then as well. So I says to her when they were all drinking after work on Tuesday over at the Monte Cristo, I says to her I said Lisa, you can fuck off I'm gettin a taxi home so I am."

"I'd say there were a few sore heads the next morning."

"Their own fuckin fault."

I put my bags on the ground and leaned on the bar.

"Howayeh." The girl turned to me.

"A pint of Stella, please."

The guy from the country touched her on the shoulder.

"I'll move them barrels for you so, Michelle," he said to her and moved off into the pub gloom.

"Thanks, Pa'."

I drank the Guinness while Michelle and Pat closed up around me, a selection of books in a pile at my elbow, the streetmap of Paris spread out in front of me and the notepad and pen beside it. I really was a pro; I realised that all the while I had been living in Northumberland Road, in those days and nights that passed in an indistinguishable blurred haze, I had also been engaged in an apprenticeship, and now my level of skill with the books surprised me. I didn't take any specific or directed *sortes* yet, but used them to get a sense of the lie of the land, as it were, how things stood in Paris in terms of the books, possible shapes and symmetries I should look out for. When Michelle told me it was time for me to get going, they had to close up, I had a series of notes jotted down, and the first few leylines dividing the map. It was two in the morning and I had nowhere to sleep. Calmly, I decided to let the books lead me. As Michelle stood with a sweeping brush in her hand, and a sweating Pat mopped up behind the bar, I took some *sortes* and cross-referenced them with my map and guidebook to decide where to go.

I waited out on the boulevard Gouvion-Saint-Cyr with my two bags, still in a T-shirt with the heat, and hailed a taxi.

"Rue de la Roquette, vers place de la Bastille," I asked the North African driver, the first words of French I had ever spoken outside Dublin, and I was amazed when the scrap of language I launched landed safely and had the effect of sweeping me off down towards the lights of Paris proper through the Arc de Triomphe. Although my surroundings had not yet begun to shine with the gloss of Pour Mieux Vivre again, and the world had not yet started its slow slide into unreality, as the taxi flew me towards the centre, despite the cars and mobile phones and plastic signs in random English, Paris was already for me the city of Balzac, of Rimbaud, of the *belle époque*, of Madame de Lafayette, already the city, I thought with a brief but nauseous wave of sadness, of Chris's films.

I opened the window to get a better look at Haussman's façades, behind whose shutters tousled-hair teenagers were being seduced by sixty-year-old women smoking sans-filtres, the small square windows peering out from the metal roofs, eaves white with pigeon-shit, where silent, drawn young women made coffee, planned literary careers, and had erotic dreams about their fathers. For me, any of the buzz-cut young men who stopped their motorbikes beside us at traffic lights, the warm wind flapping their white T-shirts under their black leather jackets, could have been from a Balzac novel, zooming directly out of a poem. The taxi sped along the *voie rapide* on the right bank and I saw for the first time the lime-coloured waters of the Seine, the Eiffel Tower receding behind, and the thin turrets of the Conciergerie, against a sky so filled with spotlights and lamps that you could hardly tell it was night.

The taxi deposited me where I, intuiting the instructions of the books through the filter of the map and guidebook, had asked, on a street just behind Place de la Bastille. The synchronicities had been wise in the bar they had chosen for me, "Objectif Lune" (the title, in fact of a TinTin book I had once read in Patrick's house), since it was advertised as being open all night, whereas the rest of the cocktail lounges and *bars Américains* in the vicinity all seemed to be closing down, and groups of expelled drinkers were throwing bottles and shouting in the street. The doorman, a middle-aged African man with an unassuming and apologetic face, who looked more like a primary school teacher than a bouncer, wished me good evening and asked me how I was, a password against the uncontrollably drunk, I supposed, and when I replied satisfactorily, he pulled open the door to allow me and my baggage in. The narrow bar was packed, and it was with difficulty that I pushed my way through the people, knocking with my bags against pints, Pernods, and shoulders to get to the bar. The place boiled with the heat of the crowd jammed between its walls. I put my bags on the floor and squeezed in between two different groups, two middle-aged men with dishevelled suits and double whiskeys and a little gang of thirty-something men and women. The barman was a tall black man in his mid-thirties with a perfectly sculpted goatee, a shining shaved head, and two gold hoops in his ears. He moved back and forth behind the bar in an entirely unrushed manner, as if he were ladling out gazpacho to his cousins in the garden on quiet afternoon, instead of mixing mojitos, piña coladas, and Cuba libres to a steamy and smoky mass leaning over the bar and roaring through the noise of talk, laughter, and music for his speed and attention.

When he brought me the pint of Stella Artois—new drink for a new phase—I had ordered, I turned around to look at the clientèle properly, leaning with my elbows on the bar behind.

At the table behind them sat two men, one bleached blond, maybe twenty-two, the other around forty, plump and sly. In my synchronicity-sensitised mind, I could almost see the words *www.gay.fr* floating in hypertext around them. They were the result of an encounter over the Internet—I was sure from the way they were taking each other in physically for the first time, but talking intently as if already beyond chit-chat flirting, that the meeting in Objectif Lune was the physical manifestation of an earlier exchange, the word made flesh.

In the right-hand corner at the back I discerned an obvious group, five male American students, physically bigger than everyone else in every way, wearing flip-flops, backwards baseball caps, and sports clothes (*"PRINCETON: GO TIGERS!"*). Their friend was making his way over to them with a tray of clear shots, which he distributed to great brouhaha, collegiate ribbing, I supposed. They banged the little glasses on the table, shouted some rhyme, or slogan, clinked them together, downed the liquid, and started shouting again while they went back to their beer.

I drank my own pint down quickly, then ordered another. I wondered what the crowd would throw up, who among the loud sticky mass would prove to be significant, and let the conversation around me flood through my ears, allowing the shards of French, English, and Italian to divide, collide, and amalgamate in my mind, an ocean of synchronicities crashing up with regularity on the shore, but nothing I heard was suggestive.

I drank there until well after dawn, when I walked out with my bags, blinking, into the bright sun of a city nearly awake and working. I was sick and exhausted, and there was no trace of the insomnia I had expected to flow immediately through my system, no sound of papal choirs or suggestive bells, and most of all no indication of where I would sleep, let alone live. I bought a litre of water and a nem in a Chinese traiteur, and a coffee and pain au chocolat in a boulangerie next door. I must have looked like the grimy punks I passed who sat laughing, drinking, and begging in groups with their dogs on the streets around the Bastille, but the businesslike vendors made the exchange without blinking. I sat on a bench beside a canal and opened the book bag. I was dehydrated, nauseous, and falling asleep; worse, I found I had no idea what I should ask or plan, what exactly I had come to Paris to look for. A few desultory synchronicities led me vaguely east, and I wandered, like a lost desert traveller, heaving my bags along with me. My senses were overloaded with Paris, women swathed in lavishly coloured African wraps, tiny sleeping fuzzy-haired children entwined impossibly in the fabric, intense young men throwing butts into the gutter as they strode through the traffic, and the dark-haired, short-black-dress mysterious young women of French films, clattering in their heels down the stairs of métro stations, or rummaging in their little handbags for cigarettes or lipstick as they walked. But my own mind and tricks with the books failed to interface with the reality. I was in a horrific no-man's land, gone from the world of the living but not quite back in the other one. My eyelids drooped and my stomach turned. When I got to Place des Vosges, I went into the park, staggered past the couples, tourists, and children, staked out a spot on the grass well-covered by the shade, threw my bags down as a pillow, and consigned myself mournfully and heavily to the turf.

I slept gratefully, peacefully, and unafraid, as if in a hotel. I dreamt of Dublin, and when I woke up again I thought first of all that I was in Stephen's Green surrounded by Ians, Chrises, and Darinas on their lunch. I sat up in shock when the sun seemed too hot, the trees too sparse, and the buildings I saw through the railings improbable. I felt the deep imprint of the grass criss-crossing my cheeks and slowly accommodated myself to where I was. It had been hours, the sun had moved to the other side of the meridian. It struck me that I really was homeless, drinking alone all night and sleeping in parks.

When I stood up, brushed myself off, and drank down the end of my warmed Évian, the first thing I did was go to a phone box where I called Sandycove reverse-charge. Patrick had hand-delivered the letter to them that morning. They were not as frantic as I had feared, instead full of difficult questions about the friend and the flat and how come it was so sudden, why I hadn't rung them instead of making poor old Patrick come all the way out from town with a letter, what had I told them in the EBS. They asked me if I had a phone number, I said there was a problem with that, but that I'd keep in touch. When I hung up and left the phone box, which was like a metal oven, I sat down against a pillar in the arcades of the Place des Vosges where people were selling paintings and knick-knacks to the tourists. I took out my books, but I had no stomach for *sortes* yet, so I just flicked through the Rough Guide like anyone else, looked at the section on the Marais and worked out how to walk to the gay section. Pulling the damned bags behind me, I walked through the seventeenth-century hôtels, Chinese delis, and Jewish bakeries until I found the main gay drag, rue Saint-Croix-de-la-Bretonnerie, sight of many of my hallucinations of Paris in the high days of the *sortes*. I stopped at a trendy spot on a corner and sat at one of the round tables on the street, surrounded by twenty- to sixty-year-old French and American gay men, sitting in twos, fours, and sixes, eyes darting back and forth with every entry or exit to the place.

I ordered an American coffee from the muscular young waiter who came around but didn't react to my slightly flirtatious looks and interaction. Oh come on, his manner said wearily, we all are gay men in a gay bar, can we give it a rest for a moment. Plus, I realised, I had travelled from Dublin, gone drinking, and slept in a park without washing or changing my clothes. Anyway, it was time to get down to business. When I paid him for the coffee, I took out my notepad and biro, with the notes I had made in the James Joyce the night before. *Why did I come here?* I had written at the top of the page, and then, after transcriptions of the various synchronicities the question had provoked, the answer, "To find John, Sarah, Luis (in that order). To go to the next level." I took out the map of Paris on which I had begun to trace some lines the night before, and seeing them criss-cross symmetrically before me, I had again the sense of a hidden order being brought to the surface, of blowing the dust off obscured forms and bringing them into the light, x-raying a mediocre painting and finding a lost masterpiece. My train of thought was constantly interfered with by something around me, a woman in a waitress's apron smoking on the street corner, holding her elbow with her free hand, a middle-aged man straddled on a stationary motorbike flirting with a young skinny man with green hair. I scanned the upper floors of the buildings in front of me, hoping to see a silhouette or some other sign in one of the small roof-windows, and looked out for one in the brisk traffic of gay men moving in front of me.

"How should I get myself started in Paris?" I asked, and chose a point on the map as my answer. My finger landed on the Orangerie museum, which at first did not ring any bells, so to speak. I understood the intention when I repeated the question and asked a book:

All the murders took place in an area of 3 sq km (1 sq mi), covering the areas of Whitechapel and Stepney, and the City of London.

But of course. I closed the books, and with a nervous look around the bar I sang out, as loud as my embarrassment would allow, the lines:

"When will that be?" say the bells of Stepney.

As heads turned to identify the English-speaking lunatic, my attention was arrested by a figure coming through the crowd to the bar. It was a visual disturbance I recognised from several times before, a flicker of familiarity emerging from the crowd. I craned my head and looked from side to side, and then there seemed, not to arrive, but to materialise inside the bar, as if steam rising from the crowded bodies, the fair-haired, toned form of Pablo Virgomare. He raised his eyebrows in greeting and flashed me his white-toothed villain's smile. He was leaning at the bar, smoking. I cleared my books and papers back into the bag and pushed my way through the customers to him.

I threw my bags down at his feet when I reached him. His fashion and clothes were as elegant, impeccably presented, and expensive as ever. He was wearing a white linen shirt with half the buttons carelessly open, long shorts halfway past his knees, and open-toed leather shoes. He sported a slim golden ring on a blond-haired toe. I had never found an appropriate formula of greeting him: I always checked him out in doubtful detail to reassure myself of his reality, noted every detail of his tanned skin, green eyes, and chic outfits, the slight scar above his right eye; I confirmed the human quiver of his flesh, but never said hello.

He looked me up and down himself, regarding my grassy dishevelled appearance, laughing and shaking his head. He pulled me towards him, kissed me warmly on the lips, then pushed me back in front of him while he looked at me, like a grandmother inspecting her soldier grandson home on leave from the front. I waited for him to speak, but instead he signalled to the barman.

"Deux citrons glacés au vodka, chef," he ordered in lazy, confident Dublin French.

I opened my mouth to ask him questions, but he tutted me into silence and held up a finger, and we stood there leaning against the bar until the waiter brought the drinks, which Pablo paid for. He held the little glass up.

"Saol fada, gob fliuch agus bás in Éirinn," he toasted flippantly, "Long life, wet beak and death in Ireland," and we clinked and drank.

"Okay," I said, "I need to find a place to live and then—"

He began to recite, in a tone of romantic reverie:

"Oh to have a little house!"

"To own the hearth and stool and all!"

I continued to drink my lemon-drop, wrinkling my nose at the bitter taste, and said nothing. Pablo wiped his lips with the back of his hand, then sighed in a tone of getting down to business.

"Go to the American Church and take the place rented by Madame de Montvrai."

"Montvrai?"

"Vraiment."

A doubt swelled in my chest, and I decided to ask.

"But Pablo . . . will I find them? What is it all about?"

He left a twenty-euro note on the bar to cover his drinks and gave me a kiss on the lips.

"You know the routine. Send me a song."

He took himself off through the bar, whistling his signature tune, receiving, I thought, a flutter of admiring looks as he went. I tried to watch him go, but as always, his way of moving was somehow distracting and he seemed not to disappear, but slowly to dissipate, to become incorporated piecemeal into the activity of the street.

I took his advice, of course, and spent the rest of the afternoon hanging round the American church on the Quai d'Orsay. I looked down through the notices but could find no Montvrai offering a room.

The sun was beginning to set, and I was getting nervous. Occasionally a group of Americans or Australians would come by to look at the noticeboard. The books replied obscurely to my consultations.

Finally, a small man in a scruffy trenchcoat shuffled up to me and asked me if I was looking for a room. He was almost bald, his few remaining greasy tufts combed back in perfect, glistening furrows. He picked his hairy red nose while he waited for my response.

"Non, je cherche une Madame de Montvrai," I hazarded.

"Ah là, Montvrai c'est ma patronne. She's my boss. You heard about her from other Americans, I suppose."

"Irlandais."

He shrugged to let me know it was of little matter.

"Does she have a room?"

Yes, he said, a studio in the eleventh. Five-fifty a month. He had been charged by her with finding a foreign tenant. Only foreign. The French, he said, were protected by crazy laws, you couldn't shift them once they had a foot in the door. He hoggered and spat into a grubby handkerchief.

"How long do you want it for?"

Of course, it was hard for me to know the answer. It depended on how long it would take me to find John, then Sarah, and then on when and where they would take me after that. I said I'd take it until the end of August for the time being if that was okay. Enjoying speaking French in Paris for the first time, I went on to explain that I knew it wasn't long, only I was looking for two missing friends. I was engaged in sort of detective work, you might say, and. . . .

"*C'est vos oignons,*" he said. "End of August is fine."

I followed him as he made his slow and mechanical way back on two métros, repulsed by the odour the heat caused to rise from beneath his coat. The apartment was not far from where I had gone drinking on my own the night before, I was glad to see (both because it was a sign that the synchronicities were working, and because it meant I would have somewhere to pass the time during unsociable hours). It was located just northeast of the Bastille, beyond the cocktail bars and takeaway joints, on a street of Arab cafés, Indian general stores, and Chinese wholesalers. It was a pale stone nineteenth-century building, fronted by a glass door with curled ironwork, between a small hardware shop and a laundrette. The man told me to wait in the hall beside the mailboxes and went into a room on the right where I heard him talking to a woman. She came briefly to the door and looked at me, for no more than two seconds, a white-haired woman with pearls, then she went back inside. A few moments later the man reappeared with a bunch of keys.

"*Alors,*" he said. "She needs a deposit of one month in advance. You pay two-fifty for the rest of July and five-fifty on the first of August. The code for the front door is 45-39-45. *Comme la guerre.* Don't forget it." My room was five flights up, one of two peeling blue doors off a dark and uncarpeted corridor running under the sloped roof of the building.

"In the room next door, there's another American boy," the

man said as he handed me a key. He indicated to me to open the door, so he could check, it seemed, that I was capable of it. The flat was small and musty, bare floorboards varnished a very long time before. There was a narrow old bed against the wall on the left, a wooden chair with a lamp balanced precariously on it posing as a bedside table. In the back right-hand corner there was a minute, linoleum-floored strip of kitchen (two hotplates, a sink, and a rough wooden table with a vase full of dirty water on it), and against the back wall there was a single battered leather armchair and a bockety set of bookshelves. The two windows on the right looked onto the street, small windows with dead plants hanging outside of them, framed with tin eaves on which I could hear pigeons scraping and cooing. In between the windows was a plastic desk with a garden chair.

"Lit, douche, WC," the man said mechanically, indicating a cubicle in the left-hand corner, below the bed, modestly veiled with a dirty yellow plastic curtain. "Au revoir." He pulled the door shut behind him and left me to my own devices.

I threw my bags over onto the couch, and once again thought about things starting anew from an undressed bed in an empty room, with only Oranges and Lemons as a guide. I looked around the small space that Pablo had so unequivocally, and presumably not without good reason, sent me to. This was command centre: from this desk between these walls, looking down at that Indian man selling brooms and mousetraps, I would seek out and find John and then Sarah and then others like them, track down that life I wanted back. I dressed the bed with the sheets I had brought. There was no pillow, and there was a dark patch on the wall at the top of the bed where the hair of years of sleeping tenants had brushed against it. I unzipped the book bag and unpacked the volumes meticulously one by one onto the shelf, alongside the few yellowing, speckled volumes already there, some translated Agatha Christie, Simenon, and a tourist guide in Spanish and Basque to the town of Durango in Biscay.

I sat on the bed, mesmerised by the slim row of books. Contained here was all the possible information I could get about John, Sarah, and Luis, who could be anywhere in this city, in any of the rooms on any of the floors of any of the long stretches of elegant stone buildings. I was in a no-man's land, between the life I had recently renounced and the coloured-glass world I longed to return to. The potential energy of the printed ink on these pages contained my only portal back. From this room I would seek them out; from this room I would go out to rejoin them.

I walked over to open the windows and let some air in. The street below was busy and active, Indians, Africans, and Arabs coming and going, buying and selling, eating and drinking. The dirty air was slightly powdered with spice. The view above stretched across an infinity of rooftops, windows, white satellite dishes, and aerials. Studded with small white lights, the black Tour Montparnasse rose up beyond them, a mysterious god, sleek and soundless, solemnly flashing a regular, inscrutable message of red light into my room. I sat there as darkness fell, watching its ancient communication, profound and obscure, punctuating my first night with a primordial hellenic heartbeat.

At around eight or nine, I was starving and could put off the beginning of the adventure no longer. I picked five books and threw them in the sports bag, took my wallet, and left the apartment. I was met in the passage by a short guy around my own age, well-built, with a crew cut and flip-flops, a saddle-bag slung over his shoulders. *Le garçon américain*. I didn't want social chitchat getting in the way of my plans, delaying or interfering with my vital enterprise. I was an arrow flying through the sky toward a single, distant point, and I did not want to be blown off course, especially not by the clichéd witterings of a spoilt young American in Paris. I thought of ducking quickly back inside to avoid him, but he had caught my eye and greeted me, so, resigned to the encounter, I waited for him outside my door.

"Bonsoir," he said in a heavy American accent.

"Bonsoir."

We shook hands.

"Keith Balfour."

"Niall Lenihan."

"Oh, you're American?"

"Irish."

"You the new guy next door?"

"Yes."

He put his key into his lock and pushed the door open with his foot.

"So what are you doing in Paris?" he asked.

"Looking for a friend," I said.

He laughed. "Well, *that* sounds intriguing."

"Not really."

"You wanna come in for a scotch?"

"No, thanks. Actually, I'm in a hurry."

He looked me up and down. I had left the bag unzipped and he could see it was full of books. He smiled quizzically.

"Get some reading done, huh?"

"That's right."

He raised his eyebrows and smiled again.

"Well, be seeing you round, Niall."

"Yes. . . ."

"Au revoir!" he called after me, as I hurried down the steps, zipping the bag closed as I went.

I ate a nutella crêpe purchased at a street corner for my dinner, then walked around my part of Paris, partially of my own volition, partially with synchronous consultation, which I performed in cafés en route over a glass of beer and a cigarette. The evening air was warm and smelt of garlic and trees, for me always since the smell of Paris. I walked along the quiet streets off rue de la Roquette, past green neon pharmacy crosses and small grocery shops with aproned men standing in the doorways, past the chic spacious apartments of *bonnes familles,* and, above them, little rooms like mine. I walked back up my street, rue du Chemin Vert, passing the building where a little square of light under the eaves was Keith Balfour at his endeavours, whatever they were, up past patisseries with queues to buy the morning's baguette, and then as far as the Père Lachaise cemetery, walled city of the dead, lugubrious home of Balzac, Proust, Jim Morrison, and Oscar Wilde, locked against the moving lights and chattering voices of the living, passing quickly by outside on boulevard Charonne. Again and again I thought I saw them: John standing joking with some girls outside a restaurant, leaning with one foot against a tree, like a rakish local corner boy; Sarah buying cigarettes in a tabac near the Bastille; John running a white hand through his oily black hair as he wove his way through the beeping cars, crossing Boulevard du Faubourg Saint Antoine; Sarah, filthy and cackling under sheets of cardboard at the entrance to the métro in République. Always the visions fell when I looked a second time, and the outlines of my missing companions were air-brushed back into the evening scenery.

Sent by the books, I returned to Objectif Lune. I was earlier than the night before, the regular bars were all still serving, so it was almost empty and was offering pints for the price of a demi until midnight. I chatted to the barman, the tall black guy from the night before. He was interested to hear I was Irish, he had once had a girlfriend from Kilkenny, he said. Fiona was her name. She had taught him to count to ten in Irish. *A haon, a dó, a trí, a ceathair, a cúig, a sé, a seacht, a hocht, a naoi, a deich.* He told me there was another Irish guy who drank in Objectif Lune, maybe he would even come in tonight. John! I thought immediately. If it was him, it would explain why the books had dispatched me there twice now.

The barman introduced himself formally; his name was André.

"Niall," I said and shook his hand.

His face lit up and he exclaimed:

"You have the same name as the other Irish guy that drinks here, the one I was telling you about!"

Disappointed, I asked him if he was certain. I repeated and spelled it, convinced that it must be a false memory, a recognition produced only by the similarity in our accents and the foreignness of the names. But André was absolutely sure, they had been chatting for weeks now.

"Yes, we talk all the time. We even talked about how it is the same first name as the tall footballer who used to play on the Irish soccer team. . . ."

"Niall Quinn," I said.

"*C'est ça, voilà!* I'm beginning to think you're all called Niall, *les Irlandais.*"

This evidence was irrefutable: it was not John. I fell into despondence again, and hoped I wouldn't have to make Irish-abroad small-talk with this Niall some evening. I asked the books, but the augury was ominous and obscure:

They've murdered a boy already. Now it's you.

I drank there all night and awoke the next day sweaty and clothed on the bed, the sun from the south-facing windows shrivelling up my dehydrated brain. The pigeons scraped and fought outside as I slowly stirred myself to the kitchen, where I stuck my head under the tap and gulped down water until my stomach was too full to take any more. My body was racked with hangover, quivering fingers and aching bones. I jumped into the rickety shower, head thumping, and in less than twenty minutes was sitting scrubbed and paracetamolled in a café two blocks down towards Bastille, sitting at a table with a double espresso, sparkling water, croissant, six books, a notepad, biro, and street map. I asked several specific and, I thought, intelligent questions which got me nowhere. Finally, I asked:

"How can I find John and Sarah?"

You would have a better chance of lighting it if you held the match nearer.

I weighed this. Tracing the sentence as an analogy, the match could refer to the *sortes,* the light I needed to see my way in the dark. Holding them nearer perhaps meant reading them more closely? But then I had the idea that "the match" could be read to mean "the couple," Sarah and John, and that I should "hold," that is, consider, them to be nearer. It struck me that if they were indeed close by, in my area of Paris, the eleventh arrondisse-ment, it would explain why Pablo had guided me there. Excited, I finished and paid for my breakfast, put the books in my bag, and left the café. My plan was now to consider them to be nearby, and so I decided to wander around the district guided at every turn, at every step if necessary, by the *sortes.*

It was a tiring and hot but initially not hopeless odyssey. I hiked up and down the scruffy streets within the triangle formed by Bastille, République, and Nation, by old white women walking poodles, hip young men carrying guitars, a Latin American couple singing for money at a métro station, then back and forth through the leafy avenues of the deceased in Père Lachaise. Although it was an exhausting trek around in circles, the *sortes* constantly seemed to be on the point of yielding something. I was led to the bell of an *S DE VERE* on rue de Bagnolet, but when I rang, the only response was a dog barking in an echoey room, which I took as an unlikely sign. Stranger still, a series of synchronicities took me to a church of Saint-Jean-Bap-tiste, where a choir inside was rehearsing *Miserere Mei,* although Ash Wednesday was eight months away.

When I consulted the books after a ham and cheese baguette and two oranginas, they seemed to send me explicitly down rue de la Roquette towards the Bastille, and then, (*"Frankly, Miss*

Price,"), to the Franprix supermarket. I walked into the white hum of fridges, shivered a little with the air conditioning, then took a synchronicity, ostentatiously, so that the security man would not think I was slyly secreting apples or brillo pads in my bookbag.

There are some pretty men gone to the bottom

I took this as a statement that the search was over: a pretty man, John, was waiting for me at the bottom of the supermarket. This made most sense, since it was in keeping with the working hypothesis that he was physically close to where I was. Pablo had very deliberately sent me to this part of Paris; the forward and back all afternoon must have been my slowly circling in on John, a hound after a fox who has crossed and recrossed the land. I had gone in circles, but I had not lost the scent, and now had run him to earth. I began to make my way down the aisle, away from fruit and vegetables, towards the deli counter at the back.

Some pretty men. I slowed my pace. More than one of them. Sweat pricked my back, and the refrigerated air seemed to grow even cooler. It could only mean that John was here with Luis. I walked slowly, creeping up alongside the frankfurters and chicken fillets, keeping close to the shelves. I imagined them together, John sullen, sexy and dishevelled, Luis middle-aged, perfectly groomed and tanned, salt and pepper hair, in an impeccable suit and a tie, a leather briefcase, expensive slip-on shoes with little tassels, the two of them trailing through the grocery store together on a book-appointed errand, four green eyes darting back and forth across the shelves. My heart pounded in my chest. And when I found them? The next level.

I inched along, hugging the shelves, certain they were around the corner at the bottom of the aisle. I stopped a few feet from the corner and listened. I could hear the low mumbling of two male voices from the other side, just out of sight. And they were speaking English. I froze, then pulled another book from the bag. I crouched down on the ground, out of sight against the display of crisps on the corner. As I flicked through the book, I was walloped all of a sudden in the back by a metal object. There was a crashing of glass. I fell forward in pain, my bag flew out of my hand and went skidding down the aisle, scattering the books on the ground. I'm being murdered, I thought, I have gone too far and Pour Mieux Vivre is having me assassinated.

"Oh, shit, hey, sorry, man! You okay? Ah, shit, sorry, man! We didn't . . . hey, it's my Irish neighbor . . . jeez, Niall, I'm really sorry . . . you okay?"

Keith Balfour, saddlebag at his side, was down on his hunkers with a hand on my shoulders, looking concernedly into my face. I caught my breath and stood up. Keith got up and walked around the aisle picking up my possessions. He handed me my notepad and biro and replaced my books in the bag one by one, checking out the titles as he did so. Standing over me was another American guy, wearing a Princeton T-shirt and a backwards baseball cap. He was pushing a supermarket trolley, which is what had come around the corner and whacked me. It was piled with crisps, crackers, twenty-packs of bottled beer, and large bottles of vodka and gin, the clinking of which had been the sound of glass I had heard.

"I'm fine," I said, "really." I took the bookbag off him and zipped it up. "Just watch where you're going," I snapped.

Keith stared at me, then broke into a half-smile. "Sure thing. I apologise. But, if you don't mind me saying, you did seem to be . . . hiding."

"I was looking for something," I said. "I was bending down to get it."

Our three pairs of eyes turned to the lower shelf I was pointing to. It was entirely empty, except for where an indecisive shopper had changed his or her mind on the way out and deposited an unwanted sack of cat-biscuits, *Minourriture*, lonely exile from the pet-food section.

"Well, in the future we'll watch out for shoppers in the shadows," Keith said, still smiling. "By the way, this is Ryan."

The bulky guy pushing the trolley held out a hand the size of a baseball glove, and we greeted each other.

"Ryan, this is my new next-door neighbour. Niall, from Ireland."

"Sorry about the cart in the ass, dude," Ryan said. "Two Irishmen brawling over a bunch of beer, happened before, huh?"

"I was going to call in, or leave a note," Keith said, nodding at the book bag, "to tell you I'm having a kind of party tonight. It might get kind of late and loud, you know. I hope that's cool with you. I mean, you should come by. There'll be a couple Irish guys Ryan knows."

"Irish like me or Irish like him?" I asked obnoxiously, nodding at Ryan. They laughed good-naturedly.

"Oh, fresh from the Emerald Isle," Keith said. "Not just heritage-hungry Americans. Come by. Around nine or ten."

"I'm busy," I muttered, and hurried around the corner away from them.

My prey had flown in the time I had wasted with the Americans and their booze-filled trolley, that much was sure. As I left the supermarket, I cursed Keith and his Irish-American sidekick aloud for wrecking my chances at the eleventh hour. I stayed in the apartment for the rest of the afternoon, books, map, and jotter open on the desk, head bent over in the little pool of light, trying to regain the trail I had lost. I plotted on the map with dotted lines of biro the ways the books had led me, to see if I could make any sense of it, like a detective in a film following the path of a deranged genius serial killer. My route could have been construed as a kind of capital Z turned on its side, I thought, but this meant nothing to me. I went back over the scores of synchronicities I had got throughout the course of the day, from *held the match nearer* to *pretty men*, tracking running themes and imagery, looking for anagrams, initials, or other clues, cross-referencing my results with fresh questions I asked of the untried volumes left on the shelf, *sortes* about *sortes* about *sortes*, all to no apparent avail.

At some point, I heard Keith and Ryan come clinking back to the flat, and for the next several hours I heard hoovering, furniture shifting, conversations on a cell phone, long ones in American English, *I think Stacey's coming, you can, like, walk over with her*, short ones in American French, *la métro c'est Saint Ambroise, oui, oui, c'est ça*. Later, I heard and smelt them come in with takeaway Chinese food. At half-eight their friends started to arrive and I had to listen to all the *hey dudes* and backslapping at the door, and squeaky American girls enthusing about the mixed drinks inside, *oh my god these margaritas are SO awesome*. For an hour or two I concentrated on my work enough to exclude the noise, but when it was finally a real crowd-noise, and when the music, Eminem or something like it, started thumping the floor, I took a synchronicity to see what I should do.

I went down, and drank my fill, and then came up, and got a blink of the moon, and then down again.

Clear enough: I gathered my tools into the bag and went down towards the Bastille, once more, to get drunk in Objectif Lune. I continued working for a little while at the bar there, while André, who told me that the other Niall was not there tonight, looked into the distance and moved to the music. Around midnight, it became too full for my consultations to be practical, so I packed away the books again and watched the crowd. I was saved from my anxious thoughts by a rapid-moving knot of Irish accents that came in laughing and slagging from the street and moved to the corner of the bar. The group consisted of four men and three women, all around John and Sarah's age. One girl was the leader of the group, with a loud, rather braying voice and a Cork accent. Every time the group had to make a decision (what to drink, how much to drink, whose round, stay or go, stand or sit, etc.), or sometimes just because she was in the mood, she would call out a slogan she had devised either for all her nights out, or, I dearly hoped, just for this one:

"Who rules ye, lads? *The wan from Clon.* Tell me who it is. Loud and clear, boys, all of ye. Who is the bee's knees?"

"*The wan from Clon,*" the others, a shy group who clearly didn't know her or each other too well, would all reply, at first with residual enthusiasm, then, as the night grew late and the battlecry more frequent, with a note of hesitation, boredom, even obedient shame.

For almost an hour, I observed this theatre, fascinated by the spectacle of the Irish rendered odd and exotic. Finally, after some scrutiny and whispering, the Corkwoman came over and spoke to me.

"Are you Irish?"

"Yes."

"Well then, come into the parlour and *fáilte romhat!* I'm Gráinne, from Clonakilty. But I'm known in Paris as—"

"I heard. Niall from Dublin. Sandycove."

"I *knew* you were a feckin Dub! I told ye, didn't I? What did I say to ye, lads? Who knows what's what? Who, lads? The wan from Clon, that's who."

Annoying as the Wan from Clon was, the alternatives of tossing and turning in bed while the Americans listened to gangster rap and downed shots of JD next door, or of glaring off into space and let-ting my head reel with thoughts of the ghosts I was chasing, were not particularly appealing either, so I picked up my pint and bag and joined the Irish. I asked Gráinne if she knew the other Niall.

"Not to the best of my knowledge," she said. "Hang on. I tell a lie. Tall dark-haired fella?"

"I don't know, André just told me there was another Niall."

"Yes, there's another Irish fella drinks here all right, who's called Niall to the best of my knowledge."

She herself had been in Paris for five years, circulated in exclusively Irish circles, and claimed to know all of the young Irish, or at least those who, as she put it, "participated." In a flash of joy, I decided that Gráinne, grotesque parody though she was, was the person whom the books had been sending me to. She was to be the guide, the Virgil who would help me negotiate this complex world and lead me, eventually, back to Pour Mieux Vivre. I told her my mission, the search for a missing Irish friend.

She hadn't come across John, *to the best of her knowledge,* she said, using what was clearly a preferred phrase. I asked her about Sarah and she shook her head again. I should come to Harry's Bar on the corner of rue de Rivoli on a Friday or Saturday night and ask around the Irish there, she said. She would think about how to go about finding them in the meantime. I also told her I was looking for a stopgap job to cover my rent, and she told me of a French cake and snacks chain whose Champs Élysées branch had a tradition of hiring Irish people. She knew the floor manager, Aisling. If I mentioned the words the Wan from Clon, I would be sure of any job that was going.

"It's a system we have. That's the way I tell them it's a good egg I'm after sending. It's a code."

I thanked her.

"You know what to say, now, that you were sent by the Wan from Clon?"

I told her I understood, but she eyed me suspiciously.

"Don't say Gráinne," she said, a hated word she pronounced between inverted commas, as if it were a insult in a foreign language she had heard men shout at her in the streets of her holidays. "It's our code."

I wrote down the name of the place before I left, saying I was sure our paths would cross again in Objectif Lune, and if not, some Friday or Saturday night in Harry's. I gave her my address and told her that if she did come across or hear about anyone matching the description of my friends, she might send me a postcard. None of this, the fact that I was a nineteen-year-old on a lone manhunt in Paris, or that I had no means of contact except postcards, surprised Gráinne from Clonakilty, who, it seemed, in her years of socialising with the Irish in Paris, had seen it all.

I was outraged to see Keith Balfour's light on when I arrived back at the flat, and to see the red-tips and silhouettes of two guests smoking out his window. I tiptoed past his door, which was ajar, allowing the sound of rap music and young American chatter to spill into the corridor. I lay on the bed in my clothes, smoking and listening to the murmur of the end of the party next door. I was becoming a real smoker, I thought. I opened the bag at around half-two and had started reconsidering the day's research when there was a tentative knock at the door and I heard the low voice of Keith Balfour.

"Yo, neighbour. Hello, you awake? Hello? Niall?"

I sighed, threw the books aside, and opened the door to Keith. I saw his eyes flick past me and look around the room, at the books and map on the floor. I repositioned myself to block his view.

"We were going to move on to the Irish stuff," he said, holding up a bottle of Jameson, "and I saw your light on and, you know, thought it would be a shame not to invite you in."

"Look, thanks, but, um, it's not a great time . . . I have a lot to do. . . ."

"I also think," he said, leaning in, "I also think I might have found your friend."

"What? Really? Where is he?"

"Come in for whiskey and I'll tell you."

I hesitated.

"Hold on a second," I said, closing the door on him. I picked a book off the ground and flicked through it.

*it was plain to both of us he was in deadly earnest; and so Alan
and I, with no great fear of treachery, stepped onto the deck.*

I threw it on the bed and went back to Keith, waiting with the
bottle outside the closed door.

"Okay," I answered, to his amused and quizzical face. "I'll
come in for a drink."

His place was a little bigger than mine, and far better furnished, full of what Americans called their "stuff," posters, chairs,
bar stools, a basketball hoop, *Princeton Class of 2005* pennant,
neon *Budweiser* light, lava lamp, a pine bookshelf, and next to it a
tall computer desk with a desktop and speakers where the music
came from. In contrast, my room seemed rather like an abandoned barn. Keith had a double bed against the left wall, on
which Ryan was sitting with a glass of whiskey talking to an Asian
girl who was leaning against the wall with her eyes closed. Two
blond girls, the ones I had seen smoking from the street, were sitting on the window ledge, laughing and drinking. When they
moved, the sprinkled white lights and red flash of the Tour Montparnasse would suddenly come into view. A sofa and some armchairs surrounded a low table in the centre of the room, piled
high with empty bottles, glasses, and ice-trays. A group of
around six people, all American-looking, were draped on these,
drinking and smoking, and there was one other guy kneeling at
the table and rolling a joint.

"People!" Keith called when we went in, banging the side of
the bookshelf with his hand for attention. "People, listen up! This
is Niall, next-door-neighbor from Ireland. Make him welcome,
fatten the calf! Niall, you know Ryan, that's Julie, Shannon, Brad,
Mike, Noah, Joel. . . ." He went through the names, the girls all
smiled brightly, the men raised a hand and said "hey," then
everyone, thankfully, went back to their conversations.

Keith poured Jamesons for him and me, and we went and
stood at the other window.

"Cheers," he said.

I returned the toast, against the distant backdrop of the tower.

"So you think you found my friend."

"Straight down to business, huh? A cousin of Ryan's came by, his name was, um . . . Ryan! Hey, *Ryan!* What's your cousin's name?

"Johnny."

"Oh, yeah, Johnny."

I raised my eyebrows in hope, even if it was hard to envision John accepting an invitation to a party like this. Keith went on:

"Yeah, well, not him, but his buddy. He was with a friend from Dublin. We got chatting, anyway, and he said he thought he knew you."

"His name . . . what was his name?"

"Let me think a minute . . . man, am I bombed. He said he knew you from high school or something."

"From college, you mean?"

"I'm pretty sure he said high school. His name was . . . oh, something short. Ian! Yes, that's his name, Ian."

I paused for a moment to take this in, with a mixture of disappointment and high curiosity.

"Yeah," I said, "from high school. No, he's not the one I was looking for."

"No? I figured maybe not. He's only in Paris for a few days."

That's a relief, I thought to myself as I looked out at the tower, and at the dark city still not yielding up its secret hiding places.

"Still quite a coincidence, huh? We knocked on your door a bunch of times, but I guess you were out. . . ."

"Yes. When is he leaving exactly?"

"Back to Dublin tomorrow. Like I said, we tried to find you. He was freaked out by the coincidence. More than you seem to be!"

"I'm used to coincidences," I said. "I'm plagued by them, in fact. Did he . . . was he keen to see me?"

Keith looked at me curiously. "I dunno, I guess . . . like I said, he was pretty taken aback by the coincidence."

"And did he," I began my last question, the last consultation on this matter. "Did he have a girlfriend? With him?"

"Yeah, they were having like a romantic couple days in Paris I think. Lisa?"

"Laoise, yeah," I nodded, "That sounds right."

We drank in silence. The smell of the joint behind us was making me dizzy.

"So that wasn't the one you were looking for, I guess."

"No. Thanks," I added.

"No worries, man."

They passed the joint over to us. Keith took a long drag, I shook my head. He gave it back.

"So," he began again, blowing the hash-smoke out the window, and looking away from me, off towards the tower. "So who *is* the friend you're looking for? What are you really doing? With the books. I've watched."

"I'm a student of literature. I read," I said, rather dismissively, and then, before he could respond, "What do you do?"

"Me? Oh, also a student of literature, as you say. I'm going into my senior year at Princeton. I study English. I've just spent a semester and the summer in Paris."

"Doing?"

"Gathering material for my senior thesis."

"What is it, creative writing?" I asked, with just a touch of European disdain.

"Kind of. Creative non-fiction."

"What's that when it's at home?"

"I'm doing a sort of journalistic thesis."

"And why Paris?"

"Come on, why not? But then when I was here, I thought I'd do this thing about ex-pats in Paris. You know, debunk the myths of the Lost Generation. But then it spread out. You see that drawer over there?" He indicated the computer desk. "It's full of tapes. Tapes, tapes, tapes. I've been interviewing people in Paris since I came."

"Who?"

"Oh, anyone who can do a proper interview in English. Dozens and dozens of them."

"And you'll turn it into your thesis?"

"That's the theory. My bet is that when I get back to Princeton, they'll gather dust and I'll write an English thesis about *The Great Gatsby* or *Bartleby the Scrivener* like the rest of 'em. Speaking of books. . . ."

I shook my head and put the glass down. He was not going to let up.

"I have to go to bed."

He didn't say anything, but got up and walked me back to the door.

"Thanks for inviting me," I said. "Enjoy the rest of the night."

He smiled and shook his head. "You think we're philistines, don't you?" he said quietly. "War-mongering Philistines."

I opened my mouth to protest, but he said, "It's okay, really. Maybe we are."

From behind him, I heard a guy's voice call out:

"Hey, what kind of Irishman turns his back on a roomful of scotch?"

"Bye," Keith said, offering his hand.

I shook it, but remained just long enough outside the door to hear him answer his friend.

"He's not doing too well since Ryan slammed into him with a plurality of bottles."

Twelve

This phrase from Keith's lips stunned and upset me, of course. The duplications and reduplications were now too much for me to deal with or untangle; it was becoming clear that things were maintaining a fiction of their own, and I was at a loss. I stood outside the door for ten minutes wondering whether or not I should go back in and talk to Keith, then decided not only to go home but that the best course of action would be to shun him. Things were complicated enough as they were. The next day, I focused on the question of money. I followed the Wan from Clon's tip and took the métro from Bastille to Franklin D. Roosevelt on the Champs Élysées and found the French fast food outlet ("La Brioche Dorée") she had told me about. I heard two girls, dressed in the uniform of red checked blouse, white apron, and red hairband whispering behind the counter in Irish accents. I asked them for Aisling. She wasn't there, and they sent me out the duty manager instead, a pleasant and bumbling French man in his early thirties who said there were no vacancies. I shamefacedly produced the four syllables of her shibboleth:

"C'est the Wan from Clon *qui m'a envoyé."*

"Qui ça? . . . zaouanne fromme Clonne . . . ?"

I repeated it, and he looked confused. One of the Irish girls said something to him and his face lit up.

"Ah, Gráinne!" He changed his tune immediately and told me there were four Irish students working for him already, all sent by Gráinne, and they had so far done a "bon travail," he said; since Gráinne had sent me, he could now reveal that one of the French girls was leaving, to prepare for her law exams (he added proudly, as if one usually graduated from the mops, aluminium ashtrays, and tartes framboises of the Golden Brioche to the wigs and parchment of the Palais de Justice), and I could take her place; I should start in three days.

He gave me the details, I gave him mine, then I rushed straight home to the books. I saw Keith coming down the road from the other direction. I realised we would meet at the door, so I turned in a side street and idled around until I was sure our paths wouldn't cross.

Back in my room, I sat down and began to work in a concentrated fashion. The answer to my first question, *Ten green bottles,* drove me mad with fury and I flung the book across the room. I spent the evening until sunset mooching without success around the gay streets of the Marais, ending with a beer in the bar where I had had the iced vodka and lemons with Pablo. I brooded on my lack of progress so far and fixed on the idea that since my arrival in Paris, Keith Balfour had been destroying all of my efforts to find John, his malign activities capped by the ridiculous fact of his uttering the magic phrase. In a dark, unreasoned corner of my mind, I began to regard Keith as a kind of enemy antichrist, a demon sent to thwart me in my attempt to return to Pour Mieux Vivre. I saluted him coldly when we passed each other in the corridor over the following days, as I went out to work at the Brioche Dorée.

The job there was tiring but manageable. Most of the work

was shovelling croissants into paper bags and ringing customers up on the till. The trickier aspects of the job included the whipped ice-cream machine—harder than one might think to swirl sustainably into a cone; the making of espresso in the machine; the transubstantiation, by microwaves, of frozen fris-bees into croque monsieurs; and the glazing (the eponymous process of *dorer*) of raw baked goods before they were slid into the ovens behind us.

They put me on what they called *fermeture,* French for "closing," though, like so many of the objects and concepts of the Brioche, untransplantable from its context, so that the Irish called it fermeture even when speaking English, reshaping it with Hibernian vowels and consonants so that it rhymed with "furniture."

After fermeture, having scraped off the last flakes of almond triangle from between the grooves of the display glass, sat on the counter between the upended tables to smoke a cigarette with the rest of the fermeture team, usually two thirds Irish and one third French, Sinéad, Laure, Paul, Aisling, Karim, Jennifer, and having turned down their requests to go drinking with them next door at the Monte Cristo, I arrived home at two or three in the morning. I was knackered when I got back, my feet swollen from eight hours of standing behind the counter in the Brioche, and I had no thoughts of insomnia. But I was determined to set a routine of getting straight down to work on the *sortes* hunt. I was in Paris for a reason, and it would be absurd, I told myself when my aching bones and tired head protested, if working in the café to finance the stay there prevented me from looking for John. I sent a postcard to my parents, ostensibly for Ciara's birthday, but really because I didn't think I could manage all the lies of a phone call, and told them I had found a job and made friends with an American.

In reality, however, his magic words thundering in my ears, I did everything in my power to avoid the American, and in fact this activity became almost as central to my efforts as finding John, as if the one implied the opposite of the other. When the Brioche started to rotate me on what they called *le planning,* as was only normal, between early mornings, *ouverture* (06h–14h), regular days (09h–17h), and *fermeture* (17h–02h), I asked Aisling if she could put me permanently on fermeture: working the night shift meant that Keith was almost always in bed by the time I got home, and I was able to work in peace. Aisling, not surprisingly, thought it was a weird request, and most likely illegal under French labour law, but I badgered her until she acceded to it and I became a permanent feature of fermeture, the vampire of the Gilded Brioche, a quickly acknowledged expert in the ways and means of shutting shop, the closure king. The few times I was forced to do other shifts, I had inevitably encountered Keith at some point, as I usually did at four in the afternoon as I left for work. On those occasions when I came back from fermeture and saw his light still on, I would go and drink with some books and notes in Objectif Lune until I was sure he was asleep. I never saw the Wan from Clon there, to thank her for sending me in the direction of the job, and André told me that the other Niall no longer drank there.

My routine, when not interrupted by these trips, or by Aisling insisting on putting me on a different shift, consisted of some hours of *sortes* and planning in my room, which became, as Northumberland Road had, an indispensable centre of operations from which to make charts, strategies, and plans. I would put them into practice with long dawn walks around east-central Paris, exhaustively following leads and hints and joining up dotted lines which existed only on my street map, now covered with a spider's web of pencil and biro, its margins crowded with annotations and observations. I found nothing concrete, only tormenting signs that something was still at work, some pattern in play, such as being led to an apartment block where the initial letters of the names on the bells formed an acrostic of "Sarah"

(*Solange NARDINI, Alain ILLIERS, Rachid ALSHAKRY, Anne-Claude LISÈRE, Henri LAVALLE*), or ending up in conversation with a drunk Irish gay man in the Marais called John. Beyond such gimmicks, I was always, in the Pour Mieux Vivre sense, sober: I had no visions, no unreal experiences, no blurring of boundaries, unless you count the extraordinary frequency with which I was led into the vicinity of acquaintances from Dublin on their Ryanair trips to Paris. I had no insomnia; on the contrary, I hungered for and jealously guarded my daily sleep from six in the morning until two in the afternoon. I ate in sizeable quantity, if not great variety, subsisting almost entirely on the surplus, unsold food from the Brioche which—one of the perks of fermeture—we were allowed to take home in plastic bags. My diet consisted only of flans, strawberry tartelettes, tuna baguettes, cold croque monsieurs and, of course, glazed brioche.

Keith's sentence about the bottles tortured me if I allowed my mind to turn to it for a moment: which was why I didn't, and why I kept up this murderous nocturnal schedule in avoidance of his society. But of course, I could not account for everything, and one night, about a week into my established routine of fermeture, synchronicities, and wanderings, I came home and saw his light on. I crept by his door, hoping he wouldn't hear me, and went to my books and notepad as always. I had not yet chosen my first synchronicity, however, before there came a knocking at the door.

"Niall? Niall? You awake?"

I chose the passage before answering:

I'd been right all along. I figured out the pattern

Gritting my teeth, I walked over and opened the door.

"Keith."

"Hey. I just got in. I saw your light on from the street and I thought, hell, how many of us can there be in Paris who are still up at three in the morning. Nightcap?"

"No," I said, surprised at my own firmness. "No, thanks, I'm working. I have a job in a café during the evenings now, so at night I have to. . . ."

"Oh, come on. After the party I have, as your Myles na gCopaleen would say, a plurality of bottles. . . ."

What was I to do, faced with this? I tried to convince myself, as Keith waited for me to respond, that it was just an impossible coincidence quite outside the economy of the *sortes*. And then it struck me that that was precisely what John must have tried to think about me back in the days. No, the fact was that with Keith, the apostolic succession was continuing, and if I disliked the form it took, the system was nevertheless greater than me, and I had to accept it. Like Luis with Sarah, Sarah with John, and John in his turn with me, I knew this thing would not go away. I could clench my teeth and scuttle down back alleys and tire my eyes out with sentences and paragraphs of cryptic advice, but it would keep knocking on my door, as I had kept knocking on John's.

"Okay, just the one," I said, knowing full well we were facing into a plurality.

He poured out two little glasses, and we sat on the armchairs, facing each other across the bottle. I was looking towards the window and the tower.

"Cheers."

"To old friends," I replied. "Showing up where you least expect them."

"To old friends."

We knocked the whiskey back, at his instigation, and he poured a second round, which we sipped.

"Where are you from?" I asked him.

"Marin County, California."

"Don't think I've heard of it."

"Just beside San Francisco. Over the water from Alcatraz. Rich suburb. My father is a plastic surgeon. And you?"

"Ireland, as you know. Dublin County. Over the water from Dalkey Island. And do you want to get in to journalism? When you're finished in Princeton, I mean."

"No. I want to do this thesis with the interviews, but I think when I'm done I'd like to get into publishing."

"Oh, nice. A good industry."

"Not much dough, but anyway. You?"

I shrugged. "Seems like a long way away."

"Something involving reading?" he suggested.

"Possibly. Did you do any interviewing today?" I asked politely.

"Not really. Just Americans."

"Philistines," I said, and he laughed.

"And you?"

"Did I interview anyone? Only the customers in the café, *Do you want that fizzy or flat.* Americans too, mostly."

"No, I mean did you get any of that outdoor studying done? Did you get any closer to finding your friend?"

"Look . . ." I said. "It's a party game. I use it as a kind of . . . meditation. That's all, a party game."

"Show me."

"No."

"Why?"

"Because . . . because . . . I wish no one had ever shown it to me, Keith." A nauseating revelation, a half-truth, but nauseating for all that, hit me.

"Don't use my name like that. You sound like a killer in a horror movie."

"Sorry."

"Please show it to me."

I took a sip of the whiskey, looking out at the tower, and then another. He thought that I was fully within the mysterious system he had glimpsed me employing; he was not to know that I was lost, fallen into the crack between two worlds. There was still a chance, of course, to spare him everything. But confronted with Keith's face across the table in the Paris night heat, I had a flashback to Kehoe's pub on South Anne Street in December and to myself pestering and pushing the reluctant John. It's not all about me, I thought, it is beyond my control. I had served my apprenticeship and moved on. Now I had been appointed to initiate the Princeton English major.

"Okay, stand up," I commanded. He got out of his chair. "Now ask a question."

"What should I ask?"

"Anything. Something you want to know."

"Like my future?"

"If you want."

"Okay."

"What?"

"I've asked it."

"No, Keith, out loud. It's not like a birthday candles wish."

"Remember what I said about the name thing?"

"Sorry. Ask out loud."

"Okay. What job will I have? Now what?"

"What job will Keith have?"

I continued quickly with my instructions:

"Now walk over there to the bookshelf," I said, and was surprised to see someone following my orders instead of the other way round, for a change.

"Now what?" Keith asked, standing absurdly with his face to his bookshelf.

"Right. Now turn around towards me. Ask the question again."

"The same question?"

"The same question."

"What job will I have in the future?"

"Now, we have decided that the answer to the question is on the bookshelf."

"We have?"

"We have. Run your hand along the books, without looking, yes, like that, until you feel you've picked the right book. When you've picked one that seems right, the one that just *feels* right, flick through it, without looking at what you've chosen, and choose a passage with your finger."

"At random?"

"Stop your finger wherever feels right."

"Okay." He had picked a fantasy novel. He looked at it. "How much should I read?"

"Read out the line your finger stopped on, then read back and onwards a bit and decide yourself if you need more from either side. It'll be clear to you."

"I picked the title of a book," he said. "From the list of other titles by the author. On the last page."

"Read it out."

"*The Mists of Avalon*. Doesn't mean anything to me."

Of course. I was not good at initiating, I thought. I had done it all wrong. I squeezed the bridge of my nose, in the manner of a frustrated, wise, and experienced initiator, and shut my eyes.

"No, sorry. It's usually not a good idea to try to predict the future exactly. It's a question of phrasing more than anything. What they're saying is, the future is shrouded in mist."

"Who are *they*? Man, you are freaking me *out*," he laughed.

I ignored him.

"Put the book back—not in the same place, or you'll remember where it is and the choice won't be properly random. Right. Now ask something else, something to do with the present."

"Like?"

"Oh you know, like about a girl or something."

"How do I feel about Rebecca? That's the girl I was seeing in Princeton before I left for Paris."

"How does Keith feel about Rebecca?"

He chose.

"Now, sir, I was for France; and there was a French ship cruising here to pick me up; but she gave us the go-by in the fog—as I wish from the heart that ye had done yoursel'! Well, that doesn't mean much."

"Come here, show it to me," I said. He handed me the book and sat down again with his whiskey. My old Jedi eyes needed only to glance lazily at the text before it coalesced into an obvious meaning in front of me. "Oh, come on, it's clear. You're in *France,* for God's sake. The French ship cruising to pick you up would be, you know, some other girl you met here who you thought would, you know. . . ."

"Okay," he conceded, "there was this one girl, Cécile."

"But in the end she didn't go for you, right?"

"Right. She *gave me the go-by,* I guess."

"Very good. Now, they are saying that you wish what's her name, Rebecca, would do the same. Leave you alone. Fall out of love. It's her they're addressing when they say *ye had done yoursel.* See, I told you it was obvious."

Keith was quiet, took the book off me and looked over the passage again, sipping his whiskey and nodding.

"It's true," he admitted. "That's exactly how things are with Rebecca. And it's what I thought when Cécile gave me the push. You're right, I mean they're right."

"I told you."

"Yeah . . . but who's *they?*"

I took a deep breath and told him the little I knew. How they used to use Virgil and the Gospels, all I could remember from what John and then Sarah had told me the first time I had done them, without any of the names or specific historical cases she had had at her fingertips, though I did remember Saint Augustine's line, as Sarah had quoted it, in Latin *"tolle, lege"* which made me feel learned. This moment of Keith's induction, a process which I had been enjoying up till now, caused a wave of doubt to swell within me. For an initiator, the level of knowledge I had was hopelessly inadequate. The thought struck me that for Keith, I would be the only available source of information about the systems that would soon come to dominate his life, though I myself knew nothing. Given this, I wondered with rising sadness and panic, how could I, or anyone else, go about finding anything about this thing, the blind leading the blind leading the blind.

But this part of the story did not interest Keith. He was interested only in what I believed the books were doing now, in how I used them in my life. I was evasive.

"Okay, then," he said, standing up and facing the bookshelf. "When Niall is talking about synchronicities and he says *they*, who does he mean?"

"No," I said. "You can't ask that. They. . . ." I trailed off.

Keith just grinned at me, pulled a volume of the shelf, and read:

There is much doubt about who they are and how many there are—whether two different names for sibyls, for instance, actually represent two persons or one. Some traditions give us as many as ten sibyls: the Persian, the Libyan, the Delphian, the Cimmerian, the Erythraean, the Samian, the Cumaean, the Hellespontine, the Phrygian, the Tiburtine. Others, applying a Mediterranean version of Occam's razor, suggest there is only one, appearing in multiple guises. And in the most famous and haunting of these stories, a sibyl destroys two thirds of the books of her wisdom.

He was taken aback.

"Wow," he said, and read it out again slowly. He sat down and took up his drink. "Amazing coincidence. Incredible."

"I told you. They tend to be especially explicit with the skeptical. Ask something else."

We asked the usual, about inner realities, other people, general questions of a philosophical nature, and so on. The *sortes* maintained the uncanny relevance they always had, though nothing was so obviously on the mark as the sibyl passage, and Keith, to my great surprise, didn't make the leap I had to asking specific factual questions. I left him at dawn, and when I looked behind me through the door and saw him sitting slumped in an armchair surrounded by piles of discarded books, I saw the perfect figure of the newcomer, the fresh convert, and I thought *Jesus Christ, what have I done.*

All evening at work in the Brioche, as I made *cafés serrés* for men in suits en route from the office on the Champs-Élysées to their lovers' apartments in the fifteenth, and served croques to drag queens as their main meal to sustain the night's clubbing, I imagined Keith alone in his apartment pulling down book after book, asking question after question, slowly working out just how much more there was to the whole thing than what I had told him. After fermeture I hurried home: I expected him to be up, waiting for me, a heap of consulted books on the ground, the beginnings of a green gleam in his eyes. I wondered, guiltily, if together the two of us might even be of sufficient number and expertise to start passing the books back and forth by candle-light. I thought that we might even be able to find Sarah, John, even Luis, together. Selfish hopes, I thought, as the taxi sped me along the right bank towards Bastille . . . but then it would be impossible to keep him away once he started, he would want to go to the next level. He might already be wandering the streets, books in hand, listening to fragments of conversation around him. And soon he would start asking the questions whose answers I had wanted from John, what's behind it, who started it, what does it mean, where does it go, and I would have nothing to give him.

I was surprised, then, to see his windows dark and curtained when I closed the door of the taxi and looked up at the top floor of our building. In my own room, I lingered for longer than usual at my desk with the map, books, and notepad, expecting his return and knock on the door. *Niall, show me more, I need to see more*. After hours had passed and there was still no sign, I was even concerned that he had taken things too far, and was already lost in the city, fallen into the gap between life and fiction. But a low snoring which began to come through the wall sometime after four let me know that he was there, and in fact that he had already been there, asleep, when I had arrived in from work. I reached for the books.

You've set me whirling round, but we must go step by step

Wise words. All the same, I did feel a light but definite sense of letdown and loneliness at the sound of his snoring, and instead of setting out into the dark hours alone with my *sortes*, I took myself step by step to Objectif Lune for a few pints of Stella to last me through to sunrise. I had no company there, but André the barman did tell me that the other Niall had finally shown up again earlier that night and was asking for me.

It was two days before I saw Keith again. The following night there were goodbye drinks for Sinéad in the Monte Cristo after work. She had failed one of her exams in UCD and had to go home to repeat. She had been the one who had trained me in, guided my first ice-cream cone and watched me sugar my first almond triangle, and so, in my current mood of initiations and apprenticeships I made an exception to my strict routine and went for Piña Coladas with the rest of the night's fermeture team to toast my erstwhile instructor. I got the first métro home, and the sun had crept over the houses when I arrived back at the flat. The next day was my day off. I spent the afternoon out with the books searching for John, or any trace of Pour Mieux Vivre, with no tangible results. I ate tortellini boiled in the packet at home, and invented all manner of excuses to stay there, in the hope of seeing my next-door neighbour: my curiosity with regard to how he was getting on since his induction into the books was overwhelming. He came in around seven; I didn't call on him, I wanted to see if he would come to me, just as the books had sent me time and time again after John and Sarah. Sure enough, at around ten, his knock came on the door.

"Evening, neighbor," he said when I opened to him. "Fancy a glass of something Irish?"

I looked at him carefully to see if I could notice any change. He did look a bit dishevelled, and that might just have been a flash of green at the back of his eyes, but the poor light in the corridor made it impossible to tell.

"Sure."

His flat was neat and untroubled-looking; most striking of all, his bookshelf was intact and orderly, and a bookmarked volume lying on his pillow was evidence of regular reading habits.

"Sit down." He put out the usual little glasses and uncorked the green bottle. "So," he said eventually, "so, I have some questions to ask you."

"I thought you might."

I had determined to be a better inductor than John had been to me, and I sat back, ready for a long night, promising myself to answer everything as honestly as I could, not to hold anything back, as had been done to me, to be open even about the severe limits of my knowledge.

"I'd like to know more about what you do with the books, and I'd like to know more about the friend you are looking for."

"Okay. Would you like to formulate a question to ask the books?"

Keith looked surprised. "Um . . . do you think it's necessary?"

"No, no, of course not. Fire ahead. Sorry, ask away."

"I mean, if you find it helps you think," he said apologetically, "I mean, go ahead, feel free." He gestured towards the bookshelf.

"No, really," I said firmly, feeling like the only one at lunch to have ordered a glass of wine. "Just ask."

"Well . . . that's what I wanted to ask. The books first of all."

I started talking to him about the mechanisms of the *sortes,* tactics I used, strategies "they" used in return, the way results came about by combining different answers, the use of maps. After five polite minutes of this, he interrupted me gently.

"What I meant was more how you came across the game yourself. What led up to it, you know."

I began with the party in November, obviously enough, with my waking up from a drunken sleep and hearing Sarah, John, and Fionnuala asking the kinds of questions I had got him to ask the other evening. He interrupted me again and asked me who the people were. I told him that John and Sarah were the friends I was looking for, that they were the ones who had initiated me into the game.

"And Funla?"

"Fionnuala. She's just a girl in college with me."

"And these other two, John and Sarah, you knew them before, right?"

He wanted to know how, exactly, and he wanted to know exactly how well I knew Fionnuala, how she and I had met, how we got on. Every time I launched into the story, he would bring me back a little, enquire about some fundamental or detail and ask me to explain it. Where was Ranelagh. When did John pull me up off the pavement. Before or after I had met Sarah in the pub. In the end, I went all the way back to the day I left home in Sandycove to move into college, but at the mention of Ian he stopped me again.

"Is that the guy who was here with Ryan's cousin? Coincidences all over the fucking place, huh? Tell me about him."

Keith was easy and unembarrassing to talk to. I said I had been in love with Ian at the end of high school. As I talked a little more about it, Keith got up and opened a drawer in the computer desk. He came back with a dictaphone. He held it up to me and raised his eyebrows, asking permission. I hesitated for a moment, then said:

"Sure, why not. If you think you can use it for your thesis. . . ."

"Thanks. . . . So let's go back to the beginning. . . ." He switched it on.

I started by telling him about the evening in Baggot Street when I abandoned my fragile new life, along with the people who had put it together, and had returned to the world of strange games and secret systems they had saved me from. I talked about this for a few minutes, then Keith interrupted me and asked me to go back to the beginning, nine months before, when, as I told him, it was all words.

We talked, or, more, he got me to talk for nearly two hours, in so much detail, and with so much backing up to explain the antecedents of so many characters and incidents, that at the end of the two hours we had only got to the moment at the party in Anna's house in Ranelagh where I had asked where my parents lived and got the line about Paris fads and Sandycove milk. The tape clicked off, and we took this as a sign to go to bed.

"Thanks a lot for that," Keith told me at the door. "Come by next time you feel up to it so we can do more. I'd love to get the whole story."

Confused, but not unhappy, I went back to my room, abandoned the books and maps to their own devices, and caught up on sleep.

After fermeture the next day, Keith's light was on but I did not go in, and went back to my own *sortes*. I could hear him next door, typing at his computer, while he clicked the dictaphone stop and start and whirred it forward and backward. Fascinated, I listened to the noises, and didn't go out on my walking trail until he had stopped working and gone to sleep.

A few days passed in this way, no visits from Keith, but the incessant sound of him typing and using the dictaphone was audible, for hours, through the wall. I wondered if he was using the tapes of his interviews to find synchronicities, fast-forwarding to a random place and typing what he heard into the computer.

It was around this time that I began to get the sense off my own synchronicities I took to search for John that someone, a man, was searching for me. Again and again it came up in the *sortes* I chose, sometimes explicitly, sometimes as a kind of background noise, a figure, a man, who was seeking me out. I took it to be a sort of static generated by Keith and his interest in my "story," but it was an unsettling feeling. So much so that I was relieved when Keith came knocking at my door at midnight on my next day off and took me away from the books.

He asked my permission once more to turn on the dictaphone.

"Now, when we left off last time, you had just told me about this first experience with the synchronicities, when you say the name of your home town came up. What happened then?"

I told him how there had been a ragged and unpleasant end to that morning, and then we talked about what had happened after that, how I had tried out the *sortes* on my own in my rooms, then gone home for dinner with my parents and Ciara. I told him about my story getting accepted for publication in a Trinity literary magazine, about how I had seen John at the party, how he had run away. I described how I had used synchronicities to chase him down to the 1937 Room and then made him go for pints in Kehoe's. I now came to the moment I had, excitedly, been anticipating telling Keith: how it had been my utterance of the phrase "a plurality of bottles has often induced this in me" that had convinced John to come back and tell me about the group. He failed to show any visible surprise or recognition. When I recounted, a few minutes later, how the same phrase had convinced Sarah to bring John into the circle, I paused to let it sink in, but Keith just looked expectantly at me while the spools of the dictaphone tape went on turning.

I went on to tell him everything John had told me about Pour Mieux Vivre. This, again, was the part I expected Keith to ask about with most eagerness, what I knew of the origins and significance of the organisation, its history, practices, and meaning, but he seemed more interested in what followed, my first forays into the gay scene, Christmas at home, my return to college. Pablo he accepted without comment or question, or even much interest, but he made me go over other parts of that time, insignificant moments which I had not thought about in so long, a lift into town from Jim McVeigh after a glass of wine with Patrick and Paula, the night in the George I first met Chris Mooney.

We left off just before the dawn at the beginning of Hilary Term when I had spied on Sarah and John from my window in Botany Bay. The tape snapped off and Keith and I made some chitchat, about him and Paris and the Brioche, before I left his room and went straight to bed.

I returned to my own *sortes* after fermeture the following night, as Keith again typed and typed on the other side of the wall, but I was assailed with references to this person looking for me, hunting me down, seeking my scent. Passage after passage mentioned it, and gradually it began to make me feel intensely lonely. I knocked at Keith's door and said that if he wanted to go on with the interviewing, I was free.

"Sure thing. You certain that's okay? I mean, I don't want to keep you from your work. . . ."

"No, it's no problem," I said. "It's not going so well anyway."

That night we covered my first real *sortes* experience with Sarah and John in Anna's house in Ranelagh, with the music and the visions, an important moment which filled the whole time until bed. The next night after fermeture, I didn't bother with my own *sortes* and went straight in to Keith; and the next, and the next. As much as I had enjoyed telling lies to Deirdre Carr in Stillorgan, this narration of the truth to the red light and turning spool of Keith Balfour's dictaphone in Paris became the centre of my thoughts, the endpoint of every day, the raison d'être, if the truth be told, of my life in Paris. Keith was friendly but unsentimental about the project. He switched on the dictaphone as soon as I arrived and got straight down to business, pausing only to pour the whiskeys we drank to keep my near-monologue company. He interjected less and less, as I began to get the hang of his methods and the focus of his interests, and was able to predict which points would need clarification, what aspects of Dublin life he would want explained, which relevant memories I should fill in. With regard to the more extravagant events I related, they did not elicit any noticeable reaction from Keith: he expressed no surprise, skepticism, or belief, and he was happy for me to brush over them in favour of filling in the personal end of my story. This was painful for me to revisit, at first, most especially the meetings with Chris, but the whirr of the recording device and Keith's patient, factual interruptions had the effect of distancing me from the story, and I told him everything, the interior of Chris's flat, his accent, the names of his friends, his childhood party-piece.

Keith mostly sat in front of me with his legs crossed, taking the odd note in a pocket-book, checking the tape didn't run out. I stopped looking at him as I spoke, as I had done in the beginning when it felt more like a conversation, and instead began to keep my gaze fixed out the window at the steady unvarying pulse of the Tour Montparnasse, the only knowledge still left in the world, flashing its patient, alien signal, forever secret, and forever, alas, indecipherable.

By the end of the week, I had given him more than seven hours of interviews. I had reached the point where Sarah and John had more or less hauled me out of a trad session in O'Donoghue's. Perhaps it was the troubling parallel of the preceding section, in which I had tried to convert Paula to the *sortes*, guilt at the neglect of my original project, or just a desire for a break from talking about myself, but after fermeture the following night I knocked at Keith's door to say I couldn't come over. He said it was no problem, I should just stop by next time I was free.

In my own room, I opened the neglected books and decided, without any great conviction, to scout around for John, and received, as I expected, stronger signals than ever that I was being looked for myself:

It was this that put him in some hope I would maybe get to land at all, and made him leave those clues and messages which had brought me (for my sins) to that unlucky country of Appin.

Frustrated and disconcerted by this, I closed the books again and decided to go into Keith. I was disappointed, almost panicked, to find his light switched off and the sound of snoring coming through the door. I went back to my room, but the books and their sinister implications glared at me from the desk, so I went back to Objectif Lune, where I hadn't been in some time.

Gráinne and another girl were leaving as I arrived. I told her that her byword had got me the job in the Brioche and I was grateful.

"To the best of my knowledge," she said, "no one has ever been refused who said those magic words to them. Who's the woman to see you right? Who? Who?" she bellowed. I joined in the refrain, *"The Wan from Clon,"* and we said goodbye. She called to me over her shoulder as she walked down towards the Bastille:

"Oh, you'll find your namesake inside! Niall *a dó*. Remember where you heard it first! From the. . . ."

The bar was half-full and I sat up at the bar, where André greeted me and asked me if I would have the usual. I said I would.

"That other Irish guy with your name is here tonight," he told me as he pulled the pint. "At last you'll meet."

"Where?"

"There. He's in the toilet, he'll be back in a second. See, he left his stuff."

He nodded to the empty stool behind me. Left on the bar in

front of it was a little pile of books and an open jotter, with a
biro tossed on top of it. I looked over at the page. It was divided
into two columns. I nearly fell off my stool when I read what
was written. The one on the left was headed "Sarah," the nearer
one "Niall," and underneath them notes in a poky handwriting I
recognised. I leaned in as close as I could without attracting
André's attention. I read:

"Greenaway" R. DU CHEMIN VERT
"Let them eat cake," (Fr. *'brioche')—a bakery? N works in
bakery on r du c.v.?*

As if this wasn't sufficient evidence, I took the top book from
the pile, a legitimate casual gesture of bored curiosity in a bar, I felt,
and looked at the flyleaf. *Kidnapped,* by R. L. Stevenson. And underneath: *John Bastible, age 11, 74, Marlborough Road, Donnybrook,
Dublin 4, Ireland, Europe, The Earth, The Milky Way, The Universe.*

Finally, the books had brought us back together. I took a slug
of my drink, ready for the reunion and the next chapter of the
story, but then, when I saw the light at the back of the bar from
the toilet door being opened, and the dark shape of "Niall"
moving through the crowd back towards his seat, an indescrib-
able dread rose up in my chest, a panicked fear for my Paris routine, my quiet life in the Brioche, and, most of all, for Keith's
interviews, which I knew would have to stop as soon as I clapped
eyes on John. As the figure made its way up the bar back to his
books, I pushed back my stool and ran back out onto rue de la
Roquette.

I knocked on Keith's door the next night, my day off, but he
was out, and I walked to Oberkampf where I sat drinking,
smoking, and checking books alone in a strange bar, coming to
terms with the discovery that, after all my looking for John, John it
turned out was the one looking for me, giving his name, for whatever reason, as Niall to the people in Objectif Lune. I had come to

Paris to look for him, but now these taped sessions with Keith had become inexplicably important, and I had to hide from John until they were finished. I asked the books where he was, how close.

That he was from the neighborhood could be confirmed by following his itinerary on a map, since as I said after the first crimes discovered in the tenth arrondissement, *all the rest had been committed in the eleventh, in a more and more limited space, in the immediate vicinity of the municipal hall and of the Place Léon Blum.*

I rushed home from fermeture the next night and went straight to Keith's door, without even changing out of my pink and white checked *Brioche Dorée* shirt, flakes of pastry still in my hair and on my grey waiter's trousers. I was relieved to find him in.

"Hey, man!" he asked, "what's the panic?"

"John. He's in Paris, in the area, the eleventh. He's tracking me down, fast. He's using my name for some reason. He was within twenty seconds of me in Objectif Lune last night, he—"

"Hold on, hold on!" Keith laughed, reaching for the whiskey. "I thought you were looking for him!"

"I thought I was, until we were about to meet. I realised that, you know, well, I want to finish this up first," I answered, indicating the pile of tapes on the computer desk. "I know that when he finds me, it'll have to stop."

"Why? He won't allow it?"

"I won't allow it. They won't allow it. It won't be possible."

We did another hour's interview, all the way up to the night on the surface of the Grand Canal. I wanted to go on, but Keith said he was tired, I should come over tomorrow and we could continue then. I told him it was urgent, and he laughed.

"I'm sure you can stay away from this guy if you think it's so necessary. Why don't you out-synchronicity him? And I'm not leaving Paris myself for a couple weeks."

He told me to relax, we could continue tomorrow.

"There's enough time, Niall, enough time."

While I was on my break at the Brioche the next evening, eating my sandwich at a table on the upper floor, as I often did in order to escape the incessant jingling of the tills, Aisling came up and said there was someone downstairs asking for me.

"Who?"

"An Irish guy. Tall, good-looking, black hair. He says his name is Niall too. He says the something from 'Clon' sent him."

"What did you tell him?"

"I said I'd get you."

I thought for a moment, then said:

"Aisling, can you do me a huge favour? Can you go back down to him and say you were confused for a second, that I was working here but have left?"

She laughed. "This is like a detective story. Why do you want me to tell him that?"

I made a big show of awkwardness and embarrassment, gave her significant looks.

"Oh!" she exclaimed, her eyes widening. "You mean . . . ?"

"He's my ex," I confided, as if reluctantly.

Her eyes widened. "Oh, so you're. . . ."

"Yes. Don't tell anyone, will you?"

"Oh, of course not. Not a soul. And don't worry, I'll get rid of him for you."

Pleased to be at this crossroads of bohemian sex-lives and thriller skulduggery, as well as having something, I knew, of a taste for lies, I was certain Aisling would successfully put John off the scent. I stood at the window, at an angle behind the bin where I could not be spied from the outside, and looked out at the pavement between our shop-front and the little roadside area of parasols and tables belonging to the Brioche, and waited. In a few moments I caught my first glimpse of John in Paris, skinny and scruffy, ambling in a slow resigned way, an Adidas bag, full of books, I had no doubt, slung over his shoulder. He looked for all the world like one of the wretched sun-weary Africans who tramp the streets of European cities with bags of sunglasses and cheap watches. He stopped and looked up for a moment at the windows of the floor I was on, narrowing his eyes. Failing to see me, he turned around and began to plod up the Champs-Élysées, away from the Brioche, but the sight of him and the aura of Pour Mieux Vivre which surrounded him was momentarily overpowering, and for a moment I thought I might give in and run down the stairs and after him.

Over the next number of days, I could feel him always close, never more than a few dozen steps from finding me. I changed my routine, went to work by the wrong métro lines, and made the taxis that took me home take unnecessary detours. Every evening as soon as I arrived back from the Brioche, I went straight in to Keith to be interviewed. He continued at his unhurried pace, determined to leave out no detail of the story, however superfluous, at the expense of advancing what I thought was the important and interesting narrative, that of the *sortes* and Pour Mieux Vivre. His enthusiasm for the interviewing had not waned: on the contrary, he was even more curious about my story and serious about the project than he had been at the start. Now, though, I felt a real desire to bring it to completion, and knew that the taping and telling would stop as soon as John found me. I stayed away from synchronicities, except on the days Keith was unavailable, out with American friends or doing other interviews. On these evenings and nights, I would ask the books about John, and found him always near and approaching.

I would sometimes catch sight of him just before I was about to walk into him. I managed never to been seen by him, however, quickly hiding behind a car or crowd, and would watch him through the window of a café or bar, muttering questions to himself, picking passages from a heap of books on the table in front of him and taking notes on a jotter and map, just like myself. When I marked out on my own map the locations and dates of where I spied him, it became clear that they formed an inward-moving spiral whose eventual centre was my apartment building.

As John grew ever closer, street by street, block by block, and closed in on my home, where I could never hide from him, I grew frantic in Keith Balfour's interviews. I told him I was going to resign from the Brioche (as I knew would happen anyway when John did catch up with me and we left on whatever journey or transformation would be necessary to find Sarah and Luis) so that he would be able to interview me at any time of the day. He laughed, as he always did, and told me to calm down, we could do a few late nights and finish it that way.

"I mean, we'll get to the Paris stuff before too long, right?"

Keith presumably thought I was mad, but took this fact in his stride as if it were of no more significance than my hair colour or accent. He was indifferent to the truth or otherwise of the basic thrust of my story, but almost passionate about the details of everything I mentioned. Whenever I began to digress into excursions with my theory of the *sortes,* the identity of Luis or Pablo, or the mechanisms of our "sessions," he would usually cut it short and elicit information instead about his favourite topics, Patrick, Paula, Chris, Fionnuala, and, especially, Ian. For Keith, as for Deirdre, Ian was a figure who remained mysteriously at the centre of the whole account, and it was a strange idea for me to think, as I spoke into the dictaphone, that he had sat in the same room I was in only weeks previously.

The night we held our last interview, quite literally the eleventh hour, we were surrounded by the packed suitcases and boxes of Keith, who was leaving for Princeton the following morning. On my way back from fermeture, I had spied John sitting in a café on rue du Chemin Vert, a few blocks from our building, holding only a single book, a sure sign, I recognised from my own long experience, that his search for me, like the dictation of my adventures to the American, was coming to a close. I was ready now to finish off the story for Keith and depart with John into the underworld, in search of Pour Mieux Vivre.

I began by repeating, in more or less the same words, the incident in Baggot Street when I had written the three letters and come to Paris. Keith asked me about my meeting with himself, the run-in in Franprix with him and Ryan. After I had told him my version of this, and explained the significance of his uttering the phrase "a plurality of bottles," he stopped the tape.

"Well, I think this is where I came in. We're done," he said, and rewound it, five minutes of my high-speed voice squeaking backwards. "You know I never said that, though, the thing about the bottles."

This was his first intervention on a matter of factual truth.

"Oh, you did," I said, "twice. But it doesn't matter."

"You're right," he said, as the tape clicked to a stop. "It doesn't matter."

He took it out with a snap and put it with the others. The only things left not packed were his computer, speakers, and printer, and the little pile of miniature cassettes, beside a large padded envelope labelled "Niall Lenihan (Sandycove, Dublin, Ireland) neighbor, Paris, Summer 2004, 11 hours."

We had a last glass of whiskey and toasted the future.

"Thanks for the material," he said. "I'll send you a copy of the thesis, if I ever write it. Do you want me to change the names?"

"No."

"And, of course, if you ever come Stateside, you know, like look me up. There's a futon with your name on it. Princeton's not far outside New York, you know. And with a bit of luck, I'll be in residence in the metropolis next year."

"Likewise, if you need to escape the philistines again, there's always Dublin."

"There's always Dublin," he repeated. "There's always Dublin. I like that. I'll keep it in mind."

As we shook hands at the door of his bare room next to the pile of zipped cases, I wanted suddenly to beg him not to go, to save me. I could almost hear the steady tramp tramp of John, his relentless and regular step coming to take me back.

"Bye."

"Bye."

I had never in my life felt so alone as I did that night lying on my back in the sagging bed of my studio, watching the lights of cars pass like clockwork over my ceiling, the noise of typing, printing, and final packing coming from the next room, the sound of my cherished tapestry and my last company about to flee and leave me to my wordy fate.

The following day, as I left late for what I knew would be my last day at work, I stumbled over a package balanced against the outside of my door. It was a thick envelope with my name handwritten on the front of it. Thinking it was a goodbye present of some book or other, I picked it up and threw it into my bag with my books, Brioche uniform, and cigarettes, thinking I would open it on the métro on my way to work. But the métro was too packed with rush-hour passengers on their way home from work, and as I was late, it wasn't until my break at half-nine that night, when I was sitting out at one of our pavement tables smoking and watching the busy Champs-Élysées night pass me by, that I opened it. It was a mass of printed pages in Times New Roman twelve point double-spaced, three hundred and sixty-five, according the page numbers, ending with the words *"a plurality of bottles."* They were accompanied by a floppy disk and a folded piece of squared French jotting paper, which I unfolded to read, handwritten in unjoined letters of felt-tipped pen:

Paris, August 26, 2004

Dear Niall,
Here are the transcripts of our conversations. I don't think I will
be able to do anything with them, but maybe you will. Why don't
you tidy it up a bit, put some kind of form on it, when you have
time, and send it to me in Princeton? Add a twelfth hour: make
it an honest day's work.
It has been a pleasure, really. Now good luck!

Keith

kbalfour@princeton.edu
Keith Balfour
c/o Dept. of English, McCosh Hall, Princeton University,
Princeton, NJ-08544, États-unis.

I stared down at the traffic moving east toward the Arc de Triomphe and allowed myself a last lash at human regret, nostalgia, and loneliness before putting the package back into my
bag. During fermeture I told Olivier, the day's duty manager,
that I wouldn't be coming back. There was much fluster and
fussing, but when he took out the planning and saw that I was
off for the next two consecutive days, he calmed down. Business
was slowing anyway as the tourist season died. He even led the
fermeture team to the Monte Cristo to see me off with a piña
colada like everyone else. They all, my colleagues (my "day-
friends," as I had once heard a drag-queen say in the George),
were curious about why I was going. I tossed out the usual lazy
lies which I balk at repeating once more in these pages. I found
some way of saying, which was true, that I had been sort of
between things and was now returning to an earlier plan I had
had. I took a cab outside the Monte Cristo, waved goodbye,
and sailed off to my insomniac exile.

John was sitting on the doorstep of the building when the taxi dropped me off, around three that morning. He stood up as I shut the door behind me, and the taxi disappeared down towards the Bastille, taking the last remnants of my regret with it. One look into the green spark at the bottom of his dark eyes was enough; I was back again. I felt myself falling deeply, quickly, like someone who has taken a strong sleeping pill, Alice down the rabbit-hole. The Paris of Keith, of the Golden Brioche and its rite of fermeture, the Paris of the Wan from Clon, flew by me, and I found myself returned at last to the place I had left Dublin to get to. We didn't greet each other. John reached out a white hand and grabbed my shoulder, and I looked back at his eyes and ruddy face. He was gaunt and red-cheeked, his hair was matted and tangled, and his clothes, used to covering a much bigger frame, hung off him like flags. We stood for a moment in the warm night, like old lovers, eyes locked together, a breeze blowing intimations of autumn around us. I punched in the door-code, and he followed me in and up the stairs.

Leaning against the door-frame, he looked with mild curiosity around my room, while I packed my essentials, passport, some clothes, and of course books from the shelf. I hesitated over Keith Balfour's package. Feeling that its presence might disturb the flow of the journey I was about to undertake with John, and knowing that the tapes were safely archived with Keith in Princeton, New Jersey, I decided to leave it behind, a packet of *sortes* for the next inhabitant of Madame de Montvrai's attic room to find. But when I was stripping my bed, and saw John idly pick the package up and put a finger in between the pages to choose a synchronicity, I pulled it off him and put it in the bag with the books.

Then, as I zipped the bag shut, John and I exchanged our first words:

"Where to?" I asked. "Do you know where she is?"

"I have something to tell you first," John said, now shimmering before me, as if in the heat-blur of an aircraft. I was enjoying the feeling of submission again, to John and to our systems. It was for this that I had walked away from Baggot Street; finally I had found it.

"What, John?"

"Something I found out. With the books."

"Yes."

"Luis."

"Yes?"

"There is no Luis. At least, Sarah never met him. It was a lie she concocted. She e mailed him all right, but they never met. She never met him and she never went with him, anywhere. He was never in Augsburg and he never came to Dublin."

"Are you sure?"

He stretched out his hand towards my bag of books, a granting of permission to consult. I unzipped it, pushed aside Keith's package to get to the books underneath it, and chose:

That destiny is just a story, that oracles are narratives.

"Luis . . . the reason . . . there is no Luis. She never met him and she never went with him," I whispered. "Anywhere."

"Sarah believed," John replied. "She added the story of the two meetings to help my unbelief. She left to find him, whoever was behind it."

"Can we find her?"

"I think so. I think she's waiting for us. Come."

We wandered, for days, maybe weeks, in some other sense for years: if we had been sailors we would have been salt-caked, scarred, and scurvied. I do not remember where we slept, if we slept, what we ate, if we ate, what we said, if we spoke. John and I moved ceaselessly through a dreamed, foggy place, where the air was heavy and blind, where every jangle of coins in a beggar's cup was a sibylline annunciation.

We walked our way to the end of the night on the trail of

Sarah. Ringing the bells of empty apartments, mooching in library reading rooms, drinking in likely brasseries the books assured us she had been in recently, we traversed Paris. Guided by the *sortes* and by candlelit rituals we tried to perform between the two of us, we threaded our way through the gays and Jews in the Marais, the cinema queues on Place de la République and rue des Écoles, the transsexuals dancing at the Folies Pigalle. We walked the pavements of the refined neighbourhoods of the north, elbowed through the mainstream nightlife of Oberkampf and Belleville, hours and hours of quick footsteps with no words passed between us, by the closed shutters of cheap Greek restaurants on rue de la Hachette, along the boulevard Saint-Michel, through Luxembourg, Denfert, through the Montparnasse cemetery, the Parc Montsouris, by the banks of the river.

Maybe one or both of us at times would have thrown himself over the Pont des Arts into the dark water, to feel with relief the cold Seine, unafraid and invisible, surround his body, but we were afraid the splash would have been a prelude to an unwanted scene, a rubber ring thrown by a Swiss tourist, plump and pleased, flashing red lights of an ambulance, a good-looking and efficient young paramedic checking for a pulse, the sympathetic French of the hospital social worker, who smiled as she said she had visited Dublin once, visited Trinity College, how it was "très bien fait."

And so we pushed on through the city, which became ever less Paris and more a palimpsest of Paris and Dublin. At the end of the Roman rue Saint-Jacques, instead of the Tour Saint Jacques, the O'Connell Street Spire rose up before us. Parisians themselves were half-transformed into the dramatis personae of my Dublin: on a corner of rue des Rosiers, instead of the late-night customers at the falafel restaurant, I saw Paula joking and laughing with an Italian waiter at a branch of Dunne & Crescenzi; when we stopped for an Orangina on a hot evening on rue de Rivoli, I listened to Andrea chattering outside what looked like Renard's on South Frederick Street about her experiences as an au pair in Neuilly ("I swear I was their fucking *slave,* like practically a Filipino or whatever"); I saw Chris dive, naked and muscular as a swan, from one of the turrets of the Pont Neuf; Fionnuala danced to France Gall in the basement of a gay club called Banana while I sat drinking in the corner; I saw Patrick marching in full French military uniform, sweaty blond hair covered by his helmet, scarlet feathers unmoving in the still heat, down the Champs-Élysées in a parade. The Dublin postal sorting codes overlayed themselves without apology on top of the arrondissements: out in the fifteenth where we should have found the church of Notre Dame de l'Arche de l'Alliance, we stumbled on the Church of Saint Thomas the Apostle of Carpenterstown, Dublin 15. When we went to view the Tour Montparnasse in the *sixième,* we came to Sandford Road and played video games in Jason's of Ranelagh, Dublin 6 with boys in Gonzaga uniforms; in the Marais' gay fourth, we saw the Merrion Road stretching leafbound southwards from Ballsbridge, Dublin 4; when we walked up rue du Temple, in the first, past the Chinese jewellery wholesalers, it reshaped itself to Capel Street, where a small child in a school uniform and 1980s sandals bellowed out the words of the first verse of *Báidín Fheilimí* in his quavering, high-pitched voice and working-class Dublin accent.

That July day in the flat on Baggot Street when I had made my decision, I had known how it would be to go back; I knew I would find John, and I knew what kind of placeless delirium he and I would wander through on our search together. And so, as we made our way through this dark, double-exposure city, we never for a moment doubted that, although they led us to shadowy, deceptive visions of Dublin, our books and rituals would eventually bring us to Sarah.

We were not wrong. Using maps of both cities, we began to discern patterns in the visions and directions. Abstract and impossible, they were nevertheless mutually, mutely perceived by both of us, and we began to recognise the lie of the land, understand the direction in which the wind was blowing. And so the tale of two cities began slowly to deliver up its secrets. Over a series of long nights in Objectif Lune, at a table covered with books, maps, pen and paper spread over the table underneath our pints, we narrowed the zone of enquiry down to a single district, number 16, Ballyroan or Passy, and to a single bridge across a river, over the Dodder at Rathfarnham shopping centre, or straddling the Seine between the Eiffel Tower and Avenue President Kennedy, and then to a single street, rue de l'Alboni, and to a single building, number one.

The morning we satisfied ourselves that our calculations were correct, we had a long breakfast of pastries and coffee in a café on rue du Chemin Vert. We planned the métro route we would have to take there, and then for an hour spoke about other things, things we had never spoken of before, our fathers, Ian, Anna, home. And then, at around eleven, as if by pre-arranged, synchronised consent, we snapped that conversation shut forever and left to go to Sarah and the next level.

The road below the métro station in Passy was covered in damp brown leaves, and the wind that blew spoke of new schoolbooks, pens, and copies; I had been in Paris for a season. Number one, rue de l'Alboni was on the corner, the entrance underneath the Pont Bir-Hakeim, fronted by a door of frosted glass and curling ironwork. The front door was unlocked, and we walked into the lobby. From here, a glass door led to the stairs and lift. Beside it was a panel of bells for the individual apartments, and we looked through them until we found the last of our *sortes*:

Sarah Ní Dhuibhir, P.M.V.

John pressed it and we both stood back. There was a long pause. I peered through the net curtains of the concierge's room opposite, and saw the concierge peering through them back at me. As John was about to press again, there was an anonymous click and buzz, and we went through the glass door. We took a tiny lift, groaning to the sixth floor. This top floor, like mine in Bastille, was dark and uncarpeted, a gloomy corridor of rough wood with two small blue doors on each side. There was no name on the left-hand door, and there was a sound of male voices speaking a foreign language behind it. Affixed to the door on the right was a tiny printed card with the letters *P.M.V.* embossed on it; from behind it there was silence. John rapped twice on this door, and we waited.

A woman's voice called out, in Irish.

"*Tar isteach.* Come in."

It was her, oracular sound of ages past. John, gaunt and green-eyed, hung back, as if in fear. I pushed the door open, and we went in.

We were standing in a small round room, barely furnished with a battered leather sofa and a striped green pull-out bed, folded sheets and a pillow laid neatly on the end. Sarah was standing with her back to us, looking out one of three tall double windows giving onto the Seine and the Eiffel Tower, which loomed directly in front, dominating the view. A cigarette smoked away in her hand.

"I'm glad you've come," she said without turning round.

To her right, in front of the middle window, there were three boxes full of papers, and next to them, a desk with a closed laptop, a bowl of tangerines, an old lemon, and a small pile of obsolete centimes.

"Are you okay?" I asked her.

She tossed her cigarette out the open window onto the wind, pushed it noisily shut, then turned to face us. She looked surprisingly fit and healthy, perhaps a little thinner than before, and just as pale. She was wearing black trousers and a black T-shirt.

No one made any move to hug or kiss anyone. She looked at us blankly with her big grey eyes.

"I'm glad you've come," she said again. She walked over to the couch and sat down. "I have something to tell you."

"We know, Sarah," John said. "I found out. You can't find him. He slips through your fingers like air. You made up the meetings."

Their eyes met for a prolonged moment, until Sarah broke it by looking away from him. She got up and stood at the window again, staring at the Eiffel Tower, bland and vulgar in the early afternoon light. A barge piled with sand moved slowly by.

"Well, not quite," she said. "I found this place. He . . . they were here. This is where they printed out our reports. The printed them all out. But I was too late. They knew I was coming. Now they're gone. We have to find them."

"Are you sure this is the place?" John asked. In answer, Sarah pulled a sheaf of pages out of one of the boxes and handed them to him.

John turned them over carefully with his strong white hands, handing them to me one by one as he was finished. They were printouts of e-mails, from Sarah's account, all in Spanish, but as far as I could make out, an episodic series of descriptions of our sessions in Northumberland Road.

From: "Sarah Ní Dhuibhir" nidhuibhs@tcd.ie

To: "Luis": laninahillen@eurosur.org

Sent: 1st April, 2004, 18:56:40

Re: jueves

Empezamos con una lectura normal, como solíamos antes, dos libros, dos voces

"Why . . . why did they print them?" I asked. "I mean, if he never met. . . ."

Sarah ignored me, and said to John:

"There's more. Look at what they did to them."

John began leafing through the pages. I saw him blanch and

recoil in shock. I held out my hand and, shaking, he handed me the page. It was an account, I thought, of the night with the statues on top of the Bank of Ireland (*"que empezaron a moverse"*), and the word *"PUTA"* was scrawled in blue crayon across it. John continued to pass me pages. Every single one had been defaced in blue crayon by vulgar scribbles and slogans. On one page there was a crude sketch of three people. *John, Niall, Sarah,* was written underneath. They were matchstick figures with massive genitalia, the men with penises bigger than themselves, Sarah a collection of rough circles. We went through page after page. Sarah and John, or gross sexualised representations of them, figured everywhere. I appeared in only a couple, one of a stick man, John, buggering another, me, with the word *"PÉDÉ"* scrawled across the top. There were many of Sarah in sexual positions, with *"puta"* and various multilingual versions of it written all over Sarah's meticulous Hiberno-Spanish. It was clear that various hands, not one, were involved, both from the jumping between languages and from the style of cartoons and writing.

I gave the pages back to John and he handed them over to Sarah, who put them back in the box.

"So," Sarah said. "They have gone. They knew I was coming, and they fled the nest."

"So we find them," said John. "Wherever they are, however long it takes."

"Yes," I joined in. "We find them. We go to the next level."

"Very well," Sarah said. "Put your books on the shelf."

John and I opened our bags, and we added our books to the small collection in the bookcase. After a moment's hesitation, I took the last remaining item in my backpack, the sheaf of Keith Balfour's transcripts, and placed it on the shelf with them.

"Niall, you first," Sarah instructed. *"Tolle, lege."*

"No," I said. "You, you choose."

John nodded. "Yes, Sarah, it should be you."

Sarah turned her head from the bookcase and looked out the

window at the pale blue sky, straddled by the iron girders of the Eiffel Tower. Her hand moved up and down the pile, and stopped, eventually, on the package of Keith's pages. Without looking, she opened the envelope and moved her hand back and forth over the thick stack of printed sheets, before choosing one and pulling it out. She ran her fingers over it, as though browsing through a Braille index, and read out the passage she had chosen:

> " 'Okay. Where do my parents live?', I asked. The answer I chose was: 'We can drink it black, Stephen said thirstily. There's a lemon in the locker.'
> " 'Oh, damn you and your Paris fads,' Buck Mulligan said. 'I want Sandycove milk.' "

Sarah thought for a moment, looking from the sheet to the window and back again. She thought for some time and then spoke.

"I have it. We go to Italy. *Damn your Paris fads* is a clear injunction to leave Paris. *My parents* must refer to the leaders of the organisation: they themselves have just left the city, after all. And while I have been misled in the past, I am certain that their headquarters is in Rome. Rome is where our parents live in another sense too: it is the home of our spiritual parents in the form of the individuals of antiquity who employed the technique of the *sortes* and recorded details of the practice for us. I think the reference to lemons is as simple as a description of southern Italy, famous for its lemon groves. '*Kennst du das Land, wo die Zitronen blühn,*' '*Do you know the land where the lemon-trees grow,*' as Goethe puts it. The sandy cove I read as the bay of Naples. The idea of lemons in a locker is an image which brings to mind gold in a safe; in Rome, or maybe Naples, there is something valuable for us to discover. What do you think?" she asked after a pause.

"I agree," John said. "It makes sense. We follow them to Italy. Southbound it is!" As they talked excitedly together about the meaning of the passage, my mind drifted from what they were saying to a *bateau mouche* passing by on the river outside. It gave four long low blows of its horn. *Eye ooh ah oh.* From the left bank of the Seine, the inevitable music drifted in to me through the open window, tinkling fairy voices. We were to leave this place, go far, seek out. Follow the allroads away southbound to the next level.

And then, I had a doubt. A sense of something unfinished troubled me. The boat blew its horn again, a sound that seemed to respond to my misgivings, to offer the missing line, the last verse.

you revealed to me the hidden secrets of your wisdom

No, that was not it.

Followed by the eyes of Sarah and John, I went to the shelf, pulled a page from Keith's papers, ready to take a synchronicity of my own.

As I prepared to choose and read, the *bateau mouche* blew its horn four more times, mournful and long like a cathedral bell. As the last blow sounded, across the rippling water came the forgotten phrase, the last line, the simplest, most obvious realisation of them all:

I do not know
Says the great bell of Bow.

A mist cleared from the world. I looked at my companions and told them it was over. I wished them the best.

"It has been a pleasure, really," I said. "Now good luck!"

From Dublin airport, I took a bus to O'Connell Street, walked up to the Green and took the Luas to Rathgar, where I found the McVeighs' house empty. I left a note for Patrick and walked from there into Ranelagh, past the gates of Gonzaga and through a small throng of thirteen-year-olds in my old school uniform, treble voices thin against the rush hour. The day dimmed as I made my way down Eglinton Road, where I had once so often been close to weeping for a hallucinated love. I stood at the bus stop just down from Donnybrook church, opposite the whizz of the traffic on the Stillorgan Road. At the gate of the church, a frantic black cluster of condolence and greeting must have been the last group of latecomers for a removal. The bells began to intone the start of the service.

"When is the next 46A due, do you know?" I asked the old woman standing at the stop next to me.

"Abracadbra," she said, pointing to its green shape coming out of town towards us.

I climbed into the bus and paid the driver. *I do not know,* I heard first in the bells beyond. But after I had ascended to the upper deck, I paused on the top step and listened again. Through the traffic on the late grey air, I began to discern the first strain of something old and sad, the last strains of something new. Before I could fully make it out, however, the 46A had closed its doors behind me and had moved back off down the dual carriageway again, outbound once more, through the traffic lights, through the years, south.

Acknowledgments

These pages seem a slim thing to come out of all the help and energy from other people which it took to produce them. First off, I would like to thank Keith Wallman of Carroll & Graf, whose creativity, patience, and solidarity brought this book into being; first too, come Elaine Markson, along with Gary Johnson, who have been faithful, persistent friends of the book and the writer since the beginning.

I owe an immeasurable debt to those who read and commented on the many early drafts and versions, and who provided companionship and support for the book along the way. In Dublin: Léan Ní Chuilleanáin, Caitríona Ní Dhubhghaill, Helen Finch, Carmel McCrea, Colin McCrea, Killian McCrea, Rónán McCrea, Rachel Magshamhráin, Gary O'Reilly, Francis Sweeney. In Princeton and New York: Michelle Clayton, Maria DiBattista, Ingrid Horrocks, Paul Muldoon, Ricardo Piglia, Elaine Showalter, Erika Thorgerson, Éric Trudel, Don Weise, and especially Edmund White.

This book is dedicated with love and thanks to Ludovico Geymonat.

About the Author

Barry McCrea is from Dublin, where he studied Spanish and French at Trinity College. He has taught comparative literature at Yale University since 2004. This is his first novel.